The Knave Of Hearts

Part 9 of the Red Dog Conspiracy

Patricia Loofbourrow

The Wedding

The hall burst with riotous color. Men, women, children from all over Merca, nay the world, had come to celebrate the marriage of one of their own. Zeppelin pilots in their ceremonial uniforms, the Travelers' Board in full regalia. A banner at the far end: Vig And Natalia Forever.

I sat in the left corner nearest the door, staring dully at the spray of flowers on my table. Apparently one didn't wear full mourning to a wedding in Bridges, so instead I wore Anna Goren's deep purple dress and veil. With the crush of dignitaries in the room, no one gave me any notice.

But I was well-guarded.

My loyal footman Skip Honor stood behind me, dressed in his finest. The housekeeper of my apartments, Mary Spadros, sat beside me to my left. Her husband (and my apartments' butler) Blitz sat beside her, their little daughter Ariana bouncing in his arms.

Acevedo Spadros III, just a month old, lay sleeping in his pram to my right, his nursemaid Daisy beside him. His guards — two men close by, two more stationed farther away — had been assigned the task by my husband Tony.

One of these was Tony's first cousin and right hand man, Ten Hogan, also called Sawbuck. He loomed a few feet away from Acevedo, looking bored. Sawbuck had wanted little to do with the boy, not even visiting when he was born, and had only given him a glance when assigned the duty.

Tony hadn't wanted me to bring the child. Tony's parents insisted.

"It'd be too much for you or me to go," Roy had said. "Particularly since they don't want us." Though he lived in our quadrant, Vígharður Vikenti had a particular dislike for the Spadros Family.

"But since the Travelers' Board will be there, in our quadrant, one of us must attend. And who better than our new little Heir?"

I thought it a masterful move. Vig and I were old friends, and who could fault a new mother for bringing her babe?

The calculated irony of it all.

The room buzzed with lively conversation. Families laughed, children ran about. Everyone seemed so alive.

I felt in a half-world, neither living nor dead. My bleeding had stopped. My color had mostly returned, my strength almost what it had been. But even at the wedding of two dear friends, I felt a terrible lonely emptiness inside.

Acevedo slept now, with the noise and bustle around him, but at Spadros Manor he cried day and night. Dr. Salmon called it colic, and said it should abate on its own "in a month or two."

Another two months of this and I feared I would go mad.

At times I wished only to die. The one thing which stopped me was the vow I made to Jonathan Diamond before his death: to find a way to be happy.

Jonathan had died after carrying me from a trap meant for him. His cry when he fell, dropping me into that cobblestone alley, ever rang in my head.

Why did you leave the house?

Tony's words kept repeating. But little Ante, the messenger boy, said he'd seen Josie. I'd only wanted to help find her.

Don't you see what you're doing? How long will you go on like this? How many more are dead because of your 'help'?

My eyes stung.

Seeing Jonathan's face before me with his twin Jack's deep voice, his cutting tone ... it only made the words more painful.

If only I'd paid attention to little Ante, he'd be alive.

Yes, the boy had tried to stab me but he was a boy, and a small one at that. He just wanted to avenge his brother.

If I'd only been stronger. If only I'd been able to bear the pain.

Why did I let Jon carry me? If I'd been more forceful, stubbornly refused to let Jon do it, he still might be alive.

How many more are dead because of your 'help'?

A waiter came by. "Some wine, mum?"

I shook my head, looking away, but in my heart I wanted the whole bottle, and all its kin.

Blitz gave me a quick glance. "None for this table, thanks." He'd brought Ariana's little tall chair, and set her now into it, then handed her a hard biscuit to gnaw on. Once the man left, he said to me, "Sorry about that."

I'd just recovered from bleeding near to death. Drinking would have only made things worse.

That was what my mind said. My heart thought perhaps death would at least bring me a chance of being with Jonathan once more.

I gazed at Acevedo, asleep bundled in his pram.

And I felt nothing.

Daisy and I exchanged a glance. She doted on the boy, tending to him day and night, with soft cooing and various amusements, nursing him as often as he wished. Barely a month after his near-death in my womb, his dreadful pallor had turned to rosy cheeks, his hair coming in full, dark brown and wavy.

He's a strong child, Dr. Salmon told me. Barring any tragedy, he should live to become a mighty Heir.

The doctor had given a full interview to the *Bridges Daily*, one of many articles trying to sate the frenzy around the boy. After his birth, crowds had choked the streets outside of Spadros Manor, I suppose hoping for a glimpse of him.

Yet so far, no one seemed to have noticed us here.

The wedding itself had been private, Travelers only. I'd paid to rent the hall: my gift to Vig.

We came to the reception hall early to escape the rush and only a very few reporters had been there. Setting up their cameras, they seemed not to notice our entry. But we'd have to leave sooner or later.

I owed Vig my life. Yet everyone around me died. Would Vig be the next?

A man shouted, "They're here!"

The crowd hurried over to the door on our side of the hall.

I sat unmoving. From where we were, we'd be able to see most everything.

Vig had no brothers, no sisters. His mother had died of a coronary after Roy's men destroyed Vig's saloon in retaliation for not informing to Roy on my whereabouts. But Natalia's parents were there, her sisters and brothers, aunts and uncles, with a host of children.

They all looked so happy.

The wedding couple strode in, an easy joy upon their faces I'd never seen in either of them before. Arm in arm, they greeted the cheers, beaming with delight.

Natalia's dress was white satin, with heavy embroidery of gold and red. Her dark hair was tied up in a headscarf to match, beads and jewels spilling down her shoulders. It was then I noticed many of the women there had similar, if less festive headscarves on.

And I'd never seen Vig wear such a splendid suit before: the finest blue silk, a suit worthy of a Patriarch.

Where did he get the money for all this?

Led to the front, the wedding couple were seated at tall chairs at a rectangular table draped in white, like a King and Queen overseeing their court.

Then the feasting began.

Whole pigs, sides of beef, dozens of roasted fowl and other platters were brought to the tables on each side. Chefs created plates for each person, which waiters brought first to the wedding couple, then to the room in order of their distance from them.

Blitz chuckled. "We'll be here a while."

It didn't matter. Nothing mattered anymore.

Musicians played, people talked. And I saw where the money came from. As maidens carrying large deep baskets danced slowly by, the men at each table deposited large bills and wads of cash into them.

Blitz turned to me, laughing. "Apparently, this is their tradition!"

When a girl danced around our table, Blitz had his dollar ready. I hoped he and Mary could afford such expense.

The food was good, dishes I'd not had before. People sang songs I'd never heard before, speaking in languages I didn't understand. It was strange, it was so new to me. But it was all beautiful.

Jon would have liked this so much. Tears threatened to return. I felt real pain, deep in my heart.

Mary said, "More tea, mum?"

I took it. I didn't care. Everything they offered: food, drink. I knew Mary and Blitz wouldn't betray me.

Yet I felt divided.

I'd have to leave eventually. I wanted so badly to return with Blitz and Mary to my apartments, have the peace and quiet of life in my dear little home. To be free.

But I feared for them. Everyone around me died. Even Jon.

Nothing had been so fortunate for Blitz and Mary as for me to be forced to leave. Perhaps they'd survive whatever new horror the Red Dog Gang planned for me.

This made me think of my dear friend Josie, who'd suffered unimaginable torment because of me.

Why had they kidnapped Josephine Kerr? Could it have only been to kill Jon?

Tony's men had found me and Jonathan dying beside the warehouse where Josie had been trapped. They found the little messenger boy Ante's body.

But Tony's men never found Josie. I could only hope she'd made her way to that place she spoke of, somewhere safe where her chains might be removed.

I'd sent messages to her home and received no reply. Her betrothed Etienne Hart, my half-brother and the Hart Inventor, had never returned to Spadros Manor, nor would he accept my mail.

And we'd heard nothing at all from the Diamonds.

In those weeks of lying bedridden, I considered well what Julius Diamond had done at the crossing a week after his son's death. In the Families, denying men that Jonathan had named his closest allies the chance to attend his funeral was unforgivable.

But from all Jon had told me, Julius Diamond hadn't been a good father, nor even a kind one. After so many years of grieving his son's imminent death, to have it come so suddenly, without warning ...

Tony said I was only excusing the inexcusable. But what might I have done or said in the man's place?

None of it mattered, not really.

Someone took Josie. Someone forged a letter from me to lure Jon there. They even hit me on the head and took me there, heavy with child. Then they herded the three of us to a point where ...

We had a clear escape. If I'd only been stronger, been able to bear the terrible, unnatural, searing pain, we might have made it to safety without any loss of life.

Acevedo stirred, then let out a sigh.

Those people went to immense effort to bring us there. The plan spoke of a precise mind, someone who knew everyone involved. The play had been carefully staged, even to the way Ante stepped back from the curb outside Spadros Manor, drawing me towards him and my imminent capture.

But what was the point?

They didn't want me to die. From the writing Tony's cousin Sawbuck and I had found on the note in my dead friend Marja's hand, these people needed me alive for some reason.

So why do this?

They couldn't possibly know about the condition inside me — Dr. Salmon had called it previa — that threatened to tear my child from my body and suffocate him before he even drew breath. Not even the doctor had known until he saw the afterbirth.

He'd gasped then, and turned pale, that old, old man who'd delivered both Tony and Roy in his day.

But the Red Dog Gang did know about Jon. The whole city knew about his illness. They knew he and I had a bond. They knew if I called, he would go to me.

And they used that to kill him.

Daisy reached across Acevedo's pram and took my hand. "They say everyone cries at weddings."

From down the long hall, Vig had been watching me. I forced myself to smile.

A waiter stood beside me. "Finished, mum?"

All the other plates had been taken. I nodded, and he took the half-empty plate and moved on. The room swayed, just a bit, when I stood. "I'm going out for a smoke."

Mary took my left arm. "Let me come with you."

We went past the guests, past the large dance floor. Vig rose, leading Natalia by the hand to start the first dance.

They looked so beautiful, so happy.

Past the kitchens, a narrow back door opened onto an equally narrow back alley, which stretched a full block in each direction. At least thirty men stood at either end: Travelers' men, Vig's men, Tony's men. I almost laughed, wondering if they were managing to get along.

Mary pulled me to the left, speaking quietly. "Look, it's that man. The one who came to the house that night."

It was then I noticed him, a dozen yards my right. Tall, wearing workman's clothing covered by a full apron, smoking a cigarette. His skin golden, well-muscled arms revealed by rolled-up sleeves. His eyes, just as green, just as hypnotic as I recalled.

A thrill ran all the way to my sex as our eyes met.

For the first time in a month, I felt alive.

And in spite of everything he'd said and done, I still wanted him.

The Dance

Mary's voice held fear. "Mum, maybe we should go back inside."

My eyes were fixed upon him. "No, it's fine. He won't hurt us. I've known him since I was born."

Joseph Kerr strolled over. Gods, he was beautiful. "Never expected to see you here!"

My heart pounded. "I'm sure you recall my housekeeper, Mrs. Mary Spadros."

His eyes never left mine. "A pleasure."

"Whatever are you doing here?"

Joe had the most glorious smile. The smile of a free and happy child, so radiant that you couldn't help but smile too.

Joy and liberation lay in that smile, a smile of someone who felt utterly safe and free.

It pulled me to him.

Joe chuckled fondly. "I've been hired by a catering service. I spend my days with dishes. Washing, stacking, traveling beside them, carting them around." He took a drag from his cigarette, then handed it to me, like we used to do when we were young. "It's not bad. And I've been saving. Once my sister's married, if her husband or his father wish me gone, I'll be able to take care of the house on my own."

He and his sister lived in their grandfather's home in Kerr quadrant, far to the north-west, past the island that lay between us.

Mary still gripped my arm, face concerned.

I took a drag from the cigarette, then said to her, "Would you let us speak in private for a moment?"

She let go and curtsied. "Of course, mum." Retreating past the steps, she clung to the railing.

I handed the cigarette back. "How's your sister?"

He glanced away. "The manacles she bore rubbed deep; the doctor says through the skin itself. He's put poultices upon them, but she still must keep them bandaged."

I gasped. "Even a month later?"

Joe nodded, eyes solemn. "They're improved, very much so ... but he fears she may bear the scars for life."

My eyes filled with tears, picturing those beautiful wrists ruined. "Who would do such a thing?"

Joe shrugged, his eyes golden-green pools of light. "But you're in terrible danger. Her fiance has been enraged, blaming you, forbidding her to send a message. Once he even cried out, 'I will see her suffer!'"

The intensity of Joe's words broke the spell of his eyes. I'd learned not even a year ago that Etienne Hart — Josie's fiance — was my half-brother. My own brother wanted me to **suffer**?

Joe took my hand, his demeanor suddenly urgent. "Thank the gods you're here: I didn't know how I might warn you." He let my hand drop. "Mr. Etienne has given us a butler." He chuckled at that, then his face grew solemn once more. "But it's only to put a watch on our mail, so we don't send word to Spadros quadrant."

This didn't surprise me, with what I'd seen so far. Inventor Etienne Hart was an enormously powerful yet somewhat unstable man. And if he blamed me for his fiancee's kidnapping and mutilation ... "Thank you for telling me."

Joe took a drag on his cigarette then handed it to me. "Congratulations on your son, by the way."

I scoffed quietly, then pulled at the cigarette, blowing out the pain. "The creature has cried constantly since birth. They call the condition colic. Apparently it's normal." I breathed in the smoke once more, then handed the cigarette back. "My head pounds. I can't sleep. I can't think." Then I let out a sigh. "I suppose I should be grateful. Some never receive the Dealer's Gift at all."

"You don't have to be grateful; the whole thing sounds a horror." He turned away. "With this job, I have money now. If you ever really want to get away from this, we can find somewhere to be free."

A rush of relief came over me. All I wanted was my life back, away from crying babies and sleepless nights. I wanted back in my apartments, helping other women find their loved ones. But instead I found myself torn up, inside and out, back living with a man I'd been forced to marry.

Then Joe was beside me. "I love you, Jacqui," he said softly, "more than he ever could." He put his hand on my arm. "This whole thing was never meant to happen. Let go of him. Let me take care of you."

A burly middle-aged man came from the back door and bellowed, "Yosef! Past time for you get back here."

"I'll be there in a minute, Mr. Barkis."

Mr. Barkis rolled his eyes and went back in.

A man dressed in black moved towards us from far down the alley. And I didn't want Tony to know I saw Joe. "I mustn't be seen here."

Joe's face softened. "That's one of our men." Then he shook his head, just a little. "What kind of life is this? What kind of marriage is this? He's got you afraid of your own shadow!" He took my hand in his. "You don't need him. And he's got his heir. He doesn't need you anymore." He looked down at my hand.

Then our eyes met, and I saw myself mirrored in them.

"I need you, Jacqui," Joe said earnestly. "I love you. I want you beside me forever." He stopped then, as if gathering the courage to speak. "I have friends who can hide us. Just say the word, and we can be gone tonight."

Tonight?

I wanted to go with him, truly I did, but something about really doing it right then frightened me. I hurried inside, Mary following.

We moved past the kitchens, then Mary grabbed my arm. "What did he say to you, there at the end?"

"Nothing. It was nothing." I kept going.

She pulled me aside. "Did you see his hands?"

"What about them?"

"He's not been washing dishes, mum."

Anger surged through me. But I spoke close to her ear as we went along. "That's ridiculous. He might have just started, or perhaps he wore gloves of some kind. Why-ever would he say so if he wasn't?" I pushed through the crowds and back to my seat.

She said nothing, but sat quietly holding Ariana, face concerned.

I still felt angry. How dare she malign a man she barely knew? The entire matter was none of her concern.

The dancing went on for hours. Cake went round, and more food, more drink. And my anger dissipated, the emptiness returning.

I didn't dare go back out for a smoke, not wanting to encounter Joe again. I might promise him things I should not.

The Red Dog Gang hunted me. They'd killed almost everyone I cared about. They'd terrorized and maimed Josie. What would they do to the man I loved, the man who'd devoted himself to me?

I couldn't take the chance of anything happening to him.

Daisy took Acevedo to nurse in a back room, and returned with him sleeping as if exhausted.

Vig and Natalia came to our table; Blitz and Mary rose. "Please, sit with us," Blitz said.

Vig grabbed his hand. "My good friend," he roared over the crowd. "When you come play to us again?"

"I have a wife and child," Blitz said, "and a household to manage."

Vig patted their clasped hands. "Maybe you find a night to visit me. For old times."

Blitz grinned. "Perhaps I will."

Vig dragged Blitz over. "Here. You dance with my wife. I have words for your Lady."

Natalia looked quite amused.

"With pleasure." Blitz offered his arm to Natalia. "Mrs. Vikenti?" And off they went.

Mary glanced at me, then took Daisy's arm. "Let's look at the flowers." So off they went.

Vig sat in Mary's chair. "So, my buddy friend, how you doing?"

I hadn't heard him call me that in so long.

"Uh oh." Vig leaned his left elbow on the table. "I don't like this. Why you crying? What's wrong?" He looked at Acevedo, asleep in his pram. "Good strong boy." He glanced at me. "You look well." He took my chin in his right hand. "Tell Vig what troubles you."

"I ruined my liver," I sobbed. "We'll never be able to have that drink I promised you."

"Ah." His hand dropped to his knee. "Well, I'm a married man now," he chuckled at that, glancing away, "so probably for the best."

"I'm sorry for everything: Roy destroying your saloon, your mother dying, everything. I've brought you nothing but pain."

"Nonsense." Vig handed me a napkin. "Yes, my mother die. She was old woman, and yes, I miss her. Very much. But everything is rebuilt. All is forgiven. The scoundrel got us new piano, better than old one. You rent this beautiful hall for our wedding. Come on, now. Why so sad? Tell me true."

My fingernails never really recovered after Jack Diamond captured me; they'd grown back pitted and bent. I wiped my eyes, feeling hollow. "I don't know. My friend just died. Maybe that's it."

Vig nodded. "The Court Keeper. I heard this." He put his hand on mine. "I heard also that he was good man."

"The best."

"Good man die, it sad, yes? But he'd want you happy." He ducked his head to peer into my eyes. "Yes?"

I nodded, remembering Jon's last words to me: *Promise me you'll find a way to be happy.* "He would."

"So dance with Vig. One time offer!"

That made me smile, and a new dance was starting. But as we danced, I couldn't help recalling a tiny wedding, far off so no one might interfere, as I was forced at gunpoint to marry Tony.

The Reports

By the time we left, it was late. Most of the guests had already gone, but the mass of reporters out front seemed unabated. When we stepped onto the walkway, Tony's men formed a wall around us, four of them around Acevedo alone.

Fortunately for little Acevedo's guards, the reporters only wanted to harass **me**. "Any comment on the Hart indictments?"

"What indictments?"

The man's face turned amused. "The counterfeiting ring. It was in the papers."

Blitz kept pushing me along. "The Lady of Spadros has no interest in the doings of Hart quadrant."

I smiled to myself. *Good one.*

The reporter seemed at a loss, yet another man pushed along with us. "What about the rumors of your husband being seen with the Diamond spinster?"

I stopped, horrified. *Gardena.* "Whatever are you talking about?"

"He's been noted going to Diamond quadrant over the betters' bridge, numerous times, and not down Promenade, either. He's been followed all the way to the Main Road. He'd hardly take that way to go to Diamond Manor, now, would he?"

I gaped at him. They'd learned about Tony visiting Gardena at one of their Country Houses. Would this bring them to learn about Tony's son Roland?

"Is your husband having an affair, my Lady?"

Tony? That was so preposterous I laughed aloud. "Certainly not."

A number of reporters spoke at once.

"Why is he going there so often, then?"

"Do her father and brothers know?"

"Who's he seeing there?"

"What's his connection with Miss Diamond?"

"Is Spadros intending an alliance with Diamond quadrant?"

Blitz gripped my arm. Under his breath, he said, "Come on, Mrs. Spadros, let's get out of here."

Honor was already at the carriage door. We bundled everyone inside to the shouts of the reporters.

"Good gods," I murmured. That last question had brought rioting to Diamond quadrant once already.

Blitz and Mary sat watching me. I glanced over at Daisy. "Is Acevedo well?"

As if on cue, he stirred, letting out a cry. Daisy took him up and began rocking him.

Ariana pointed a chubby little finger at him. "Baby."

"Yes," Mary said, "that's your cousin Acevedo, our baby Heir."

***

Tony had retired to his rooms by the time I got to mine, so after my lady's maid Amelia Dewey undressed me, I lay in my bed alone.

Acevedo began to howl.

I put the pillow over my head. My head ached. I felt exhausted. But I couldn't sleep.

Those reporters.

Sooner or later, someone would have made the connection. Looking back, I'm surprised it took as long as it did.

By all accounts, Anthony Spadros had been besotted with Gardena Diamond since well before his betrothal to me. Which, it seemed, had been forced on him by Roy as well. And one Grand Ball, Gardena — whose father seemed ready to forbid her to marry at all — bedded Tony, hoping for a child, which she got.

This foolish tryst had caused all manner of trouble from then on. But everything had been resolved ... until now.

I'd been one of many to suggest, nay, beg the Diamonds (most notably Gardena's oldest brother Cesare) to make a plan as to how to present young Roland Spadros to the city before something like this happened. As far as I could tell, my entreaties had been ignored.

If Diamond quadrant accepted the boy as their own, all would go well. But if they found the boy's birth certificate (which Gardena's father had marked indicating that Tony violated her — again, preposterous) ... then the two quadrants might find themselves in open war.

And if the populace of Diamond quadrant thought they were avenging the rape of their Family's only daughter, even Julius and Cesare might not be able to stop them.

I turned up the lamp. I needed to tell Tony about the reporters.

I had to be quite careful what I wrote, as anyone coming in here might see it. After some thought, I made a notation upon a pad on my bedstand: *Diamond*.

A soft knock at the door to my closets, then Tony came in.

My husband was a pale, ordinary-looking man: not particularly tall or short, heavy or thin, and the striped pajamas he wore made him look even more ordinary than usual. "I saw your light on," he said. "How was the wedding?"

I scooted over, still lying down. "I never saw so many different kinds of clothing in my life."

He climbed in beside me, sliding his arm under my pillow. "I'm glad you got to attend." He kissed my forehead. "You've seemed so melancholy lately."

A rush of emotion came over me; I turned to face the wall, Acevedo's screams in the distance. My life felt like a nightmare.

Tony raised himself on his elbow and began gently rubbing my lower back. "All will be well, my love." He kissed the back of my head. "We'll get through this."

He kept rubbing my back. A bit of desire I thought long lost stirred in me. But of course it was too soon for that: the doctor said at least two weeks after bleeding's end, and I'd only just stopped spotting.

Tony's hand went round to my poor sagging belly, still stretched and marked with stripes of pink. His hand cupped the folds there.

"I'm grateful for what you've done for me and my Family." He chuckled then. "Even though he's noisy right now, I'm still so grateful for him. But I'll be glad when you've recovered your slender waist."

I felt bitter. He obviously had never seen a woman naked who'd given birth. Very few regained a smooth flat belly, and those who did still had their mother's stripes, faded white. As little as men wanted to admit it, that was just part of the price women paid for a child.

One more loss in a world of hurt. I felt so lonely and sad that I began sobbing, right there beside him.

"I never meant to make you cry. I love you as much now as I ever have." He lay beside me, and I clasped his hand in mine. "Shh ... just rest now. The day makes all things brighter."

He was beside me, warm and comforting, his face by mine, kissing my shoulder from time to time.

Finally, then, I was able to sleep, even though Acevedo still cried.

Yet at the last, I thought of Joe. My beautiful, quiet, peaceful Joe.

***

I woke when Amelia pulled open the curtains, the morning sun streaming into my eyes over the edge of the other side of the big U-shaped building we lived in.

Spadros Manor was a strange place, really.

I stretched, yawned, and Amelia turned towards me. "Sorry to wake you, mum. Mr. Anthony asked Mrs. Molly and Miss Katherine to breakfast."

Tony's mother and sister. I felt disgruntled. "Very well."

Katie — a girl just turned sixteen — was as reasonable as most girls that age were. But I really wasn't interested in seeing Molly that day. Well, to be honest, ever again.

Molly Hogan Spadros had forced me to bear Acevedo in the first place. She took my morning tea which prevented a child and replaced it with one which did nothing. Then she maneuvered my husband and I to be alone together — though we'd been entirely estranged — and like a fool, I bedded him.

Then when I finally found a midwife who might remove the thing, Molly intervened. What she threatened the woman with, I'll never know, but the howling mess down the hall was the inevitable result.

My head hurt. It always hurt in those days, from the time I woke to the time I finally slept. I'd asked the doctor about it shortly after Acevedo's birth, and was told I couldn't take anything: all I needed were liquids and rest.

If the horrid thing would ever stop screaming.

For an instant, I considered Joe's offer. I felt sure that if I might get one night of sleep, one day of peace, then I might feel well again.

But then Honor knocked, coming in with my "provisional" tray — tea and toast, paper and mail. In all the years I'd known him, he'd never so much as glanced in my direction when bringing it in.

Amelia began arranging my paper and mail. "I hope you're well?"

"As well as any day." I yawned, getting out of bed; the sudden motion made me dizzy.

Amelia hurried over to help me into my robe.

I said, "Is that a new ring?" The ring was golden, with elm leaves carved into its face. It looked real, not some cheap copy.

She blushed. "My Mr. Dewey gave me this for our anniversary."

"Oh! Congratulations. What it is now?"

"Twenty years, mum."

*Tony must be paying Peter Dewey **very** well.* "I'm happy for you." I took her hand, examined it. "It's lovely. I wonder where he got it."

"If you like, I can ask. Gold would suit your complexion."

Amused, I put on the pendant Jon and Mr. Hart had given me: the Holy Symbol of Mr. Hart's Family, rendered fat in silver thread. Of course, I couldn't wear the Hart Symbol in public, but at home …

I wore it under my bodice, close to my heart, feeling it was one of the last things I had that Jonathan had touched.

The three pressed daffodils he'd given me with it were framed beside my bed. A fond smile at them, and after visiting the toilet-room, I went to my tea-table. As I munched my toast, Acevedo whimpering in the distance, I wondered why Molly should want to visit in the first place, much less for breakfast.

Amelia began making my bed as I paged through my mail.

None of the letters were from Josie. Most involved my business as an investigator. Despite numerous requests to have business mail sent to my apartments, it seemed no one dared do it. I sighed, packed those into my green and gold paisley carpetbag, and turned to the paper.

The headlines were about the counterfeiters — some mid-card Hart Associates — but I was surprised to see Mr. Thrace Pike mentioned as the prosecutor for the case. The thin pale face and dark eyes of the young former *Bridges Daily* reporter the night he'd vowed to defeat the Four Families swam before me.

Nothing seemed to deter the man: not poverty nor disappointment nor the scorn of all around him. He'd even abandoned his devotion to the Bridgers — the fanatical religious sect he'd grown up in — to pursue his goal. In the time since he turned to the law, the man had done very well for himself, particularly since he'd left his grandfather's defense firm.

Thinking of the older man soured my mood. I still owed Doyle Pike a good deal of money, although not nearly so much as before.

Returning to the paper, I continued to read. Apparently one of the Hart Apprentices had discovered a new kind of Party Time that didn't taste like cinnamon sugar.

I didn't see that it would make much difference other than to the sellers of cinnamon rolls (who'd always been looked upon with suspicion) and those few police in Bridges who actually cared about enforcing the law.

The Bridgers, of course, were furious; the Letters to the Editor page was full. One asked: *How might we keep ourselves and our families free from the drug without being able to taste its presence?* Another quoted the Holy Writ: *A befuddled mind plays their Hand to the ruin of his partners.*

I was reminded then of the man who I still thought of as my father: the former Party Time addict Peedro Sluff, now dead.

Six weeks after his murder, the police still had no leads on who might have shot him in his liquor store. And no one had helped with our inquiries, even though he'd been under Spadros protection.

The fact that someone murdered a man placed under the Spadros Patriarch's protection was disturbing in itself. But this was only the most recent. A police detective in the pay of the Family. The Spadros Inventor — a distant cousin of Roy's. And now Peedro.

It hinted that Roy's hold over the Family was slipping.

I didn't know what might happen if it did, if people began to believe they didn't need to fear that ruthless cold-hearted sadist, didn't have to follow his commands. But none of it would be good.

I needed to help Tony understand how dangerous this all was.

The people didn't want me here — at best I was a scandal, a Pot rag. They felt forced to accept me out of their fear of Roy, nothing more. Plus, the Red Dog Gang seemed to be targeting me. The safest thing for Acevedo would be for me to stay at my apartments.

But I couldn't have him learn that I'd been forced to bear the child. He'd need Molly's help with the boy, and the last thing I wanted was for him and his mother to become estranged from each other. I already knew how painful that was. "Amelia, might you hand me that pad by my bed and a pencil?"

"Yes, mum." After handing me the items, Amelia went into the bathroom; the sound of running water came forth.

Below the word *"Diamond"* I wrote, *"apartments."*

Then I returned to the newspaper. Cesare Diamond had made a speech about the dredging of the South River. It wasn't clear whether he'd thought up the slogan, "Bringing Our People Home," but I had to admit it was clever.

Unfortunately, it kept the first Spadros-Diamond War in everyone's minds, which when added to recent events, didn't seem good.

Why hadn't Julius Diamond just sent a messenger any time in the week after Jonathan's death to tell us not to come to his son's funeral? Why force me to get out of bed after almost dying in childbirth, let us come all the way to the betters' bridge with a newborn, only to publicly turn us aside?

Maybe Tony was right: perhaps I was wrong to forgive him.

On the next page was a long article: over sixty "chaste" young women in Hart quadrant, some as young as fourteen, had been struck with an unexplained fever. Many of these women had died, leaving grief-stricken and bewildered families.

That this writer used the word "chaste" amused me. But otherwise, the article would never have been printed at all.

In the Pot, the first thing we would have considered in such cases was womb fever. The malady was common in brothels, which was why the Cathedral insisted the men be inspected and bathed before allowing them to visit the women, so as not to spread contagion.

But a sudden, deadly fever in women who had never bedded a man? This puzzled me.

Another point in the article interested me. Only in a few cases had any of the family members caught the fever themselves, all sisters of the deceased who'd shared the same bed.

The article gave warning that young women suffering fever should sleep in a room away from other women in order to stop the spread.

Yet this raised more questions. Many of the women in the slums suffering this fever had slept two or even six to a bed yet the rest never fell ill. And the disease seemed only to attack women.

Was there some strange new contagion afoot?

The Intrusion

A flyer had been slipped in the back:

MORE FAMILIES SLIP TO OBLIVION

Blood Tea Interruption Is Ruining Us

The Pot has never been so full as the interruption to the supply of what the ladies somewhat indelicately call "blood tea" has meant the expansion of the poor, and for some, the fall to exile.

Men already unable to afford the mouths they must feed are now forced to add more through no fault of their own.

Why have we put our livelihoods and futures in the hands of one man's ingredient, one method to gain control of our budgeting? This situation not only risks our standing and honor, it risks moral decay and the future of our heirs.

We demand an investigation into how this has happened, and put forth petitions to the Cultural Correctness Committee for alternate assistance.

People for a Better Future

I sat back, appalled. Molly had to have done this. In her single-minded obsession with me presenting her son with an heir, she'd doomed the entire city.

Who was this "People for a Better Future" group? Why had they suddenly become the champions of the city?

How did they get access to the *Bridges Daily* to slip these inside?

Amelia came in with a bundle of my clothing over one arm, which she set upon the bed.

As she lay out my clothing, I folded the flyer and slipped it into my carpetbag. Another mystery.

I recalled the Hart symbol on one of this group's earlier pamphlets, something I'd never been able to adequately explain. "I'll be going to my apartments after morning meeting." My business partner Master Blaze Rainbow (who I always thought of as the first name he'd given me: Morton) had asked to meet.

"Yes, mum," Amelia said, over the sound of running water. "Mr. Pearson told me." John Pearson was Spadros Manor's butler, as well as Mary's father.

It was the first time I'd gone to my apartments since the baby's birth, and I looked forward to it. "I'd like to wear my charcoal dress."

It was still a bit tight on me, and had been patched and mended many a time ... but I liked it.

"Of course, mum."

"Can we get a Memory Boy here before I must leave?"

"I'll have Mr. Pearson try, mum."

I smiled to myself, relaxing.

"Time for your bath, mum." Amelia glanced at the bed. "Oh! I forgot your stockings and house shoes."

She headed back to my closets.

I went into the bathing room. "And my wrapper, if you please. I feel a chill."

Amelia cried out!

Clutching my robe to me, I rushed to my closets: Amelia's husband Peter stood there.

"Goodness gracious, you **startled** me," Amelia said.

I peered at him. Peter Dewey was Spadros Manor's stable-master. "Whatever are you doing in there?"

Peter stared at me blankly, apparently unable to give answer.

A noise past him, and Tony's manservant Jacob Michaels came peering around. Michaels was quite short for a man, and gave the impression of being quite young, although he was much older than I. "What's going on here?"

"Mr. Dewey was just leaving," I said firmly. "And I'll be speaking with Pearson about this."

Peter tipped his cap as if out on the street instead of in my private chambers. "Sorry to disturb you, mum." He turned round, going past Michaels through Tony's rooms, and out the door to the back hall.

Amelia's face was crimson. "I don't know what's gotten into the man. He's **never** done something like this, **ever**! To come upstairs! And into your private **rooms**!" She sounded ready to cry. "I'm so very sorry, mum."

I felt puzzled about why he was there. I didn't want to ask in front of Amelia if anything was taken. But Michaels and I exchanged a glance, and I had the feeling he'd been thinking the same thing.

***

Tony was already at the table when I went down to breakfast; Molly and Katie were nowhere to be seen. He smiled when he saw me. "Get your food and sit by me."

When he spoke like this, he usually either felt quite fond of me, or had something in particular to say. Today, it seemed, it was both. He spoke quite softly, close to my ear. "What's wrong, Jacqui?"

I shrugged. I'd been feeling pretty well up to then, but at his words melancholy swept over me.

"I worry for you," Tony said. "You grieve **all** the time." He took my hands, seemingly heedless of Pearson and the servants standing by. Yet he spoke softly. "I loved Jon too, more than any other man —"

Oh, dear. I hoped he'd never said that in front of his cousin Sawbuck, who was completely besotted with him.

Tony kissed my hands. "But Acevedo's your **son**. He needs his mother. Miss Daisy is trying her best, but —"

I nodded. She was trying to tend him, to the point of exhaustion.

"— she's not his mother, and never can be." He squeezed my hands. "We need you, Jacqui. I need you. Please come back to us."

I didn't know what he meant, but I nodded just the same. Other than the wedding, I'd not left Spadros Manor, not even to go on the veranda, since I'd come home from trying to attend Jonathan's funeral. Today would be the first time to return to my apartments.

Pearson had stepped out during the exchange, and returned to the door. "Mrs. Molly Spadros and Miss Katherine, sir."

Tony gave Pearson an amused smile. "Show them in."

Most decidedly late. So **that's** how Molly wished to play this.

Molly Hogan Spadros was buxom, with a mass of raven curls spilling down one shoulder. Tony's sister Katherine was slender and taciturn. She normally had long wavy auburn hair, but had cut it to her chin and dyed it black a year or so earlier.

To everyone's dismay, Katie dressed much as her father Roy did: black trousers, a white shirt, a black vest. Her only nod to womanhood was a row of round black beads which hung below her open button-down collar.

Tony and I rose. He bowed, whilst I curtsied to Molly's rank as the Queen of Spades. In my bitterness, I thought: *If I had the power, I'd banish Molly from the quadrant.*

But I smiled warmly at Katie, and came round to take her hand. "I'm so glad to see you."

Katie seemed startled by that, but sat beside me. After an instant of hesitation, Molly chose a seat across from Tony, Pearson holding the chair for her.

Tony said, "I hope you're both well?"

Molly didn't wait for Katie to answer. "We are. And you?"

She'd directed the question mostly to me, so I answered directly to her. "As well as might be expected."

I felt pleased to see her flinch.

Tony glanced at us both. "Would you care to select your meal?"

We rose once more as Molly and Katie went to the buffet, and waited until they returned. My food was about cold by this time, but I ate it anyway.

Since Tony had asked Pearson to run the morning meeting, after breakfast, we went down the hall to the parlor. Tony and Katie went ahead, with me and Molly walking a few steps behind.

Tony said to Katie, "Do you have old Burch this term?"

"No," Katie said, "still Miss Lila."

"But —"

"I'm to get another year of deportment," she flicked her collar, "I suppose as punishment for this."

Tony laughed.

Molly took my arm, pulling me close. "Roy wants to see Acevedo."

I extricated myself. "So?"

"Anthony won't allow him over."

I stopped, lowered my voice. "What possible way do you think I might sway that?" Molly started to speak, but I stopped her. "If I had anything to say about it, you'd never set foot in this house again."

Tony and Katie stood beside us. "Is something wrong?"

Molly had the grace to look abashed.

"Nothing," I said.

"Then let's go to the parlor. I have a surprise for you."

To my astonishment, Daisy stood in the parlor beside a crib holding a sleeping — and praise be the gods, quiet! — Master Acevedo Spadros III.

The boy looked quite the young cherub. Molly and Katie pushed forward to coo and smile at him.

I turned to Tony. "However did you arrange this?"

"Your Miss Daisy said she knew a trick from her grandmother," Tony whispered, "so I allowed it just this once."

I felt concerned. "Is it harmful?"

"I don't think so," Tony said, "but I'd not want to do it again."

The boy opened his eyes: dark blue like Tony's, shaped like mine. He looked up and smiled, big and toothless.

"He's adorable," Katie said. "May I hold him?"

I smiled fondly at her. "Of course you can. Put your hand behind his head to hold it up for him."

So Molly and Katie sat on the sofa whilst Katie held the baby. Tony and I sat in the armchairs, watching them.

"Finally quiet," I said softly. "Too bad we can't have Daisy perform her magic every night."

Tony chuckled.

After a bit, Acevedo began to fuss.

Daisy said, "I'll need to go feed him."

Katie leaned forward. "Can I go with her?"

We all looked to Molly: she nodded. "It'll be good for you, Katie." Her tone clearly stated what she had to be thinking: *to see what you'll be giving up if you continue this path you're on.*

Katie rolled her eyes, but followed Daisy and Acevedo out.

After that followed a full half-hour of awkward small talk before the three returned. Katie carried Acevedo, looking rather awe-struck. She kept saying, "I never imagined such a thing!"

Daisy began blushing furiously, and looked quite uncomfortable.

Tony only seemed amused. "Dear sister, that's not something you generally speak of in front of gentlemen." He then took my hand. "I know you wanted so to be able to nurse him —"

Why was he saying this in front of everyone?

He spoke to Daisy. "— but you seem to have found an admirable substitute. Well done."

Daisy looked as though she might faint. Being spoken about at all in front of uppers was rare enough, but to be praised by the Heir in front of her Queen?

I smiled at her. "We'll ring if we need you."

She curtsied to the floor. "Yes, mum. Thank you, mum. Sir." Then she rushed out.

I said to Tony, "The poor girl looked ready to die of fright."

Katie stood there awkwardly, as if not sure what to do.

"She's a good one," Tony said to me. He turned to Molly. "You've chosen well." Then he reached out to Katie. "Here, let me take him."

Perhaps he was getting heavy, because Katie handed him over with some relief then sat beside her mother. Acevedo stared blankly around him as babies do.

"Get a chair and sit by me," Tony said to his sister.

So Katie sat beside Tony, and they amused themselves with baby-talk whilst the boy tried to focus upon them.

Molly said to me, "Would you care to walk with me?"

I surveyed her with suspicion. "Perhaps."

Tony and Katie didn't rise when we did, encumbered with and focused upon the baby as they were. Molly and I proceeded to do a turn around my excessively large parlor.

Molly said quietly, "Why are you behaving like this?"

I said, just as quietly, "Behaving like what?"

"I thought Tony was deceiving me. But you never so much as smile at your boy."

I shrugged. "What do you wish me to say? I bear the child no malice, but ..."

"This isn't right. Can't you at least pretend to love him?"

"Like I've had to with your son?"

Tony glanced up, startled.

I'm sure he didn't hear what I said, but I lowered my voice just the same. "Do you even care about me at all? Or am I just a broodmare for your ambition?"

Molly stopped to stare at me, mouth open. "Jacqui, I —"

"What you've done is unforgivable. You have your Heir. That's what you wanted me for, isn't it?"

"Jacqui," Tony said from across the room. "What's wrong?"

Molly turned to Katie. "Perhaps it's time for us to go."

"But —" Katie said.

"No," said Molly. "We've been here long enough."

Acevedo arched his back and began to cry when Tony handed him to me. So we rang for Daisy, who stood just outside the door.

We followed Molly and Katie outside. They got into Molly's piano black carriage with her silver Queen's Seal upon the door, and left.

Tony turned to me. "What was that all about?"

I felt weary. "It's an old argument, between her and I alone."

"I won't have you argue. I love you both, dearly." He took my hands. "I want to see you happy."

But how might I ever be?

The Affidavit

A carriage pulled up: red, with the seal of the Memory Boys upon its side in gold. The horses were Hackney stallions, like those that pulled the taxi-carriages, but the tack on these horses was red and gold.

Tony said, "What's this?"

"I called for a Memory Boy before breakfast. Pearson must have told them it was urgent."

"Is it? What's going on?"

Acevedo's howling could be heard even out here. I took his hand, just for a moment. "Nothing bad, I hope."

A grown footman wearing the red jacket of the Memory Boys came round to open the carriage's door, but the outfit he wore more resembled livery.

I said softly, "Are you available later today?"

He shrugged. "Anything you need, I can make the time for." He smiled at me. "You know that."

Did I?

The Memory Boy Werner Lead came bounding from the carriage, accompanied by his two older brothers.

Werner's formerly white-blond hair had turned golden. His two older brothers, both dark-haired, were now becoming men, with the soft beginnings of beard upon the eldest.

Werner pressed forward, coming as usual to the bottom of the stairs. His two brothers, both armed, stood several paces behind, watching everything but him.

Tony said, "You honor us with your haste, Memory Boy."

Werner gave us a happy smile. "I do like riding in carriages! But the honor is mine. What message does Spadros Manor wish sent?"

Memory Boys brought messages much too secret to write. But in Bridges, everyone reported to someone, and I didn't know who Werner reported to, not yet. I smiled at him. "It's nowhere near that formal. The message is to Mr. Paul Blackberry of the *Bridges Daily*. We merely wish to meet with our old friend at his convenience, on a matter dear to us all."

Werner nodded, but I could see the gears turning. Even with a simple message like this, the boy was learning much. Perhaps too much. "To Mr. Blackberry: we wish to meet with our old friend at his convenience on a matter dear to us all." He bowed. "Very good."

I handed him a dollar. "This again should you return his reply before true night falls."

His eyes widened. "Thank you!"

Tony chuckled as the boys hurried away. "You're too generous by half." He took my hand, and we went to one of the small tea-tables beside the front door and sat. "Now, what's this all about?"

Acevedo wailed in the distance.

I sighed. "There have been several pamphlets and fliers over the past year or so from a group calling itself 'People for a Better Future'." I glanced at him. "I sent one of them to Roy; I don't know whether he told you about it."

Tony shook his head.

"On the face of it, most sound innocent. But lately they've been becoming more pointed against the Families. I found the last one in the back of the *Bridges Daily*."

Tony's eyes widened. "Surely Mr. Blackberry has nothing to do with this!"

"But if someone's using his paper to harm us, he needs to know."

Tony drew back, blinking. "I completely agree!" Then his eyes narrowed. "That Bridger fellow used to be with the paper. That Pike fellow, your lawyer's grandson."

"Former lawyer, I'll have you know." Mr. Doyle Pike had threatened and blackmailed me in the past, and I wanted as little to do with the man as possible.

"Whatever. Isn't the grandson with the District Attorney's office now? Could **he** be behind this?"

"Hmm." I wasn't sure what was in Thrace Pike's mind. He claimed he'd left the Bridgers to join his grandfather's firm. Or at least that's what his grandfather said. Thrace's wife Gertie — definitely still a Bridger, no matter what she claimed — seemed not to know anything about this group. "I've not seen him since the fire."

"Wait. He was there? At the warehouse?"

"Yes. He was one of the men who rescued me." I shuddered, remembering how he spoke, the passion in his voice, how he dared once more to lay hands upon me. "I don't understand how he of all people even knew I was there."

Tony had a slight frown on his face. "That is the oddest thing I've heard in some time. And he didn't explain?"

"No, I ran out. Then I saw you." The memory warmed me.

Tony took my hand. "That was the most fearful night of my life, yet the most wonderful." He beamed. "To learn we were to have a **child**!"

I felt bitter. What a disaster that'd been so far.

My carriage pulled up: the plain carriage, piano black with black horses like the rest, but with no markings to indicate the rank of those inside. In broad daylight, not much of a disguise, but it was particularly good when going somewhere at night. I rose. "Master Rainbow wanted to meet with me ..." I shrugged. "I've no idea why. And I have some correspondence to write. But this shouldn't take long. We can speak about it more later."

Tony smiled fondly at me. "My love, I await your return."

***

On the way to my apartments, I thought about what Tony had said: *"My love."*

Jonathan often called me that, and the thought brought back tears.

Why had the Red Dog Gang wanted Jonathan Diamond dead?

It couldn't possibly be just because we were friends — he was much too powerful for them to dare this without good reason. Had he seen something he shouldn't? Had his position as Keeper of the Court threatened them somehow?

My head hurt. I felt exhausted all the time. My mind went round and round, unable to grasp onto an answer, and that in itself made me weep. I'd been like this ever since I was taken. I feared I was losing my mind, and it frightened me.

But when I got to my apartments, Morton was there, and I felt glad. A man barely taller than I with light brown hair and a fondness for wearing brown, when we met in the parlor of my apartments, he seemed happy to see me. "I have good news!"

The ringing of a messenger's bell whizzed by. This reminded me sharply of little Ante. Why would the boy work for the Family he thought had murdered his brother? Were all those years of service just for the hope of revenge? "I'm glad to hear it. Please, sit down." Blitz had brought tea, and I took a cup. "What's happened?"

"I found Albert Sheinwold. Or to be more precise, he agreed to meet with me."

"Oh." We'd been searching for the man for a couple of years. "That's wonderful! When did this happen?"

My sudden question seemed to have taken him off guard: he was in the midst of drinking, and quickly swallowed. "Last week. Yesterday, we met with a notary, and he's given an affidavit to it all." Morton shook his head. "The whole thing's incredible. He told me about Zia, how she'd killed all her informants, what she said about her partner's death — or shall I say, murder —"

"Murder?"

"It sounded as if she had him **killed**!" The thought seemed to dismay him. "I'd heard rumors of this, but ... to hear the man testify to it in person ... good gods." He sat silent, for several seconds his face downcast, then murmured, "Was I to be **next**?"

This certainly seemed alarming. But from what I'd seen and heard of her so far, not particularly surprising.

Then he sighed. "Now all I have to do is get his statement to the Feds. They'll have to believe me now."

"If you need an invitation into Clubb quadrant —"

Morton waved me off with an amused smile. "That won't be necessary. I live there now, remember?"

I put my hand to my forehead and rubbed it, feeling weary. "Yes, I'm sorry. I do remember."

"That's quite all right." He chuckled. "I never thought in my wildest dreams that I'd end up living there."

Although he looked nothing like anyone in the Hart Family, from what he'd said before it sounded as if Blaze Rainbow had grown up in the Hart lands. His family had owned property there. Living in Clubb quadrant must be disorienting at times, particularly having to be in hiding, away from your own people.

Morton said, "May I ask something perhaps personal?"

"Of course."

"Are you well? You look so pale. And you weren't at Master Jonathan's funeral."

A rush of emotion. "I'm as well as I might be, under the circumstances." If Morton hadn't heard about how we were turned away at the bridge, he didn't really need to know about it now.

"Congratulations on your son, by the way."

"Thank you." But my mind was on my earlier thought. Now that I had him here, perhaps I could get the answer to a question that had bothered me for a while now. "There's something I never understood."

Morton glanced up. "What?"

"That meeting you told me about when we first met. It was you, Zia Cashout, Frank Pagliacci, and the detective. Mr. Bower. Right?"

"Yeah. So?"

"Why would you, a man who's lived in Bridges all his life, think that a man with the DA's office and a police detective would help a couple of private investigators meet up with an informant?"

"Like I told you: they claimed they believed the man had information that would help them bring down the Families. The only way he'd talk is if he saw you first."

Yes, he'd told me this before. But it was then that it hit me: he'd been a Hart all his life ...

Morton was playing both sides!

This explained why he never went to them for help. And what could he have possibly said to the Hart Family if they'd caught him, one of their own people, in their own quadrant, discussing with the Feds as to how to destroy them? "So why the whole charade with taking David Bryce? Why would you believe any of that? It was not only cruel, but unnecessary: they could have just come to me directly and not tell me about the 'bringing down the Families' part."

Morton's head drooped, and he put his elbows on his knees, studying my coffee table. He shrugged. "I guessed they thought you'd be guarded, or just go to your husband. They never really explained it." He sighed, still looking down, and he sounded dismayed. "I trusted Zia. She'd done this longer than me. I thought she and I were partners, that we were there to protect each other." He shook his head, put it into his hands. "I was a complete fool."

Sitting there, watching him, I was reminded of what he'd said, shortly after I first met him: *I never played a rough man before.* And I remembered thinking before we rescued David that he must have been entirely new at this.

And I felt moved. He'd not only been betrayed to his enemies, but it'd been by someone more experienced, someone he thought would keep him safe.

Yet something still didn't feel right. "What did you do before you started all this investigator work?"

Morton laughed, sitting up. "Sat behind a desk, mostly."

A gentleman, shuffling paper?

Then I recalled all the work Tony did before we hired the accountant. "Protect that affidavit well, Master Rainbow, if you mean it to protect you."

I hoped he had more than a piece of paper for protection from the likes of Frank and Zia. Otherwise, it was a certainty that this venture would end up with him dead.

The Son

The doorbell rang; I heard Blitz answer it. From the footsteps that approached, I knew who it was well before Blitz announced him. "Mr. Charles Hart to see you."

Morton's face lit up, and he rose.

Mr. Hart seemed equally pleased. "By the gods, Master Rainbow! It's wonderful to see you." The two shook hands. "Whatever are you doing here?"

As if he didn't have spies upon us both at all times.

Yet that thought reminded me of what Jack Diamond had said: *I don't even have to put spies on you! I simply follow the chaos and I know exactly where you've been.*

And I wondered how that madman fared. "Master Rainbow and I are business partners. As you most likely already know." I smiled at him to soften my words. "To what do I owe the honor of your visit?"

"I'd like to take you to luncheon," Mr. Hart said. "If you feel well enough. You're invited too, Master Rainbow, of course."

"I have a prior engagement, but please, enjoy your outing."

"Thanks for calling on me," I said to Morton. "Please let me know if there's any way I might help."

"I will," said Morton.

I called out, "Blitz!" When he emerged, I said, "Let my husband know where I've gone, will you?"

"Of course. When might you be expected to return?"

I glanced at Mr. Hart, not knowing what he had planned for me.

"Oh, I'll have her back here before tea-time for certain," he boomed. "Safe as can be."

Blitz grinned. "Very well then. Have fun!"

Morton, Mr. Hart, and I went down the front steps. Mr. Hart's carriage sat there, white with the seal of the Hart Patriarch raised in silver on its side. We'd been asked not to park in front because the street was much too narrow for anyone else to pass, but who'd tell that to the Hart Patriarch?

"My carriage is on Scoop," I said. "Where might I meet you?"

"I've sent your carriage home," Mr. Hart said. "It'll be back to bring you home for tea." He grinned. "It's no trouble to return you here."

"A good play!" Charles Hart bringing me back to Spadros Manor might cause a great deal of trouble if Roy Spadros learned of it.

"I'm so pleased you think so." He turned to shake hands with Morton. "Anywhere we might take you?"

"Don't trouble yourself on my account," Morton said. "I plan to enjoy the day." He tipped his hat and strolled the opposite way, towards the Backdoor Saloon.

He said he had a prior commitment. What was he really up to?

Half the neighborhood was in the street gaping. Mr. Hart turned to me. "Shall we?"

So I got in.

The inside of his carriage was a fiery red, entirely covered in the finest velvet. A gift for his grandfather, he'd said once, made long ago.

We traversed the streets, making our way towards the Main Road, then towards Market Center. I wondered if Mr. Hart intended to take me to that one restaurant he seemed to like so well.

Why had Morton agreed to work with Frank Pagliacci? It obviously wasn't any animosity towards Mr. Hart. And in all other things, Morton had been quite loyal — well, to me at least — even putting his life in danger.

Perhaps I'm just a sucker for a pretty face, he'd said the day we rescued David Bryce from Frank and whatever hell the boy had suffered at the hands of that fiend. Which made me wonder from time to time if he'd become my business partner for some other reason than financial.

But Morton never acted as a man pining over a woman would, never became familiar, never imposed upon me in any way. He never even had any animosity towards Tony, and though at first Tony had definite jealousy towards Morton, they seemed now to be friends.

That Tony and Morton should become friends was another matter I didn't understand, and I suppose at that point in my life, I wanted to.

Mr. Hart's carriage continued on past the Hedge, that fence of yew and iron surrounding my home, which was now in the hands of the Red Dog Gang.

Melancholy filled me, recalling my great-grandmother, the Eldest of our people, who now lay dead.

The discussion with Ma at our meeting in the park before Acevedo was born had made one thing very clear: the neglect of my duty to help my people had left them open to the Red Dog Gang's influence. I'd made little progress on that account, and it bothered me. What could I do to make them want to get rid of the villainous Black Maria?

Black Maria seemed a direct threat to the Cathedral, and I wished I would have thought to ask Ma about that when I saw her. The whole meeting had gone horribly wrong, leaving me with more questions than answers.

"I felt surprised to learn you were out in public so soon after giving birth." Mr. Hart sounded somber. "How are you, Jacqui, really?"

I shrugged.

"We're all worried for you."

I scoffed. "Did my mother-in-law put you up to this?"

"What? No. I've not seen her in some time." He squinted slightly, as if in some thought. "Briefly, at the last Grand Ball. Of course, we didn't so much as speak."

Of course not. Roy still harbored fury at the very mention of Mr. Hart. To have his wife speak with the man might have thrown him into apoplexy.

This made me wonder what Roy thought of me meeting with his most hated enemy like this. However did Mr. Hart arrange it?

Mr. Hart had leaned forward, elbows on his knees, now gazing at the floor. "In some ways, Jonathan Diamond was closer to me than my own son. His death now, when he had so much to live for, it ... it grieves me deeply."

He loved Jon, too. How did this happen?

"What the two of you must have had ... it only comes once in life, most rarely so. For some, never. I know how you must mourn him —"

And I did. Jon was the one man who knew everything, understood me without my having to speak. He knew how to make me smile when the world was at its worst.

I loved him. I loved him with all my heart. I never admitted it, even to myself, until he lay dying in that alley. But I loved him.

And like all the rest, he lay dead.

"— but your son is only young once. Don't let grief cause you to throw away the good life you could have. The life Master Jonathan would surely have wanted for you."

That moved me more than Tony's words ever could. I gazed out of the window at the gray water as we rode along, Market Center a pale blurred outline in the distance.

I wiped my eyes. Where was Jon now?

For a while, I'd thought that since Acevedo was born as Jon died, that somehow he'd gotten Jon's cards.

But Acevedo seemed to want nothing to do with me. Had I disappointed Jon, caused him to hate me somehow?

Surely not. I could see nothing I might ever do that would make Jon hate me.

So whose cards had my baby gotten? Why did he cry so? Why did he pull away, arch his back, scream when I tried to hold him?

I could never know. All I knew is that my best friend was dead because of me. "I think Jon's death was intentional."

Mr. Hart twitched. "Hmm?"

"He was lured there with a forged letter supposedly from me. We were hunted in that warehouse, herded and terrified, when the whole city knew Jon was dreadfully ill. They hounded him to his death." I turned to the window. "And I want to know why."

"I don't understand."

"It was a set-up. Miss Josephine was kidnapped then they demanded I go there to save her. But they didn't know that I didn't know about the Cathedral. Whatever it is that they want from there. Besides, my husband wouldn't let me leave in any case. So they had to get me there another way. Thus, my kidnapping."

Mr. Hart nodded, his eyes intent upon mine.

"But she was being kept cruelly manacled, in the most abominable filth ..." the thought of her beautiful wrists permanently scarred enraged me, and I forced myself to focus, "yet left entirely unguarded, with items nearby that either of us could use to free her. Then the men 'just happened' to return. And there were only three ways out of the building. They had to know where we might go, and they'd be fools to leave those ways unguarded, Yet they did. They had a boy in their thrall who hated our Family, who they'd promised might have a stab at me —"

Mr. Hart gasped in horror.

I snorted. "This wasn't my first time facing a knife-hand, sir, and he was half my size. I was in little danger. The point is that they treated her horribly, but when we got her free, they made no serious effort to capture us."

I put my hand to my forehead: if only I'd seen it then! If only I'd been stronger, my mind clearer. "The entire thing was for show, to terrify and dismay us. To see if they might force one of the three of us into doing or saying something rash that would lead to our doom."

And Jon had done just that.

"I heard Master Jonathan carried you from the building."

I nodded. "He might have saved my life." The Family searched for me, both our Families did. But they had no idea which building we were in until we emerged. "I could have bled to death in that warehouse, the child inside me." I stared at Market Center's shoreline, trying to compose myself. "Jon collapsed once, before the terrible pain began. What if he'd died right then?"

Mr. Hart looked appalled. "No one would ever know until your bodies were found. What a risk you took, going inside!"

"All I knew was that Miss Josephine lay bound in there. She was calling out. She's —" I remembered our kiss in the meeting room on Market Center. "— **more** than a sister to me. How could I stand by?"

Mr. Hart turned his face to the window and didn't speak for some time. "I have many questions about this kidnapping, Mrs. Spadros. I too question the circumstances around it."

I felt a great sense of relief: I wasn't mad to question it. I hadn't felt I could speak of it to anyone, not even to Tony. My head hurt all the time, I couldn't sleep ... even the carriage ride made the world sway, my stomach turn, as if my whole existence was unstable somehow. I can't explain it any better.

But someone else believed the whole matter wasn't right. "I don't know what to do."

We passed the bridge guards and turned right, towards the bridge to Clubb. The restaurant he loved so well lay nearby.

"Let's get something to eat," Mr. Hart said. "There's something I wish to discuss with you."

The inside of the Kournikova had walls covered in two tones of mustard-brown split by a golden edging. Thick reddish-brown carpeting covered the floor. Round tables filled the room, surrounded by chairs upholstered in Paisley, woven in green, gray, gold, and brown. The tables, covered in white, lay empty but for one small square one in the center, set in white and silver.

Delicious smells filled the air. We sat, Mr. Hart's men standing guard at each corner, much too far away to hear us speak. I wondered what Mr. Hart had to discuss with me that required such secrecy.

Our food was delivered at once; we ate in silence. I had so much in my mind then that I felt numb. Why kill Jon? What use did the Red Dog Gang have for the Spadros Pot? Why involve Josie in all this? Could it all just be to terrorize me? If so, what had I **done** to them?

"My son is obviously unsettled at the attack upon his betrothed," Mr. Hart said quietly. "He wishes to have greater say in the doings of the quadrant, I believe so he can improve security."

"Do you think that's wise?"

"I do."

I laughed, feeling rather unsettled. "Your son rushed past my guards to my bedroom in the middle of the night carrying a box with a **finger** in it!" The fact that he did this still astonished me. "Is he mad?"

"Etienne can be impetuous, it's true," Mr. Hart said. "But he's capable of leading. And it's well past time he did so. "

I didn't feel convinced.

Mr. Hart must have sensed it, because he leaned forward, his elbows on the table. "What you want is for me to choose between my daughter and my son. How can you ask that? How can either of you ask this?" He leaned back. "I want you both to be happy." He glanced away. "This situation, this ... animosity between you two threatens everyone involved." Then he faced me. "I must keep you all — you, him, my wife and your mother — I have to keep you safe from the man whose only goal is to kill us."

This startled me: I'd forgotten about the man Mr. Hart so feared, the one who'd been blackmailing him into silence.

"We **must** resolve this issue between you two. And if giving him more power makes him feel that I don't value you over him, then —"

"So it's as I thought: he believes Acevedo is a threat to his claim."

Mr. Hart shrugged. "I'm honestly not sure how he might."

I hesitated, fearing how he might take the news. "I've been warned of a wildcard in Hart quadrant."

"Oh?"

"I don't want it to be Mr. Etienne —"

Mr. Hart scoffed.

"— but there's something not right about him. He frightens me."

Mr. Hart sighed then, his shoulders drooping. "I was rarely home when he was young. Now he feels I never once valued him, perhaps because of his poor vision."

I nodded.

"Everything I do, he takes as proof. Even my affair with your mother is proof I didn't value him, reasoning that I went out to create a more worthy, more capable heir, one without impediment. In his view, every day I was gone I was with your mother. Every night I was gone I was with you, being a father to you, even when you weren't even yet born. Perhaps it is a form of madness, this terrible envy he holds inside, but it's one I brought on by my actions. His sight may be poor. But he's a strong, brilliant man, with a sound body and a charm over men I never had and don't understand. In that way, he's much like my grandfather." He looked away. "Within his keen mind, though, hides a bitterness which I fear will be his undoing."

I sat back, appalled and grieved at what Mr. Hart had just said. To live your life feeling so unworthy ... it was too much an echo of my thoughts growing up. "I'll try."

"That's all I ask, Jacqui. We can be a family. A real family. But it will mean all of us being more than we've been."

I nodded slowly, trying to understand. Trying to picture Inventor Etienne Hart not mocking me, not trying to accuse me of harm. "How is Miss Kerr, by the way? I've not heard from her."

He seemed downcast. "Her doctor says she will recover. Terrible thing, that."

"May I ask a personal question?"

"Of course, Mrs. Spadros. Ask anything you wish." He chuckled. "Most things I might even be able to answer."

I understood that. He was a Patriarch of a rival quadrant, after all. "Nothing like that. I just wondered ... why do you dislike her brother Joe? I saw him washing dishes for pay."

Mr. Hart's eyes widened.

Something was very wrong between him and Joe, but I didn't know what. "Why won't you support him? From all accounts, you and his grandfather are close."

Mr. Hart's expression became guarded. "That situation isn't something I can discuss in the slightest."

"What situation?"

He shook his head. "No. I won't even begin. It's not even entirely my story to tell." He raised a hand. "Please. Let it go."

I felt taken aback. What could possibly be wrong? "Very well."

He waved to the waiters, who picked up our empty plates. "Anything else?"

"No, I've eaten plenty, thank you."

He let out a quiet laugh. "Let's get you back to your apartments then, before we're discovered here."

Very few knew Mr. Hart was my father, and upon seeing Mr. Hart send flowers and visit my apartments, some had come to an unsavory conclusion. For reporters to find us luncheoning together might cause trouble we didn't need.

On the way back, Mr. Hart was quiet, pensive. Finally, he said, "When can I see my grandson?"

"Oh," I said, dismayed. "I don't know!"

Mr. Hart seemed to retreat into himself. "Forgive me. It's a great deal to ask, all things considered."

"I don't know. Something's ... I don't want to say wrong, but ... different. About Roy."

"Like what?"

I spoke softly, aware of the driver and footman, who were surely listening. "He's been quiet, almost reasonable. Concerned. He used to only be angry with me but now ... " I was having trouble finding the right words. "It's almost as if he wants to help."

Mr. Hart's tone was bitter. "You've given his Family an Heir."

I thought back. "No, it started before that. And he's lost weight. His hair has gone white. I don't know if he's sick, or what. Oh, I shouldn't be telling you any of this, especially in here. But —"

Mr. Hart sounded alarmed. "I'm glad you did, and not because I plan to harm him." He shook his head. "Do you realize what would happen to the city should Roy Spadros die? His son must be ready to seize the reins at once, and with great force. He'd be one man trying to steer a monstrous stampede." He glanced aside, then back, speaking quietly. "I can only help you so much, even if I dared do so openly. But you must speak with your husband about his plans for the succession, and at once." He bit his lip, looked away. "I could send help if needed," he looked at me then, "men who resemble your people enough to not be remarked upon —"

I felt suddenly afraid. Might he use this knowledge he'd just received to seize our quadrant?

"They would be sworn to your aid, Jacqui. I'd never send anyone to harm you. Either of you." He glanced away. "I know now I was too eager, too enamored with the idea of an alliance with your husband. I spoke too soon, and too forcefully, in a place where he'd surely feel threatened." He turned to face me. "Please give him my apologies."

I nodded, not sure what to say. The idea had only terrified Tony then, and I wasn't sure it'd be received any better now.

The carriage pulled up to my apartments, and Mr. Hart put his hand upon mine. "Please consider all I've said."

"I will. Good afternoon to you."

A navy-blue carriage of the Court stood in front of Mr. Hart's, pulling away as I climbed the steps to my apartments. I knocked on the door. The chip off one corner of my sign advertising my investigator business seemed to have fostered a crack in the painted wood. I wondered if Blitz might be able to fix that for me.

Mary answered the door. "Oh, hello, mum. There's a gentleman here to see you."

The Consultation

The "gentleman" wasn't a gentleman in the strictest sense of the word, but rather Assistant District Attorney Thrace Pike. As Mr. Pike owned no land, and worked for his living, Tony would have called him a tradesman like his grandfather.

But even still, the man did look like a gentleman should: top hat, fine suit, new shoes, even a fine leather briefcase. "I'll have to say, Mr. Pike, that your position in life seems to have changed for the better."

A bit too much for the better. I wondered where he was getting all this money.

He smiled, his eyes never leaving mine. "It's a pleasure to see you."

"Would you care to join me for tea?" It was a bit early for tea-time, but I felt sure Mary wouldn't have trouble setting something up for us.

He didn't seem to be disturbed in the slightest. "Most certainly. There's a matter I'd like to discuss."

These men and their discussions! I got him seated on the sofa, went to inform Mary of the change, sent Blitz to tell my carriage I'd be delayed even further, and relaxed finally into an armchair. I wondered why he was here, in light of all that had passed between us. "I hope your wife is well?"

He didn't flinch, or lower his eyes, or even blush. "Entirely. We have a new home upon Market Center. Did you know we're expecting another child?"

"Already?" The last I'd seen her, she'd just given birth to their son. But that was two years ago. Or was it three? "So this is your third?"

"Fourth. My second son was born last summer." He smiled broadly. "But enough of me." He leaned forward, elbows on his knees. "How are you, Mrs. Spadros?"

He seemed so sincerely interested in my welfare that at first, I was too surprised to speak. "I'm ... well! Thank you!"

He leaned back, relaxing. "I'm glad." A slight frown came over his face. "I felt surprised to see you arrive in a Hart carriage."

I chuckled softly. No way could I tell Mr. Pike that Mr. Hart was my father. So what else might I say? "I might remind you that I'm not just this woman you see before you. I'm the Lady of Spadros, and at times I must deal with the other Families. It's as much my job as," I laughed, just a bit, "fighting against them seems to be yours."

His mouth fell open slightly. "I see." He licked his lips, then took a deep breath. "You sit here now. But I know you must return to them."

I nodded, wondering where he was going with this.

He spoke softly. "How trustworthy are your people?"

"Here, in this house? I trust them with my life."

He nodded slowly, then hesitated for some time. Then he spoke quietly. "If you could get free of the Family, right now — just walk away and let the whole thing crumble behind you ... would you?"

Mary came in with the tea service then, for which I was entirely grateful. Because I immediately thought of so many things at once I should never have been able to answer.

Leave Tony? Be able to see Joe as a free woman? Never see little Katie again?

And what would this mean? Did he mean for me to just disappear, bringing a horrible frantic search, like when Jonathan went missing? If I were to suddenly vanish, everyone would blame another. It might even mean war. I didn't want to bring harm to Mr. Hart, or Gardena Diamond, or even the Clubbs.

This was too close to what Joe had suggested, whilst being much less desirable.

My mind was in a whirl. But by the time Mary poured our tea and left, I had my answer. "If no one were to be harmed, of course."

Mr. Pike fetched his tea-cup and saucer. "I think I've found a way to do that. A way that might make things better for you." He blew on his tea, took a sip. "Obviously it wouldn't be today, and it's too soon to share any details. But I wanted to hear your thoughts."

"In principle. I'd be able to answer more when I heard your plan."

He beamed. "All should be in order soon, you have my word." He leaned back, cup and saucer still in hand. "I've devoted myself to the question ever since we met together that night in the Plaza."

Really? That was four years ago!

Interesting. And his fervor on this particular point — particularly after his emotional display on the night Jack Diamond captured me — felt more than a bit disturbing.

But I didn't want to dissuade him. Perhaps his plan — whatever it was — would have merit. And if somehow he was working with our enemies, well, what he told me might come in handy. I reached for my tea-cup, placed a small sandwich on the side of my saucer, then sat back. "I appreciate any help you might give me."

We sat sipping tea. The sandwich — bits of pork creamed in white sauce — needed seasoning.

"Oh," Mr. Pike said. "I happened to speak with my grandfather —"

Hmph, I thought. An utter scoundrel whose only interest seemed to be money.

"— and he mentioned something you might find of interest. Do you recall Dame Anastasia Louis?"

How might I forget her? She got me tangled in a scheme which ended in destruction of the zeppelin station and financial ruin for the city. Then **I** got blamed for it. "Of course."

Mr. Pike leaned forward. "My grandfather found her will."

"Her will? However did he find that?"

"No idea. But she left everything she owned to one of her young men! Can you imagine? A woman of her age, taking up with a man hardly older than you!" He seemed scandalized by the prospect.

I recalled Mr. Blackberry of the *Bridges Daily* telling me once about Dame Anastasia and her young men, dozens of them around her all the time. It seemed she'd been carrying on like this for decades before her untimely demise. "All we can hope for is that she found some joy in her liaisons." I felt melancholy: though she betrayed me, I'd regarded her as a friend. "Her cards have passed to the Shuffler now."

***

After tea, my head hurt, and I felt a bit dizzy. I wanted to lie down, but I'd moved my bed to the Manor when I realized I had no way to prevent Acevedo's birth. So after Mr. Pike left, I got in my carriage to return to Spadros Manor.

On the way, I lay on the bench seat and thought about Dame Anastasia, and what Mr. Pike had discovered.

Tony had looked into how the carriage which took me had gotten past the blockade at the end of the street the day of my abduction in front of the Manor. His men at the far corner said no one had come past them, but they saw a carriage pull out between Dame Anastasia's former mansion and our property.

So Tony sent men to speak to the new owners, a quite elderly couple: Mr. and Mrs. Daudizu. Or that was what the name sounded like to his man; the couple never actually wrote their names down. The couple claimed not to own any horses; they hired a carriage on the few times a year they went out.

Tony's men searched the house, the very clean stables, and the property. Yet they found no trace of the Red Dog Gang.

However, they did find tracks of a carriage and horses in the wooded field Dame Anastasia used to own which lay beyond the house itself, but before our property began. Evidently someone had hidden the carriage there, waiting for the opportune time.

"The old couple probably never noticed them," Tony said. "These scoundrels! To use old folk in this way, knowing they'd come under Family scrutiny ... it's despicable."

Still suspicious, Tony had his lawyer, Mr. Trevisane, check who owned the property and the passage of title. It showed that Dame Anastasia had sold the mansion and acreage directly to the couple.

Which is what she'd implied to me. This suggested that the property had changed hands before she died, not after.

Lucky for us all, I thought at the time. I'd never met any of her "young men," but if even one was anything like Frank Pagliacci, we'd not want him — or any of his men — living just next door.

Tony set men to watch the old couple's grounds just in case, but the men hadn't seen anyone of interest. The couple seldom left, and had few servants.

So I wondered: might this will of Anastasia's tell us anything new?

My carriage must have gone over a particularly large bump, because the jolt sent a spike of pain through my head.

"Sorry about that, mum," Zeus said through the speaking bell. "There was no way to go round. I'll have the men for this street look into that."

I sat up, grasped the bell on my end. "Thank you."

I could almost see Zeus tip his cap in my mind.

Old Zeus had been recommended by Jonathan when my former driver had been shot — by the Red Dog Gang — and I couldn't have asked for a better one. He knew the city well, and seemed to know the best routes anywhere.

Thinking of my former driver and the circumstances around his death made me wary. I peered out, looking for any danger.

My back window opened. Honor said, "Is all well?"

"Yes, I'm fine. That just reminded me —"

Honor gave a bleak chuckle. "I was reminded as well. No, it was just a sinking in the road. We'll get it fixed up, never fear."

***

When we returned to Spadros Manor, the wind had kicked up; as I went to lie down the windows whistled and rattled. The boy was crying, of course, but Daisy had the doors leading to his room shut, and from the sound of it was rocking him.

I woke to Amelia shaking me. "Sorry to disturb you, mum, but it's time to dress for dinner. I told Mr. Anthony you were asleep, but he insists on taking dinner in the dining hall. He wishes to speak with you beforehand, in private."

Acevedo wailed in the distance. I felt bleary, off-balance. But I let Amelia dress me, fix my hair.

Once done, I went through our closets and into Tony's room.

He stood facing away as his manservant Michaels brushed his dinner jacket. And I had a chance to look round Tony's room, really

48

look at it. It was spare, the bedroom of a man who was hardly in it. My portrait hung upon the wall, as did a portrait of his mother. A certificate of tutorial hung above a long row of well-read books. By his bed, a notepad and a locked leather-bound journal lay beside a fountain pen, atop a short locked cabinet which I knew held all he had of his son Roland.

Tony turned to face me. "There you are! Did you sleep well?"

I shrugged.

Without ever looking at him, he said to Michaels, "That'll be all."

Michaels gave me a glance as he bowed, then he left to a side door which led to his rooms, the door clicking shut.

Tony smiled, but it never reached his eyes. "Why did you not tell me that Joseph Kerr was at the wedding?"

My head hurt, I was tired, Acevedo was screaming, and right then, I felt angry. "You dragged me out of bed for **this**? I didn't think it was important, that's why. I went out back to smoke and he was already there. He's got a job ... washing dishes or something."

Tony rested his hands on my arms, peered into my eyes. "You know I love you, right? Do we have something here, together?"

"Why are you asking this?" I shook off his grasp, turned away. "We have Acevedo. We have our home here." I turned to him. "What more do you want from me?"

I recalled Joe's words: *He's got his heir. He doesn't need you anymore.*

Tony and his mother seemed inseparable. Could he have been somehow involved with her scheming?

Tony sighed, put his hand upon his forehead. "Never mind." He let his hand drop, took my arm. "Let's go down to dinner."

We went out of his door to the hall overlooking the back gardens and down the winding marble stair.

Joe was never this needy, this inconsiderate. If only I'd recognized the meaning of Joe's sign upon the windowsill in my study that night I left here the first time, and gone to our place in the Old Plaza by his ancestor's broken statue in the Pot. We might be in another city by now, with a real family — not this forced monstrosity.

The stair emerged between the breakfast room and the dining room. Our long dining room was paneled in white, the doors to the veranda at its midsection.

Jonathan and I had sat in those very chairs after the Queen's night dinner party, so many years before.

Gods, I missed him. To this day, I miss him still.

The wind outside howled, and the doors rattled. Barring any word or gesture from Tony to do otherwise, I took the foot of the table, Pearson there to hold my chair.

Though no tears came, I felt so much grief that I could hardly breathe. Jonathan had been everything to me. He was my one advisor, my one true friend, the compass of my life ... and now he lay dead. His dying request was that I find a way to be happy.

It seemed impossible here.

As our Chef, Monsieur Sabacc stood beside the roasted ham in his full Chef's uniform and tall white hat to do the carving, and this time, Pip Dewey, Amelia's son, stood in a similar regalia (and much shorter hat) to assist him.

Tony sat watching me.

Finally, I got myself under control, began to think. It wasn't like Tony to have me awakened, or to insist on eating down here when we could have easily taken dinner in our rooms. He'd brought me here for a reason.

"I got a letter from your lawyer," Tony said.

I didn't think it important enough to correct him in front of the servants. "Oh?"

"In regards to Peedro Sluff."

The man I'd thought until recently was my father. "I wasn't aware they were acquainted."

"Mr. Pike owns the shop. Apparently we're Mr. Sluff's next of kin."

"Oh. I didn't know." Why was Doyle Pike, a lawyer, owning shops? At the time, it seemed strange to me.

"He would like Mr. Sluff's belongings removed so he may rent out the shop."

"I see." All those lovely liquor bottles ... "I'll take care of it."

Tony's eyes widened. "I didn't mean you had to do it personally. I only thought —"

Why did he even bring it up then? Why not have his men take care of it? "Don't bother yourself over this. I'll see that it's taken care of."

Tony's eyes narrowed. "Very well."

The servants brought our second course, and we ate. What was Tony doing? Why bring up Peedro — a former Party Time addict who owned a liquor store in the slums — in front of the servants?

"My father wants to see Acevedo," Tony said. "And he wishes to do it when you're here, so he might speak with you."

Good grief. What might I have to say to that man? But even if he'd been living on 1st Street instead of being the Spadros Patriarch, Roy Spadros had a legal right to see his grandson, and if we ignored this, he'd only become more insistent.

If dealing with whatever he wished to say to me was part of the round, then ... "Fine. He can come over whenever's convenient."

I thought he'd be happy, but instead, Tony frowned. "I don't want him around either of you." He stabbed at his food as if it offended him. "I won't have him here, interfering with my servants —"

In a flash, I realized why Tony insisted on eating down here. He wanted to say this where the servants might hear.

Had he learned what Roy Spadros had done to Amelia? I glanced at Pip, yet the boy seemed undisturbed by the conversation, gazing placidly in front of him.

"Do you hear me?"

Tony's question broke my reverie. "You don't want him here."

"Exactly. What's more, I don't wish you to go to his home either."

I didn't see much call to do so. "Very well."

That seemed to mollify him, and he resumed eating, the wind howling loudly enough to drown out Acevedo's crying.

Pip began to carve, with Monsieur giving quiet instruction. The boy's hands were sure, quickly cutting fine thin slices, as if he'd been practicing for some time. The slices were put upon plates, vegetables added, and presented before us.

So this was a test of sorts. "Excellent," I said to Pip. "Thank you."

Pip faced me, bowed his head only, without meeting my eye, and returned to stand beside Monsieur.

Monsieur did allow himself a very slight smile. Ham was my favorite, as the household generally knew, and this was delicious.

We finished our meal in silence. Afterwards, Tony brought me to his study to sit by the fire. "We need to talk."

"I thought we'd been doing that for the past two hours."

"How are you planning to dispose of Peedro Sluff's belongings?"

I shrugged. "Like Anna Goren's, I suppose."

The wind gusted, and sparks flew from the fire.

"I — I'm just concerned. Are you going to be able to deal with going into a liquor store? Handling the bottles?"

I remembered when I'd been so desperate I'd grabbed a bottle of bottom-shelf swill and almost fought with Peedro when he wouldn't give it back to me. In front of Tony.

But things had changed. "I'll be fine. I'll have Mary and Amelia to help me."

Tony nodded, yet not looking convinced. "There's something else."

"Roy."

"Well, yes." He glanced away. "He showed me the pamphlets you sent him. We think it's best that I publicly separate myself from him. So far as I can, of course."

"Of course." Tony could have sent out a press release, or done any other such thing. But servants talked, and by the end of the week half the city would know that Anthony and Roy Spadros were becoming estranged from each other.

"Trouble's coming about some of the things he's done," Tony said. "I can feel it. I want to implement your idea about money for the holidays at once."

I'd suggested we give the people money on each holiday, not to be counted towards their Family fees: a nickel for anyone in the Family, a penny for those who hadn't yet joined. And Midsummer was coming soon. I rubbed my temple. "That's a good idea."

He smiled at me. "It's **your** good idea. I've got a meeting set up with my main men tomorrow."

My head was hurting so bad. Acevedo's crying could be heard even in there.

A door slammed in the hall; pain spiked through my head.

Tony said, "What's wrong?"

"My head hurts all the time."

"Still? I thought the doctor said that was from your bleeding. And not getting enough liquids. And that it would go away in a week or so." He considered the matter. "But it's been a month!"

"And I've not seriously bled in a while."

Tony rang for Pearson. "Call the doctor at once."

Pearson looked at us both. Not seeing any immediate mayhem, he replied, "Very good, sir." Then he left.

Tony took my hand. "You've not been sleeping either: you look so pale and worn." He kissed my fingers. "This has been more difficult than I expected. I spoke with Miss Gardena about the colic, for any help as to how to soothe Ace's pain. Did you know Roland had none of this?" He sat back, and from his face I could tell he was at a loss. "I'm most grateful that sweet child never went through this torment."

I nodded, which made my head hurt worse.

We sat there for a while, fingers intwined, until the doctor arrived.

Dr. Salmon was an ancient thin man, a private surgeon who'd been with the Family for generations. When he arrived, he took us to my bedroom, where he had me lie down. He pressed upon my belly, looked at my eyes, and felt my head and neck.

Then we returned to Tony's study. "She's in no immediate danger," he said, "but I'm puzzled. When did this malady begin?"

"I've felt unwell ever since I was taken," I said. "When I awoke in the courtyard of that warehouse, after I was hit on the head."

Dr. Salmon and Tony gaped at me.

Tony said, "You were hit upon the head?"

"In all the rush to save you and the child," Dr. Salmon said, "nobody mentioned a blow."

"No one told me," Tony said. "All I knew is that she'd been taken." His face fell. "Most of the men there that day are dead."

His cousins, his friends. "I thought you knew."

"Gods, what a horrible day," Tony said. "I hope we never see another of its like."

Acevedo wailed in the distance.

Tony said to the doctor, "What should be done?"

"Well," Dr. Salmon said, "this changes everything. And it explains her symptoms perfectly. You've never gotten a chance to heal."

At that, I recalled how Morton had to stay in bed a full week after his blow to the head, and how worried everyone was for him.

"Since you're no longer bleeding," Dr. Salmon said, "It's safe for you to take salicylate for this; it should help. Come to my office tomorrow morning to have x-rays of your head and neck done." He stopped then, his head tilted to the side. "And she needs to sleep. I have a few things we could try on that account."

Tony blinked. "You mean my son? What things?"

"Well, there's the tried and true: opium —"

Tony said, "Now wait just a minute —"

"— or if you prefer, vodka."

"Absolutely not," Tony said, "to either of them."

The doctor sat, hand to chin. "I've heard a tincture of fennel might help. An old wives' tale." He shrugged. "We could try that."

"Fennel," Tony said. "That's a plant, right?"

"Exactly," Dr. Salmon said. "A vegetable with dinner. Probably soothes the stomach, or perhaps babies like the flavor. Who knows? If it gives her a few hours' rest, it's worth it."

"Yes," Tony said. Then he asked, "Why does one child suffer and not another?"

"No one knows the answer, my boy. Babies are strange little creatures." He chuckled. "I'll give you the tincture tomorrow."

Pearson's wife Jane had some salicylate in her storeroom, and the headache did improve. For the first time in a while, I felt hope.

Maybe, finally, things would get better.

The Pretense

The next morning after breakfast, the news spoke of a massive blackout in the Clubb slums, which as of the time of printing, still had not been fixed.

We again had Pearson do the morning meeting as Tony and I went to Dr. Salmon's to have my neck rayed. Then we sat in the doctor's office to await his word.

The office, like the doctor, looked very old. Wooden furniture worn at the arms and seat by years of sitting, books and their cases fraying. No dust, everything shone, but even the air felt ancient. "The doctor's been with us for a while, hasn't he?"

Tony chuckled. "Delivered my father, or so my father tells me. By the look of him, though, he might have delivered my grandfather."

Dr. Salmon laughed as he came in the door. "I'm not quite **that** old. But I did know your grandfather as a boy." He sat leaning upon the edge of his desk. "We did a bit of school together; his grandfather insisted he go. But Vedo was never one for books." He grinned, tapping his chest. "That was me."

I couldn't believe my ears. "So you knew his grandfather? The first Acevedo Spadros?"

He smiled fondly to himself. "I met him a few times, when he'd retrieve Vedo from school. He was a nice old man. Looked like a teacher. Not nearly so fearsome as everyone made out." He glanced at Tony. "You favor him, sir. I can see him in your eyes."

Tony seemed taken aback. "I'm honored."

"From all accounts, he was a kind and brilliant man."

At that, Tony laughed. "No one has ever called me brilliant." He took my hand. "I'll leave that to my wife." An introspective look crossed his face. "I like to think I'm kind, however poor an asset that may be here."

Dr. Salmon gazed solemnly at Tony. Then he straightened. "Your wife's x-rays are good. No injury to the skull or spine."

I said, "That's a relief."

"Try to rest as much as possible. Use the salicylate when you first start to feel the headache, but wait an hour before you decide you need more. It takes time for the body to take it in, you see."

I nodded, the room wavering just a bit.

"A warm bath before bed will help as well. I'll have my nurse give you a list for your maid. Once treated, these things generally clear up in a few weeks."

"We're grateful," Tony said. "And the fennel? For my son."

"Ah, yes," Dr. Salmon said. He rose, going round to a cabinet behind his desk. He opened the wooden doors, where an array of bottles sat, choosing out a brown one with an eye-dropper, which he handed to me. On it the words, "Tincture of Fennel" stood printed on the white label. "Three drops at night should do the trick. If he's still having trouble after a week, just call, and I'll come see to him."

When we got home, I gave the bottle to Daisy, who opened it: the smell of alcohol wafted forth.

Daisy and I exchanged a glance.

"Mr. Anthony said no alcohol," Daisy said. "What should I do?"

I wanted very much to taste it myself. "Let's do as the doctor's prescribed for now. Perhaps it'll help."

"Yes, mum."

After luncheon, I went to sit in my study, more to be alone than anything else. I put my head in my hands. I felt so tired.

What did Molly give Mrs. Crawford to make her betray me?

I might never find the answer to that one. It was just one of so many questions I still had.

But none of that mattered right now. First I had to get well. Then I had to get my life back.

I had my properties: the apartments Dame Anastasia gave me and Anna Goren's old shop. People hired rooms in one, and I received rent every month from the other. I was paying my debt to Doyle Pike little by little: in a year or so, I could start rebuilding my savings.

But what might I do now?

I got out a pen and paper. More business cards, for a start: I was almost out of them. Then contact my informants to see if they had any leads, anyone who might need my help.

A terrible thought came: could Molly be telling people not to use my services? I wouldn't put it past her.

A knock, and Amelia put her head in. "Mr. Anthony wishes to see you, mum."

When I went to Tony's study, to my surprise Monsieur and Mistress Anne, who ran the kitchens, stood there before him.

Mistress Anne was a thin, middle-aged, sharp-tongued spinster. I enjoyed her humor, and was quite pleased to see her. I hoped she wasn't being reprimanded.

Tony reached out his hand. "Draw up a chair and sit beside me."

Monsieur got a chair for me and held it as I sat, then returned to stand beside Mistress Anne.

Tony said, "Monsieur Sabacc and Mistress Anne are here to ask permission to marry."

I'd thought for a while that they'd fancied each other. "How wonderful!" I glanced at Tony. "If you wish my opinion, I think it a splendid idea."

Tony grinned. "I think so, too." He rose, shaking Monsieur's hand. "My best wishes to you both." He glanced at me. "Please, sit down."

Monsieur gaped at him, taking a step back. "You do us too great an honor, sir."

Tony smiled to himself. "My wife has taught me many things. One has been that some deserve more honor than they believe." He gestured to the chairs. "Please."

So after an instant of hesitation, they sat.

"I'll continue at my home across the way," Monsieur said. "The only change will be for Mistress Anne to join me there. Otherwise, your kitchens will remain as efficient as ever."

"Good to hear," Tony said. "And how do you wish to handle the wedding? How long will you be absent for your honeymoon? To be most specific: what do you need from me?"

"Only your blessing," Monsieur said, taking Mistress Anne's hand. "We can care for the rest."

"Well, you have it," said Tony. "You've done excellent work for us. Tell me of the dates and we'll be there."

***

Apparently, the next place Monsieur and his betrothed went was to inform the staff, because the entire household was abuzz about it.

Perhaps the noise soothed Acevedo enough for him to sleep, because he did. I felt a headache coming on, so I took the salicylate and went to lie down.

Now I understood. The headaches weren't from the baby crying. The blow to the head did it. Both things were fixable.

My mind was so weary, so jumbled then, that it's no wonder I made the decisions that cost us so much. There are a great many things I'd change in my life, if somehow I might use that mythical machine that brings you backwards in time.

When I woke, Tony sat at my tea-table, a full tea set before him. He smiled at me. "Hungry?"

"I am." I put on my robe over my housedress and joined him there.

"Here, let me serve you."

I sat astonished as he put food upon my plate, set it before me. "Thank you!"

He returned to his chair, took my hand. "I would, if I could, take you and Acevedo to a place where we might live a normal life, where a man might fill his wife's plate at tea-time without it being seen as strange." Tony seemed pensive. "How I long to live a simple life, free from all this ..." he waved his hand around, "pretense."

58

It reminded me of my advice to Josie before Acevedo was born. "Tony, you're the Spadros Heir. You can make your life within these walls whatever you wish. Can't you?"

He smiled as if speaking to a child, then said, "I've told the men about the money. For the holidays. They were quite enthusiastic about the idea: they think it'll get more men to cover the slums."

It made sense. A nickel meant little to those on 100th Street. But to those on 10th ... that was half their Family fees for the month. "And they know they're not to count it in that month's fees?"

"Yes, my love, they know. I think the merchants will be pleased as well. Your friend with the fabric shop, for example. The people will have more to spend."

I hadn't considered that aspect of the matter.

"My father won't like it, of course. He thinks giving people anything makes them weak. But —"

"Wait. You didn't clear this with Roy?"

"Why should I? Ever since that event last year, he's given me entire control of the quadrant. It's my money, given to me by my men, to do with as I choose. His cut of the take won't change, so I can't see what business it is of his anyway."

My goodness. "You have complete control of the quadrant? Why?"

I thought Tony might be offended, but his gaze turned inward. "I've been asking myself that ever since he told me. It's so unlike him. But all he'd say was, 'it's time.'" He peered at me. "It frightens me, yet it also makes me glad. Too long have my people suffered under fear and torment because of his brutality."

"Once he told me it's better for people to fear you than love you, because love can turn to hate so quickly. Fear overcomes hate, makes men obey gladly rather than suffer the consequences."

"That does sound like my father." Tony sighed, slumping forward to put his elbows on the table. "I hate making men fear me. It feels wrong." He glanced up at me. "Yet another thing I wish one day to be free of."

"But we may have to one day." I recalled what my friend Josie once told me: *never let anyone get the upper hand, or they will kill you.* "Just because we don't like it doesn't mean it won't become necessary."

Then I recalled what Mr. Hart had said about power. "What will you do if Roy should die?"

Tony leaned back then, his hands behind his head, his gaze upon the ceiling. "If my father should die." Then he sat up. "I don't think this is something to be discussed here."

Where others might be listening. "Care for a stroll?"

The large bell sounded overhead, the one used to summon every man, woman, and child on the property to the front of the Manor. I felt alarmed. "What's wrong? Has something happened?"

Tony smiled. "Just something Pearson's taking care of. Be at peace: we're in no danger."

I let him remove my robe, get my wrapper from the closet, and put it on me as running footsteps and shouts came from below. He moved slowly, as if waiting for the commotion to settle. And it did. Pearson spoke, and the sounds of a group moving out of the front door and away gradually subsided. The front door shut.

Tony said, "Let's go now."

The front hall was quiet as we went down the grand stair, along the hall past his study, my study, the breakfast room, into the dining room and through the veranda to the gardens.

The sun was setting. Flowers were beginning to bloom, their scent lingering in the warm humid air. We strolled through the gardens in silence, then out to the meadow.

As we picked our way out through the meadow, murmurs came as of a crowd far to the right, past the copse of trees beyond. Then the sound of a far-off slap. "What's going on over there?"

Tony said, "Nothing to worry yourself over." He quickly added, "You asked what I would do should my father die." He shrugged. "Bury him. Lead my people."

This sounded good. It sounded terrible. "I had a discussion with Mr. Hart the other day —"

"When you went to luncheon with him."

Of course, Tony knew I went to luncheon with him. "The prospect of Roy's death seemed to dismay, even terrify him. He said —"

Tony turned to me. "You spoke to him about **that**?"

"Tony, he believes ... how did he say it? That you'd be 'one man trying to steer a monstrous stampede.'"

Another slap, not quite so loud. "And what did this paragon of virtue believe I should do?"

"He said, and I quote: 'he should seize the reins at once, with great force.' I feel he's right. People obeyed Roy because they feared him. They don't fear you." I peered at him, not knowing where he'd been or what he'd been doing all those days he'd been off tending to the Business. Suddenly his words took on new meaning. "Do they?"

"Of course not. For better or worse, I've tried to be an actual leader, not a tyrant." He turned away. "What if this whole way of doing things — the hierarchy, the street captains, the Family fees, the way some live in poverty and others in wealth — what if it's all wrong? What if those people in the slums and Pot might live without all this suffering?"

"I don't know." The prospect of such momentous change daunted me. I recalled what Eleanora Bryce's new husband Mr. Highcard had said to me once: *Change comes at a price; great change is sometimes too costly to bear. Would your people say change was worth the cost?*

"I'm not fierce like you, Jacqui. I'm neither brave nor strong, nor do I believe in this," he waved his hand around, "thing we've constructed. But I'm here." He took a deep breath. "I have the reins. But I have no idea what to do with them." Then he shook his head and sighed. "I wish Master Jonathan were here. He always had good counsel."

Tears came to my eyes. "I miss him too."

Another slap, this time a bit louder. Tony's hand went to his forehead; it was if he hadn't heard me. "The only thing I know is that if I help my people, they'll want to help me make things better." His eyes pleaded with me. "Does that make any sense?"

Oh, gods, Jon, what should we do? Tony had just told me he had complete control of a quadrant with no plan to secure it should Roy's health fail. "I think so." What would **Jon** do? "Mr. Hart pledged men to our aid should we need them —"

Tony stared at me in alarm.

"— with his vow that they'd be there to aid, not to take advantage. I don't think he'd do anything to harm me directly."

"And once his men were there, securing the safety and love of the people ..." Tony took a deep breath; another slap sounded in the distance. "If we couldn't hold our land in the first place, how might we force them to leave?" He hesitated, and when he spoke, his voice shook. "I went to the Dealers, as you suggested. The people are a handsbreadth from starvation, being hunted by this Strangler fiend, and terrorized by their own police. They hate us, Jacqui. Even the Dealers I spoke to had disdain in their eyes for what we've allowed here. My carriage was pelted with stones, even as my men whipped the protestors away." He thrust his hands in his hair. "I've pledged my help. But I don't know if it'll be enough!"

He sounded close to panic. I tried to make my voice soothing. "What did the Dealers suggest?"

"Repairs and security for the lower slums, particularly at night. Another food distribution center, this one for the East side, so we might have more groceries open. Allow them to rebuild the Western poorhouse, so they might aid the people there. It went on and on." He sighed, letting his hands fall to his side as another slap sounded. "I do think I was able to convince them of my sincerity, there at the end." He shrugged. "For all the good it might do."

Jon would always offer encouragement, no matter what insanity I planned. "Tony, you mustn't despair. You plan a good work. But it might only be accomplished in Acevedo's time. If this is what you want, you can't let what people think of you stop that."

He took hold of my arms, head down. "Your being here means everything to me." He leaned his head upon mine. "At times I marvel that you love me." He crushed me to his chest, which startled me. For a moment I stood there, until I had the presence of mind to put my arms round him.

Did I love him? I wanted to support his plans. At times I desired him, even though we might not act upon it until my body had healed.

Perhaps I never knew what love was then. I was so young, with so much to understand. All I knew to do was to rest my head on him in the moonlight and listen to the slaps far away.

The Mystery

"You had Pearson horse-whip my husband!" Amelia's face was a mask of grief and rage in the candlelight. "Why?"

"I did no such thing." So that's what those "slaps" were about. "I merely told him your husband was in my rooms, as I said I would."

"He did you no harm," Amelia said. "You should have known what would happen."

I thought using a horsewhip on men was barbaric. But I could never forget Amelia not warning me of Molly's scheming. And the last thing I wanted to do was undermine Pearson to his servants. "Mr. Dewey chose to come up here without being summoned. He knew the rules. Do you know why he came here?"

Amelia's face fell. "He wouldn't tell me."

"And that's the problem. There are reasons downstairs servants aren't allowed here. Is he a spy? Did he steal, or break something? We don't know. Where is he now?"

"Confined to our rooms for a week. To let his back heal, mostly. But my girls are distraught, saying they won't work either." Her face grew suddenly afraid. "Of course, they will, mum, I'll see to it."

Would Pearson have children whipped as well? Tony seemed to let Pearson do whatever he wished when it came to the servants, and I wouldn't put it past the man. "Thank you. We've had enough turmoil here for one day."

Mr. Dewey had been horse-whipped. In my name, merely because he'd been in my rooms. And now those little girls were in danger.

Once she left, I lay in bed, head pounding, and wept with frustration. There was nothing I could do!

***

Fennel seemed to be what Acevedo needed, because although he woke from time to time as babies do, the night was quiet enough for me to finally sleep. When I woke, to my surprise Tony lay there beside me.

Or rather, he sat up in bed, still in his pajamas, two ledgers and some papers upon his lap, a fountain pen in hand. He smiled when he saw me. "Good morning."

"Whatever are you still doing here?"

He chuckled. "I'm glad to see you, too." He made a notation upon one of the papers. "I told Ten to handle the added security in the slums. He's got men going door to door to recruit with the promise of the extra nickel now instead of at the holiday. They've got an interest in keeping their families safe."

"But surely if they didn't want to be in the Family before —"

"Yes, Ten said that too. In case we don't get enough men, I'm offering their street's fee as a quarterly bonus to anyone who volunteers to cover night security. Of course, that'll be part of their take. They'll still get their holiday bonus for free."

"Sounds good." We'd been taking in enormous amounts from the Casino every month, so I thought we were likely to have plenty.

"The doctor said you should rest. Is there anything I should —?"

"I was thinking of going to my office this afternoon."

Tony tensed up. "Any particular reason?"

"I like it there."

"But Jacqui, the doctor said —"

"It's restful there. No babies crying. It's quiet. Besides, I have some things to do." Jonathan had suggested I keep a journal after I almost died of drink, and not wanting any of my enemies to discover it, I'd hidden it at my apartments. I felt I might write some, if there were time after completing my office-work.

"Very well." He put the papers into one of the ledgers and closed them both with a snap. "When do you think you'll return?"

I shrugged. "I'll probably stay for tea."

He turned away, ledgers in hand. "I'll let Pearson know."

Tony probably wanted to spend the day together. "Is there something you needed me here for?"

He didn't look at me. "No." He went into his rooms.

I wasn't sure what was going on. But I got up and rang for Amelia to start my day.

***

When I got to my apartments, Mary met me at the door. "Oh, you just missed her."

"Missed who?"

"Come inside," Mary said. She led me to my study and closed the door behind her. "An old fishwoman. She's come to the kitchen door twice now asking for you."

"That's odd. I don't know any fishwomen."

"She claims she's one of your informants, with urgent news. She did seem familiar." Mary shrugged with a tiny shake of her head. "I'll try to get her name the next time she arrives."

"What did she look like?"

"Very old, mum, bent and wrinkled, with white hair."

Another mystery. "I don't know who she could possibly be."

"Maybe she has a case for you?"

I laughed. "We can only hope."

Mary went back to her work.

Why were there no cases? Not even anyone coming by, or asking to be put on my list for when I might begin work again.

I considered this for a while.

In the Cathedral, a woman new with child was allowed to rest as long as she liked. She and her children too young to whore were first in line for the shared table. But the longer she waited, the greater the chance that her supplicants would choose another. So most returned to their calling as soon as strength returned.

Even after so long in the quadrants, I still didn't understand all the quadrant-folks' customs. Perhaps waiting longer was part of them.

Or perhaps — as I suspected — Mr. Doyle Pike (and/or his many sons) had been dissuading anyone likely to offer me a case. The interest mounted with every day I failed to pay him.

I set my carpet-bag next to my desk and got out the mass of mail I'd received since the last time I'd been there, putting it into a pile on the left corner of my desk. If this kept up, I might have to get a basket for my desk just to keep my mail from sliding around.

I had a huge floor-basket back at Spadros Manor full of various items which might give me clues to the Red Dog Gang's actions, along with the letters that had been stolen from me several years back. They'd not been moved during the time I was away, and I'd never found the time to look at them since I'd returned.

I'd planned to do more work on that particular mystery while I lay abed. But Tony had decided that during my convalescence, I should spend my time on thank you cards to those who had sent gifts, with personal letters to those on my list who didn't — those who I hadn't been able to visit as yet.

Tony thought the fact that they hadn't sent gifts indicated that they held animosity towards us.

I picked up another envelope. My bank statement for the month I'd been indisposed had been — of course — sent to Tony. He'd given it to me unopened, more than a bit annoyed at the bank defying his wish to have my mail actually sent to me. But that was life in Bridges.

I opened the statement: the apothecary who owned Anna Goren's former business had sent his rent to my account on time.

Relieved, I paged through the rest of the mail. I hoped to see some reply from any more of the aristocracy on my list, but there was none.

I sighed. I'd have to go to them.

It was what they wanted, all of them — the Lady of Spadros, in their homes, apologizing for her earlier misdeeds. It was so petty.

It was life here.

I began opening the rest of my mail. The woman who'd sent the beautiful knitted blanket for Acevedo, Mrs. Minerva Karayi, had turned in her cards. I wrote a letter of condolence, then put a note on my list of things to do as to the date of her funeral.

Perhaps I should have Tony hire me a personal secretary, someone to open my mail, deal with my bills. But I doubted he'd want to pay for any work to do with my business.

Jon would often recommend someone in cases like this, but he was gone. There was no one to either help or advise me: I had to do this on my own.

Thinking about this reminded me of my plans to return here, to stay at my apartments permanently. Try as I might, I couldn't think of a way to do so without bringing Tony scandal, particularly with Acevedo being around.

I might need to consult with that horrible Doyle Pike after all.

I stretched, deciding to go out front for a smoke.

Joe was at the bottom of the steps, holding a bouquet of wildflowers. "Hello, Jacqui."

Part of me felt glad to see him, pleased at the simple, heartfelt gift. Another part worried about Tony's reaction should he learn Joe was here. A third part felt annoyed that Joe would just show up without invitation when I wanted a quiet moment alone. I lit my own cigarette. "I hope you're well?"

He leaned upon one of the railings. "I am now."

I smiled to myself, sitting on the top step. With him standing at the bottom, our faces were around the same level. "I take it you don't have to work today."

"A dinner-party tonight. But I always have time to see you." He came up the steps, sat beside me. "Are you well?"

"I'm feeling better."

Joe smiled fondly, took my hand. "I'm glad." He stroked my fingers with his thumb, gazing at them. "Were you ill?"

I sighed. "Headaches. When I was taken the day we found your sister, they hit me on the head. The doctor didn't know. But it's being cared for." I felt as though I had a new lease on life.

"I wish I'd been there to care for you." Joe tucked a curl of hair behind my ear. "I'd not have let it go a month."

I shrugged. Tony was only there a short time with me each day; it surely wasn't his fault. "How's Josie?"

"She wants to know when you might help with her dress."

I smiled to myself: Josie was such a dear. And so brave, to continue on with this wedding I wasn't entirely sure she wanted, even after all that she'd suffered.

"Tell me what happened that day," Joe said. "When you saved Josie from those fiends. I want to know. I want to know everything."

Tony never even asked.

So I told Joe what happened: the boy I'd murdered, the terror as I thought I might die, the horrible grief I'd borne over Jonathan's death. I found myself sobbing in his arms. I pulled away, took out my handkerchief. "I'm sorry."

"Nothing to be sorry for. I will always be here for you, Jacqui. No matter what."

I felt an instant of bitterness. Joe had left me to die, left me to face that trial alone.

"I know now that I was wrong to choose my family over you. I was wrong to leave you here alone. I thought he'd protect you, that he'd take you somewhere safe, or at the very least, that you'd be safe here. But I want to be here for you. I love you, Jacqui. I want to spend my life with you. Let me prove myself to you. Give me another chance."

I didn't know what to say.

"I didn't grow up with all your advantages, a home and a Ma. I've not always been the person you know I could be. But when I'm with you, I'm a better person. I need you. And I'll be here whenever you need me." He took my chin, his beautiful eyes gazing into mine. "Please, Jacqui. Let me take care of you the way you deserve."

I took his hand from my chin. "It's not that simple, Joe."

"It **is** that simple." He gazed out at the narrow street. "Things have changed, Jacqui. My grandfather can't hurt you now. We can be free." His manner became animated. "Walk with me to the end of the block, Jacqui. Turn a corner. Get into a taxi-carriage." His eyes captured mine, his mood sobered. "It really is that simple. Send the man a note after we're safe and gone, if you must." He shrugged, glanced away. "I'm not sure what you're waiting for."

"You don't understand."

"Then help me."

How could I explain it? So much had happened that he knew nothing about.

I had a business. I had obligation for doing what I said I'd do: caring for Peedro's things, helping Tony with our supporters. Most of all, I'd made a vow to destroy the Red Dog Gang. To avenge all the people they'd murdered because of me. I wanted nothing more than to finally see Frank Pagliacci, put the pistol Jonathan had given me in the man's face, and deliver the justice my people deserved.

Besides that, I had a whole quadrant who depended on me. Who I'd hurt. How could I just walk away from all that without making things right?

Joe got up, still holding my hand. "When you're ready to love me, just say the word."

That threw me off balance so that I almost cried out *no, don't go. I do love you.*

But I couldn't say that, not here. Not with Tony's men probably standing right in the alley around the corner a few feet away.

Joe gave a slight smile, but it never reached his eyes. "I love you, Jacqui. I always will." Then he let go and walked off.

I put my head in my hands, heart pounding. What was I to do?

***

I went inside for tea in my parlor. I'm sure Blitz and Mary knew something bothered me, but they never asked about it.

The shadows lengthened outside as I sat there, cup in hand.

What **was** I waiting for? I felt sure Joe loved me. He'd never do anything to harm me. I trusted his judgment. If he said he had a place where we might be safe, then he had one.

So why did I not go?

I wanted to understand.

Had everything that happened these past three years done something to me inside? I didn't mean the pain when I sat, the low cramping pains inside my belly, the issues with my bowels. Those had left weeks ago. I meant inside my heart. Inside my mind.

A few years earlier I'd have died rather than allow a little boy to be smothered, much less do it by my own hand. Had my Cards been damaged somehow?

Did I **want** myself to suffer?

Could that be why I'd stayed with Tony? Acevedo didn't need me, no matter what Tony thought. I could have brought my bed back here, returned to my apartments at any time. Daisy certainly cared about him much more than I did, and as long as a child knew someone cared about him, that was all that mattered.

The clock struck six. The doorbell rang.

After a moment, Blitz returned, with Morton close behind.

I said, "Good evening. Would you care for some tea?"

"Don't know if there's time." Morton held a letter in his hand. "I just got this from Sheinwold. He wants to meet with us both on Market Center at half past."

Hmm. "Let me see that."

Morton handed me the letter, then sat in an armchair beside me, about a foot away.

We were to meet in the alley behind a tavern called The Twenty-Eight. We had just enough time to get there if we left from here, right now. But by half past six, it would be twilight, in a perfect place for an ambush. And something else caught my eye.

The same curl-up to the "t" as in the forgeries we'd suffered through the years. The same starts and stops in odd places. The same slight shake of the hand.

They expected us to drop everything and rush there. They'd lured Jonathan Diamond to his death this exact way.

And Morton could identify them.

I gave the letter back to him. "This is a trap."

Blitz turned pale.

"But perhaps we might trap Zia instead. Blitz, get everything we can muster in the next five minutes and let's go."

Blitz went to the front door, took out a brass whistle from under his shirt, and let it blow.

Everything we might muster turned out to be three carriages, four horse-men, and twenty-seven armed men on foot. My street's captain, an Associate named Mr. Eight Howell, wanted to go along, but I stopped him, leaving three of the men to stay with him. "You need to be here in case this is a diversion for some attack on our street."

For a second, the man seemed confused, scratching his big bushy beard. But then he nodded. "You've got a good head for this." He gestured to the others, who now looked at me with new respect. "Good hunting."

The fully-laden carriages set off as horse-men cleared the way. Charging across the bridge to Market Center, we galloped to the tavern.

But when we arrived, police swarmed the area. Constable Hanger came to my carriage window, speaking sharply, angrily. "If you're looking for Albert Sheinwold —"

"How could you possibly know that?"

He hitched his chin over his shoulder, where a mass of police worked, surrounded by an ever bigger mass of gawking spectators. "He's just been found dead."

The Coincidence

The former Bridges police detective and Spadros Family man Albert Sheinwold looked older than the portrait I kept in his file. He lay face up in the narrow brick alley strangled, with crimson lips marked upon his cheek and a Red Dog Gang card in his breast pocket.

I peered at the card, then at him. "Just like the rest."

A motion, out of the corner of my eye. Morton had collapsed onto the wall, face white.

Blitz hurried to Morton, sitting him upon a crate. "Never fret, sir. Such a sight would unnerve any gentleman."

Constable Hanger nodded at me, speaking just loudly enough for the four of us to hear. "Exactly the same." He pointed to his own collar. "The marks on the neck. They're the same." He stopped for a moment, as if deciding how much to tell me. "I served under the detective running the original Strangler cases — those boys. And I helped him with the files. This has been done by the same hand."

"That's not it," Morton panted in reply to Blitz. "I knew it in my mind. That Frank Pagliacci had to be the one murdering these men. But ... I met with ... I supported ... a serial killer!" He put his face in his hands. "Dear gods."

Constable Hanger gave Morton a surprised glance. "What were you doing here?"

Morton had his elbows on his knees now, his hands clasped in front of him. "I got a message that Sheinwold wanted to meet us. But I just met with him a week ago to get an affidavit notarized."

Constable Hanger stalked over, grabbed Morton by the lapels, lifted him upright, and slammed him into the stone wall. "You blundering fool! I've kept him safe for over two years, and in just two weeks you've killed him. Did you deliberately lead them to him, or are you utterly incompetent?"

I grabbed the Constable's shoulder, pulled him back. "Stop this. He needed Sheinwold alive!"

He let go with a disgusted motion. Morton adjusted his jacket.

I looked at them both. "Now everyone just calm down."

A brown-skinned man wearing a tweed suit came over. "What's all this commotion?"

"Nothing," Blitz said. "Your dead man's a Spadros Associate who's been missing for some time."

"Hmm," said the man.

I nodded. "I'll send word to Mr. Roy that he's been found."

Morton stared at me, mouth open. The man — most likely the detective on the case — nodded and walked away.

I said to Constable Hanger, "Can we speak with the detective on those cases?"

Constable Hanger scoffed, closed his eyes as he shook his head. "He's dead. Murdered not all that long ago. He worked for you — I thought they'd at least tell you about that."

"Wait — he was the detective found dead? The same one as —?"

The Constable nodded. "The same."

"Good gods." The detective investigating the death of Major Blackwood's lawyer. And this detective had investigated the Bridges Strangler murders as well? This last part had to be why he'd been killed! "We're going to need everything he had."

"Your husband has most of it," Constable Hanger said. "But if I find anything else, I'll have it sent over."

Tony had most of it? Why didn't he tell me?

I felt someone watching. In the thickening crowd, a very dark-skinned man with black hair dressed in black stood in the shadows wearing dark spectacles. As I turned towards him, he turned away.

Blitz said, "What is it?"

I pointed. "Over there, a man. Dark of skin, wearing black." There were men of all sorts in the crowd, but the day was warm and none wore black. "I didn't get a good look at him, but I'm pretty sure he's been following me." I remembered how men in brown followed me everywhere right after little David Bryce went missing.

"I don't see him," Morton said. "But I'll keep watch."

Tony had men watching over me. And Jonathan said he had men on me as well. Could this be one of Jon's men?

Constable Hanger said, "Mrs. Spadros, it'd be best if you and your men left."

"Whatever for?"

An older woman yelled, "Did you people have him killed, too?"

The crowd muttered, glancing at each other.

The Constable leaned over to speak in my ear. "Rumors have gone wild about Mr. Roy's involvement in the murder of Anna Goren ever since your husband deemed it a Family matter. The Spadros Family is not loved here." He scoffed. "Not that they ever were."

Passers-by began glaring at us as others ran up from a distance.

"Thank you, sir." I turned to my men, feeling shaken. After all this time, to find Sheinwold dead. "Come on, let's go."

We got back in the carriages as quickly as possible. I sent a horseman to give Roy the news, then had my driver Zeus take us back to my apartments.

No one spoke on the way. Morton looked less pale, yet glum.

What was happening on Market Center? I'd never seen such a mood in the crowds there before. Did they really believe Roy killed Anna? Why would he do so? She'd just been an apothecary who'd helped me.

But Constable Hanger told me Roy had been to her shop an hour before her death. I never did find out why.

Once we arrived at my apartments, I said goodbye to Morton, who looked somewhat improved, and set off for Spadros Manor.

The card in the pocket was excess: the whole scenario stank of the Red Dog Gang. Someone knew Morton and I searched for Sheinwold;

with the letter and the circumstances, I should have realized before we left that we'd find him dead.

This man who directed the Red Dog Gang was devious. At every turn, he'd outwitted me! And each time they killed, it was someone important to me, someone I went to meet, done seemingly only to cause me grief.

Which meant spies, in and around the places I frequented. We'd taken care of the spy-hole in back of my apartments. But we'd never found who spied on me outside my apartments, nor who spied on me for the Red Dog Gang around Spadros Manor.

Much of what had happened had to be distractions to keep me from investigating what the Red Dog Gang was doing.

So what **were** they doing?

***

I asked for dinner in our rooms. Alan Pearson, our night footman, brought the evening news with dinner. While we ate, I told Tony what had happened. "This is the first real proof that this former Federal Agent is working with Frank Pagliacci. Before this, it was just the word of Master Rainbow — who I'm not always sure is telling me the truth — and that disgraced police detective Mr. Bower."

"You're sure that was her lipstick?"

I recalled knife-fighting with her in the alleys of Market Center. "I'm sure. She's got orange-red hair, so you wouldn't think red would look good on her. But that particular shade does."

Tony exclaimed, "What a ... cruel and dastardly thing to do! To kill a man, then kiss him?"

"Cruel and dastardly are good words for Miss Zia Cashout, from what I've seen so far."

Tony snorted.

"Do you by chance have anyone on Market Center? A dark-skinned man? I've seen him watching me a couple of times now."

"No," Tony said. "Well, yes, I have men on the island. But none that are dark of skin." He chuckled. "I save those men for excursions into Diamond."

Spying, you mean. "Maybe he was Jonathan's man."

Tony seemed confused.

"A man wearing black, dark of skin. I've seen him twice now. I thought maybe he was one of yours, or perhaps Jon's." I shrugged. "I didn't get a good look at him, but I told Blitz about him, and Master Rainbow as well."

"Good."

"I'd certainly feel better if I knew he was Jon's man."

Tony gave a slight shake of his head. "A man's first loyalty is to himself. Just because he got an order from Master Jonathan to watch over you doesn't necessarily mean his heart bears kindness towards you now that Jon is dead. If he once belonged to Mr. Julius, the man might even blame you for Jon's death." He unfolded the evening edition of the Bridges Daily and turned the paper towards me. "Did you hear about this?"

HART PATRIARCH PRESS CONFERENCE

"No outsider shall ever rule this quadrant!"

I stared at the headline. "Mr. Hart said he wanted to reassure his son of his standing. Perhaps this means he's decided not to ...?" I left the words hanging: "... *consider Acevedo for the succession?*" I didn't know who might be listening.

Tony shrugged, speaking softly. "It'd mean little in any case. Would Hart quadrant ever accept Spadros rule?" He turned to the paper. "There's lots of speculation here as to whether he meant some interference from outside the dome."

"I'd never considered that." The Feds were always a danger. If they got the idea that we couldn't run the dome properly, they had the right and obligation to seize it, scattering us and all our people to the other domes in permanent exile.

Tony continued to read. "Another power outage in Hart."

"Hmm." I sipped my tea.

Tony turned the page, and something dropped onto his lap. "What's this?" He put the paper aside and retrieved what looked to be a pamphlet.

"One of those tabloids, I presume. Did Mr. Blackberry ever reply?"

Tony blinked. "No." He sighed. "I'll have Ten pay him a visit."

I hoped little Werner hadn't run into trouble. It wasn't like the boy not to run back at once, particularly when money was involved.

Tony began reading the pamphlet then laughed. "Someone's finally figured out you were born in the Cathedral."

I chuckled. That was stated in open court years ago.

Then Tony's eyes narrowed. He leaned forward, began squinting at the page, turned it, and the squint became a decided frown.

"What is it?"

Tony turned the page, then closed the pamphlet and leaned back with a sigh. "They claim my father has impeded the city's repair."

"What?"

He held up the pamphlet. "You're from the Cathedral, which used to be owned by the Dealers. Now you're with my father, and the Dealers refuse to help fix the city. Therefore, my father has used some influence over the Dealers to forbid them to help."

"You mean blackmail?"

Tony shrugged. "Whatever. The point is that they're accusing him of intentionally harming the city."

"It couldn't be that the Dealers are making their own stand," I said bitterly. "Poor little brainless women can't do a **thing** without some **man** ordering them around."

Tony's voice was steady. "Yes, there are some who think that way. But it's more likely they don't want to believe that the Blessed Dealers would work against the good of Bridges. They'd rather blame my father than question what these women are really doing."

What **were** they really doing? "Anna Goren and Inventor Call were both murdered, seemingly by the same hand, just before they were to reveal something big, something that would help fix the city. That's too much of a coincidence."

"And the Dealers seem ready to let their people rot in jail rather than to say what they know."

"I can't believe their Director's still there! Even with the protests and everything. Why not give them some false information?"

Tony said, "Maybe anything they gave would reveal more than they dared."

"But what could be so important as to go to all this trouble? To murder the Spadros Inventor over? To allow the slums to be in cold and darkness over? To risk even losing the city to the Feds?"

"Unless the entirety of the Dealers' leadership have suddenly gone mad," Tony said, "it's something terribly important."

And that something focused upon the Cathedral. Some knowledge, some book? Again, I wished I would have asked Ma more that day at the park. "I've never seen anything there to explain this."

Tony rose wearily. "I need to send this to my father." He kissed my forehead. "I'll return shortly."

So I rang for dinner to be taken away, and for Amelia to get me ready for bed.

Then I lay there unable to sleep for all the questions. Did Tony really have everything on the Bridges Strangler, and not told me about it? Why?

And if Tony and Roy had all the information, why not go after Frank Pagliacci themselves? Surely someone in all the thousands of Family men could learn something about the man's whereabouts.

I felt as though I were missing something, something important.

But I never was able to figure it out before exhaustion overtook me.

***

Since I'd finally been going out, and felt much recovered, the next day I took up the list of Spadros supporters that Tony insisted I must meet, and ventured forth.

They all seemed astonished to see me. "So soon? It's been barely a month since your confinement! And you look so pale."

I felt as good as I might, given all that had happened. And looking pale? I'd been indoors for a month. "I wanted to come here to show you how much the Spadros Family values your service. To give apology for my neglect of you over the years."

After several of these supplications, I felt a bit weary, so I stopped at my apartments for tea-time. It was out of the way, true, but I did feel more restful there. Little Ariana toddled towards me, Blitz and Mary were all smiles, and no one would be whipped.

We sat, as we once did, around the kitchen table for tea. And in the midst of eating, the kitchen bell rang.

"I'll get it," Mary said. She opened the door, then looked back at us. "It's that fishwoman again."

I chuckled, amused. "I'll see her." If she were one of my informants, I'd know at once. If not, if she were simply some madwoman, or some reporter in disguise trying to get a 'scoop', I'd simply call out to the men who had to be at the ends of the alley, and have the creature escorted away.

I took the door handle and peered out. "May I help you?"

Twilight was falling, and the alley was beginning to dim. The old woman stood hunched over, one thin lined hand on the banister to the side steps, her face hidden by the ragged shawl she wore. But when she looked up at me, I could hardly believe it.

It was Dame Anastasia.

The Informant

I went down the steps, closing the door behind me. How could Dame Anastasia Louis be here? "I saw you **die**!"

She smiled at me, eyes twinkling. "You saw the zeppelin explode, that's all."

"That's all? That's **all**?" The man to my right at the end of the alley looked over at me, and I lowered my voice. "I went to trial for your **murder**!" Then I took a breath. She had something to tell me. "What happened? How are you here?"

"In the zeppelin station, I got this feeling." She looked around. "Too many people knew I was leaving, and when. So once we climbed the stair and were in the hallways, I told my nephew to bring your gift to my rooms. I told him I would visit with my friend I'd seen in the crowd and meet him for dinner. Instead, I went down to the luggage area. It was almost time for departure, and the hatches were open. No one was there. Just for an instant, but it was enough. I hid behind the baggage carriages, clinging underneath as they began to return, hoping I was wrong. But in the explosion, the carriage lit ablaze." She pulled up her sleeve, and the skin had been badly burnt. "I managed to escape in the early rush and confusion." She hung her head. "And I've been hiding ever since."

"But you could have come forward! Told them what you knew! Testified against Frank —"

"He blew up an entire zeppelin just to kill me! What do you think he'd do if he learned I still lived?" She glanced around, then faced me. "I have to tell you what I know before it's too late."

"What do you mean, too late?"

"You're important to them somehow. They had this entire plot: isolate you, break you down to have you under their control. And if that didn't work, kill you."

That first part sounded like what I'd thought. "If that didn't **work**? What was their real goal? I don't understand."

She looked away. "I'm not entirely sure I understand it either." She sighed. "Or perhaps I didn't want to."

I felt entirely confused. What good would breaking me down do? These people must believe me much more powerful than I actually was. And why had Anastasia never warned me of it?

"But once I overheard Frank talking to someone about whoever it is calling the play. I think it's a woman."

My mind reeled. A **woman**, directing these men to torture me?

"He kept saying 'she'," Dame Anastasia said. "I'm quite sure of it. Be very wary of a woman suddenly wishing to make acquaintance."

I nodded, thinking of that day Judith Hart suddenly showed up at my home before Acevedo was born. She claimed she wanted to ally, against her own son if need be. She'd come to the bridge to Market Center a few days after Acevedo's birth, before Jon's funeral, asking to see the boy. I didn't find out about it until after she'd left: the doctor had told the staff not to allow any visitors.

I didn't trust her then; I certainly wouldn't trust her now. "Roy Spadros and I have been in discussion on this topic, and from the evidence we've gathered, the leader of this is certain to be someone quite old, probably of great fortune."

"What makes you say that?"

"The person know things from the past that few could." Insight came to me in a rush: the situation with Mr. Hart. "They have great power in the city, and influence over many. Plus, they're using blackmail to obtain what they know."

Dame Anastasia frowned, her eyes distant. "Do you think this woman could be one of the aristocracy?"

"Why do you think that?"

She spoke slowly, carefully. "Mrs. Maria Spadros — Mr. Roy's mother — was a daughter of the aristocracy. After the Coup, most of the aristocrats lost everything: their lands, titles, and much of their fortunes." She took a deep breath. "Her parents probably hoped to gain influence by marrying her to Acevedo Spadros II." Her demeanor became quite serious. "But they never forgave the Spadros Family for her disappearance. They still live. And the way they speak of it! There's real venom there."

I knew little of Mrs. Maria Spadros other than the horrific rumors about her, and nothing at all of the parents. "Could Mr. Roy's grandmother be trying to destroy him?"

"I don't know," Dame Anastasia said. "All I know is that whoever Frank reported to was a woman, and that she wants you broken."

How could the Director of the Red Dog Gang possibly be an old woman? And why target me? Maria Spadros disappeared before I was even born. "Why are you telling me this? Why come here now?"

"Frank suspects I'm alive." She retrieved a wrinkled tabloid pamphlet from her waistband. "It's about me, published last month at the anniversary of the explosion." She snorted. "It's nothing you don't already know, but it calls me a 'licentious whore'." She chuckled, tucking the pamphlet into her waistband. "I think he wants to smear my name, in case I should reappear accusing him of his crimes."

That did sound like something Frank would do.

"I wanted you to know." She became somber, eyes fearful. "In case he finds me."

"Anastasia, come inside. Let me call my husband and his men. We can protect you."

She shook her head. "No one can," she said wearily. "Not anymore." She took a deep breath. "Don't look for me; I won't be in this disguise again." She hobbled down the alley and away.

Perhaps I should have called her back, told the men to capture her. But those burns ... she'd gone through so much to bring me this bit of news that I think pity for her stayed my hand.

I went inside.

"Mum," Mary said, "who was it?"

"One of my informants," I said, which was the honest truth.

Dame Anastasia could have warned me about Frank's plot and never did. She had abandoned her great-nephew to his doom. She'd left me to take the blame for the zeppelin explosion and the financial disaster she caused, staying hidden all this time, when she could have come forward with the truth.

Yet she'd risked her life to bring me this information.

Mary said, "Mum, are you well?"

"I don't know, Mary." I sighed. Why focus on destroying me? What had I **done** to them? "I don't feel as if I know anything anymore."

***

Once back at Spadros Manor, I showed Pearson my list. "Who are the aristocrats on here?"

He perused the list, checking off a few names. Too few. "There, mum. Is there anything else?"

"Did you learn why Mr. Dewey was in our rooms?"

"No, mum, he won't say. Both Mrs. Dewey and Master Michaels insist nothing was taken. Mr. Anthony said not to pursue it further." His tone said he thought that to be a mistake.

"Thank you, Pearson. Has the evening news arrived as yet?"

"It has. Shall I bring it to your study?"

"That would be wonderful." What Dame Anastasia had said came to mind. "I'd like everything you have on Mr. Roy's grandmother."

He blinked. "His who?"

"His mother's mother. Whatever we have on her."

For the first time since I'd met him, the man seemed completely taken aback. "Um … yes, mum, at once."

I went upstairs and rang for Amelia. How could an old **woman** be leading all this?

Dame Anastasia's evidence was slim, yet sounded definite. A woman did seem to be involved, at least in Frank's case, along with many men. Yet a woman in equal partnership with all these men, nay, directing them?

But then I recalled Morton's letter about Birdie, who had seized the High-Low Split of the Spadros Pot, calling herself Black Maria: *she seemed quite definite in her bearing, as if used to commanding men.*

Not even the Dealers commanded men!

Then I recalled Ma, back home, at the Cathedral. No man would dare defy Ma, at least, not to her face.

But that was in the Pot. These were quadrant-men. And from all accounts, this Black Maria was rather young, not much older than me.

I puzzled over that as Amelia got me changed into a housedress.

So perhaps this old woman had other women below her, women like the former Federal Agent Zia Cashout, or this Black Maria.

But could she possibly be commanding Frank Pagliacci and his men? Directing their movements? The one behind all this torment?

If so, what could her motivation possibly be?

I went down to my study, leaving the door open. The evening news lay on my desk, along with a hot cup of tea and a small tea-pot.

To my surprise, the headline read:

DISTRICT ATTORNEY SCANDAL

The Bridges Strangler:

They Hanged The Wrong Man

An exposé in multiple installments

Introduction:

We at the Bridges Daily have a shocking true report: how a fiend has been allowed to walk our streets — unchecked, unpunished, backed by corruption in the highest levels of our government.

It began with the disappearance and murder of a young girl almost two decades back. Over the years, dozens of young boys' deaths were passed off as suicides. An understaffed, poorly trained, and nearly unfunded First Precinct of Spadros quadrant tried to bring this man to justice, only to be blocked at every turn.

Soon, even the tabloid papers were calling this man the Bridges Strangler, and the people of the slums began to fear for their lives. After one such attack, a Constable was blamed for the deeds entirely without justification. He managed to escape with his life, but others weren't so fortunate. Photographers and reporters who tried to collect evidence were hounded to their deaths. A Detective on the case broke down under the strain.

In the meanwhile, a man of the Pot was quickly tried and hung, yet identical strangulations have continued unabated.

These facts are well-documented, good readers, and entirely accurate. We promise a detailed installment every week.

But we warn you: this report will be disturbing.

Next week: Part 1 — A Policeman's Girl Murdered

So Mr. Paul Blackberry came through. Even though he couldn't link it directly to the Mayor, the Mayor would certainly be implicated, since he was the District Attorney in most of these cases. "We might finally get him!"

Amelia came in from the hall. "Get who, mum?"

"That damnable Freezout." I showed her the paper.

Her eyes widened. "Ohhh." Then she gave a delighted smile. "That old scoundrel deserves it."

"Did you need something?"

She curtsied. "Time to dress for dinner, mum."

***

After dinner, I asked Tony if we might take a stroll in the garden. There, I related my theory that the aristocracy might be involved with the Red Dog Gang, without mentioning Dame Anastasia.

"However did you come to this idea?"

"An informant," I said. "One who mentioned that Roy's grandparents — his mother's mother and father — are still furious about his mother's disappearance."

Tony's eyes widened. "I've never met them; my father forbade it. He said once they were the worst kind of people ..." He let out a laugh. "Which is saying something, coming from him."

"Yes." The heinous acts of Mrs. Maria Spadros — even if a tenth of the rumors were true — didn't come from nothing. "But why target us? Why hurt my friends? I've never even **met** your grandmother."

"It makes no sense," Tony said, not looking at me. "Unless there's something we're missing."

We walked for a while, then Tony said, "I asked my father what he needed to speak to you about, but he refused to say."

Could it be about Mrs. Crawford? I knew Roy would be angry at what she'd done, particularly since it was against his express wishes. And I couldn't tell Tony about any of it: he had no idea that his mother had forced me to bear Acevedo. "Maybe I should go to him, since you don't want him here."

"I think that's a bad idea," Tony said. "I won't forbid it, but I urge you to reconsider, especially with these pamphlets linking you."

The one about the Dealers. "Let me think on it," I said. "But it could be something important. Perhaps he's learned something about the Cathedral?" I really couldn't understand what he might know, but if he felt it so important ...

"Very well," Tony said. "But be discreet. We can't have it get out that you're going there, not now."

"Tony ... I know you have information on that man of yours, the detective who was murdered. But why did you not tell me? I could've helped you."

Tony shook his head, not looking at me, face sober. "I don't want you involved with this right now. You have enough to worry about." He clasped my face in his hands. "You need to rest. Get well. Grieve."

Oh, Jon ... A rush of melancholy; I blinked back tears. "What did Ten say about Mr. Blackberry?"

Tony smiled to himself, let his hands drop. "He received the message, but has as yet found no suitable time to meet. With this exposé, he's been quite busy. I suspected this to be he case when I saw the news article, and told Ten he could relay our concerns regarding his paper. He did."

"And?"

"Mr. Blackberry's as concerned as we are, perhaps more so. He's started an investigation of the packaging department. Hopefully, we can at least keep these miscreants from using the *Bridges Daily* to provoke sedition."

I laughed. "At least little Werner didn't get waylaid, as I'd feared."

Tony kissed my forehead. "I love that you hold such concern and kindness for children."

It made me remember little Ante's dead body. His pale face. The way he'd clawed at my arm, trying to free himself.

Yet I also sighed internally at his tone, waiting for the rebuke hidden there. And in a moment, it came: "I wish you felt more concern for our son."

So predictable. "Are you done? Because I don't wish to speak about this." I turned and walked into the house, leaving him to stand there in the twilight.

I couldn't take this anymore. I needed to get out. I needed to be free to focus on what really mattered: taking down the Red Dog Gang.

But I couldn't just dismiss what Dame Anastasia had told me. The situation with Roy's grandparents might not even be as dire as a vendetta about their daughter: it could be a simple as hating that their grandson's heir had married a Pot rag. If they had fallen in with Frank Pagliacci and were trying to turn the rest of the aristocracy against the Spadros Family because of me, then I needed to do something about it.

I went to Pearson's station. "I'd like a list of those in the aristocracy yet not Spadros supporters who might be amenable to seeing me."

His eyebrows raised. "Yes, mum. It'll take some time, but I'll have the list to you as soon as I can."

I'd go to them myself. If I could split even one of them away from the Red Dog Gang, it would help.

Once I'd done all these meetings for the Family, though, my obligation to them would come to an end. I needed to be able to retire to my apartments with as little scandal as possible, so I could then focus on what was happening to my people in the Pot. Tony wouldn't like it, but I couldn't think here. I couldn't breathe here. I felt chained, as chained as Josie had been in that warehouse.

***

Acevedo slept more that night, but once day came, he'd begin to cry.

Tony didn't speak to me at breakfast, which was well, as I had nothing to say to him either. My head hurt, so after morning meeting I went to lie down. At noon, I was awakened by a knock at the door. "So sorry to disturb you, mum, but Mrs. Molly's here to see you."

I lay facing away from the door, but I didn't move.

"I can have her come up here if you prefer."

"Very well." I didn't move, and eventually I heard Molly try to tiptoe into the room. "What do you want?"

"I just wanted to see how you were," Molly said.

"Well, now you see me. You may go."

"Jacqui, don't do this. I'm your mother —"

I turned to face her. "No, you're not. You will never be my Ma. You're nothing but a ruthless, conniving, scheming bitch —"

Molly flinched.

"— who's done nothing but use everyone around you. You got what you wanted." I gestured towards Acevedo's screams. "Now leave me alone."

She stood there, tears in her eyes.

"Go," I said, "before I have you thrown out."

The door closed with a sharp click.

Good. I wanted to offend her. Maybe that would keep her away from me.

I put the pillow over my head, fuming. How dare she think she could have things go back to how they were, after what she did? Not only did she betray me — in direct defiance of her Patriarch — but she involved an innocent old woman in her schemes. And she tried to get Amelia to participate as well.

Maybe I shouldn't be so hard on Amelia, I thought. She might have been afraid of what I might do if she told me.

As if summoned, Amelia poked her head around the door. "Would you like your luncheon in here?"

"Yes, that'd be best." I didn't want to go downstairs now, particularly since there was a good chance Molly was still here.

So I had my luncheon in my bedroom. I was almost finished eating when Pearson knocked. "A letter for you, mum."

I opened it: a printed card from Josie, inviting me to tea tomorrow on Market Center!

Pearson hadn't moved.

"I've received an invitation to tea tomorrow," I said.

"Very good, mum. I'll have a carriage ready." He bowed and left.

I hated Molly. But her mentioning my Ma made me feel bitter besides. Ma had never once come to visit me, even though I almost died whilst delivering the child she helped force upon me.

It was then I noticed Acevedo wasn't crying.

Was he well?

I went to his room: he wasn't there. Daisy wasn't in her room, either. And his guards were gone.

Fear struck. Where was my baby?

I went out back to the veranda: no sign of them.

Alarmed, I hurried out front.

Daisy stood a few feet away. There sat Tony, and Molly — who held Acevedo, propped up on her lap.

A carriage went by. The baby laughed!

"Ace loves the carriages," Tony said. "Who would have known?"

The Exchange

Molly stayed until time for Acevedo's feeding, but said she'd come back the next day.

At tea-time, I told Tony about Josie's invitation.

"Why are you going to meet her?"

"Tony, she's been badly hurt. Apparently, her doctor told her she'd be scarred for life."

"So you **have** seen Master Joseph."

"So?"

"Why do you keep seeing him? What's going on between you?"

I didn't know. "Nothing. He just wanted to visit."

His face changed, as if he'd come to some decision. "Your maid will accompany you."

I shrugged. "It's at a restaurant, so she'll be downstairs with the servants. But if it makes you feel better —"

"It does."

Then I realized: Molly would be here around tea-time, not at home. "Have Pearson call my plain carriage. It should be safer."

Tony nodded. "Good idea."

"Maybe invite your mother for dinner as well."

He shrugged. "She probably won't want to stay quite that long, but I'll suggest it."

Molly would simply think Tony wanted to spend more time with her, and she probably would stay until at least six, half past if she wasn't too concerned about dressing for dinner with Roy.

I'd have a short span of time to visit Roy between leaving Josie and Molly arriving at her home. If he wanted to discuss Mrs. Claudete Crawford, as I suspected, it was best done with Molly ten miles away.

***

The next day, I took my plain carriage and met Josie at a small cafe upon Market Center. She'd gotten an outdoor table which faced the street, although well back, so we might sit along the wall and watch the carriages pass by.

Whilst her twin had dark hair and golden brown skin, Josephine Kerr had blonde curls and the lightest complexion. I would say pale, but only health glowed in her countenance. She had a sunny smile, and if I didn't know about the bandages covering her wrists, the thickness around them under her gloves wouldn't have been noticeable as she held out her hands to me. "I hope you're well?"

"Entirely," I said. Turning to Amelia, I said, "You may go."

Amelia curtsied and left.

Josie and I sat. I said, "I hope you're well also."

"I am," she said. "My wounds improve daily. I don't dare look at them — the thought terrifies me — but Joe has kept careful watch. He schedules his work so he might be there when the doctor arrives."

"How are you paying for all this?"

She beamed. "My Mr. Etienne pays for everything."

"I'm grateful." I gingerly took her hand, not wishing to hurt her. "Did Mr. Etienne ever learn who took you? How did you escape?"

She glanced away. "Must we speak of this?"

"Of course not. It was a terrible thing." I felt chastened. "I'm sorry to have disturbed you."

The beautiful smile returned. "All is forgiven, my sweet love. I could never, ever stay angry with you."

Heat rushed to my cheeks, there in front of everyone, and I put my hands in my lap. A rather elegant-looking liquor store lay across the wide road.

A waiter came up. "Your tea, ladies."

As the sandwich stand was set up and the tea was poured, I couldn't help thinking of that day in the warehouse. Had I been wrong to urge Josie to leave us?

If she'd stayed with me, between us we could have gotten Jonathan to safety. She might have been able to help him with me in my distress, preventing him from feeling forced to carry me.

Why did every decision I make go wrong? What was I missing?

"What troubles you, Jacqui?"

I shook my head. "Too many things."

"Then let's just sit here and watch the traffic pass. I find it soothing." A mischievous smile came over her. "Plus, it amuses me to see what some people wear, believing they look their best."

I smiled to myself, putting some small sandwiches on my plate. "That is amusing."

She sighed, relaxing into her chair, and blew on her tea. "What a lovely place this is." She took a sip, added sugar, then sipped again. "I love Market Center. This is the most wonderful place in the world."

"I've never traveled." I doubted she had either. "But it indeed is pleasant."

"I wish everywhere might be like this. No Family men spying upon you, no having to search your cushions or miss a meal to pay for your fees every month. The city working well, without the power going out all the time."

I shrugged. "I never thought much about it."

"They have the right idea here, at least in my view. No one tells the merchants here that they'll 'protect' them for a price. And the crime here is rare. They only need one police station for the entire island!"

"That does sound good."

"Well, that's how it used to be," Josie said. "I'd give anything to make things right again."

A laugh burst from me. "Like when the old tyrant was King?"

Josie hunched into herself. "You used to wish for the old days, and feel sorry for my grandfather. Now you call his ancestor a tyrant?"

"I can do both," I said. "The first Polansky Kerr was a tyrant, from what they tell me —"

"That's it exactly," Josie said. "Who tells you? Of course the Families will say anything to make what they're doing seem right. But my grandfather told me that his mother only spoke of her grandfather as a kind man, only wanting to make things better for his people."

I didn't know what to say. "That was long ago. I'm not sure we'll ever know the actual truth of the matter." I rubbed my forehead, wishing I'd brought the salicylate.

"Jacqui, what's wrong? You don't seem your usual self today."

I shrugged. Maybe Joe hadn't told her. "When they took me, before I came to you there in the warehouse that day, they hit me in the head so hard I fell asleep. Ever since, I've had terrible headaches."

"Good gods," Josie said, her face horrified. "I had no idea."

"Yes." I felt weary. "And my son has something called colic. It makes him cry all the time. Both have gotten better, now that the doctor has become aware of the situation —"

"That's good."

"— but that's just on top of everything else that's going on."

Josie leaned forward. "Like what?"

Should I tell her? "A group of men have been harassing us. Stealing our shipments, attacking us. They're the ones who framed me for the zeppelin explosion."

Josie gasped, hands to her mouth.

"They've tried more than once to kill me, and they've killed ... " I tried to count. Anna Goren, Madame Biltcliffe ... "several of my friends. They killed Marja, just because I loved her."

Josie became very still, then tears came to her eyes. "Oh, no."

"I've been so frightened they might attack you next, or even Joe." I took her hand. "It weighs upon me. I fear they were the ones who took you, which is why I asked about it." I felt at a loss. "That's all."

"My poor darling. Why did you not tell me of this before?"

"I never wished to add to your burdens. You have your sick grandfather to care for, his affairs to run, a wedding to plan." I glanced at her wrists, damp white calico peeking out from under the gap between her glove and sleeve, a bit of pink liquid soaking it. "And now you're so terribly injured —"

She glanced down, pulling her sleeve over the bandage. "Think nothing of it." She took my chin. "Listen to me. I have survived much worse." She let go, leaned back in her chair. "I won't have you worry on my account. Now eat, before all this goes stale."

The tone in her voice made me laugh, and I took her advice. The food here was good. "There is one thing which troubles me."

"What is it?"

"Remember that first time you visited? Oh, a few years back. Someone put a threatening card upon our front step. They'd have had to come in past our gate, past your coachmen, and to our step. Do you recall me asking about it?" At the time, I'd thought it to be the work of Jack Diamond, but he seemed to have nothing to do with it.

I'd seen her numerous times since the day I asked, and she'd never mentioned it. But then, I'd forgotten to ask about it during those meetings, so I couldn't put the fault on her entirely.

Josie sighed, not looking at me. "I do, and forgive me for not speaking of it until now. It was ..." She straightened, her eyes red. "They went into Spadros shortly after you asked about it, and were taken by that Strangler."

"They were?" I could hardly believe my ears. "Why didn't you and Joe tell me?"

She shrugged, looking away. "There was so much going on at the time ... and my grandfather was so ill ... I'm sorry, Jacqui." She sat, eyes upon her plate. "They were our cousins."

I felt horrified. "Oh, Josie, I'm so very sorry."

She nodded, eyes still downcast.

"If it makes any difference, I think this Strangler and the ones who've been threatening us are working together."

Josie looked up then. "Oh?"

I nodded.

"Hmm," she said. "It would make sense, them both being in your quadrant." She took up some strawberry jam and put it onto her toast. "Would you like more tea?"

I took some, then sat considering what I'd just learned. Did these coachmen see who put the card upon our front steps? Is that why they were killed?

And which of our men stood gate guard that day? We'd only had a few guards on the property back then. But I couldn't remember. I'd been drunk that day, quite decidedly so, and let much go by that I should have recalled. At the time, I'd been afraid to ask, not wanting Tony to learn what I was doing.

So much death might have been avoided if I might have had the courage to do things differently.

But what might I do now? This Strangler seemingly had the free run of our quadrant, supported by the Mayor himself, allied with the Spadros Pot and factions in both Clubb and Hart.

Not to mention the spy in Diamond, that (as far as I knew) had yet to be caught. Cesare seemed to think Jake Bower was the last spy, but he had caught him well before the attack upon their Country House.

If an aristocrat was behind these threats, it explained where they got the money to do all this. And if Frank Pagliacci, high in the ranks of the Red Dog Gang, was not only the Bridges Strangler but being funded by the aristocracy ... how might we stop such a fiend?

"One thing that is passing strange," I said. "The more I look at this, the more I believe that a **woman** is leading these men!"

Josie stared at me, mouth open, then scoffed. "A woman? That's preposterous! Outlandish!" She frowned as if puzzled. "What pathetic sort of man would ever let himself be led by a **woman**?"

I shrugged. "The evidence is leading that way so far."

She laughed, shaking her head. "You and your silly ideas. That's what makes me love you so. A woman, leading men?" She chuckled, leaned back. "To be honest, I'd never even considered such a thing."

By then, I was feeling more than a bit foolish for suggesting it. "Why not? My Ma owned the Cathedral, and the men there did whatever she asked. The Clubb Inventor is a woman, and her Apprentices follow her lead."

"Oh," Josie said, looking abashed. "The Clubb **Inventor** is a woman? I never knew!" She seemed to be re-evaluating her position.

"I'm surprised your Mr. Etienne never spoke of her; he's been introduced." I smiled at her fondly. "Perhaps things are changing in this city."

She leaned forward. "**Really**? This seems hard to believe." She hesitated. "I never saw your Ma command the men."

A laugh burst from me unbidden. "She most certainly did."

"And the Clubb Inventor really is a woman?"

"Really. Her name's Lori Cuarenta. I've met her more than once. She's not all that much older than we are."

Josie gaped at me as if completely dumbfounded. "I don't understand. How could a woman be in charge of ... directing ... **men**?" She paused, blinking, her head downcast. "And they don't have a man that **appears** to be in charge, that gives the actual commands."

"No, they don't. Not at all." I shook my head, chuckling just a bit.

She sat quietly, staring out at traffic for some time. It really seemed that she felt disturbed about something. Then she turned to me. "So what does this mean? Why would a woman send men to kill you?"

I felt someone watching me. A motion in the corner of my eye: a man, dark of skin, wearing black. All I saw was the edge of a long coat, to the ankles, and he was gone in the crowd.

"Jacqui, what is it?"

"Someone's been following me. I think I just saw him."

Josie looked around. "I don't see anyone watching us."

We were actually lucky that no one else had recognized me yet. Normally, I couldn't sit facing a street like this or the space beyond the low wrought iron fencing around this little dining area would have already been taken over by shouting reporters. I finished my tea. "Well, our good fortune won't last forever. I so love sitting here with you, but I'd not like this afternoon spoilt. And I have somewhere else I must go." I took her hand. "I'm so happy to see you looking well."

She smiled at me. "I'm happy to have seen you too." She got her handbag, then gestured at the store in front of us. "I must be going as well: my doctor will be by shortly, and I need to pick up some things for Joe from across the way."

I smiled to myself, feeling a great fondness come over me. *Joe.* "Tell him I said hello, will you?"

***

To my surprise, Roy was at home when I arrived at Spadros Castle; he actually seemed glad to see me in his parlor. "Please! Sit down."

My eyes went to the portrait, four by three, of Katie as a young girl. Molly claimed he drew it from memory.

He glanced over his shoulder. "You like it? Katherine says it embarrasses her." He laughed. "Everything does these days. I suppose it goes with the age. At that age, most things my parents did embarrassed me."

He'd never spoken of his parents. "What did you wish to discuss?"

Roy hesitated. "I had nothing to do with the tea."

"I gathered that."

"I know you must be angry —"

I gritted my teeth.

"— and I think you know who did it. My wife won't tell me. They went against my express wishes, and I must know."

"Why? Why do you care? You've got what you wanted, and —"

"Do you think I wanted to **force** you to bear my grandson?" He sighed, looked away. "This is wrong. What's happened is wrong. I won't be here forever —"

Suddenly, his eyes looked weary, as if he held on by mere will, a will that was fading.

"— and you, Anthony, Acevedo ... they're the future of this Family. I want you to care for my Family because they're yours, too." His shoulders drooped. "But I don't think you see it that way."

"Why should I? You took everything from me: my home, my mother, my life, even the man I loved. You forced me to marry —"

"But I didn't force you to return to him. And I certainly didn't force you to bed him. I presume you did that part on your own."

He had a point.

"I want to help you. Tell me who did this to you."

"You know who did this to me: your wife."

He glanced away. "For various reasons, I can't ensure justice for you in that case. But those who participated in the plot must be found.

They acted against the Lady of Spadros, who one day will be this quadrant's Queen. I can't let that go unpunished."

I'd never considered this. One day, I would be **Queen**?

"Or shall I question your servants instead?"

Fear surged through me. "No!" Amelia would be terrified at even being in the same room with the man who'd violated her. "Please. No. I've already questioned them."

"What of that woman who left right after you discovered you bore the Dealer's Gift?"

Mrs. Crawford. I needed to go to the Spadros Country House and speak with her before this all got out of hand. "Just leave this to me. Please. You must promise not to harm her."

He let out a breath, glancing away. "Very well. I won't harm her."

"Why were you and your wife at Anna Goren's apothecary shop the night she died?"

He glanced away. "Obviously, we knew about the tea. I only wanted to learn if you did it on purpose, or if this Miss Goren had been working with our enemies to deny the Family an heir. I thought it more proper to bring my wife with me. Of course, the woman denied knowing you at all —"

A twinge of pain. But she'd only been trying to protect me.

He laughed. "But when we showed her the packaging you'd put in the trash-bin, she had to admit you'd been there to purchase." He peered in my eyes. "I had nothing to do with her death, I swear it. You must believe me."

Did I? The clock struck half past six, and I rose. "I must go: I don't want Mrs. Molly to find me here."

His face turned amused, and he rose as well. "Then we must speak another time. I have much to tell you."

Why didn't he say so at the beginning? Puzzled, I got in my carriage and sped away home, hoping Molly wouldn't notice us in the twilight as we passed each other.

***

When I returned to Spadros Manor, Pearson met me at the door. "The key to Mr. Sluff's shop has arrived," he said, handing an envelope containing it and the address on a card. "When shall I schedule you to be there?"

I considered the matter. I'd been working my way towards the center of the city with my visits of late. "Move my calling times to after the morning meeting. I'll have luncheon at my apartments then do afternoons there instead. I can't imagine he'd have too much to pack up. Perhaps a week's worth?" That would actually give me four days, with having to be "at home" on Wednesdays. No one had been coming to call when I was "at home," but Tony seemed to feel that would improve in time.

"Shall I send men with you to crate the bottles?"

All those lovely bottles. I mustn't think of them. "Yes, that would be for the best."

"And how do you wish to dispose of them?"

It took me a moment to come up with an answer: I was sore tempted to have them brought to my apartments, even knowing Blitz would have refused to have them there. "Offer them to my husband's men as gifts. Sawbuck should know who's the most deserving."

"I presume you mean Master Hogan."

I grinned. "Yes, exactly."

Pearson gave a slight bow. "I'll contact him right away."

***

The next day, Pearson sent four men, along with Mary and Amelia and a flat-bed horse-truck piled high with empty crates and boxes.

I'd never seen Peedro's front door locked, so unlocking it left me disoriented. Inside, the room smelled of old dust. The bottles glistened in the afternoon sun, golden liquid clinging tenderly to the insides.

"We'll get these cared for, mum," the oldest of the four said, a man of perhaps fifty. He gestured to the others. "Come on, boys, let's let our Lady get to her work."

Amused, I went past the bar where I'd stood whilst Peedro taunted me with a bottle. The rickety stool he always sat on still stood behind there. A door next to the bar led to his private rooms.

Nothing on the walls. A narrow, unmade bed. A pile of old newspapers, a closet full of worn clothes. A battered cabinet tall as I was, stuffed with tattered files for his business. Receipts, bills yet unpaid. A dirty, unfinished wooden table with one chair and no coverings sat in the midst of it all. But on the table, he had a thick binder, full of news clippings ... of me.

All I had done, from the reports of my being there, my betrothal, my wedding, my doings. One of the many portraits I'd had done to be distributed to the shops for sale. Everything about the trial, some things underlined, almost as if he'd been trying to learn something.

He'd acted all those years as if he cared nothing for me, even felt disdain. But this spoke louder than any words or actions as to how often he'd thought of me.

Had he felt guilty, ashamed at what he'd done? If not, then why compile this? Perhaps he'd lied so long about me being his daughter that he'd come at last to believe it.

Amelia stood by the closet. "What do you want done with this?"

I said, "Give the clothes to the poorhouse. And sell the furniture."

Mary said, "I'll take care of that. And the racks out front?"

"Yes," I said. "The racks, the shelves, the cash register. Sell it all." I wasn't giving Doyle Pike one stick of it. "Put the money in my account." Something about the underlining struck me as purposeful. And I recalled this man used to be a police detective. What had he been up to? I closed the binder. "Bring this to my office."

"Yes, mum," Mary said.

I turned to the cabinets. "We'll have to go through all of this."

Mary put her hand on my arm. "Are you well, mum?"

I didn't know what she meant. "I feel well."

She glanced at Amelia. "This was your father, mum. Are you sure you want to go through his things right now? Are you sure you want to do this here?"

The men in the next room were grunting, the bottles clinking as they went. I could hear the liquid sloshing. "It's as good a place as any." But I fancied Mary could hear my heart for its pounding. "I'm going to go out back for a smoke."

"I'll come with you," Mary said quickly, walking me to the door past Peedro's bed.

It opened to a few steps down, into a short, narrow alleyway, not even ten yards long. The door sat a few feet from another, wider alley to my left, with the street to my right, making an H. The afternoon sun angled towards me down the wider alley on my left; if anyone were to come from that direction, his shadow would be easy to see. Funny to say, but this little alley seemed cleaner than Peedro's whole home.

Mary seemed worried. "Should I stay here with you?"

I waved her off. "I'll be fine; I just need some air. You go on, get those clothes taken care of. Anything you find out of the ordinary, put on the table for me to look at later." I got a cigarette from my handbag and lit it. "The sooner we get this done, the sooner we can leave the rooms to that old vulture."

Mary chuckled, but she left the door propped open with the chair.

Just to be sure, I stepped down the little stair and went to the brilliantly lit larger alleyway on my left, peering up and down it. A bit dirtier, but just as empty. I strolled to the other end; people walked past on the sidewalks. I heard the voices of a couple of men, close by.

"— nicer than here, even the slums."

"Yeah, and them rickshaws during the train outage. Smart!"

"Kind of makes you wish you lived there."

Realizing my smoke would give me away, I returned to the left side of the stair where I began, just out of the sun. And I recalled my trips to Joe's grandfather's house there in the upper Hart slums. It **was** nicer there than here. Why was that?

I stood there smoking, enjoying the silence, the golden light. Out of the beam as I was, the brilliant sun to my left bathed the bricks and cobbles in a lovely color. Almost the color of bourbon.

Perhaps I focused upon this more than I should've, because suddenly a pale-skinned man stood to my right, directly in front of the little stair, and for a moment I couldn't see him clearly. He smelled faintly of sardines. I squinted at him. "May I help you?"

He chuckled, spoke softly. "I'm sure you remember me, 'Miss Ogier.' Or else you will, in time. But what I want?" He grabbed my arm. "I want you to tell me where my aunt is."

The Assailant

It occurred to me that I might scream and instantly have two women, the four men inside, and the carriage-men outside rush to me for aid. But they'd come through the door beside me. The man had three ways out of this alley, and I wanted answers.

I knew this face: the man at Dame Anastasia's factory, over three years before. But this was no bumbling fool. Whilst his ears were still big and his skin still poor, he'd lost weight and no longer wore spectacles. His hair was clean and he dressed as a gentleman, entirely in black. "I don't believe this!" It was Dame Anastasia's great-nephew, Trey Louis. "What are **you** doing here? However did you escape?"

His face turned amused. "Why does everyone act like you're some genius? My Lady, you ask entirely the wrong questions. But if **this** is what you wish to know ..." He scoffed, shaking his head. "It became clear to us both that we were being used as discards."

I gasped.

He snorted. "We weren't sure when the blow would come; she suspected we'd be found dead in whatever city we left for. So we'd planned it for weeks: make a big show of leaving, then sneak off the zeppelin and take another flight out."

She'd spoken of being afraid of Frank, of not wanting anyone to know where she went. So this made sense.

Then he shook his head. "I knew the instant she knew that something was wrong. I'd felt it too, but her reaction only confirmed it for me." He glanced away. "I have to admit it hurt when she handed me the package." He took a deep breath. "She's not really my aunt, to be honest. Just another part of the play. But she picked me up as a boy, then after all these years, left me to die." Then he straightened, the set of his shoulders telling me he wished to speak no more of her betrayal. "So I gave the package to a porter to bring to our rooms and left the zeppelin as I'd planned, telling the hatch attendant I'd forgotten something. I saw Anastasia hide herself, under a carriage no less! Most unlike her. Yet it was then the situation became clear: in alarm I ran away from the station, for the trees beyond. I suppose I was lucky: other than a few scrapes, I escaped the blast unharmed. We had a meeting-place planned in case we got separated, but she never showed up." He focused on me then. "Now, where is she?"

The glare from the alley now annoyed me; I shook my head, taking a step towards him. "I thought she was aboard the zeppelin, too."

Trey Louis snorted. "You lie so very poorly. I knew she'd go to you. I've kept watch over the places you frequent these past three years." He tapped his temple. "But she's good. She fooled my men with that last disguise. If she hadn't gone to your back door the third time, I don't think they'd have even mentioned it." His manner became earnest. "I have to find her. Where is she?"

"I swear, I don't know."

He frowned at me.

"Yes, she visited. But I don't know where she next went. She said she wouldn't use that disguise again."

He nodded sagely, gazing into my eyes.

I felt a bit guilty. "You didn't really think I meant to marry you ... did you?"

He began to laugh, but quietly. "That whole thing was a set-up, Mrs. Spadros. I was stationed there to deflect any questions about the project. I recognized you before you even spoke. We had a good laugh about it, really ... me, Anastasia, even Frank. We found it all quite amusing. You're a young, gullible fool," at this, he scoffed, "entirely unconvincing as an actress."

Now I felt mocked, and it made me angry. "How dare you? By your own words, instead of alerting the pilot, you left hundreds to die, me to take the blame for it, and ... and your only concern is confronting your aunt? And you mock me for trying to learn the truth?" I couldn't take it all in. "And it sounds as though you bear no animosity towards Frank for trying to kill you."

"Oh, no, he didn't try to kill me, not at all. It was all that little hussy Maria, or Birdie, or whatever her real name is."

"Oh, is **that** what he told you?" The man clearly was still under Frank's thrall.

He nodded. "I don't know what hold she has on him, but if I were him, I'd kill her in an instant."

Interesting. "Tell me about this woman."

"There's no time. Frank sent me here to fetch you. You're in serious danger, both of you. He wants to get you to safety."

Frank wanted to get me ... to **safety**?

"He and my aunt had a falling-out, and she's obviously poisoned you against him. But trust me: all he wants to do is to help."

I scoffed. "He's a multiple murderer! How can you support him?"

He sighed. "Frank said you'd be difficult." He grabbed my arm, pulling me towards him and to my left.

"No." I pulled away, towards the wall, the sun blazing in my eyes. But his grasp was too strong.

"Don't fret," Trey said, pulling me towards the bright alley. "My carriage isn't far."

"No!" Things were getting out of hand! I screamed, "Help!"

Out of the glare to my left, a sharp movement, and Trey Louis lay upon the ground clutching his head. Mary appeared at the door, calling to the men inside. Trey scrambled to his feet, blood on his face, and ran off into the sunshine.

The men came bursting past her, and she pointed up the alley. Two gave chase; the other two stood round me.

Trey's top hat and a splatter of blood lay upon the ground.

Mary said, "Who was that man? Did he hurt you?"

"No," I said. "But he wanted to take me." I stared at her. "He almost did." I moved closer to the stair, glancing over my left shoulder. "Someone saved me."

The men looked up and down the alley beside me and shook their heads. Amelia came to the door and gasped, hands to her face.

"Let's get you inside," Mary said. "We've had enough excitement for today."

***

"And you have no idea who it was? The man who saved you?"

We sat in Tony's study before dinner, in his armchairs, and he held my hands.

I shook my head. "It must've been a man, but I only saw an arm with some weapon." I tried to picture the scene. "The sun was," I held up my hand forming a ball in its direction, "right there." I tried to recall more. "It could've been a left arm. And he wore black. And black gloves." Something tickled my mind; I leaned back, considering.

"What is it?"

"He smelled familiar. But I can't place it. And he was taller than me, by a good bit."

"Well, this solves the mystery of the man in black, at least as far as his motivations." Tony stood. "Come with me." He led me out to the veranda, and we sat there in the twilight. "Who was this man that tried to take you? Why was he there?"

I sighed. "Dame Anastasia and her great-nephew were on the zeppelin, but they escaped before the explosion."

Tony stared at me, mouth open.

"She was ready to let him die! She fears Frank will find and kill her. Her nephew — well, I guess he's not really her nephew — made it out, yet he hunts her. And he's in thrall to Frank Pagliacci as much as anyone might be."

Tony leaned back. "I won't ask how you know this 'nephew' —"

I shuddered, surprised. "I never said I —"

"Amelia heard someone speak through the open door before you cried out, but she didn't question it." His tone said he hadn't decided how to punish her. "You should never have been left unguarded."

"Don't blame them: the alley was empty. I told them to go inside. The door stood open." I peered at him. "Should they not have followed my orders?"

"No, they shouldn't, not when they're impulsive and foolish." He took my hands. "I don't say this to chide you. But what if this benefactor hadn't been there? You'd be in the hands of scoundrels who want you dead."

I shook my head. "He claimed I was in danger. That we both were. Dame Anastasia and I. That Frank wanted us taken to safety."

Tony gaped at me.

"Dame Anastasia was most specific. The note Ten and I found in Marja's hand was clear. They need me alive." I felt weary. "But they want to destroy me," I tapped my chest, "inside. I wish I knew why."

Tony frowned. "It almost sounds as if they're divided."

"Hmm." He did that on remarkably little information. "The man denied Frank being involved with any of it. He blamed the other one, the woman they call Black Maria. He said **she** exploded the zeppelin."

Dame Anastasia had worked with Frank Pagliacci. She'd bedded him, she'd introduced the aristocrats to him. Then when he turned on her, she defrauded the city and fled, leaving me to die.

Tony had turned away; he sounded bitter. "For any of these villains to survive ... yet a good man like Jonathan lies dead —"

"Yes," I said. "It feels —"

"Unfair. Entirely so."

We sat listening to the crickets, each, I suppose, with our own grief, until our retainers came to dress us for dinner.

***

It only took a day more for the men to crate up the bottles. For most of that I stayed well away, several men standing guard at every turn.

Peedro Sluff's rooms took me a bit longer.

I attended Minerva Karayi's funeral with Acevedo, carrying the blanket she'd made for him. Her husband wept when he saw us.

Over the next few days, I sorted the papers in Peedro's cabinet, seeing what he still owed, and what was still owed him.

Mary readied the sale items, interrupted a few times by workmen arriving to cart off this or that. Amelia, moving a bit more slowly, busied herself with cleaning the place, and I tried to piece together this man's life.

He'd been married, his wife filing for divorce — a rarity in Bridges — when he was sent to the Pot. She'd later remarried, and died in childbirth. His parents had turned in their cards. He had no children.

Except, it seemed, me.

Strangely enough, there was nothing in his house about his former cases, particularly the one which had ruined him. Perhaps he didn't want to be reminded of that horror. But the story of little Trina Bower stuck in my mind. Peedro had been seen by Mr. Jake Bower — or so his wife said — in the area where the girl was later found.

Planting the child's body where Peedro had been seen by the girl's father was as good a way as any of dividing these two men. Had Peedro come close to finding her killer?

Something about that troubled me, but as yet the meaning of it wasn't clear. What was clear was that Frank Pagliacci had motive to want Peedro dead, particularly as more and more attention was being paid to Frank's crimes as the Bridges Strangler.

But no cards of the Red Dog Gang had been found. The police never reported any fingerprints in his rooms other than Peedro's own. And two months later, they still had no leads.

I looked over the big piles of old papers on Peedro's table, some tattered and yellow. "Bring a trash bin," I said to Amelia. "Most of this has to go."

***

The next installment about the Bridges Strangler was in the evening paper, and it was entirely about Trina Bower. The title:

A Policeman's Girl Murdered

The child's photo sat there.

> A pretty girl of ten, Miss Trina Bower went outside with the other children to play with her toys at a policeman's party in the Yuletide of 1885.

> She wasn't seen again until some months later, dead of strangulation, with the most vile crimes done upon her young body.

Gods, I thought. I hoped someone had contacted Reina Bower to warn her. And I wondered if she and her Constable had ever gone to see Mr. Blackberry as I'd suggested.

No matter; he seemed to have more than enough information.

The piece went on, detailing the months-long search, copies of letters from the Spadros First Precinct begging for help from City Hall which never came, the suspicion on a police Detective, who later fell into disgrace, then ruin. The true killer was never found.

> This poor child's story starts a chain of crimes lasting through to today, good folk. With each report, we hope to enlighten you as to the kind of villain allowed to walk our streets even now.

> Next week: Part 2 — For Years, Boys Go Missing

Heart pounding, I put the paper away. This went beyond shocking, and I knew most of it already. Mr. Blackberry was putting his life on the line just by allowing this to be printed.

But then I thought: if he or anyone on his staff should fall dead, it would only make City Hall — and by extension, the Red Dog Gang's dummy Mayor Chase Freezout — look worse.

They had to distract people from this report. What would they do?

I didn't know, and the question frightened me.

***

A few days later, I was in my study after tea, looking over the police files from Peedro's murder case. I'd asked Tony to let me see them (without the pictures, which Tony refused to let me have).

I'd pictured a single shot, but the reality was a bit stranger.

Someone had emptied a .38 revolver into him.

The excess of this spoke of a personal affront being avenged. But who had intimate reason to kill him ... other than perhaps me?

Jack Diamond stood at the top of my list.

Peedro had murdered Jack's friend the same night Peedro sold me. Jonathan's twin brother had abundant means, a good motive, and as everyone thought him dead, plenty of opportunity — not to mention the best alibi possible. Thousands witnessed his funeral procession; no one would ever consider him as a suspect.

I was beginning to regret keeping silent about Jack still being alive. But until I knew more about why, what he'd learned that was so vital, who he feared so much, that the man had to fake his own death ...

I wouldn't be the cause of someone else being murdered. I wouldn't. Not even a scoundrel like him.

Peedro Sluff used to be a police detective, which certainly made for a lot of suspects. The Detective Constable assigned to the case had been investigating this line of thought for some time, and had come up with several names. However, all had good and legitimate alibis for that night. But Peedro used to also be a Party Time addict, and as such, could have made a number of enemies in the Pot.

I made some notes to take with me back to my office at the apartments. Such a shame. Just when the man had gotten free of the drug and was making his life good again — to be murdered!

A knock at the door. "Mum," Pearson said, without opening the door. "There's a man outside asking for you."

The man turned out to be Joseph Kerr. Tony had told his men not to let him past the front gate, so I put on my wrapper — now rather large for me — and went out to meet him.

I'd been hesitant to even go to the front gate ever since I'd been taken from there. Not that Joe would be part of any such thing, but even so, it made me remember all that had happened that day. But I took up my courage and went to him in any case.

The men guarding the gate opened it for me, and I stepped onto the sidewalk. Joe stood there in the late afternoon sun, dressed in a tweed cap and workman's cotton. His hair, his eyes, his skin, just as beautiful as ever.

But he wasn't smiling.

"Good evening," I said, wondering what troubled him so. "I hope you're well?"

"Oh, Jacqui." For the first time ever, I heard fear in his voice. "Something's terribly wrong. It's Josie."

The Sickness

Josie? "What is it? What's happened?"

"She's had a sudden fever."

I gasped. The women's contagion?

He looked seriously concerned. "The doctor doesn't know what's caused it. He says the wounds on her arms look fine. But she's out of her head, and her skin feels like she's on fire."

Out of her head? "You must return to her. Don't leave her side." The air felt chill; I pulled my wrapper around me. "I'll come at once."

He let out a breath, visibly relaxing. "Thank you."

Thank the gods, Tony had come home early that day.

I ran towards the Manor, up the steps. Honor stood there, barely opening the door in time. Pearson, at his station, glanced up as I burst in. "I must have a carriage."

"And where might you be off to?"

"Hart quadrant. And call Amelia; I must be ready to leave at once." Without waiting for a reply, I ran to Tony's study and entered without knocking.

He looked up. "What's happened?"

"Tony, we must go. Josie's taken fever, and she's frightfully ill. The doctor doesn't know what to do for her."

Tony blinked. "So why must **we** go? Surely her doctor knows more than we do about such things."

I realized my mouth was open, and shut it. "She's one of my dearest friends. She's been struck with fever. Many women in Hart quadrant have died of it. Why would I **not** go to her? With all that's happened, I thought you'd want to come too. Besides, there are things we do for fever in the Pot that a quadrant-man might not know."

Tony burst out laughing. "Very well, go. I'd wager this fever is nothing more than another play to get you out of your home." He waved at me dismissively. "Go. But don't forget I told you so."

"You think she's lying? Pretending to be ill? That her brother would come all this way —"

"Ah. Yes. Now I see it. Joseph Kerr came here and told you his sister was so terribly ill that you had to go to him."

"Why are you acting like this? Why do you assume he'd lie about something like this?"

"Because I became very well-acquainted with Joseph Kerr when I had him in my safe-house," Tony said. "He's a lying, conniving snake, who'd do anything to strike at me and mine. But if I forbid it, you'll only run off after him. So I'll say this: you will go with outriders. You will not go into that house alone. And under no circumstances are you to stay the night. Is that clear?"

I felt furious, but I knew better than to protest: he might decide I couldn't go at all. "Perfectly. But when I come home with news of her illness, you best remember I told you so."

Tony snorted. "That'll be the day." He strode to the door. "Pearson!"

Pearson hurried up. "Yes, sir."

"Ten horsemen are to go with her. Two plus Honor and Amelia are to accompany her in. And either Honor or Amelia must stay at her side. You hear? They're not to leave her side for any reason."

"I'll inform them, sir."

"I don't care if the Floorman Himself commands it, they are not to leave her side. Do you understand me?"

"Yes, sir."

Pearson never glanced at me, but I felt humiliated. When he returned to his station down the hall, I turned to Tony. "How dare you speak to him about me as if I were some rebellious child?"

"You are a rebellious child," Tony said, "and some days I wish I'd never married you."

I felt stabbed in the heart. "Why are you saying this?"

Tony didn't look at me. "Because it's the truth."

Pearson glanced over at us, and I lowered my voice. "I've loved you, Tony. I've bedded you. I've borne a child for you. I've given up my health, my body ... I've almost died for you, more than once."

"No," Tony said. "Everything you do is for yourself. I don't know why, or what you're getting out of it, but I know it's not out of any love for me. Or you wouldn't have anything to do with the man who almost destroyed me."

I took a step back. "I don't know what to say. What if your cousin Ten lay dying with fever? Would you not go to him?"

"The matter would be entirely different."

"Different how?"

"Ten hasn't tried to ruin your life."

"This is ridiculous. Josie hasn't tried to ruin your **life**. She barely knows you! Anything she says or does has nothing to do with you. And anything Joe might have done ... well, it's between he and I. You don't enter into it."

"I'm done with this, Jacqui. If that's truly what you believe, then you're better off with them." He went back into his study and shut the door in my face.

What was **wrong** with him? Why would he say these things to me?

Something else was bothering him. Something making him angry and upset enough to lash out at me.

I knew from experience that he wouldn't tell me what was wrong until he was ready to, so I went upstairs to get changed. I still needed to visit Josie.

I only hoped it wasn't too late.

***

By the time we got to the Kerr's brownstone in the upper Hart slums, night had fallen.

I shouldn't have been surprised to see Etienne Hart's carriage there. His coachmen snapped to attention as I passed. Unlike his father's white carriage, Etienne's was red, with the mark of the Heir in silver upon its sides.

Miss Susan, Josie's housekeeper, answered the door, then showed us into the parlor. Etienne Hart had been pacing, and stopped mid-stride when we entered, turning to face me.

Inventor Etienne Hart was an overweight man in his fifties with auburn hair, a round pale face and strange, multi-lensed spectacles. "What are **you** doing here?"

"Visiting one of my closest friends. I hope you can say the same."

My answer apparently took him by surprise, because for once he didn't have some biting retort.

He had no men in the room, so I gestured to mine to stand aside. The two horsemen Tony had assigned to guard me took positions beside the door, whilst Honor and Amelia stood behind me and to one side, but casually, as if simply enjoying the decor.

Etienne Hart's eyes narrowed. "Why do you need so many retainers with you?"

"This is my husband's doing." Since he outranked me, I couldn't sit whilst he paced, and had to turn to speak to him. Which was quite rude on his part. "Why do you hate me so much?"

He scoffed, continuing to pace. "Hate would imply I cared. I don't hate you. I pity you." He stopped in his tracks. "I despise you. You're just a painted-over discard, unfit to be called Lady of anything."

Out of the corner of my eye, I saw one of Tony's men tense up at the insult, and I shook my head slightly. "I'm genuinely curious. What do you mean, discard?"

He began to pace once more. "The Spadros Family murdered my grandparents, my uncles, my cousins. But that wasn't enough. They had to seize you so they might take my quadrant."

My first reaction was shock: was that why Roy took me? Then I felt alarmed. Very few knew that Charles Hart was my father. I went to him, spoke quietly. "Why are you saying this in front of them?"

He laughed. "You think I care about what they think?"

I spoke quietly. "You may not care about that, but there's a reason our association is kept secret. If you need to know why I suggest you ask your father."

That seemed to get to him. "Very well."

"I truly would like there to be peace between us, despite your actions. Why do you believe my baby's a threat to you?"

He scoffed. "Your squalling brat is irrelevant." Then he pointed off towards his home. "I still don't believe you innocent of my wife's death. And I distrust my father's sudden alliance with you." His arm dropped to his side. "All he must do is claim you as his own, and a couple of 'accidents' puts your husband over half the city."

"What?" I couldn't believe what I was hearing. "You truly believe us capable of that?"

"You're a Pot rag — who knows what you might be capable of? And your husband might feign incompetence, but he was raised to rule by Roy Spadros." Etienne shook his head. "I'll die before I let you take my land. Or let you coerce my father into giving it away."

I felt sad. "You have the matter entirely wrong. Your father loves you. He intends you to rule your quadrant. No one's coerced him: he approached us to make alliance."

Rolling his eyes behind their thick lenses, Etienne shook his head.

Yet someone **was** coercing Mr. Hart ... to do what?

But I couldn't speak of that here. "Besides, I care nothing for any of this intrigue. I'd be just as happy out of the Families altogether."

He pointed at me. "You don't understand, do you? You say you want out, but they have complete control over you." He snorted. "My father. His utter lack of character is what got us here in the first place."

I didn't like what he was implying. "My husband is angry at your actions, true. But given the chance, I think he'd choose peace."

Etienne scoffed at that.

"I've known my husband since the age of twelve, sir, and one thing's clear: he's not Roy Spadros. If anything, he's not harsh enough." Then something occurred to me. "We've had pamphlets speaking against us distributed in our quadrant marked with the Hart Symbol. Could your mother's people be behind this?"

He snorted. "The Bridgers are a bunch of crackpots. But if they ever spoke out against your Family, they'd sign their names to it." He seemed to be considering this. "They might be mad, but at least they're honest."

The door opened and Miss Susan said, "The doctor says she can have visitors now. But only two at a time, and you mustn't stay long."

"Go ahead, sir," I said. "I must have my maid with me."

Etienne Hart sneered. "As I said, only a discard."

The man was infuriating.

After a few minutes he returned, looking grim. "I don't plan to leave her like this tonight."

So Amelia and I went upstairs and to her room.

Josie lay covered to her shoulders. Her face was a deep pink, her hair strewn across the bed. She moaned and tossed as if in pain.

I knelt beside her; her hand was hot as an oven. "Good gods, what's happened to her?"

A man of middle age stood by, a nurse at his side. "A sudden fever; I'm not finding any reason for it."

"What have you given her?"

"Young lady, I would certainly have heard of a woman physician in this city. I doubt you'd even understand my words."

I stood. "I'm the Lady of Spadros, but more, I'm a woman of the Pot, and in the Pot we have no physicians to heal us. She needs garlic, in her food, her drink, and in poultices upon her skin, to fight whatever contagion has caused this. You must get cold wet cloths, and ice upon her body, if you can find it this time of year. And salicylate for the fever. Otherwise, she'll die of this heat inside her!"

He gave me a skeptical look. "Salicylate might work, but —"

"If she were awake, she'd ask for the same. So unless you have something better to administer, go at once and do as I say."

The man simply crossed his arms. So I turned to Miss Susan. "You do it, then, if he won't."

She curtsied. "Right away, mum."

He scoffed. "This will do nothing except waste good garlic. I've told her betrothed to arrange her funeral: I doubt she'll live the night."

No wonder Etienne didn't plan to leave. I felt bitter, grieved. "Then I suppose other patients have more need of your care."

Miss Susan came in with a basin full of cold water and cloths. I pulled the covers completely off Josie, exposing her deep pink ankles and feet. The doctor rolled his eyes and left, the nurse trailing after.

Amelia, Miss Susan, and I put the wet cloths upon Josie's limbs, then I opened her windows wide. "She needs cold air, fresh upon her. When these cloths dry, put new ones on," I said to Miss Susan. "Do you understand? Until her fever breaks or she tells you differently. Do you have garlic?"

"I sent for some," she said. "How do I prepare it?"

"Raw," Amelia said, "grind it to a paste on a cloth, then lay it on the belly, between her breasts, on her limbs, and around her neck. Put the cloth against her skin, not the garlic itself, or it may irritate. And when you give her drink, once an hour add the juice of garlic to it."

I stared at Amelia. How did she know?

"The slums have no doctors either," she said. "But I didn't know you in the Pot did the same."

I went to Miss Susan and took her hand. "The gods bless you. My husband has forbidden me to stay tonight, but if you wish, I can leave Mrs. Dewey to help."

"Before the doctor arrived, I sent message to my sister. Her girls should arrive soon. She'll not be left alone for an instant, mum, not if I have say in it."

I went downstairs. Miss Susan's kin had arrived, and were hastily removing their coats. One said, "Might I get you some dinner, mum?"

"I'll be in the parlor; you can bring it there."

Amelia said, "I'll help with that, mum." She followed the woman to the kitchen.

So I went to the parlor, where Honor and the two horsemen still stood. Etienne Hart now sat in an armchair. Honor looked alarmed. "Where's Mrs. Dewey?"

"In the kitchen." I sat upon the sofa. "That doctor is as incompetent as he is rude. As far as I can tell, he's done nothing for her."

Etienne Hart leaned forward. "So there's hope?"

I bit my lip. I didn't want to give my brother hope, only to have that hope fail. "The fever is serious," I said. "But sometimes women know cures that men do not."

His eyes reddened, and he let out a breath. "Thank the gods. I don't think I could bear to lose her."

I stared at him. *He loves her!*

"Don't look so surprised, Mrs. Spadros. I'm just as capable of feeling as any man. And I'd not marry a woman for convenience, no matter how much my father might wish it."

Sadness came over me: Josie said that was exactly why she married him. I wondered if her feelings had changed in the interim.

Etienne said, "Why won't you help us?"

The question threw me off guard. "Help who?"

"The Inventors only want to repair the city. It's for the good of all."

"But I've told you all I know."

He scoffed. "You lived there over half your life and you know nothing? You're impeding the entire city out of some misplaced loyalty to the Cathedral, who by all accounts cast you out." He shook his head. "I and the Diamond and Clubb Inventors meet weekly. We have everyone in our quadrants from Apprentices to the lowest furnace sweeps considering ideas to fix the Magma Generators without these women. I've begged your Inventor to join us, to engage your quadrant's people to find answers. Yet he refuses. Do you have any idea why?"

"I can't say." I pictured Monte Arrow stumbling from Maxim Call's home, covered in the man's blood, weeping. "He was sorely grieved by the death of Inventor Call. Perhaps it's clouded his judgment."

Amelia brought in a tray with a large tea-pot upon it. She and one of the other women brought individual small tables for each of us, then a tea-table laden with a stack of dishes, some silverware, and a platter of various meats and sandwiches which looked left over from their tea-time many hours before. The other woman said, "If you prefer something hot, sir, we can fix more for you."

"No need," Etienne Hart said. "Focus on making my Finette well."

Finette. That was the name Josie had given when she came to my apartments cloaked and hooded a year or so before. And I recalled what Jonathan Diamond had said to me once, long ago: *not even their grandfather uses his real name here.*

Amelia glanced at me, nodded, curtsied low, and returned, I suppose, to the kitchen. The rest of us served ourselves, then retreated to various chairs to eat.

Joe had seemed so surprised and alarmed that he'd not been registered by his real name here in the quadrants. But Jonathan seemed to think that Joe didn't use his real name except perhaps with me. If he didn't use his real name here, what name did he use?

And why did Josie act as if she'd never met with, nay, even heard of the Clubb Inventor — if her betrothed met with the woman every week? "Inventor Hart?"

He looked up from his tea. "Yes?"

"Do you speak much of your work with your betrothed? I only ask because I had a conversation with her which now confuses me."

He chuckled. "What would an innocent young woman care about tedious meetings? She's clearly had no training in scientific matters — I'd have no inkling of where to even begin."

"Inventor Cuarenta is hardly a crone, sir."

"Miss Lori Cuarenta?" He shook his head. "An unnatural creature — hardly worthy of womanhood. If my investigations had not shown differently, I'd think her a dressed-up pretty-boy."

"Because she's intelligent and capable, she somehow isn't womanly? From what I hear, the path to Inventor is a long and arduous one."

He rolled his eyes. "Apparently not arduous enough, if even a woman could achieve it. Could they find no Clubb man worthy of the honor? It's an embarrassment to an otherwise reputable quadrant."

This angered me. "You know as well as I do that Apprentices choose their next Inventor. Obviously **they** thought her worthy."

He scoffed. "Weaklings and fools, the lot of them." He leaned back, tea-cup in hand. "This'll make Clubb easier to conquer, though, when the time comes."

I had nothing to say: the man sounded entirely mad.

This didn't come from nowhere, though. Did Charles Hart feel this way about **me**? Was his desperation to get me out of my quadrant due to seeing me as an "innocent," incapable of caring for myself?

After a while, I had Honor grind garlic and carry basins up and down to let Amelia eat. The men outside were rotated in so they might eat as well. One was sent with a message for Tony. But for much of the evening, we sat in desolate silence.

The clock struck eleven, and I heard Joe in the front hall.

His sister was dying! I'd told him not to leave her side! Where had he been?

Amelia spoke in my ear. "Mum, Mr. Anthony said to leave if that man arrived, and specifically not to be in Hart quadrant past the day."

I turned to Etienne Hart. "I'm afraid I must go, sir. Please call if her condition changes."

He rose when I did, took my hand. "Thank you."

Now this was surprising.

"I must ask: who has your loyalty? The Cathedral? Your Family?"

I wasn't sure what to say.

"Why are you so loyal to them? Why have you refused to come to your kin? What has the Spadros ever given you but heartache?"

I had no idea how to answer, so I curtsied. "Good night, Inventor."

By this time, Joe had gone upstairs; I managed to leave without him seeing me. And we left Hart quadrant by the stroke of twelve.

But on the way home, I pondered Etienne Hart's questions.

I didn't have answers. And it bothered me.

When Pearson opened the front door at Spadros Manor, Tony stood in the front hall, dressed for the street. When Tony saw me, he visibly relaxed. "Thank the gods you've returned."

"Why, what's wrong?"

"Did you not see it? My man told me there was a tremendous commotion upon Market Center."

"No, Zeus took us another way." We'd gone over the river at Sixth, then through the Clubb slums. In my musings, I hadn't really noticed it until then.

"The man deserves a reward."

"Whatever was going on?"

Tony shrugged. "From what I hear, it began as a protest of rumors that my father was killing people upon the island. Then it reached the government area, and the police were called. My man said he saw a full on riot, with men attacking the Mayor's home."

"The **Mayor's** home?"

Tony nodded. "They held signs saying the Mayor set a murderer upon them." He frowned. "Do they think my **father** is the Strangler?"

"Good grief," I said. "We must warn Mr. Blackberry."

"I'll send a man to my father." Tony said. "He must know this is an attempt to discredit the exposé that I commissioned."

I stared at him. "You never told Roy of it?"

Tony's face turned sheepish. "I forgot." He went to the door and outside. I followed to the doorway as he spoke to two of his horsemen.

The men nodded wearily and set off.

I watched Tony trudge back up the walkway, up the steps to the porch. He leaned a hand upon the doorpost. "The man you sent back told me of Miss Josephine's condition. Forgive me for doubting you."

I turned away from him. "The doctor was a horror. He seemed ready to let her die! He told the Inventor she'd not live the night."

"Inventor Hart was there? Did he hurt you?"

Hurt me? Why would Tony think that? "No. He wasn't even quite cross. He seemed more frightened, worried and in despair."

"To face losing two women you love in the space of a few years' time," Tony said from behind me, "would cause anyone to despair." I felt his hand upon my shoulder. "What's to become of her?"

"I don't know." I turned to him. "I just did what my mother would for any fever. Her maid brought her nieces to help." I felt adrift. What if she died? "It's up to the gods now."

Tony took me into his arms. "Oh, Jacqui, I'm so sorry."

I pulled away. He'd been up all night, ready to come to me through that mob if I hadn't returned. Yet I wasn't ready to forgive him for what he'd said to me earlier. "I must bathe, to prevent any contagion from staying upon me, or going upon you." I'd told Amelia to do the same on the way back. "Good night."

✳✳✳

When Honor came in with my tea and toast the next morning, I asked him to tell Amelia she might have the morning off.

I woke with the sun already past the windows.

To my surprise, Roy Spadros sat there.

I sat up. "Whatever are you doing in my bedroom? Get out." I put on my robe, went to the toilet-room, and locked the door. I certainly wasn't going to encourage this sort of behavior.

I stayed in the toilet-room for some time. When I returned to my bedroom, he still sat there. But quiet, pensive. "I knew you'd make Anthony strong. I just didn't know how."

Was Tony strong? I wasn't sure, and when I thought about it too much, it frightened me. I returned to bed, sitting up, and pulled the covers to my chin. "What do you want? My husband will be furious that you're here."

Roy snorted softly, an amused smile upon his face. "I wanted to see your son." He glanced away. "And I have a task for you —"

This interested me at once.

"— but first I must explain."

Something about his manner seemed quite out of character, almost shy. What could he possibly need to explain ... to me? "Go on."

He didn't look at me. "I'm going to die. But in spite of what the doctor says, I don't believe it'll be natural. And there's something I need you to do." He paused a long time. "I thought this would be easier than it is."

"Is something wrong?"

Roy shook his head. "Molly was right: it must be you who does this." For the first time, his pale icy eyes held a mixture of fear and hope. "But I don't know if you can."

Something seemed deeply wrong. "Sir, please, if you might explain what is required, I could tell you whether I am able to help."

Roy nodded, head down. Then he took a deep breath and straightened. "I will tell you how it was with me."

From the earliest age he might recall, his mother ... touched him. As he grew, she would do this night after night. Every night. Then at the moment when he reached his fulfillment for the first time, she forced him to watch as she cut herself, made him taste her blood.

"If I ran, she had the servants fetch me. As I grew older, she had men tie me to my bed." He looked away. "Later, she gave me threats. My pets. Such friends that I had. They'd die should I defy her."

I nodded, filled with horror, and with compassion for the boy trapped in such a life. "What about your father?"

"I once told my father what she'd done; he called me a liar and struck me." His voice hardened. "He often struck me, when he was home. But my father was rarely home, and when he was, never questioned why she spent so many hours in my rooms."

"I'm sorry."

"Don't be." He wouldn't meet my eye. "I was a bad child, a monster. I deserved every blow." His icy blue eyes bored into mine. "You mustn't allow this incessant crying: you must strike your son."

I couldn't breathe. I couldn't think. In the Pot, to strike a child meant immediate execution. But to abuse a child like this ... to force them to whore ... and with their own mother! It was unthinkable.

Roy sounded resigned. "It made me who I am. It gave me strength to do what I must." His eyes rose to mine. "And so I have passed this to my sons." He stared past me. "With my first, I believe I began too late. He only hated me, became spiteful. I would have taken on Anthony's training, but Molly pointed out that we wanted an heir, not a man-lover. So I let her do it." He let out a sigh. "But I don't think she followed my instruction." He took a deep breath, then gazed into my eyes, and I saw pain there. "Will **you** train the boy?"

I kept my face still, but I felt appalled. There was no way in hell I would do any such thing to anyone, much less an innocent child. I knew, though, that if I said no, or protested in any way, he would find someone else to. I couldn't let that happen. "Yes, sir, I will."

Roy let out a sigh of relief, sinking back in his chair. "I knew I chose rightly." He sat there, eyes closed, as if now his work was complete.

Fear gnawed at me. "What about Katherine?"

He smiled to himself, eyes still closed. "She's the only woman who has ever truly loved me. And I have never hurt her." He let out a sigh. "She doesn't need to be strong. She has me, and she has my men. Anthony will care for her when I'm gone." He turned his head towards me, opening his eyes, and tears lay in them. "Someone hurt my mother. And I knew if I were to make Katie strong I'd need to do it. But when I held the knife in my hand, I was too weak. In her innocence Katie stood looking up at me so trustingly. I ... I couldn't."

I nodded, relief surging inside. *Thank the gods.*

He stared back at the ceiling. "After my wedding, I had my mother brought out to the country, her and those servants who helped her." He turned his head towards me. "That little cottage you stayed at when you were ill, the one young Master Diamond brought you to —"

A shock of fear and horror went through me. The old men and women living there, without their tongues, without their thumbs ...

Roy smiled. "I knew about it all. Peedro Sluff was my spy in the Pot. After you bedded the Kerr boy, there by the statue, and promised your love, I knew it was time to keep you here."

I shuddered, picturing Peedro watching me and Joe there together.

"Ahh ... It was a beautiful torment, tearing you from your true love, was it not?" He closed his eyes, and for a long time he didn't speak. "I bound my mother. I kept her in the cottage." He sighed, and his voice was sad. "But even she screamed in fear of me at the end." He opened his eyes, staring at the ceiling. "Thank you for listening. It feels right to tell someone."

I sat there, appalled, horrified, and deeply saddened. "Thank you for your trust in me." I meant it. As terrible as it all was, it answered a great many questions.

But there was one more. "Why do you hate Charles Hart so?"

*Why did you torment **me** instead?*

Roy didn't move. "Only one man ever showed me kindness, and Charles Hart killed him, right in front of me, for no other reason than he was in the way."

"I'm sorry. I truly am." I didn't feel any bond to Charles Hart, really, even knowing he was the Masked Man. He left my mother and I in the Pot when he could have brought us out long ago. None of this might ever have happened.

"I know you think I'm evil," Roy said, still staring at the ceiling. "But beware of the Kerrs. They will show you no mercy." He got up without looking at me and left, closing the door behind him.

The Madness

Tony was livid. "I distinctly told him not to come here. And he was in your **bedroom**?"

He'd called me from my study to his right after he got home, shortly after tea. "He was, Tony. But ... it wasn't that. What he told me was even worse." I sat in front of his desk and related the conversation, and Tony looked as horrified as I felt. "He said the doctors told him he might die. How sick is he?"

"I don't know. He's never said a word about it."

"The way he spoke ... I fear he's gone mad, Tony. I really do."

"My father's not mad," he snapped. "He knows exactly what he's doing." He stormed out.

Acevedo began to cry in the distance, and I returned to my study, feeling caught in the midst of a nightmare. A man driven to insanity by a sadistic fiend, then betrayed by his ruthless, neglectful father and the power-hungry woman he adored. A man who — according to Molly — killed his oldest son with his own hands.

Now Roy wanted me to abuse his grandson? And Tony didn't think this was madness.

The things I'd learned! That Peedro spied on me, even when I lay with Joe. That Roy took me from my home specifically to torment me.

Etienne Hart's words rang in my head: *What has the Spadros ever given you but heartache?*

My eyes fell upon my list. I couldn't think about Roy anymore. With everything that had gone on, my schedule had been derailed once more. How many people might I see tomorrow?

A soft knock at the door. "Come in."

It was Tony, looking remorseful. "I'm sorry I was short with you."

He seldom apologized. What had changed? "Sit down."

He sat across from my desk. "I'll invite my father over to speak with him. To learn what troubles him so. What this illness of his is about. We can sit on the front porch, and let Ace watch the carriages." Tony gave an introspective smile. "That should make him happy."

I didn't want to coddle Roy, or appease Molly, or do anything with the baby. All I could think of was getting these visits to our supporters over with so I could get out of here. "Do what you want. I've got more important things to attend to."

Tony sighed, head down. "He may well be mad. Perhaps he's been mad all my life." He fell silent for a moment. "It would explain much." Then he straightened. "But he's my father. I care for his welfare. If there's some way, any way to ease his burdens ..." He seemed to be pleading with me. "I have to at least try."

"I think that's admirable."

He glanced down at my list there on the desk. "And you don't have to deal with him. I know you're trying your best to do what I've asked. I've gotten many letters from the gentlemen of these women you've visited, expressing their gratitude."

"Oh?" This surprised me.

He kissed my forehead. "We'll get through this. You'll see."

After he left, I sat staring for a while. *I wish I'd never married you.*

Why was I doing this? Why was I even **here**?

I sighed. I had to focus. These women might know which of the aristocrats were against us. Once Pearson got me the list, I'd have him investigate which would consider seeing me.

And then there was the matter of the Pot. Too much was changing there, and I'd been gone so long I knew I'd seem like an outsider to my people. What could I do?

All this — in my mind — paled before the question of who kidnapped Josie, and why?

It seemed like the Red Dog Gang's doing, but if so, the changes in their methods confused me. I pictured her tormented sleeping face, pink with fever, hair plastered to her face with sweat. I felt filled with fear for her, and grief for what seemed her imminent death. I wanted to return to her so badly. Not only to see her, but ...

I knew she had wine there.

I wished then that I would have hidden one of Peedro's bottles in my carpetbag to take home. Of course, I couldn't have, with Mary and Amelia and all Tony's men watching me. But back then, I wanted a drink so bad it hurt.

I needed to do something, anything, to stop thinking of this. The doctor said if I went back to drink, I'd die. I was lucky Joe showed up in the bar last year, or I might not have been able to stop myself.

I didn't want to die, not yet. I had too much to do.

There was still time before I had to dress for dinner, so I took a stroll out front, around the edges of the wide white stone porch. Down the path and around to look at the flowers there: daisies and white hydrangea, interspersed with black rosebushes. I ran my hand along the fence, past the gate.

Tony's men on the other side looked at me, but never spoke.

Far to the left, by the gate to the stables, I heard a sound.

Joe stood there. "I hoped I wouldn't have to deal with those men," he said. "And here you are."

The stable gates were shut. I crossed the cobblestone stable drive entryway to meet him. "I'd only come out to stroll the front garden. What news of Josie?"

"That's why I've come. The fever's broken." He reached through the fence, and I gave him my hand. "I have you to thank for her life."

"Nonsense." I smiled to myself, my cheeks warm. "I just did what my mother would do."

"But it saved her," Joe said earnestly. "And we're ever grateful." He squeezed my hand, let it go. "I've taken the week off work to stay with her until she's well. You're welcome to visit whenever you please. There's no need to message first." He gave me a knowing smile which sent a thrill through me. "And no one need ever know."

The way he said it made visiting without anyone knowing seem exciting, alluring. The freedom to just go, spend a day with people who I loved, who loved and understood me. "Thank you."

"I must get back to her," he said. "But hurry to us. I long to see you again." Abruptly, he crossed the street away from me and was gone down the alley beside Monsieur's home.

I stood there in the twilight, holding on to the bars, until Amelia found me, to tell me it was time to dress for dinner.

***

That night I lay in the quiet beside Tony, but I couldn't sleep. I felt so angry — at Tony for his whipsaw moods, at Josie for getting sick, at myself for time and time again not leaving. I should have left with Joe when he asked. I should have left with Jonathan when he begged me to. Everything in me wanted to leave.

Why did you go out?

Don't you see what you're doing? How long will you go on like this?

Why are you so loyal to them? Why have you refused to come to your kin? What has the Spadros ever given you but heartache?

I should never have married you.

Could I really have a life with Joe and Josie? At peace, loved for myself rather than some means to an end? A moment of privacy, in a normal home where I felt safe?

I wanted it more than anything. None of this endless abasing myself in front of people I didn't care about so Roy might continue on in his mad desire to rule a quadrant. And Tony, boxed in by his own desire, I suppose, to live up to the expectations of a man who wasn't even his father!

I loved Tony when once, long ago, he said he might take me and leave this place, be free of Roy and his schemes. But it seemed he'd chosen the yoke Roy put on him, and strapped himself in.

When I thought of all the long years of what I'd experienced that lay ahead of me, it made me sick. It made me weep, my hand over my mouth so Tony might not hear my sobbing.

***

The next I remember was Amelia opening the curtains. "Good morning, mum. Did you sleep well?"

"Not particularly." I pulled the covers over my head.

Honor put down my provisional tray as always, left.

I sighed, threw off the covers. I had to start the day no matter what my wishes might be.

The paper held an article about some meeting on Market Center with the Mayor, the purpose of which was to talk about the grievances the people there had towards the Families. I thought it odd that Mr. Blackberry would allow such things to be printed, but he had to have talked with the Patriarchs before doing so.

The Bridges Strangler had left another young man's body in the East Spadros slums. It seemed so common now that it hardly seemed news. He had help from the entire Red Dog Gang, not to mention the Mayor. For some reason, they didn't want the man caught.

Was it just to destabilize the city? Or was it as Morton had thought, that they had their own man — perhaps Frank Pagliacci himself — to step in with the promise that the killings would stop?

I wasn't sure a fiend like this could live up to such a promise.

Amelia said, "Time for your bath."

I put down the paper. "I'm sorry Mr. Roy was here yesterday. Neither of us wanted that." I took a deep breath, trying to keep my voice from shaking. "And I'm sorry my husband has asked Mr. Roy here today, after he said he would not."

Her face hardened, but she curtsied. "What Mr. Anthony does is no affair of mine."

"But it affects you. Do you want to come with me calling?"

She didn't look at me. "No, mum, I'd rather stay here. I have work to do."

"Very well." I took her hand. "I won't let anything happen to you, not if I have any say in it."

She curtsied, still not looking at me. "Thank you, mum."

***

Roy and Molly were to arrive around two and stay for tea. I'd arranged for one of my visits to be at tea-time. Perhaps I might leave before they arrived and not have to see either of them.

Unfortunately, that plan was thwarted. "You're to stay at least until they arrive," Tony said at breakfast. "And that's final."

"But why?"

"I don't like the way you've treated my mother, that's why. You refuse to see her, then when you do, you dismiss her like some maid. What's going on?"

"If anything is going on, that would be between her and I."

He seemed taken aback. "Well, she is my mother and your Queen. You must greet her properly and show some respect."

But you don't know what she did to me!

Of course, I could never say that. "Very well." Courtesy dictated I stay fifteen minutes, and I planned to stay not a second more.

***

They arrived right at two. We met them on the front porch: Roy, Molly, and to my surprise, Katie, still dressed in trousers as before. She'd let her hair grow, and had it touching her shoulders like a very young girl. And instead of a women's hat, or even a feathered fascinator and veil, a trilby — quite the fashion these days, at least for men — sat atop her head.

I curtsied low, trying very hard not to laugh. "So good to see you."

Both Roy and Molly looked at me strangely.

Tony said, "Would you care for a glass of lemonade?"

Roy said, "Of course."

We sat at the tea-tables set up on either side of the front door, the men on one side, us women on the other. Pearson and his wife Jane brought out the lemonade in tall glasses, then Jane went inside with the platter, whilst Pearson took up a post beside the door.

The lemonade was too sweet for my taste.

Daisy came out holding Acevedo. She'd dressed him in one of his many white baby gowns, the embroidered lace hem still going well below his feet.

Everyone rose; Daisy brought the little Spadros Heir before Roy and curtsied low.

Once she'd risen, she handed him to Roy, who held the boy up in his thick hands. "A fine son you have here, Anthony."

Tony smiled to himself.

We all sat, Roy tucking Acevedo on his lap. Daisy moved to stand past Tony.

Katie said, "May I hold him?"

Molly said, "There'll be plenty of time for that today."

Katie pouted just a bit, even as old as she was. Acevedo seemed quite pleased with the situation, gazing out, I presume, at the carriages passing by. Although at times, it was difficult to tell what he looked at.

The carriage of the Lady of Spadros pulled up in front of the gate, piano-black with the Lady's seal raised upon its side in silver. The very instant the clocks chimed the quarter hour, I rose. "I'm afraid I must be off." I curtsied then started down the steps, calling over my shoulder, "I hope you have a pleasant day."

Roy handed Acevedo to Tony and rose. "I'd like to speak with you, if I might. Before you go."

I turned to look up at him. "But of course."

He came down the steps slowly, clutching the black wrought-iron banister as if pained. But by the time he reached me, his face had regained its composure. Then he spoke quietly enough for only us to hear. "You remember that night Peedro Sluff shot that boy, the Diamond's retainer?"

"Yes." I could never forget. Peedro also shot my best friend, Air.

"Ever wonder why I wasn't afraid?"

Why was he stopping me to ask this now? "I have, actually."

Roy leaned close, his ice eyes, as usual, without any emotion. "Because I didn't care. Maybe Sluff was there to shoot me. Why else have a gun? But he didn't. If he had, you'd all be dead anyway. My men would have seen to that."

I nodded. It made sense.

"Back then, I didn't care about anything. Not even what all this might do to you. And I regret that now." He looked me in the eye.

"I'm sorry. I truly am." He shook his head slightly. "I don't expect you to forgive me." His eyes gazed beyond me, far away. "Perhaps it's better if you don't."

Then he gave me a rare smile. "You've grown a great deal since then. I'm very proud of you."

A surge of anger: he didn't get to be proud of me! Yet underneath I felt strangely pleased. "Thank you, sir."

"Go to your duties, then. I won't keep you."

So I did. But the change in him made the rest of the day seem surreal. I felt off-balance, speaking to these women yet somehow not there. It took until the third visit for me to feel myself. And in the carriage on the way to the fourth, I wondered if this was some play. Some way to torment me, keep him in my mind even when I clearly wanted a day to myself.

They have complete control over you.

A bitter anger rose within me. *To hell with him*, I thought. *To hell with them all.* I grabbed the brass tube. "Zeus, take me to Hart quadrant, please. The Kerr's home."

His voice sounded tinny. "Yes, mum."

The small window behind me opened up. Honor said, "We won't be able to get to your tea in time if we do this."

I didn't want to cause trouble. I didn't want to snub yet another woman. But I was tired of being manipulated: by Roy, by Tony, by everyone. Today, I would do what **I** wanted to do. "I'll send word once we get there."

The small window closed behind me with a sharp click, which was not like Honor at all.

But the day was beautiful, the sky blue, the water under the bridges clear and sparkling. I relaxed into my soft black velvet cushions with a sigh. Today was going to be a good day.

***

A man I didn't know, dressed as a butler, met me at the door.

But Joe stood in the hall. "What a pleasant surprise! Josie would so like to see you." He handed my coat to Miss Susan. "She would love for you to read to her." He glanced at Miss Susan, who began brushing out my coat. "Just like you did when we were children."

I had never read to Josie in my life. "Of course I'll read to her."

To my surprise, the "butler" now slouched against the wall by Miss Susan, relaxed, as if waiting for someone.

Joe gave me that beautiful smile of his, so full of life it gave me chills at times. "I hope your family is well."

"They are." I felt flustered, off balance. "Roy and Molly and Katie are visiting at the Manor. The weather's nice, and Tony thought they might sit on the porch out front and watch the carriages drive past. Acevedo loves the horses."

Joe gave the man a nod, and the man went into the next room. "Shall we visit Josie now?"

"Certainly." I wondered what all that was about, but I followed Joe up to her room.

Josie sat wrapped in a robe beside a tea-table, with a partially filled cup in front of her. She still looked very ill, and tired, but she smiled when she saw me.

I ran to kneel before her. "I thought I might never see you again."

She took my hand gently, the bandages still around her wrists. "Joe tells me you saved my life. I'm forever in your debt."

I smiled up at her. "Nonsense. I only did what any woman with sense would." I looked over at Joe, who stood watching soberly. "You must dismiss that doctor at once. He was ready to let her die!"

He nodded. "That's disturbing, to be sure."

"Sit." Josie looked up at Joe. "Have Miss Susan bring another cup."

Indeed, there were only two cups there, and two chairs.

"I'll get a chair." Joe went to his room next door, returning with one, and we sat with her.

"We must celebrate," Josie said.

Miss Susan came in holding a large tray. On it was another cup and saucer with a fresh pot of tea, a platter of small sandwiches, three small plates, and some milk and sugar pots. She set the cup and saucer in front of Joe, then poured tea for me and him, set the teapot down, then curtsied and left.

Joe took one of the small plates and passed one to me. Then he took a small sandwich off of the platter and bit it. Josie took a sip of her half-empty cup. "I didn't expect to see you today."

I took a sip of my tea. "I didn't expect to be here today: it was more of a spur-of-the-moment thing."

Josie smiled warmly. "I'm so glad you did." She took another sip of her tea, and I did too.

Joe took another bite of his sandwich. "Are you hungry?"

I shrugged. "Perhaps a bit." I took a few of the small sandwiches, put them on my plate. Then I drank some more tea. I felt satisfied, light. "This tea is good. What kind is it?"

Josie smiled. "I told you, we're celebrating. Joe got me some Party Time, for when I got well." She took a sip of her tea. "Seemed like you being here was the perfect time to share it."

She was such a dear. That off-balance feeling had returned, but this time I enjoyed it. "I haven't had this since we were children." We'd been perhaps fifteen. It was harmless fun. "This must be the new kind; I didn't taste it."

"Well, we knew you couldn't have wine," Josie said, "so this is the next best thing."

A great sense of fondness came over me. "You're so thoughtful."

Joe held the pot. "Would you like some more?"

And I realized my cup was empty. "Why yes, I would."

Joe poured my cup, then set down the teapot and took another sandwich. "These are the best! I don't know what Miss Susan puts in them, but she could sell these to the hotels."

The sandwich was good enough. But I wasn't hungry, not really. I loved this tea. I loved the way I felt, lighter than air. I felt free.

Josie had been watching me and rose, her face solemn. "I'll be in my dressing-room," she said, an edge to her voice. "Not that you'll need me." And with that, she turned and walked out.

"Joe," I said, "what's this about?"

Joe took my hands and kissed them. "Josie's giving us a gift. Time to ourselves, without anyone seeing or judging us." He traced the side of my face with one finger, and his touch warmed me. "Time to be free, to be who or what we want to be."

The raw need in his voice and eyes took my breath from me; I couldn't speak.

"I love you, Jacqui." Joe drew me close, and kissed me.

Oh, gods, I thought.

He took me to her bed, to his lap. His hands moved over my body, pressing me to his, and I kissed him back, overwhelmed with the clash of my fantasies and the all too sudden reality of him in my arms.

I have no idea how long we kissed, but the longer we did the more urgent it seemed. Then somehow we were standing; my dress loosened, and my breasts were free from my corset, and I flung the restraints off, panting with need for him, and lo! his body was free as well, and we loved each other with abandon, there on Josie's bed.

But there came a thought: *this will kill Tony*.

And I looked into Joe's eyes, my body full of rising desire, so close, so desperate for its fulfillment after so long without, expecting, needing to see love in his eyes, yet instead ... I saw triumph!

And I felt confused.

What did this mean?

What had I done?

I let Joe finish, because he seemed to have such a need to do so, yet it brought no joy to me. He cried out, and fell upon me for some time, panting, then rolled away.

What had I done?

I lay there, tears blurring my sight, feeling betrayed and guilty both. I wiped my eyes. "I must go."

Face covered in sweat, Joe lifted himself upon an elbow, glancing towards the door. A white sheet of paper folded lay on the floor, as if it had been pushed underneath the door.

He stood before me naked. He'd shaved; he was as hairless below the belt as a child. And at the bottom of his belly, low almost to his manhood, was a tattoo of a horseshoe the size of my hand, its arms pointed down along each side. He stepped into his trousers, went to the door, and picked up the paper.

On the wooden floor where he'd stood lay a glistening drop of greenish-yellow.

He opened the paper, reading it with his back turned to me.

I didn't know what else to do. So I began buttoning my shoes and straightening my petticoats.

Joe sighed. "Well, things didn't go entirely as planned. But there's always the next time."

Heartsick, angry, humiliated, I untied and loosened my corset in back so I might fix the hooks around me in front. The next time? Did he just expect to have me whenever he wished? "Tighten my laces, if you please." I turned my back to him so he wouldn't see my eyes.

"Pah," he said, "this is no way to lace a corset," and with one hand on my back and two firm motions, he ripped the laces clear out of their grommets. "I'll do this up proper."

I grabbed the corset to keep it from falling whilst he laced, humming to himself as he went.

Where had he learned to lace a corset?

And I remembered Jonathan Diamond's words:

"There are five cases brought before the Court by the families of five women — from all four quadrants — who make claim against Master Joseph Kerr of Hart quadrant."

"For what reason?"

"Seduction with the promise of marriage, with a resulting child. The youngest was fifteen. Two of the children have been born, and Jacqui, they look like him."

When I had my gown fastened, I took his hands. "There will be no 'next time', Joe. I should never have come here. This was a mistake."

Joe looked at me solemnly. "Then I made the right decision."

What did he mean?

He escorted me to my carriage. I got inside. Joe closed the door and walked away without saying goodbye. The carriage started off.

What had I done?

***

When we returned, police surrounded the mansion. An appalling scene faced me: blood lay spilled on the steps, on the porch, on the walls, on the walkway, the bushes, the fence ... and bullet holes without number pierced Spadros Manor.

Amelia came running outside. "Where have you been?"

I stepped out of the carriage. "What happened?"

"Gunmen came on horseback, and in carriages. Mr. Anthony and Master Acevedo are shot, Mr. Pearson and Mr. Roy are dead!"

My vision turned gray. Suddenly Honor was at my side, holding my arm. "Steady, mum — let's get you inside."

"Pearson's dead?"

"Yes, mum," Amelia said. "He put himself in front of Mrs. Molly and the baby. Shielded them with his own body." She began to weep. "Poor Jane, his poor children."

The amount of blood before me ... covering the sidewalk, the grass. There was nowhere we might step to avoid it. A slaughterhouse on my doorstep. "Where —?"

Where were the bodies?

"The coroner's men have been and gone, mum. We were frantic, thinking you'd been waylaid. We sent horsemen out, but they said you never made it to your tea. No one could find you."

I shook my head. "I was out calling." My excuse even sounded weak to me. "How badly were they hurt? Tony, and the baby?"

"The surgeon's with them now."

Honor brought me to the parlor sofa. My boots dripped with blood; he took them off me and put my feet up. "Stay here. I'll fetch the doctor as soon as he can leave the patients."

"Thank you," I said.

"And I'll fetch Mrs. Mary. She'll want to be here."

Mary. Her father Pearson ... he was dead?

Amelia sat across the room weeping.

Pearson's death, the injury of my husband and the child ... it seemed unreal, only a story. "Did you see what happened?"

Amelia shook her head, face downcast. "No, mum." She sat staring into space for a time. "Miss Daisy told me she went in to fetch Mrs. Molly a wrap, and Miss Katie followed her. Then she heard guns, and shouts, and hoofbeats, and she became frightened. She screamed for help so loudly that I heard her from in your closets upstairs! We all ran out, the house maids in front of me. There was so much blood! And someone screamed for Jane, and she ran out, and she began to cry, 'John, John, oh, John!' and lay weeping on him, but he was clearly dead. He took ten bullets at least, one in the head; one passed through his arm and hit Master Acevedo in the hip."

Terror struck: I tried to rise. "I must see my baby."

But Amelia rushed over, pushed me back upon the sofa, and took my hand. "No, mum, wait for the doctor. You don't want to see your baby so injured. You don't want to see."

This overcame me more than her story. What had I done? I began weeping. "I should have been here."

"No, mum," Amelia said. "Don't say such things. You might've been killed!"

"I would rather die." I'd betrayed my husband yet again, and for what? A man who saw me as only a possession to be won? Some chip to be taken from another?

Amelia put her arms around me. "Don't speak like that. The doctor will care for them, and they'll be well again, you'll see."

I shook my head. "You don't understand." I sat up, sobs wracking my body.

"What's this?" Dr. Salmon hurried over to sit beside me. "Calm yourself, my dear. Your husband and child are injured, but they'll recover. Babies heal very well."

His face was blurry with my tears. "And Tony?"

Dr. Salmon nodded. "Your husband received three bullets, one in the left upper arm, one in the right thigh, and the third grazed his temple. No major vessels were hit, but his arm's shattered. It's a miracle he wasn't more seriously injured — there are enough bullet holes out there for a war."

It was all becoming clear. "This **is** a war, Doctor. Someone has started a war."

The Outrage

Katie had been sedated; Molly was in one of the guest rooms with her. Neither had been hurt.

From the sound of it, Tony was in agony: his cries from upstairs could be heard there in the parlor. But I couldn't hear Acevedo. "Where's my baby?"

"In his room with his nurse," the doctor said. "I've medicated him, so he should sleep for several hours. The nursemaid has been given instruction." Then he hesitated.

"What is it?"

"The bullet's still there. Inside him. It's in the joint itself. I don't dare try to remove it. I've sent for surgeons in Azimoff who specialize in very small children."

The bullet still lay inside him? Even Dr. Salmon was fearful of removing it? I found myself on my feet. "I must see him. I must!"

"What you must do," Dr. Salmon said, "is get these blood-stained clothes off you." He turned to Amelia. "Get her changed, and bring her to her husband. Perhaps she can talk some sense into him."

Once the doctor left, Amelia took me into the hall barefoot.

Alan Pearson stood leaning on the banister sobbing. Honor stood in the front hall with the door open, directing the terrified maids. "Pretend it's spilled wine if you must," he said, "but we have to do this. There's no one else."

I gaped at Honor, astonished.

He gently urged the frightened girls on. "Pour the buckets first to wash off the worst of it," he took one and sluiced the drying blood from the stone, "like this, then we'll start scrubbing." He turned to another. "Yes, good, that's it."

The sounds of Tony's anguish grew louder as Amelia and I went up the stairs. What was happening to him?

Amelia pulled me to my bedroom. She shut the doors to the hall and to my closets, which lowered the sound somewhat. "Master Michaels is tending to him, mum, never you fear."

"Why is he in so much pain?"

"He's been shot, mum, more than once, and he won't take anything for it. The doctor says the first shock has worn off, and he must take something," she sounded ready to cry, "but he won't."

"Call for Master Hogan," I said, "he'll —"

"He was here, mum," Amelia said. "Out front. When it happened. He arrived with several of his men just after you left." She dipped a cloth in water from the washbasin and began to wipe my face. "He's been shot too, mum, many a time. The doctor gave him something. He's sleeping."

Sawbuck was here? He'd been shot? I felt exhausted, unsteady. "Please help me undress, Amelia."

Amelia undid my back buttons, at first like usual, then halfway down my back she stopped.

"What?" I said. "Is something wrong?"

Amelia began undoing the buttons furiously. Some came off and bounced on the floor.

I turned to face her. "Amelia, stop!"

Her face was a mask of tears and fury.

I put my hands on her arms. "We're all upset by —"

She flung my hands away. "You **whore**!"

I felt utterly taken aback. "Amelia, what —"

She spoke over me. "Someone else has done your corset. You were gone much longer than usual ... was it Joseph Kerr, or was it someone else this time?"

I slapped Amelia. "How **dare** you?"

She grabbed my arm. "How **dare** I? I've served Mr. Anthony since he was born! I have watched him do **nothing** but love you."

I felt unable to move or speak.

"Your betrayal almost killed him. You weren't here to see the grief he bore, the humiliation you put him through, the agony of having to shoot the men who rose against him. He shot his own **cousins**!" She took a deep breath. "He wouldn't eat, didn't leave his room for weeks. And when he emerged from his rooms, he'd changed. The kind, gentle boy I once knew was gone. He became hard, cold, in a way I never would have thought possible. Every month you stayed gone, every report of your reckless behavior has been like another knife in his heart. Then you spit in his face in front of the other Families!"

I felt stabbed in the heart.

"He's suffered every manner of torment for your whims, but has done nothing to deserve any of it. The shame, the disgrace he's borne ... it's unbelievable. And yet he took you back into his home, accepted your story of Acevedo being his son, when everyone told him he was mad to do so."

Oh, gods. "Amelia, I—"

Amelia let go of my arm and shook her head. "Don't ever speak to me again. You've had every benefit, every luxury, been cared for, had the chance to be home in comfort with your little boy. And yet you spit on it all. Mr. Roy is dead; I can't bear to see Mr. Anthony die too. He's a good man, yet you **will** kill him." Tears ran down her face. "Me and Peter are leaving," she surveyed the room, "and good riddance." She turned and walked out without closing the door.

I stood there, stunned. What had I done?

***

After a while, I realized I still needed my dress off me. I rang for a maid and sat at my tea-table, hearing Tony's cries without any thoughts whatsoever. Finally, Honor peered in through the open door. "Where's Mrs. Dewey?"

"Gone." I felt numb. "Would you send Shanna in?"

"Yes, mum." He pulled the door shut.

I stared at the blood upon my hem. *Someone did this to us. Why?*

Shanna rushed in. She was very young, not even yet nineteen. "Oh, mum, I'm so sorry. Here, let me help you." She got me into a housedress, put the blood-spattered clothes to soak.

All the while, Tony moaned in pain, and I was too afraid to go to him. How badly had he been hurt? Would there be blood on him, too?

Shanna pried my hands from the armchair. "It'll be okay, mum. He sounds worse than he looks. Here, stand up. The doctor says you must go to him. All will be well."

I gasped: I'd been holding my breath. I had to do something.

"It's okay, mum. You can do this."

I was five and twenty. I almost cried in shame at this young girl consoling me. I swallowed at the lump in my throat and took a deep breath. *I can do this.* "Very well."

Shanna led me through my closets and opened the door.

Tony lay upon his bed, his left arm in a sling, a bandage on his head. There wasn't any blood anywhere. Relief crossed his face. "Oh, gods, you're safe."

I ran to his side, knelt before him. "You're alive," I sobbed, face in his bed. "I'm so sorry."

"Hush." He let out a grunt. "This isn't your fault. Shh. Be at peace, my love. All will be well."

"Don't they have any medicine for you? For the pain?"

Michaels came in from his rooms. "He won't take it."

"What? Tony, you have to take your medicine. Why won't you?"

"I'm fine, Jacqui, truly I am." He let out a moan of pain.

"No, you're not, the doctor even said so."

"Please, Jacqui, don't press me on this. I'm fine." He tried to reach over to me with his right hand and winced. "How's Acevedo?"

"They won't let me see him. But the doctor says he's sleeping." I let go of his hand, pulled a chair beside him. "He's calling for doctors from Azimoff."

Tony relaxed with a sigh, closing his eyes. "Good."

I kissed his brow, as far from the bandage as I might reach. "I'll learn the truth of things and return."

He opened his eyes and pain lay in them. "Thank you."

I turned to go.

"Make sure to check on Ten," Tony said. "He saved my life."

I smiled at him. "That was my next stop. If they'll let me see him."

***

Sawbuck was in the guest room next to Molly and Katie, the same room, as it turned out, as Morton had been in when he was injured three years before.

The doctor was just coming out of his room.

I said, "Might I speak with him?"

Dr. Salmon hesitated, then nodded. "He's suffered multiple bullets to the side and back —"

I gasped.

"— Nothing serious, thank the Dealer, but a lot of damage to the tissues. He's going to be in bed for some time." He shook his head. "I'm astonished there were so few dead."

"You said that before."

"You saw how many holes were out there. They had to have had Tommy-guns to do all this damage in such a short time."

I leaned upon the wall. *Tommy-guns.* I remembered the rat-tat-tat-tat from outside the Diamond Country House as we battled the Red Dog Gang there.

"Are you sure you're up to this, madam? You look quite pale."

I scoffed. "Everyone says that about me these days. I need more sun, that's all." I pushed past him and into the room.

Sawbuck had several bandages on his face and arms, and a rubber tube went to a bandage on his arm from a glass bottle of clear liquid. He looked half asleep, but his eyes widened when he saw me. "Sorry I can't get up to greet you."

I grinned at him. "Think nothing of it." Leaving the door open, I pulled up a chair beside him and sat. "Why does my husband refuse his medicine?"

He took in a ragged breath. "Long story." His face grew pensive. "He almost died of opium —"

Oh gods, I thought. *After I gave him too much of it.*

"— and ... let's just say he wants nothing to do with it."

Tony's suffering was because of me. "I'll speak with him."

I had an urge to grasp Sawbuck's hand, but I restrained myself. It'd be unseemly, plus Tony wouldn't like it. "Do you need anything?"

His speech began to slur. "The location of those scoundrels, so I can shoot them back."

I chuckled. "I'll work on it, never fear."

Sawbuck's eyes were half shut. "You're tricky," he said, "but you're a good one."

I sat there until he began to snore, then let myself out.

***

If anything, Tony was more awake. After asking Michaels to leave us, I sat beside him. "I spoke with Ten. He told me you fear the opium."

Tony's face grew evasive. "I'm not afraid of it, not like that. It's only ... I won't risk it, Jacqui."

I hesitated, not knowing at first how to say it. "There's something I must tell you." I'd been dreading this. "The night you almost died ... with the opium ... I did that."

Tony blinked. "What do you mean, **you** did that?"

I bit my lip. "I'd gotten a tip ... about ... remember we had so much trouble with that reporter? He's in the District Attorney's office now."

Tony frowned a bit, his eyes squinting as if trying to recall, then nodded. "He's kin to your lawyer-man. The Bridger fellow."

"Yes. Well, he gave a speech on Market Center. I thought I had to hear what he was saying. But your father already had men there."

"Jacqui, what are you telling me?"

"I gave you opium that night, before you put the extra in your cup." I felt horrible, the guilt I'd held in for years bubbling up, and I began to cry. "If I'd come back five minutes later, you'd be dead."

"You ... you ..." Tony seemed entirely at a loss. "You **sedated** me?"

"I'm sorry, I'm sorry," I sobbed. "I didn't want to hurt you. I didn't want anything bad to happen. But now you're suffering so, and it's all because of me."

He lay there a moment, his eyes upon the covers, but unfocused. "I can't ... I don't trust myself ... with this. Not now." He looked up at me, fear and pain and longing in his eyes. "Would **you** do it?"

"You want **me** to give you the medicine? After everything I've done to you?"

He smiled fondly at me. "I don't think you'll hurt me. Not on purpose, anyway."

That didn't make me feel any better. But I found the medicine on his dresser, read the instructions. Sat with him until he slept.

Why, after everything I'd done to him, would he trust me?

***

Acevedo's rooms were those Roy had as a child. His bedroom lay at the far end of the right-hand arm of the U-shaped building. The suite had one set of doors facing the hall, leading into a small anteroom with a tea-table and chairs; two guards sat there, rising to their feet as I passed. The door beyond led into Acevedo's room.

Daisy sat in a chair by the window, asleep, the gold of late afternoon falling across her left shoulder. My baby lay in his crib immediately to her right, face flushed, chest quietly rising and falling in the dim light.

And I felt ashamed.

I should have been there. I should have been the one holding him when assassins came. I should have been the one protecting him.

Shanna came beside me, speaking quietly. "The doctor wishes to speak with you."

We went along the upper rail and down the long stair.

Honor had been acting as butler, hovering by Pearson's station as if not wanting to disturb anything. "In here," he said, and opened the parlor door.

Blitz and Mary sat on either side of Mary's mother Jane on the sofa. Mary's brother Alan sat beside her, gripping her hand. Their other brothers stood awkwardly by. Molly and Katie presided over the room in armchairs, with one, I presume, reserved for me. Dr. Salmon paced by the mantel, which didn't ease my mind any.

Everyone but Molly rose when I entered.

I said, "Please, sit down."

I turned to Honor, who still lingered in the doorway. "For gods' sake, get these men chairs. It's wrong to make them stand when their father just died."

The looks on their faces were beautiful: some shocked, others appalled that downstairs servants might sit on the same level with their Queen. But Katie looked at me with pride, which made me feel for once as if I did the right thing. I snapped, "Well? Get onto it."

Chairs were brought from the dining hall for everyone, including Dr. Salmon, who had to be urged to sit. Then Daisy and Honor left. Only then did I sit, in a chair by Blitz, which was about as far from Molly as I might get.

Dr. Salmon said, "I called you here mainly so as to not have to say the same thing again. But it would help with the police if we had one story of what happened. And I think we all want to hear from those of you who were there."

"I only know what I saw," said Molly. "I'd asked for my shawl, and sent our Heir's nursemaid for it. My daughter Katherine has taken a liking to the girl, and followed her in." She stopped, eyes distant, as if seeing it in her mind. "I sat with Acevedo watching the carriages go by. Pearson stood by the door, as he always does, to my left. My husband and son sat on the other side of the doorway, with my nephew Ten standing farther down the porch by the pillar. His men were out in the garden.

"When the carriages came past, at first I didn't recognize the sound. Then Pearson threw himself atop me," she stopped, face horrified. "They were shooting at me! I felt the bullets hit his body!" She shuddered, then looked over at Jane. "Your husband saved my life."

Jane began crying.

"Then the baby screamed," Molly said. "Anthony was hit; he'd dropped his gun. Ten threw himself upon him." She let out a sob. "Roy was hit too, and fell. Then he looked at us all." Tears filled her eyes. "And he got up. He got up! Roy took his gun in one hand, and my son's in the other, and he fought the men himself, even as he took round after round. I saw him shoot six dead. It may have been more. But he got up, full of bullets as he was." She clasped her hands to her mouth, tears streaming down her face. "My poor brave man."

All I could do was stare at her. "How many carriages were there?"

Everyone shook their heads and shrugged.

"So many dead," Molly said, eyes wide and staring. "Bodies lay everywhere: in the street, in the front garden ..." Then she turned to me. "And we couldn't find you! Where were you?"

"Out calling," I said.

Dr. Salmon said, "Has anyone anything to add?"

No one spoke.

Dr. Salmon said, "Might I speak with both the Mrs. Spadros and the young daughter privately, then?"

Everyone else said, "Yes, of course," and left.

Molly, Katie, and I sat there. I felt fearful of what he might say.

He turned to us. "Mr. Anthony has a broken upper left arm, which has been casted, and wounds in his right thigh and temple. Master Acevedo has a bullet in his left hip, which has injured the bones there. I'll know more once I can get him to an x-ray."

Molly leaned forward. "And my nephew?"

By which she meant Sawbuck.

"Master Ten has been shot in the back and side numerous times. So far it appears the bullets went into his flesh at angles to his body. So I don't think anything vital was hit. But they're both in a lot of pain. If your nephew continues to have difficulty, I'll have him brought to the x-ray as well."

The beating of my heart slowed. I began to be able to think. I had the man here; I might as well ask. "What was wrong with Roy?"

The doctor blinked. "Whatever do you mean?"

"It's obvious he's been sick. He told me you said he'd die soon."

Molly and Katie both stared at me in shock.

This confused me. Had they never noticed? "He's lost weight. His hair's gone completely white. He seemed in pain. And he'd been acting and speaking completely out of character. My husband and I seriously wondered whether he'd gone mad. That's why my husband invited him here today, to see what was wrong. If there were some way we might help."

Dr. Salmon peered at the floor. He took a long deep breath, let it out. Then he straightened. "Mr. Roy had cancer."

Molly gasped, hands gripping the armrests. Katie only stared at the doctor, mouth open.

"He refused for anyone to know, under threat to my life. Despite all I might do, he's been in terrible pain." His face fell. "I suppose it'd drive even the most stable man mad."

I sat pondering this. Whatever you might have said about Roy Spadros, stable wouldn't have been the first word to come to mind.

"No." Katie stood, looking at us all. "You're wrong! My daddy wasn't mad! He was a good father. He was a good man! He saved Mama, and he saved Tony. How could you **speak** of him like this?" She stormed out, slamming the door behind her.

I stood, just as angry. "Good gods. You!" I pointed at him. "The girl has it right. Of all people, for **you** to speak of Mr. Roy like this!"

Dr. Salmon seemed more than a bit taken aback by my fury. "My dear, whatever do you mean?"

"You **knew**! You had to know, **all** that time, what that woman was doing to him."

He gaped at me, a surprised fear in his eyes.

"Yet you said **nothing**! You did nothing!" I pointed towards the front porch. "You helped make that man what he was, yet you can sit here and **judge** him? How **dare** you?"

Dr. Salmon sat quietly, hands steepled between his knees, head down. "I said something once. When he was five." He drew a long, shuddering breath. "She had my wife and children murdered in front of me." His eyes closed, his face reddened, and he bit his upper lip, gripping his hands together. When he recovered, tears lay in his eyes. "I could speak more, once more, and die. Or I could live, and give him what aid I was able."

I had no idea what to say, and I found myself again in a chair. We all sat silent, gazing at the floor.

A knock: it was Honor, with a message in hand. "Forgive my interruption. This came from a man riding hard from the Clubb bridge to Market Center."

I peered at him, confused. "From the island?"

Honor nodded. "Forgive me: the messenger said I must read it before bringing it to you, so I might tell you all at once." He took a deep breath; his voice shook. "At the same time as ours, there were attacks upon the other three Families. Clubb Manor by the zeppelin station was hit. Hart Manor in town, where the Inventor's mother and daughter live. And the Diamond Country House?" He looked up at us. "Some of their retainers are dead. But the uppers are all well."

Now it became clear. "A distraction. Their intent was to draw any aid the other Families might give away from us. To keep them in their quadrants whilst ... "

Molly said, "What?"

"I don't know," I said. "But something else is going to happen."

The Insurrection

Alan ran in, out of breath. "They've attacked Spadros Castle!"

Molly sat frozen in terror.

I couldn't think. Too much was happening. "Do we have anyone to send? Anyone at all?"

"We lost twenty men," Alan gasped. "Here, today." He panted for a moment, seeming calmer. "But I sent word to our street captains. They should have reinforcements on their way within the hour."

I took a deep breath. "I know your grandmother's there."

Alan paled.

Roy had seized the old woman when Tony and I were married to ensure John Pearson's loyalty. "Go. Take your brothers with you."

Alan ran out.

I went to the front door. Servants scrubbed the front porch, the stone walkway. The way was mostly clear. Behind me, bullet holes beyond number pierced the walls, but as there were no windows upon the first floor facing the street, nothing had entered the house itself.

Past the gates, police barricades had been set up, keeping back the crowds, the reporters. Ignoring the flashes from their cameras, I went to the gate. Dozens of cards lay in the street, all stamped with the mark of the Red Dog Gang.

I did this. My lack of care for my people, both in the Pot and out ... it led to all this death and suffering.

A motion to my right, and Joe came pushing through to the front of the barricade.

The policeman there looked over his shoulder at me, and I went to Joe, annoyed. "What do **you** want?"

Joe gaped at me. "Thank the gods you're safe. I thought you might be dead! They said — they said you'd been attacked! That there was blood everywhere!" He brought out a letter and handed it to me. "Josie sent me with a letter for you."

Etienne Hart, Josie's betrothed, had perfect reason to want us dead.

And I realized: they weren't shooting at Molly.

They were shooting at my son.

I threw the letter in his face. "If you thought I was dead, why come with a letter? You're a lying piece of trash, Joe. I don't want to see either of you again." I turned and stormed off.

Joe called after me. "I don't understand: what did I do? Jacqui, please tell me. What did I do?"

Honor met me on the walkway. "Come inside: it's getting dark."

Joe wailed, "What did I **do**?"

***

I had barely sat down in my study when Blitz came in, with his sidearm. "That Army man is back, and he insists on seeing you."

"What does he want **now**?" I didn't have time for this. But the man would likely keep bothering us unless I met with him. "I'll see him in the parlor. Just him, unarmed. If he protests, show him the street."

Blitz grinned. "Right away."

Colonel Righly Hanafuda, a swarthy man with a narrow face, graying dark hair, and large dark eyes, had visited some time back about Major Blackwood's murder, and apparently wasn't happy with what he'd learned since. "Mrs. Spadros, have you been lying to us?"

As he hadn't risen, I took an armchair. "Under the circumstances, sir, I can't say I'm pleased to see you. Which topic are we discussing?"

"Why did you go to that house? You claimed you didn't know the old couple living there, yet —"

"Which house?"

"The address in Hart quadrant that you claim belongs to the Kerrs. We saw you there last week, and again earlier today. Why do you keep going to see those people if you don't know them?"

"Last week my friend was sick! You didn't see her there? She's blonde, a year older than me. The doctor and his nurse were there last week as well. Her twin lives there, too."

He shook his head. "The only people we've seen go in or out are you, your retainers, and the Hart heir. The old couple answer the door. We've searched the house, and can find no one else. They give no reason as to why either of you were there." He stood, putting his fists on his hips. "Impeding a military investigation is punishable by five years in a Hub prison, young lady, so if there's anything you're withholding, I suggest you come clean now."

Blitz stood directly behind me. "Show some respect, sir."

"My apologies." He glanced at the revolver Blitz wore. "But no one seems to know where Inventor Hart is. And I feared —"

I scoffed. "You have a strange way of showing your concern." I rose. "You see what's going on here. Unless you've come to arrest me right now, I'm going to have to ask you to leave."

He left peacefully enough, but his visit only raised more questions.

The Army had that house under surveillance for months now. How could they possibly have not seen all the people I knew had come and gone? Joe, the butler given to them by Etienne ... the doctor, his nurse ... they saw not one of them? None of this made any sense.

"Unbelievable." Blitz sounded angry. "You were at Joseph Kerr's home just now. Is **that** why no one could find you?"

I felt weary. "Yes, I was there." As I pictured the triumph in Joe's eyes, humiliation flooded through me. "I should never have gone."

Blitz hesitated a moment, the anger draining from him. Then he spoke gently. "Well, hopefully we won't be bothered by him again."

But Mary's words at the wedding gnawed at me: *He's not been washing dishes, mum.*

What if Joe had lied to me about why he was there?

And why had Major Blackwood, of all people, been investigating Joe's family? What had the Major learned that someone felt worth killing him for?

What were the Kerrs involved with?

What had I done?

***

Dinner was quiet: Katie was sullen, morose. Molly alternated between picking at her food and loud weeping.

Blitz and Mary had found a neighbor to watch Ariana and decided to stay the night. Mary was taking her dinner in the servants' hall with her mother whilst Blitz stood at table with us as butler. They both looked as if they'd been crying. Mary's brothers still hadn't returned, and they had to be worried for them.

I felt not the slightest bit hungry.

In the midst of all this, the power went out. Fortunately, we had a candelabra on the table which Blitz had lit. "Good gods," I said. "Bring out the house candles."

Blitz gestured to one of the little scullery maids, who had taken over for Mary's brothers at dinner, and the girl dashed out.

A ring at the door, far off. The girl returned with a box, setting an unlit taper candle in its holder beside each of us. Honor came in, lit candle in hand, and bowed. "My Queen, Mr. Charles Hart is at the betters' bridge to Clubb, requesting entrance to Spadros quadrant."

Molly glanced up in alarm. "He wants to come **here**? To**night**?"

Everyone but her looked to me.

And I realized something else.

With Roy dead, Tony was now the Patriarch of the Spadros Family.

Which meant I was now Queen of Spades.

The Messenger

I took a deep breath, trying not to sound too shaky. "He may enter —"

Molly said, "Jacqui, no —"

I held up a hand. "He may enter, but he must come **only** with his carriage-men. Twenty of our men must guard him. And he and his men must come unarmed. Or else he can slither back to his racetrack and stay there."

Honor blinked, mouth open. "Yes, mum." He bowed and went out.

Molly said, "Why are you doing this?"

"I need to look him in the eye when I ask if he sent those men."

Katie stared glumly at her plate.

I rose. "Blitz, Mrs. Molly and Miss Katherine already have a room upstairs. See that they have whatever they need." I went to the candelabra, lit my candle, then started towards the hall. "Do you and Mary need anything?"

"We'll sort it out, Mrs. Spadros," Blitz said. "Do you want me to send word when the men return?"

"At once. I'll be in my study."

But first, I needed to go to Tony's library. I might be Queen, but I knew little of the accession. I felt sure he had a book to explain what I must do next.

Candles lit the way, but I felt glad for the one I held. Whilst my study was just next to the breakfast area, his library was the farthest from the dining room, almost to the front door. Our wide stair curled over and down to my left, making a sort of archway, whilst the doors to our various rooms lay to my right.

Just before I got to Tony's library, the front doorbell rang. Honor answered it; Alan Pearson would have fallen into the hall if Honor hadn't caught him.

I rushed over. Well, as quickly as one might with a candle in hand.

The man was dirty, blood-spattered, disheveled, and smelled strongly of fire. A lantern had been hung upon the front porch: through the open doorway, his brothers trudged up the stone path in its light, looking demoralized.

"We got there too late," Alan gasped. "There was a mob! They stormed Spadros Castle. The Castle didn't have enough men by half ... they'd sent too many here to our aid." He let out a sob. "They murdered everyone inside and set it ablaze. We got there too late. My ... my Grandma's dead!"

He began weeping. His brothers helped him to his feet and consoled him, their cheeks stained with tears.

I drew Honor aside. "Put him to bed, and see to his brothers. Let me know when Mr. Hart arrives."

"Yes, mum." He began walking back towards Alan.

I had to raise my voice a bit so he might hear. "Seat him in the parlor, and don't tell anyone else he's here."

The power came back on. Honor glanced over his shoulder and nodded. "Right."

I blew out the candle, fetched the book I needed, and went past the wide stair to return to my study.

Molly stood beside the stair, partially in shadow.

I stared at her. "You heard."

She didn't move. "Were you not going to tell me what happened to my own home?"

I went to her, tucking the book under my arm. "I thought to tell you in the morning, after you'd had some rest. That's all."

"And you were going to see that man without even telling me?"

"I told you both, at dinner."

She seemed to crumple into herself. "Katie and I must see him."

"I don't think that's such a good idea. Not if we suspect his Family in this. And particularly since she knows how much Roy hated the man. Who knows what she might do?"

"Please. We deserve to be there when you confront him. Can you give us that one honor?"

She realizes it too. From now to the end of days, she was to be the Queen Mother, pushed aside as her son and grandson seized power. As I took what was once hers. "I can. I promise, you'll be there."

"Thank you." She took a deep breath. "I never liked you, Jacqui. You never valued anything we tried to give to you. But ..." She nodded then. "Now I think Roy was right to trust you." She pushed past me and up the stairs.

I stood there for some time, trying to understand what she'd just said. She never liked me? They thought that taking me from my home, my friends, my family ... would somehow **help** me?

Eventually, I went upstairs. The doctor had stayed the night, and I passed his room, then Molly and Katie's, then Sawbuck's, all silent and dark. Then I went past the guards, to Acevedo's room.

My son slept; Daisy sat, forehead on her arms on his crib's railing as she sobbed.

I spoke softly. "What's this?" I pulled up a chair to sit beside her, put my arm round her thin shoulders. "What's wrong?"

"I vowed to you I'd protect him ... and I wasn't there."

I felt as if I'd been stabbed in the heart. "There's no way you could have known."

Acevedo whimpered in his sleep, and for the first time, I felt compassion for the child. *He's been in pain almost since birth, with so much more yet ahead.*

I kissed his small brow, feeling a great tenderness for him. "Get what rest you can," I told Daisy. "We're not nearly through this yet."

She glanced up in alarm. "How so?"

"They'll have to take the bullet out of his hip sometime. This will be a long road for us all."

I went back past the guest rooms, past my room, and to see Tony.

Michaels answered the door. "He's asleep." He opened the door wide, then went to his own rooms.

A lamp was turned to low. Tony lay peacefully in the soft glow, much as Acevedo had. I sat in a chair beside him, his book on my lap, but I could barely see him for my tears.

I felt so ashamed of what I'd done. How stupid I'd been to trust Joe after everything he'd done to me!

I could never tell Tony. What would it do to him to learn I'd betrayed him yet again?

I wish I'd never married you.

Amelia's words came back to me then: the pain he'd gone through, the ruin of his reputation. And everyone telling him not to take me **back**? That Acevedo couldn't possibly be **his**?

And now my husband and baby lay injured. My father-in-law and Pearson? Dead, along with dozens of Tony's kin.

I'd ruined Tony's **life**! How could I ever atone for this?

There seemed no way.

I grieved there, face in my hands, for what seemed only a moment, but then a hand lay on my shoulder: Honor. "Mum, Mr. Hart's here."

A glance at the clock: over an hour had passed. "I'll be right down. Tell Mrs. Molly he's here, but keep her out of the parlor until I arrive."

I wiped my eyes. Tony needed me to be strong. He deserved so much more. I kissed Tony on the forehead as I'd done his son, put the book on my bed, and went downstairs.

Molly must have moved quickly; she and Katherine were already downstairs. Katie wore Tony's pajamas with the leg-cuffs rolled up and one of my many robes. Molly was in one of my nightgowns and a robe, even managing to look elegant, if a bit disheveled.

I said, "Let me do the talking." I glanced at Katie. "Got it?"

"Yeah," Katie said.

I nodded to Honor, who opened the door.

Mr. Hart rushed to me, tears in his eyes. "Oh, gods, you're alive!" He clasped me in his arms, a bit tightly for my taste, then let go, looking at Molly and Katherine. "Mrs. Spadros, I am **so** sorry for your loss." He looked at me and Molly both, ignoring Katie completely. "I had absolutely nothing to do with what happened."

Katie scoffed.

Molly said, "This is my daughter Katherine."

Katie rolled her eyes. "You brought me here for **this**?" She walked out, leaving the door open.

"She's lovely, if ..." Mr. Hart seemed to be trying to find a word which wasn't too offensive.

"Odd might be the best word," I said, still looking at the open doorway. "And yes, those were her brother's pajamas she's wearing." I snorted quietly. "I'm not sure what's going on with her."

Molly and Mr. Hart were peering at each other. Mr. Hart had a puzzled look on his face, whilst Molly looked hesitant. Finally, Molly said, "I've gotten my answer. Good night." Then she left as well, but closed the door this time.

I turned to Mr. Hart. "You didn't travel six hours to hug me. What's really going on?"

He walked to an armchair, leaning both hands upon it. "Etienne has disappeared. There are rumors he ordered a hit on your son."

To hear it said made me quail. "This is monstrous."

"I thought I knew my son," Mr. Hart said. "I never imagined he'd do such a thing. How could he even **think** of doing something like this?" He turned to me. "I'm so sorry I didn't listen. Giving him more power must have made him think he might act without consequence." He thrust his hands in his salt-and-pepper hair. "What am I to do?"

"Would you care to stay the night?"

"No," he said quickly. "I have to get back. There's been rioting on Market Center all day, but the roads should be clear by now."

I stared at him, shocked. "I had no idea."

"That second installment about the Strangler, I suppose, on top of all that's gone on."

That explained the timing. Why had I not seen it?

"I'll return when things settle down." He came to me and clasped my face in his hands. "All that matters is that you're safe." He let his hands drop. "What of my grandson?"

As I told him what happened, his face hardened. "A search is underway for Inventor Hart. I **will** find him. And when I do, we will both learn the truth of this. Warn your men: if they see him, we need him alive. If he must be put down, we will —"

I jerked towards Mr. Hart, astonished and alarmed.

"— but if it has to be done, let me do it."

Mr. Hart would kill his own **son**?

"He may have tried to start an unsanctioned war," Mr. Hart said firmly. "I could have him confined, if the other Families agree to overlook the offense." His face turned grim. "But we don't target women and children. If my son has tried to murder a newborn baby, then ... we can't allow him to live."

***

After Mr. Hart left for his long journey home, I had Shanna get me changed, then I sat up in bed, reading Tony's book.

An informant had warned me that a Hart wildcard was in play. I'd suspected my half-brother Etienne of being this for some time, but him saying he felt just as other men did had thrown me off that suspicion.

Or had he **meant** to?

Before the Coup, when the Dealers' blessing foretold a wildcard, that child was quietly put to death. Such a man would stop at nothing, even having his betrothed Josie kidnapped to further his aims.

Etienne had confessed to framing me for the zeppelin explosion in front of Tony and the other Inventors. Back then, he frightened me. But at Josie's house he seemed, if not entirely reasonable, certainly not mad. Merely a quadrant-man worried for his beloved who lay dying.

Could he have been making one final appeal? And when I didn't respond as he wanted, did it drive him to this attack?

But he claimed Acevedo was irrelevant. Why take this step now? Why throw away all the goodwill he'd gained over the years, his titles as Heir and Inventor, for a mere chance to kill a baby?

Or had the real target been Roy?

From what Molly said, it didn't seem that way.

I should have seen the answer.

I could make any number of excuses for why I didn't grasp the situation: my headaches, the recent events, grieving for men I'd loved. But the answer lay there, right in front of me, and I didn't see it. Perhaps I didn't want to.

I blew out the candle instead, and went to sleep.

***

Other than having to get up in the middle of the night to dose Tony with his medication, I slept fairly well. I'd almost forgotten that Amelia had left until Shanna opened my drapes the next morning. "Someone found this outside." She handed me the letter Josie'd sent.

"Oh." I didn't know what to do with it, so I tossed it into my huge basket of old papers without a glance.

The morning paper was full. The burning of Spadros Castle, the shootout at Spadros Manor. Roy's obituary. I didn't want to read it.

"There's a Tenni Mitchell here to see you," Shanna said.

I thought she might visit. "Oh, yes, send her in."

Tenni was my dressmaker, a pretty woman just turned twenty. She and her younger sister Oma entered, both laden with packages.

Tenni put hers on the floor and ran to me, kneeling by my chair to take my hands. "I'm so sorry for your loss, mum."

A wave of grief. "Thank you."

She waited for me to settle. "I have two walking dresses ready-made that we can fit you for — one is good enough for the funeral."

Relief swept over me. I hadn't even considered what a Queen in mourning for a Patriarch should wear.

"I also brought three house-dresses, two hats, and six yards of black ribbon for the baby's gowns." She glanced at Shanna. "Where's your maid?"

"Shanna's my maid now. Let's see what you've brought."

The mourning gowns were lovely: a black cotton brocade, beautifully made but light enough for summer, and a flowing black silk. I got out of my nightgown and let Tenni fit me for them. Then she returned them to their boxes and me to my nightgown. "I just have to re-do a few seams and take up the hem," Tenni said. "But I can have the brocade back to you later today. The silk will take a day or two, but certainly before the funeral."

I felt astonished. "Are you sure you have the time?"

Tenni smiled to herself. "I've contacted my customers, and given the circumstances, they agreed to wait a few days for their orders."

"I appreciate this." My heart felt full. "You don't know how much."

She smiled, but tears came to her eyes. "I remember when my father died. Oma here is too young to recall him, but I remember. You've lost both yours in a year."

I had to breathe and look away, tears falling onto my robe. After the wave passed, I let out a quiet laugh. "They were both utter scoundrels, you know."

Tenni took my hands. "Yet you grieve them. It means you can. Don't let what others think take that from you."

I nodded, not sure exactly what she meant. But I wanted my mind on other things. "I hope Miss Cheisara's well?"

Tenni's head drooped. "Well of body, mum, of course."

I glanced at Oma and Shanna, then drew Tenni close. "I have faith that whatever trials you're facing, the two of you can overcome them. I am always here for you, day or night, should you need counsel."

Tenni gave several quick nods, head still down, a quick grimace coming over her face. Then she took a deep breath. "Thank you." Then her face brightened, and she spoke loud enough for all in the room to hear. "We won't keep you any longer, mum." She and Oma curtsied to the floor. Then the two collected their things (leaving the hat-boxes and a small wrapped package which had to be the ribbon) and left.

Shanna had stood there gaping this entire time. "She's so young. How is **she** your dressmaker?"

I smiled to myself, wiping my cheeks. "It's a long story."

***

My mail contained two letters: one from Cesare Diamond, of all people, the other from Alexander Clubb. Both denied any involvement in the attack in any manner, and pledged their entire support to the Spadros Family. We had only to ask.

Why had they sent the letters to **me**?

This pledge of support from the Diamonds was the most surprising: I couldn't imagine their Patriarch Julius Diamond wanting anything to do with it. Yet his Heir, Cesare, sent it anyway.

I wondered whether their household got any sleep that night just from the shouting which must have gone on about the matter.

As if on cue, off on the other side of the house, I heard a loud argument. Rather, Katie was speaking in high and frantic tones, whilst Molly tried and failed to shush her.

"I've never been a lady's maid," Shanna said over the noise, "or even much spoken to one." She hesitated. "So if I do something wrong, please tell me."

I smiled at her over my tea. "Never fear, you're doing fine."

"Next is your bath, right?"

"Yes, that's right. Amelia used to put everything out on my bed before I went in."

A knock at the door. "Yes?"

Honor peeked around the door without actually looking at me. "A man is here to see you, mum."

It now sounded like Katie was crying. Wailing, more like. I wondered what our guest downstairs, whoever he was, must be thinking of all this. "So early?"

"Yes, mum. A Master Seven Bresciane." He hesitated. "He claims Mr. Roy sent him?"

Roy might have had some mechanism set to start into motion upon his death. Many high-cards did. Perhaps this man was a lawyer? "Invite him for breakfast." Breakfast wasn't scheduled to begin for another hour, but it'd have to do. "Until then, ask if he'd like some tea and seat him in the parlor."

"Yes, mum."

Shanna and I exchanged a glance. Before that was morning prayers with the staff. Usually Tony did this, or Pearson when Tony was unavailable. "Honor, would you care to do the morning prayer?"

Honor drew back, eyes wide. "Me?" He quickly recovered, for the first time looking at me. "Yes, mum, of course I will."

Perhaps I'd upset the order of things here, but we were in unusual circumstances. And to be honest, I didn't think anyone else would be capable of leading it that day. "What's going on with Miss Katherine?"

Honor looked uncomfortable. "Mrs. Molly had asked for the evening and morning news over the past few days, and ... Miss Katherine read some things that upset her."

"Like what?"

"His obituary, for one. The *Bridges Daily* ... well, mum, it was truthful. Both good and bad. It seems our Mr. Blackberry no longer fears us. And Mrs. Molly had gotten hold of one of those pamphlets about Mr. Roy, one of the really cutting ones."

Oh, dear. "I'll speak with her later. Now if you'll excuse me, I best get ready for whatever this man has to tell me."

***

As I stepped out into the hall on the way to breakfast, Michaels approached me. For an instant, I felt alarmed. "Is my husband well?"

He nodded, looking away. "Your husband's taking his breakfast." He took a deep breath. "Your maid's rooms were searched last night, mum. Mrs. Dewey's, I mean. One of the men brought me this."

He handed me a scrap of paper:

I hope you're well. Please visit tomorrow after luncheon. Look forward to our meeting. — Joe

The imprint of my lips still showed red upon it.

Michaels swallowed. "I told the man not to speak of it, but ..."

I nodded. Surely by now, everyone downstairs had heard of it. "She'd gone through my trash, it seems."

Michaels shrugged.

"I'd like it if you'd not tell my husband."

"He saw it when you left, mum. But yes, hearing of it again —"

He didn't need to be reminded of this, not now. "Thank you."

Michaels gave three quick nods, not looking at me. "I'll return to work, then."

I grabbed his upper arm. "Thank you for caring for him."

He took a step back, extricating himself, and bowed low. "It's only my duty, mum."

***

Molly and Katie had taken breakfast in their rooms; Tony and Sawbuck were dosed and sleeping.

The breakfast area, open to the hall as it was, didn't seem a proper place to discuss Roy's final wishes. So I had the furniture in my study pushed aside and the table and buffet moved there, so we might close the door and have some semblance of privacy.

Master Seven Bresciane was a thin man, at least seventy, with pale sallow skin, big eyes, and thinning gray hair. Something about him was both peaceful and menacing at the same time. Honor said later that he'd been at morning prayers. In my musings, I never noticed .

Master Bresciane had balked at sitting at table with me until I insisted, which certainly placed him as not of the aristocracy: they thought themselves above me. And probably not a lawyer. A servant?

Blitz stood at breakfast as butler; only the three of us were in the room. But Blitz looked frightened. No — a better word would be terrified, as I'd never seen him before.

Why was he so afraid?

Food in front of us, I watched the strange little man, and he watched me. While we ate, I thought about how to begin.

Other than introducing himself, Master Bresciane hadn't said a word. I thought I'd better make the first play. "To what do I owe the honor of your visit, sir?"

He smiled an affable smile, one with a touch of humor. "Please, call me Sev. Everyone else does." He put down his fork. "Last night we had a meeting. I'm bringing you the report."

This wasn't what I expected him to say. Something about it felt disturbing. "Who had the meeting, sir? I'm afraid you have me at a disadvantage. You know much about me, yet I know nothing of you."

He nodded, yet rather than bending from his neck, the flexing motion came mid-chest. "Quite right." He licked his lips, a slight frown on his face, almost as if not sure how to begin. Which from the terror Blitz showed at the man's every gesture wasn't exactly comforting. "I met with what are now possibly your husband's men."

That startled me. *Possibly?*

Perhaps he saw the question in my eyes, because he nodded that strange body nod yet again. "They followed Mr. Roy. They followed Mr. Anthony, and by his word they followed his man, the one they call Sawbuck. But now, Mr. Roy is dead. Mr. Anthony and Sawbuck are injured and medicated." He took a small breath, then spoke to me as if I were a child. "It's not healthy for power to go missing." He sat unmoving, peering at me.

I glanced up at Blitz, who looked ready to either faint dead away or bolt from the room screaming.

Looking back, I suppose I could have done anything I wanted.

I could have chosen to let the Spadros Family go down and walked away, just as Amelia and Peter did. I could have let this man take the Family, kill Tony and the baby and everyone who opposed him in exchange for my life.

But at the time, I didn't consider any of that. I believed that I'd created this situation. And I remembered what Molly had said once: *You do things without thinking, then you leave others to clean the mess.*

I wasn't going to do that anymore.

But I didn't know if my idea was allowed here. Josie had been perfectly right. Etienne would probably have agreed with her.

In Bridges, women didn't lead men. Few even considered it.

Master Sev Bresciane sat watching me.

This man wanted to hear something specific. I didn't think what I was going to say could possibly be what he wanted. But I believed I'd made this mess. And I knew I had to try, if I could, to care for it, no matter what that cost me.

I didn't dare look at him. "Once ... when I was a small girl ... just twelve ... Mr. Roy told me ..." I swallowed, afraid of the man laughing in my face. "... that if the day came when my husband couldn't take care of the quadrant ... that I should. Do it."

I took a deep breath, feeling both foolish and afraid. "If I may help in any way, sir, I — I'll do whatever is required."

The Accession

I didn't feel until then that Master Seven Bresciane had been tense, but then he relaxed, smiling and nodding in his strange way. And then he spoke gently, as if to a young child he felt great kindness for. "This was exactly what Mr. Roy told me: that we should follow you."

"Really? He told you that?" Who was this man?

He leaned back with a gentle smile. "And if you refused, we were supposed to kill you."

"Oh." That made things difficult. This man was loyal only to Roy, and Roy was dead. I took a deep breath. I knew Family tradition well enough, and I'd read Tony's book. "You know what we must do."

He smiled that affable, kindly smile. And it chilled me. "Yes, of course I know. But I want to hear you say it."

There was always the question of who attacked us, and back then, I thought we had plenty of time for that.

But first the Family had to restore its own order. I straightened. raising my right hand. "My husband, Mr. Anthony Spadros, is Patriarch of his Family, and I again pledge my life to him as I did upon my vow-day. I will follow him unto death. Master Ten Hogan is his second, his kin and protector. When they're well, you and all who swore the oath unto death must follow them. Until then ..." I steeled my resolve. Once I'd decided, this was the only play. "I take the cloak and card upon me, to play this round in my Patriarch's name, as the gods have so intended. And this is my first directive as your Queen:

you must find, question, and kill everyone who's fled their post and betrayed their Family."

Compassion came over me, and I lowered my hand. "But leave Peter and Amelia Dewey to the last." Perhaps they might yet escape. "I think they've suffered enough."

Master Bresciane nodded, and it seemed clear to me that he understood their situation. Then he rose, offering his hand. "Here's to a hopefully short transition."

I smiled at him and rose, briefly taking his hand. "Thank you for coming to see me, sir."

I watched as Blitz escorted him out. *What a strange little man.*

I still didn't know who he was. Some messenger? But sent by who?

When Blitz returned to the room, his face was deathly pale. Sweat hung on his brow. He staggered, holding to the wall.

I rushed over, brought him to a chair. "Blitz, are you well?"

He shook his head.

I sat beside him. "Who was that man? Why do you fear him so?"

His hands shook as he looked into my eyes. "That was the Knife Man, Mrs. Spadros. Mr. Roy's right-hand man. They say if all be ready, he'll take out a man's tongue with a hot knife in five heartbeats, then return to his dinner as they drag the man screaming away." He sat panting for a moment. "He's the most feared man in the city, more so even than Mr. Roy. And he told me if I didn't support you with my life, I'd be the first on his list."

The Knife Man, here, across from me? At my breakfast table? I felt sick. "I don't understand. Why didn't he take over himself?"

Blitz looked at me. "Be glad he didn't," he panted. "Be very glad."

***

The play was in motion. My path was set: there was only one card I could place. So I rang for Honor. "Every servant in this household must be at the morning meeting. No exception."

"I'll see to it, mum." He rushed out.

I sat beside Blitz. Yes, my servant: the butler for my apartments. But he was also my tenant. My partner in business. My friend.

Why would Inventor Etienne Hart order a hit on his six-week-old nephew? The child was no danger to him even if Hart and Spadros were at open war, which we hadn't been since before I was born.

He'd even bragged: *my people play the long game.*

So why do this? Why now? "Blitz, we have a problem."

A weary laugh burst from him. "You're not kidding."

***

It took longer to start the morning meeting than usual, as we brought in the men working the fields past the meadow, the groundsmen and the gardeners, the scullery maids yawning after being up since three to prepare the way for breakfast, the maintenance men who'd been pulled to do stable-work now that Peter Dewey had fled.

I sat on the platform watching them file in, Honor and Blitz by my side. "You did well at morning prayer," I said to Honor.

"Thank you, mum."

Jane had cried through the whole thing, along with many of the staff. But I think Honor did a good job, giving a short word about heroism, family, and loss before starting in on the prayers.

The last came in, Monsieur and Mistress Anne and young Pip. The room was full: all weary, sad, shaken.

I stood before them. "I have always endeavored to tell you the truth as I could, and this will be no different. So I'll say it plainly: Mr. Roy and Mr. Pearson are dead —"

Jane started sobbing.

"— killed defending this very home. They died to spare you the slaughter which took place at Spadros Castle. All there are dead, including old Mrs. Pearson, who some of you know."

A loud wail, and a few more began weeping: many had elderly friends and family there.

I took a deep breath. "Mr. Anthony is your Patriarch now. He and Master Hogan and your Heir are injured," for a moment, I faltered. "Mr. Roy asked me to take over if anything should happen to him —"

Scattered murmurs, and people looked at each other, some afraid, some scandalized, some amused.

I spoke over them. "— and my husband was unable to lead."

I waited for them to settle. "I spoke with Mr. Roy's right hand man today: Master Seven Bresciane, who some of you call the Knife Man."

It seemed everyone in the room gasped at the same time, then there was a shocked, terrified silence.

"He has pledged to follow my command." He didn't say this in so many words, but ...

The room fell silent, and it was then I realized how very powerful that man was. I moved to behind my chair, only to grasp onto it for support. "Anyone who has fled will be found —"

A movement, from the corner of my eye: Pip Dewey's face had turned into a mask of fury.

" — so if you know someone's who's in hiding, have them return to us now. If they simply ran in fear, and had nothing to do with this attack, I will be merciful."

Many began nodding.

"For today, Mr. Blitz Spadros," I gestured at Blitz, "our Patriarch's cousin, will act in Pearson's stead. Please, for your safety, don't leave the Manor grounds for any reason." I took a deep breath. "This is a terrible time." Then I recalled what Tony had said once, long before. "But you are my Family. We can pass through this round if we work together. May the gods bless you."

Blitz came forward then and spoke about Molly and Katherine and Dr. Salmon being here for the time being. He spoke of Sawbuck and Tony and little Acevedo and what the doctor said must be done for them. The timing and requirements for meals. "Deliveries have been canceled for the rest of the week, so go into the storerooms if need be. We can't risk outsiders here until all is secured."

All eyes went to me, and I nodded. This seemed a good plan.

Blitz spoke of all the little things which make up the running of a Manor, and a look of inspired awe came across Alan Pearson's face.

"Since no one is leaving today," Blitz said, "all stable-workers should report to the front of the Manor to complete the work there."

The bullet-holes hadn't been patched yet: I felt surprised that Blitz remembered it.

"Good work, everyone," Blitz said. "You're dismissed."

Two masses of people formed: one around Jane Pearson, the other around me. Condolences, vows upon bended knee to serve, and tears.

A few, looking sad and lost, chose instead to drift for the doors.

Pip stormed out.

It took a half-hour for the room to clear. I remembered an evening, long before, the only time I ever saw Pearson cry. *You and Mr. Anthony are dear to me as my own children.*

Then I went to Jane. "I never had chance to tell you how sorry I am. In many ways, your husband was like a father to me."

Tears ran down her face. "It's too much. My John, and his little mother, and Mr. Roy, all dead. And that dear boy hurt so —"

I suppose she meant Tony. And I realized she'd seen him grow up.

"— and that precious baby!" She began sobbing in earnest. "What will become of us?"

I wrapped my arms round her. "We have the support of our men. And this house is a fortress. As long as we can keep the quadrant long enough for my husband to get well, we shall succeed."

She looked at me. "Did you really see that awful man?"

I nodded, letting go. He didn't look all that frightening to me, a thin frail man I could knock over with a blow.

"I thought he was dead! I hoped he was dead. He frightened me even as a child."

"Wait — you knew him?"

"Well, mum, he was here when I was born. Here, I mean. My mother was lady's maid to Mrs. Maria, and I was in the scullery like Mrs. Dewey's girls are — I mean, were — when I was old enough. My John was house boy, did all the fetching, and Master Seven ... he was an orphan. I think he was with the groundsmen. But I never knew what he exactly did. One day he just wasn't here anymore, and no one would tell me why."

"How strange."

"I was only a child," Jane said. "Meaning no disrespect to anyone."

I chuckled fondly. "I'll keep it between us, never fear."

Mary approached. "Mama, Alan wants to speak with us."

Jane looked at me. "My apologies, mum."

I rose, so she did too. "Nothing to forgive. You go be with your children." I wanted to see what was wrong with Pip in any case.

I found him in the kitchen, a mass of bread dough before him. I presume he was kneading it, but it looked more as if he attacked. Grabbing it high then slapping it down, punching as hard as he might over and over, with grunts and whispered shouts of rage.

I went to him. "Pip?"

He raised then slapped the mass down, seemingly unaware I stood beside him.

"Pip?" I put a hand on his shoulder. "Master Dewey?"

He recoiled from my touch, his tone biting. "What."

I spoke as gently as I could. "Pip, dear ... where's your mother?"

He spoke with fury. "Why do you think I'd know? As I've told everyone else in this place, I don't know!" He punched the dough. "And I wouldn't tell you even if I did."

"Even after everything they've done to you?"

He put his hands upon the floured table and stared at me. "They're still my parents! And my sisters are innocent in this. Do you think I want them dead too?"

I didn't know what to say. I hadn't considered them at all.

"Remember when you told me if I hadn't learned what happened to my mother by the time I became a man that you'd tell me?"

"As I recall, you were ten years old."

"Well, I learned what happened to her on my own." His face fell, and he leaned upon the table. "I don't hate them. I pity them." He gazed upon the table for a moment. "I even pity you, though you left me here without a word —"

"Pip, I —"

"— even though you promised to tell me goodbye." He turned his head to look at me, still leaning upon the table, and spoke bitterly. "You're just as much a slave as I've been."

A slave?

Before I might speak, Alan burst in. "Mum, there's something you must know."

I turned to him, alarmed. "Good gods, what's happened?"

He took a step back. "I'm sorry to frighten you, mum." He glanced at Pip, then at me. "Sorry to disturb your discussion. But I thought you should know. It might be important."

"Know what?"

He stopped then, took a breath. "When the men attacked, I was in the dining hall. My father told me to set the dinner table. He's — he was — training me. I heard the screams and pulled the mechanism for the large bell. Then I heard my mother cry out, and I ran to her." His face turned fearful. "But I remember now. The large bell never rang."

Pip and I shared a glance. Then I turned to Alan. "It never rang?"

"No, mum. If there's something wrong with it, we must know —"

In a flash, it came to me: Peter Dewey, in my closets. "What mechanisms lie in my closets? In the walls?"

Alan looked confused. "None, mum."

"Then we must begin there." I set off, Alan beside me. Up the stairs, into my bedroom, Shanna jumping up from her mending to curtsy, into my closets. Nothing. "He was here. Peter Dewey stood right here. Amelia found him." I considered this a moment. "What if he came from my husband's rooms and didn't know we were here?"

"But nothing of mechanical interest is in your husband's rooms."

I stood there considering, my dresses around me. "But if he was in the back hall ... trying to flee ..." I pictured him in the back hall, hearing someone come, becoming alarmed and going through Tony's room. Then if Michaels had heard him and gone in to investigate ...

Not wanting to disturb Tony, I returned with Alan to the hall facing the side of the house. To the right, the door to the hall for Tony's room, then the hall turned right once more. I pointed past the second door to Tony's room, past the winding back stair on the left and Michaels' room further down on the right. I spoke quietly, so as not to wake him. "What if he was really over there?"

Alan's gaze went past me. "But isn't there something right here?"

At the corner of the building right in front of us, the windows were interrupted by a panel in the back wall. Alan went to it and with a gentle push clicked open the small door there in the wall. It was cleverly hidden; I hadn't noticed it before.

Inside the panel lay many mechanisms. On one, the label said, "Large Bell NE."

The wires had been cut.

What had Peter done?

He faced me. "**Now** do you want Peter Dewey spared?"

A small sound, and I turned. Pip stood there.

He must have followed us!

I felt afraid for an instant of what he might say or do, yet his eyes only held pity. I said, "I don't know."

Alan's face turned that carefully neutral look servants got, and he reminded me so much of his father right then that I wanted to hug him. He glanced at Pip, then back at me. "We'll take care of it."

Pip's eyes narrowed in a puzzled sort of way, then pushed past us.

"Wait." I followed Pip down the winding marble back stair, unsure of what he was thinking or what he might do. "Wait."

Yet he didn't stop, and he must have known the way, for he went faster than I. We went down two flights, emerging in the servants' quarters. Pip hurried into a side door which led towards the back of the kitchens, near the stairs down to the Magma Steam Generator.

Monsieur was just coming out of his office. "Oh there you are. Whatever were you doing back there?"

Pip took the opportunity to escape through the kitchens.

I went to Monsieur. "What may I do for you, sir?"

"Oh, it's really nothing, mum. I only wanted to tell you that with all the trouble, Miss Anne and I have decided to marry privately. We'll take our honeymoon later, once things have settled."

I felt a great sense of relief. "Are you certain?"

"Yes, mum. We discussed it last night, and we felt it best to be here to help. Just until things have settled."

I took his hand. "Your kindness will not be forgotten."

He smiled to himself, his cheeks coloring just a bit. "It's really nothing. Glad to be of service."

I let go of his hand. "Your kitchen boy Pip's in a state."

"Oh?"

Maids were going to and fro in the hall, curtsying as they passed.

I lowered my voice. "I fear his father cut the wires to the large bell before he left."

Monsieur's eyes widened, and his mouth dropped open.

I looked round. "Pip claims he doesn't know where they went, and I believe him. But —"

Monsieur nodded. "Thank you for telling me. Who else knows?"

"Master Alan."

"I'll speak with him at once." He hurried through the kitchens then along the hall and up the stairs to the dining room two steps at a time.

Rather than retracing my steps, I followed him. He'd been right: I shouldn't have gone into the servants' quarters unannounced. By the time I got through the preparation room and to the dining room, he was gone.

I went through the dining room, then turned left past our breakfast area, going towards the front door. Blitz stood at Pearson's former station, puzzling over a ledger. He glanced up as I approached. "I never imagined the number of tasks for a house this size."

"Oh?"

"And it seems Mr. Pearson was secretary for the entire Family." He lifted the ledger. "The man had notes on what went on not only here, but over most of the city. An entire army must have reported to him."

And he'd confessed to me that he reported to Roy. "I never knew."

Blitz let out a breath. "I don't envy whoever takes this on."

I leaned upon the counter. "But we know what's happening." I pointed to the ledger, remembering all the other ledgers Pearson had. "It's all in there, right? My husband can use this."

Blitz nodded slowly. "How is he?"

"The medicine helps. But it makes him sleep. Which is probably for the best." I shook my head. "He'd be so upset by all this."

"And your son?"

Cries came from upstairs. "We're still finding the right dose. The doctor fears to give him too much."

"The poor little babe." He looked away. "I can't imagine that happening to Ariana. I think I'd die from the fear for her alone."

What did I feel for my son? I didn't know, and it seemed like I should. "Mr. Pearson was doing two tasks for me, and he never reported back."

"What sort of tasks?"

I lowered my voice. "I'd asked him to learn what he might about Mr. Roy's grandmother." I recalled Molly's words: how she could feel the bullets hit Pearson's body. Could Pearson's investigations have led these people to target him? "Also, I asked him who in the aristocracy not supporting us might meet with me."

Blitz looked hesitant.

"What?"

"If we go to them or even summon them after we've been attacked, we'll only look weak. You're their Queen: they must come to you."

Hmm. "Very well. But I need anything Pearson had on Roy's grandmother. And as far as the rest ... see what you can find. One day we might need the information."

I went to the door; Blitz opened it for me. Outside churned a mass of men: repairing the front wall and columns, replanting damaged bushes, buffing out scars in the front fence and gate. The street was closed, but at the corner barricades hundreds of flowers lay there, some tied to the streetlamps, with notes and icons of the Blessed Dealer, and candles stood lit.

Crates full of packages and mail for us were being moved along. I never found out who arranged it, but I learned later that each of them were being checked by the police, then moved onto a flatbed horse-truck, then taken to the far copse of trees to be checked again by some of Roy's men and their wives.

I stood in the middle of my front walk. People went round me on both sides, but I never really saw them. Could my half-brother really have sent men here to slaughter my child?

A flash, from far off. Something dripped upon my hand. I touched my face and it was wet with my tears.

Mary came to stand beside me, handing me her handkerchief. "Mum, I'm sorry to bother you. But you can't stand out here like this. It's not safe."

I let her lead me back to the house. "What do I do?"

"You rest, mum. Let us take care of things for you, at least today. We can decide about tomorrow then."

So I sat beside my tea-table staring down at the men and women who'd sworn to serve my Family as they went back and forth through the graveled courtyard I'd never set foot in.

The very courtyard where a young Charlie Hartmann — from all accounts, not even as old as I — listened to the first Acevedo Spadros make his plans to destroy my people and free them from Joe and Josie's ancestor, King Polansky Kerr I.

Whether that King truly was a tyrant, or a kindly but misunderstood man, I don't suppose any will ever know. But here I sat all those long years later.

And what I really wanted to know was ... why?

Why would Etienne Hart try to assassinate a baby?

Why would Etienne go back to the Red Dog Gang — who seemed to want to destroy the Four Families — after his father essentially gave him control of his quadrant? Did it have something to do with Josie's kidnapping? Had he blamed us for it, given them some way to influence him?

Why was Josie kidnapped in the first place? And who did it?

I'd thought the Red Dog Gang intended to drive Jonathan Diamond to his death, and it did seem so. And from what Mr. Hart had said, Etienne had motive: to remove a man who his father loved as a son.

But if the Red Dog Gang did this to torment me, why **use** Josie this way? It seemed out of their usual pattern. Normally, I went to a friend's aid only to find them dead.

This seemed an attack on Etienne in particular. For him to then return to them for help to attack Spadros Manor made no sense.

And why would Etienne attack the **other** Families? If his goal was to take over Bridges, well, even if his father agreed to it, he didn't have the strength for that. His only way to ensure he'd get the quadrant when Roy fell was to enlist Diamond and Clubb to help him. Attacking them was the last thing he should have done.

Perhaps the man really was mad.

A whispered argument in the hall. I went to the door and opened it: Alan and Blitz stood there. "What's all this about?"

Alan said, "I need to know what to tell the men —"

Blitz said, "But she needs her rest —"

I held up my hand. "Tell the men about what?"

Blitz turned away. "This is exactly what I feared would happen —"

I said to Blitz, "What? That I'd be too weak to tend the Family?"

Blitz said, "That you'd be doing so at cost to yourself." He grabbed my upper arms, and I was reminded of the night Thrace Pike had done the same. "Your father-in-law lies dead! Your husband and son are badly hurt! You need to come to terms with it all. I barely can." He let go, looked at Alan. "Surely this can wait for tomorrow."

"Not if what they say is true."

I felt confused. "What are they saying?"

"That Mr. Anthony is dead, and you reign only by the Knife Man's sufferance. That he's taken over! Every decision is going to Master Bresciane first, because no one knows what to do and he gave the first order." He took a slow, shuddering breath. "But if the people feared Mr. Roy, they're terrified of him. People are packing up and leaving the quadrant. Diamond closed their bridges, so now they're flooding into Clubb. The riots in Market Center have worsened, and there's looting in the Spadros slums."

Oh, gods, I thought. *Eleanora*! Her shop was on 2nd. Had I put her and little David in danger?

"We have to make a show of ... of **something**. Or we may not have a quadrant left to defend."

"Call Master Bresciane," I said. "This is not what we agreed."

Blitz was right: I needed someone. Someone like Ten Hogan. Someone good at leading men, someone who knew the Family. Someone to take charge.

I looked to Blitz.

He paled. "No." He took a step back. "Absolutely not. I'm out of the Family as much as any man can be, Mrs. Spadros, and if you want me back in like that, then you might just as well kill me and mine tonight. Because I'm not going back."

I wasn't going to kill them, and he knew it. "Then who?"

Blitz shrugged.

Alan looked exhausted, grieving.

And suddenly, I knew: it just came to me. I'd known the man for years. He could take care of just about anything. He was someone I could trust. "Summon Mr. Eight Howell. I'll meet with him first. Time it for an hour before Master Bresciane is to arrive."

The Move

Mr. Howell's reaction to my offer wasn't quite what I'd hoped for: "Are you trying to get me killed?"

"Whatever do you mean?"

He paced back and forth between the sofa and the row of armchairs. "You can't do this. It's a bad move." He threw his hands in the air. "We have procedures!"

"Mr. Howell, please. Sit down. I don't understand you."

He glared at me, growled, then threw himself into the sofa. "I'm an Associate. I'm not a made man. I'm not even a Spadros! You can't just put me over these men: they won't accept it."

"Can't we make them accept it? I am your Queen now, after all."

He scoffed. "It takes years for an Associate to be a made man, and even then, to rise further takes many more. These men have earned a place of trust; I haven't!"

"I understand that, sir." The grumbling Amelia always did about Mary and Blitz and even little Tenni's move from servant to owner had shown me how important a person's place in the city and the way they got to that place was to these people.

"I'm not sure you do. They'll kill me for this. If I'm very lucky, I'll survive the week. And the minute anything happens to you, I'm dead. And not only me. My wife, my children, all my friends and family, they're dead. These men you want me to lead will see to that. You want me to risk everything on a woman's whim?"

This was troubling, and more than a little insulting, but I pressed on. "It's not a whim, sir; you're more than capable. If you're worried for your safety, I'll mark you and yours specifically off limits."

"Oh, gods, no. Not that." He seemed even more distressed by my words. "I've tried my best to help you. Don't do this to me. Pick anyone else. Anyone. Please."

"I trust you, sir. Mr. Roy ordered you to follow me."

He put his head into his shaking hands. "I'm ruined if I do and ruined if I don't, it seems."

A laugh burst from me. "Ruined? I'm giving you a great honor."

"My wife won't think so. Picked to rise above all, then marked off limits? She'll use this as proof we're conducting a romantic affair."

I almost laughed. "What? That's absurd!"

He lifted his face, his eyes red. "I'll lose everything. Everything. How did I offend you? What have I done for you to treat me so?"

It was as if the man spoke another language. "What if I consult with your wife first?"

It was if he hadn't heard me. "And the other men? You're just undermining your authority with them if you do this. They'll think you don't understand them. Or this Family." His hands shook. "Please, Mrs. Spadros. I'm begging you. Don't do this."

The front doorbell rang. After a moment, Blitz came in, only a little less pale than the first time. "Master Seven Bresciane to see you."

Mr. Howell turned white. "Him? Here?" He collapsed to his knees, shaking, and vomited onto the rug.

Blitz gaped at the man. Master Bresciane, standing behind him, appeared amused.

"Let's get this cleaned up," I said, "then we need to have a talk."

***

In light of recent events, I moved the discussion out to the veranda and ordered tea.

Mr. Howell just sat staring as if he'd been subjected to some terrible shock. So I explained the situation to Master Bresciane and told him what I wished to do.

He mulled the matter over, then said sharply, "It'll work."

Mr. Howell stared at him, aghast. "You **want** me to do it?"

"You must," Master Bresciane said. "Your Queen has commanded it." He took a sip of tea. "I'll speak to the men, never fear." Then he turned to me. "What we need is a press conference. You should've done it yesterday."

The very day we'd been attacked?

"Get up there and tell people the truth. By the statue will do. Have the newspapers cover it and post flyers on every street. Tell them anyone who's left their Family that isn't in their homes by tomorrow night will be deemed a traitor, hunted down, and executed."

This took me aback. "I see."

"And you must do it today."

Today? Could we arrange it in time? "I'll send riders out at once."

The Funeral

We just managed it, me standing in the pitch dark facing huge lights below the giant golden statue of Tony's ancestor. A microphone blared out my words to the crowd of reporters there. "No one will harm you. Return to your homes if you love your lives," I said. "And stand by your Family in our hour of need."

The papers loved it.

Someone had managed a photo of me standing out in the front garden bereft, and it appeared on a tabloid with the words OUR MOTHER IN HER GRIEF.

But most of the tabloids talked about me taking over, and it wasn't all good. One put it:

A POT RAG TO LEAD US?

Another put it more bluntly.

ANTHONY SPADROS: DEAD, OR GELDED?

I had that particular establishment found and burnt, including every copy, before Tony might see them.

But Mr. Blackberry had worked overnight, it seemed, to post the entire speech in the paper, with the headline:

TRANSITION OF POWER

Spadros Queen Holding Reins

Whilst Patriarch Recovers

We'd found a print shop to do the flyers, which began appearing all over the city. And people began returning home.

The next morning (after summoning Mr. Howell's wife to assure her of my good intent), I had the man plan Roy's funeral, along with the funerals of the men who'd died for us. He'd been an excellent administrator, and I felt this the best use of his talents. Since none of us wanted really to dine in the big hall, I let Mr. Howell and his men use the table for planning.

Funeral arrangements turned out to be more complicated than I imagined. Tony was in a lot of pain, mostly from his leg. We didn't know if he'd make the five-and-a-half mile walk to the Main Road as we'd planned.

"He must walk, at the very least for the cameras," Mr. Howell said. "There are too many rumors out there that he's actually dead."

"What if we put all the reporters and camera-men along our block? That's only a mile or so."

"That might work," Mr. Howell said. "But we must get him up before then. Collapsing in front of the cameras will undo any confidence people might have in him."

So we moved the discussion to Tony's bedchamber. He still looked weak, and even paler than usual. But he was sitting up in bed, and when the pain was under control, he seemed in good spirits.

"This is Mr. Eight Howell, who I've chosen as my second," I said. "He's arranging Mr. Roy's funeral, and those of your men, and we wanted to speak with you about the ceremony."

Tony completely ignored Mr. Howell, his public emotionless face perfectly set. "My manservant has told me of your work," Tony said to me. "And my father's man has been here as well."

"Then I presume you understand all that has happened," I said, "and why we're here."

He took a deep breath, let it out. "Moving hurts more than it should. Or so the doctor tells me. How long do I have?"

I looked to Mr. Howell.

He glanced nervously at Tony, then said, "The bodies are still at the morgue, sir. We've kept them cooled with wet cloths, and Mr. Roy's body in ice. But we have perhaps a day or two before they start to putrefy in earnest."

Tony said to me, "Spare no expense. They are to be encased, and packed in fresh Spadros roses, and made to look well for their families if possible. They died for us, and I'll have their cards sent to the Shuffler with honor."

Mr. Howell said, "We can be ready four days from now."

"You've done well," Tony said to me. "Continue as you have."

He seemed quite formal, so I curtsied low. "Yes, sir."

Then for the first time, he looked at Mr. Howell. "Unless there's something else, I wish words with my wife."

Mr. Howell bowed. "Yes, sir. Thank you, sir." Then he left.

I sat beside Tony's bed, waiting for whatever he had to say.

Once the door clicked shut, Tony said quietly, "Today is the first I've been allowed to read the papers. Under what insanity did you put **yourself** forward as my father's successor?"

"Roy told me to do so himself, when I was twelve. If you became unable. And he'd confirmed it with his men."

Tony gaped at me.

I felt bitter. "It figures he never told you. One last little torment on his way out."

Tony sighed, shaking his head. "I never will understand the man. And this Howell fellow?"

Tony didn't know his own man? "Associate for my block, at the apartments. Blitz refused, and I didn't know who else to turn to. He's done well, once Master Bresciane and I convinced him."

Tony's eye widened. "So you actually met with him."

"Twice, so far. I'm not sure why everyone's so afraid. He seems a sweet old man."

Tony began to laugh, then winced. "That 'sweet old man' has been mostly how my father's kept control of this quadrant." He sobered then. "You never answered my question about Eight Howell."

I realized what he was asking, and shuddered. "Good gods, Tony! Why would you even **think** that? He's twice my **age**!" I leaned forward. "My choosing Mr. Howell was Business only. He's very good at taking care of things, much better than I."

Tony relaxed. "That's a relief."

Suddenly I felt ready to cry. "I'm so glad you're getting better. This whole thing has been a nightmare."

He reached for me with his right hand. "My poor dear. I'm so sorry this has all fallen upon you. How's our son?"

I hesitated. "What has the doctor told you?"

"Only that he's out of any immediate danger, and is being medicated." He looked afraid. "What's happened to my boy?"

"The bullet's still in his hip."

Tony's eyes widened.

"The doctor feared trying to remove it. Acevedo and Daisy are at the doctor's office right now to have his hip rayed. To see how bad the damage is. And yes, he's well guarded. The doctor sent to Azimoff for surgeons who specialize in babies, but the Cultural Correctness Committee hasn't ruled yet on whether they can even come here."

"Good gods," Tony said. "They might not help us?"

"I don't know. Mr. Trevisane has made the case that he's been the victim of an assassination attempt once already, and a zeppelin flight not only puts him but everyone aboard at a risk too great to bear."

"Well, at least lawyers can be good for something. What else?"

I sighed. "Other than the city in riot, people fleeing our quadrant because they thought the Knife Man had taken over, and a hundred of our men dead?" I shrugged. "They managed to save some of Spadros Castle from the flames."

Tony's jaw dropped, and I realized he'd never been told. "I'm sorry; it was the day of the attack. A mob." I let out a breath, feeling as if that had been several weeks ago, instead of two days. "All your father's servants were murdered. We're still trying to identify who did it, but many came from Market Center."

Tony sat there, staring, face horrified.

I let him sit quietly until his face returned to its normal before I next spoke. "But the picture Roy drew of Katie was saved."

Tony smiled fondly to himself. "I'm glad for good news, however small. It was done well." He looked up at me. "And what about Ten? No one will tell me anything."

"He was shot many times," I said, "but only one is serious. A bullet is stuck in the bone of his spine, and caused a break. He's able to move, and the sensation to the feet is well. But the doctor's forbidden him to rise from his bed until they can remove the bullet, fearing it may cause more damage if he moves."

"He's been there alone?"

"Just in the guest room; he's being well-tended. Your manservant gives him reports on you hourly — when he's awake."

"But he's been there alone!" Tony seemed the most upset about this, more so than the condition of his son. "I must go to him."

"I — we don't have a wheeled chair, Tony. Can you walk?"

"I can try." He put his legs over the side, the bandages soaking with fluid as he moved.

I hurried to ring for Michaels, and the two of us got his bandages changed. The area around the wounds looked redder than normal, and puffed shiny. "Has he had a fever?"

"No, mum," Michaels said, "and the fluid has run mostly clear."

"Good," I said. Once we got new bandages and some pajama trousers on him, I said, "Up you go."

When Tony put weight upon his leg, he cried out, collapsing back upon the bed. "Why does it **hurt** so?"

"Perhaps you need your leg rayed as well," I said. "I'll speak to the doctor about it."

Tony smiled at me, sweat upon his brow. "I'm grateful you're here." He turned to Michaels. "Both of you."

Michaels blushed a bit as we put Tony back to bed.

"I hate this," Tony said. "I should be up, to encourage my men."

I glanced at Michaels. "Might we not have him carried down? Have his main men here to meet with him? It might help."

Michaels nodded. "It'll take some doing. But we can certainly try."

So whilst Michaels gave Tony a trim and a shave, I consulted the book on makeup Dame Anastasia had given me long ago. All of Tony and Roy's main men were summoned to their Patriarch to give report. And Mary's brothers were asked to carry Tony down the back stair.

Tony's main men, two dozen in all, seemed astonished that night to see Tony dressed for the street, only a small bandage upon his temple, left arm in a cast and sling, looking well, sitting at his desk in his study. I'd set their chairs well back, so they might hopefully not notice my ministrations to his face.

I don't know what they spoke of, but Alan stood by the door and told me later that Tony supported what I'd done so far.

I felt a great sense of relief. If he'd gone against me, things might not have gone so well. At least, not for me and Mr. Howell.

Mr. Howell told me later that in front of all the main men, Tony had called him in and praised his work. "He said I'd done well to support his wife as Mr. Roy asked, and on the plans for Mr. Roy's funeral so far. He said I was to continue." Mr. Howell shook his head in disbelief. "It was a great honor to even be in the room with those men. But to be praised by the Patriarch? My wife'll never believe it!"

"Good," I said. "Now they'll go tell their men they saw Mr. Anthony sitting up and well, that he knows what's going on in the city, and that plans for Mr. Roy's funeral are underway."

Mr. Howell nodded.

"You may return to your work, sir. There's much still to be done."

***

Over the next few days, I tried to talk with Katie about whatever upset her, but she refused to speak with me, locking the door when I threatened to come in. Molly seldom left her rooms either.

Sawbuck was furious once he learned I'd taken over. He was angry that I'd promoted Mr. Howell. He was particularly angry at Master Bresciane coming here. But he seemed more angry that he wasn't allowed to rise from his bed than anything else.

I didn't have time for their problems: I had a quadrant to run. Tony might be awake now, and more alert, but he fatigued easily. So the bulk of the decisions fell to me and by extension, Mr. Howell.

As it was, many dozens of people worked around the clock until the funeral, some weeping as they went. Hundreds of cases of black Spadros roses were ordered to pack the caskets, enough to enrich half the florists in the city. Dozens of women were set to cutting the blossoms from their stems, whilst ones with little sense of smell did the actual task.

Across the street for an entire mile from Spadros Manor towards Dame Anastasia's former home, men set up stands covered with awning. The front row was reserved for our main men and their families; behind them, the reporters and camera-men.

We enclosed an area in black cloth to the sidewalks just past that, large enough to hide Roy's piano-black carriage with the seal of the Patriarch raised in silver on its side.

The carriage was Tony's now. I had them rip out the upholstery to remove the smell of Roy's cigars and re-cover it in black velvet.

Tony's former carriage, the carriage of the Heir, was now Acevedo's. Once Tony was inside his, Molly, Katherine, and I would ride in it, holding the boy.

The reason for the curtains would be in case Tony needed help getting into his carriage. It wouldn't do to have that photographed.

This was the planned procession:

First a group of men on horseback would carry our flag bearing the Holy Symbol of Spadros, black on white. Ten yards behind, a single drummer on foot hitting a slow beat. Ten yards behind him, Tony and Roy's main men carrying floral displays of grief. Ten yards behind them, the open bed carrying Roy's body.

Until we reached the enclosed area, Tony and I would walk behind Roy, me carrying Acevedo.

Molly and Katie would follow, ten paces behind. Then after thirty yards, dozens of men carrying the smaller flags of our neighborhoods and villages, representing the people of our enormous quadrant.

Thirty yards behind them, the hundred open beds carrying the caskets of the men who'd died for him, three to a row. After that, the carriages holding the families of his men who'd died.

When we reached the curtained area, Tony would get into his carriage and set off.

For the next mile, covered stands towards the Main Road were being built at a breakneck pace. This seating was Family only: the Button men, the Associates, the soldiers, the Acey-Deuceys, even the messenger boys. These thousands of men would follow with their mourning banners and displays after the entire procession had passed.

Each man needed a black rose on his lapel, a black band on his arm.

After that, a covered stand a block long was built for anyone else — uppers not in the Family, members of other Families, and so on — who wished to attend.

After that, it was standing-room only, kept back from the road by volunteers and a lot of police.

Once we reached the Main Road, we'd turn left, towards our Country House, where Roy wished to be buried. Carriages would be parked along the road for the displays, and for anyone who wanted to attend the graveside service. I imagined any taxi-carriages which happened to show up there would find a good business.

At least, that's how it was supposed to go.

When the doctor rayed Tony's leg, a bullet lay next to the nerve. Tony had surgery to remove it. Whilst most of the terrible pain went away, it meant he had to start healing all over again, two days before the funeral.

Acevedo's hip had to be casted to prevent any further damage. But it made changing and cleaning him a major challenge. I wondered how we might keep his white baby gown, now trimmed in black ribbon, clean through the ordeal. Tenni made a black under-gown, which helped hide the inevitable.

The day was hot. Tony wore the Spadros ceremonial cloak of the Patriarch, a long heavy thing of black velvet trimmed in white and silver, our Holy Symbol outlined in white embroidery. That on top of his black mourning garb was hot enough. I made sure he drank plenty of water before we set off, but even dressed and inside he began to sweat. I used every trick in Dame Anastasia's makeup book — powdering his face, then using stage makeup, then applying powder again, so sweat wouldn't cause creasing. But he still looked terrible. As we walked, even his public mask couldn't hide that he was in pain, and I felt grateful that the reporters were so far away.

I held Acevedo, but the motion made him cry. Finally, Tony stopped. "I'll take him," and he did so, resting the boy on his shoulder in front of a hundred flashing cameras.

But this meant he had that much more of a burden.

I held his arm to keep him steady. At every other step, he gritted his teeth, let out a quiet grunt.

That was the longest mile of my life.

After an eternity, the curtains closed behind us. Honor took Acevedo. Alan and Michaels held Tony as he sagged in exhaustion.

Blitz opened the door. "Let's get him into the carriage. We have maybe three minutes before people begin to wonder."

Plus, the procession still came inexorably towards us.

Once they got him in, Michaels and Blitz crouched upon the floor out of view, in case Tony might need any attention. Alan took up his spot in back as footman. They had ice there for Tony's leg and a stout dose of salicylate in water for him to drink, which would cut the pain without making him sleepy.

Sawbuck wasn't there; he still lay in bed, a board under his mattress, being turned every hour, until Dr. Salmon could get some equipment to do the surgery, which was to be under the ray machine so they might see the bullet and not cause more damage.

I took Acevedo. By this time, Molly and Katie had arrived, and got into the other carriage. Honor took the footman's spot in back. Daisy sat upon the floor out of sight in case Acevedo needed tending.

The curtains on the other side opened. Tony's carriage went off, ours following behind.

The drapes on each side were then dropped and pulled away so the crowd of men and caskets behind could pass without being hindered.

The drum kept its slow solemn beat. Katie — who at least had the courtesy to wear my charcoal dress rather than Tony's clothing — cried the whole way past the stands. At first, Acevedo cried too, but eventually he began looking around at the crowds.

Many uppers had come out, including those from Diamond and Clubb. A few of the Hart extended family had arrived, mostly distant cousins. Cesare Diamond stood in the Family box beside his wife Furaha, with his sister Gardena clutching his other arm. Lance Clubb stood beside her, face bleak. But none of the Patriarchs were there.

And of course, Etienne Hart was gone as well.

Once we got past the stands, every mile became quieter. A few reporters had run or secured carriages to get there ahead of us, so the flash of cameras became more frequent. We tried to amuse Acevedo, wave at the crowds, and put on a good face, but after a while he became fussy and had to be fed.

Shouts of "Where's the Heir?" came forth, louder and louder. I took him from Daisy, wiping his mouth on his gown, and held him aloft. But that upset him, and he began to cry again.

"Don't mind them," Molly said. "Let his nurse feed him."

So I gave him back to Daisy, and the shouting became louder. One shouted, "What have you done with our Heir, Pot rag?"

Katie leaned out of the window and screamed, "He's here with his nurse, you worthless scoundrels! Have you no shame?"

The crowd muttered as we passed by.

"Hush, Katherine," Molly said. "Have some decorum."

I turned to Molly. "What would you have me do?"

"You're doing fine," Molly said. "It's going better than I feared."

Katie stared at her mother, mouth open. "Why?"

I said, "This isn't the time —"

"Why do they hate us? Why did they write all those lies about Daddy? Why did they burn our home?"

Molly said, "Let's discuss this later."

Katie crossed her arms, face angry.

As we approached the Main Road, a commotion occurred up ahead, the crowd roaring. I turned back to open the small window behind me. "What's going on?"

"I don't know," Honor said.

We passed by several fistfights going on in the crowd, women and children backing away. I waved over one of our men on horseback. "What's happened?"

"Rocks at Mr. Roy," he said. "We got it under control, mum."

"Thank you."

The man smiled at baby Acevedo, tipping his hat to him, then went back to his post.

Katie's face was a mask of shock. "Why would they throw rocks at my father?"

Molly said, "We can talk about that later."

"But —"

"Not here," Molly said firmly. "Not where people can see."

And there were still many people here. At the Main Road the street was choked with people, carriages, and not enough of our men to clear the way. We had to stand there for a while before some of our men could move the people aside.

Then it became somewhat easier. After a mile or two, the crowds thinned. Once we were alone on the road, we stopped. The drummer and flag-bearers were put into carriages, to be taken out just before reaching one of the many villages along the way. We refreshed ourselves whilst men cared for the horses. Then I went to Tony, who lay upon the bench seat, eyes closed. His trouser leg was soaking wet, and the water and cloths in the basin were a pale red.

Tony opened his eyes when I got in. "I thought the attack was the worst day I'd seen so far. I think today has been worse."

I took his right hand. "But we survived it."

A slight smile crinkled the corners of his mouth. "I could hear my poor little Ace crying all the way up here."

"He's fine. At least so far. He's never done such a journey before."

"I hope never to do this again."

I kissed his hand, and eyes tightly shut, pressed it to my brow, emotion coming like a wave. To do this again would mean Acevedo himself had died, or one of our future children. Or perhaps Molly, although a Patriarch would never be asked to walk for any of that.

Blitz and Michaels had gotten out when I arrived, yet stood close by. "We should go," Blitz said. "We don't want to be on the road at nightfall."

As I went back to Acevedo's carriage, Katie caught my arm, pointing to her dress. "Do you like me better like this?"

I shrugged. "I like you however you are. I think you'll get a better reception with the others if you are who you actually are, not as a way to rebel against ... whatever all this you're doing is about."

"So you think I'm ... I'm throwing some tantrum, like a child."

"I don't know, Katie. I don't know what you're doing."

She let out a breath. "Just forget it."

"Why **are** you doing this? Why did you take up with the Red Dog Gang? They're —"

"I'm not the only girl there," Katie blurted out, as if that made any of this better.

This surprised me. "Who else?" When she said nothing, I continued. "You know those cards in the street? They were Red Dog Gang cards. Your precious Frank and his men were the ones who killed your father."

Her face turned angry. "That's not true! Frank would never do that! He loves me! He promised no one would be hurt!"

"After what you saw at the Diamond Country House, you really believe that? Well, he lied. Just ask anyone who was there." I shook my head. "You need to think about whatever you told him. About the Family, about our homes. Anything you know about them might help. We need to know so we can get them before they do this again."

"You're mad if you think I'm going to betray my friends."

"Friends don't send carriages full of gunmen to murder your father and brother. Just think about that."

She turned away in a huff, and didn't look at or talk to me the rest of the way.

Why hadn't they questioned her already? Roy's plan to let these people make a wrong move, brag about their accomplishments, or whatever else he'd planned ... it'd failed spectacularly. But Katie could tell us much about them — if we could only get her to talk.

***

Despite our best intentions, it was fully dark by the time we reached the Spadros Country House. Katie had fallen asleep, and moved unsteadily. Baby Acevedo looked around in the lamplight, eyes wide.

The place was everything you'd expect a country manor to be: large, white, with grand columns and an expanse of well-cropped meadow, white sheep grazing, orchards in the distance.

Other than the building itself, the place made me think of the Diamond Country House, although I thought ours more relaxing.

The servants I'd remembered here were much older now. Some, I didn't recognize. They bowed and curtsied low as I passed.

My room was next to Tony's. He had to be carried up the stairs by four men. "I'll care for him," Michaels said. "And I'll come for you when he's ready."

"Thank you," I said. "This means so much to us."

He gave a shy smile, not looking at me, and bowed, returning to Tony's room.

Shanna and Mary (along with little Ariana) had arrived before the funeral, and all was ready. A warm bath and my housedress on, and I felt much better.

Mary said, "Where would you like dinner?"

"In Mr. Anthony's room, if he's well enough."

"I'll check with his manservant."

I thought about how fragile I'd been at Katie's age, and I hoped I hadn't been too hard on her. "Send a bouquet to Miss Katherine's room, with my compliments."

"Yes, mum."

"And send Mrs. Crawford to me."

Mary paled. "At once, mum."

She went out, and I surveyed the room.

The walls were white, with moldings along the walls six and twelve inches out from the sides and ceiling on all panels, in the ancient pre-Coup way they called Deco. Lace white curtains were coved by sheer white curtains, and those by thick white woolen drapes trimmed in black. My bedding was much the same, sheets and coverlets and blankets trimmed in white lace and black embroidery.

It all seemed smaller than I remembered.

By the time dinner arrived, Tony had been bathed and dressed, and was asleep. His bed was set up differently than at home, so his good hand was close by. I sat beside him, holding his hand, wondering how things had gone so very wrong.

***

The next day, we buried Roy, and Pearson, and our men. It was a quiet ceremony, far out in the area reserved for the servants. Just the families of the men, which of course came to many hundreds of people. But no reporters, no cameras. Just us.

Someone had found a cane for Tony. He walked with a decided limp, but he was on his feet. The families of his men would see that he'd survived. Much of it was theater, but some of it was Tony insisting he could make the walk.

At first, I didn't understand why they'd bury Roy out there. But Master Bresciane had already spoken to Mr. Howell about Roy's wishes. Mr. Howell had refused to make the trip, but had gone to Blitz just before the funeral, to ensure all went as planned. "Apparently the men should go first," Blitz said. "Roy wished to be buried last of all." His face got a thoughtful, puzzled expression. "He made all the arrangements for his folding as if he should die in violence." Then his eyes grew moist.

"What is it?"

Blitz hesitated, then shook his head. "Nothing. I only wonder if he knew something we didn't."

"That's certainly possible. He thought he'd not die in bed."

"Well, I wish he would have told all of **us**," Blitz said bitterly. "Perhaps John Pearson's life might have been spared."

I thought upon this. "Pearson loved Mr. Roy. He told me in not so many words. They grew up together as boys. And he told me he loved us, me and Mr. Anthony, as if we were his own children." A rush of emotion came over me. "I think he'd be quite pleased to have died saving Roy's grandson."

Blitz looked down, nodding. "He was a good man. I didn't have a father, Mrs. Spadros, not really, and I ... just wish I could have had him as one for a bit longer."

I smiled at him. "Me too."

After the two-hour ceremony of names read and prayers said, the caskets were lowered all together, then Roy's. He didn't want to be buried near his parents or his son, but with anyone who'd died for him. That alone made me cling to Tony's shoulder weeping.

Tony's eyes were dry. "A tragic end to a wasted Hand," he said quietly. "He could have chosen to rule this quadrant in any way. He could have chosen peace and prosperity, but instead chose terror and brutal violence. I grieve for Pearson, and for the men who died for us. But my father?" He shook his head. "A part of me is glad to be finally free of him."

I patted the hand which held his cane, and we wandered the graves, moving towards the reception. And my eyes fell upon an old gravestone: Eunice Ogier.

Tony said, "Who's that?"

"A woman who was kind to me, back when I was a child." I dusted off the stone, left a penny there. "She'd known Mr. Acevedo. The first one, your ancestor."

Tony's jaw dropped. "What did she say?"

"She was a small child when they first met, four or so. But he told her they'd have a place there as his family after the Coup destroyed their home." I smiled to myself, remembering how she'd cry at night over his death. "She loved him very much."

Tony nodded slowly, eyes down. "I want people to love me, Jacqui. To serve willingly, not out of fear. To believe in what we're doing." He looked at me then. "Is that so wrong?"

"Not wrong at all." But growing up in the Pot I'd heard of the atrocities of the first Acevedo Spadros, and I wondered if as long as men like the Knife Man existed, if ruling in peace was really possible.

***

A huge banquet out in the fields came next. Molly had forbidden Katie to wear trousers during the funeral, but Katie had found black men's clothing for the reception — from the length of the trousers, probably something of a much younger Roy's — and defiantly relished the stares and whispers around her.

We sat at the center of the head table, me on Tony's right, Molly at his left. Katie sat beside Molly, and as Mr. Howell had refused to make the trip to the Country House, the spot beside me lay empty.

This had the effect of Molly seeming the center of attention, her place beside Tony secure. I felt grateful that no reporters had come out with us, as anyone with half a brain could see what she was doing. If people got the idea that Tony was merely her dummy, we could have another revolt on our hands.

Molly was becoming a major problem. Although she was no longer in power, she still quietly wielded a great deal of it.

I had to do something, anything, to get her to step aside.

Tony smiled at me, took my hand. I always sat to his right, him being left handed, but with the cast on he had no choice but to try and eat with his right. It made things not as awkward as you might think. "I'm glad you're here with me," he said.

"Where else might I be?"

He gave a tiny shake of the head. "Anywhere in the wide world, my love." He squeezed my hand. "I'm grateful you chose to be here."

After the banquet, most returned home, Blitz and his family amongst them. We gave Tony and the baby a night of rest before making the long trip back to the city proper.

When we returned to Spadros Manor, the stands and drapes had been removed. The way had been cleaned. The many thousands of tokens, flowers, and candles had been moved past the stables to the far copse of trees as a sort of memorial.

Mr. Howell met me and Tony at the gate. Molly and Katie went past us. "They've got one like this at Mr. Roy's place," Mr. Howell said, "but we had to post guards to keep people from smashing them."

"If you can, seize the miscreants," Tony said. "And —"

Mr. Howell nodded. "Already done, sir. We've got them in holding for you," he glanced at me, "to decide what should be done."

A crowd had gathered with the rumor we'd come back to town, and were watching us.

Tony said, "Let's get inside." In the parlor, he said, "Find out what they know. They could be just dullards expressing anger at my father, or they could be trying to stir up a harsh reaction."

Mr. Howell nodded. "I've instructed the men not to let themselves be provoked."

Tony handed me the cane and clapped the man on the shoulder. "Good work."

He bowed. "Thank you, sir. It's been an honor."

Tony hesitated. "We have offers from all three quadrants for aid should it be needed. If we need it let me know. But **only** if we need it, you hear? And only what we need. I'll not have my quadrant invaded under guise of kindness."

Mr. Howell let out a laugh at that. "Understood, sir." Then he hesitated. "I had some woman from the Dealers here today. They said —" He scoffed. "'We understand the situation but remind the Spadros of his vow to provide security for his people.'"

Tony and I exchanged a glance. "Good gods," Tony said. "A week after major upheaval? That's typical." I still held his cane; he ran his right hand through his hair. "Ask each quadrant for five men. **Spadros**-looking men; I don't want another panic on our hands. Move five of ours down there and put ten on each side to patrol nights."

"That'll help," Mr. Howell said. "I'll let the precinct know what we're doing. Maybe they can chip in some extra of their own if we," he rubbed the fingertips of his right hand with his thumb then winked, "offer a bit of inducement."

"Good." Tony took the cane from me. "Anything else?"

"The matter of payment for the merchants, sir. I have a box of purchase orders need your signature, now that you're up and about. But that can wait for the morrow."

Tony smiled. "Good chap. Come by when it's convenient."

"Yes, sir. Thank you, sir." With that, he left.

Tony turned to me. "Where do you want to have dinner?"

"In the dining room is fine. Unless you're too tired."

"No," Tony said, "I feel better. Now all we have to do is get through Ten's surgery tomorrow —"

"That's tomorrow?"

Tony nodded. "Michaels told me on the trip out. Whatever mechanism the doctor needed for the surgery arrived at his office overnight, but out of my care and concern for Master Ten, he feared to operate until I'd returned from the countryside." A small smile touched his face. "That was kind of him."

But perhaps not so kind to Sawbuck, who still lay abed. "Will you go with him?"

"Tomorrow? I don't see the need to be there. I won't be allowed inside in any case." He smiled at me. "But thank you for the reminder to see him; I think I'll try the stairs."

I watched him go up one step at a time, not willing to put much weight upon his injured leg. And I remembered all the times I'd heard Sawbuck say he would die for Tony. That he **would** die for Tony, as if it were preordained. As if he found himself with no other choice.

I wasn't going to spill Sawbuck's chips or reveal his hand. But I was tired. Tired of all the lies, all the secrets, all the deception. I decided that, at least on my part, that the truth had to finally come out.

The Debacle

After dinner, we all sat in the parlor: Molly, Katie, Tony. Molly said, "I hope you're well."

She was merely being polite. I said, "I'm well, thank you."

But I didn't feel well. Not exactly ill, but my belly hurt, low and aching, and I felt more tired than I thought right.

But we had ridden many miles that day. Perhaps I wasn't fully recovered from all that had happened to me in the past two months.

Katie had found a set of men's house clothes from somewhere, and looked very pleased with herself when she saw I'd noticed. But then she looked a bit shy. "Thank you for the flowers."

I smiled fondly at her. "You're very welcome."

After her attempt at politeness, Molly sat sipping tea. She'd asked for port, but I then learned that Tony had removed all the alcohol from the house when I returned and told Pearson not to buy more.

Not something I wanted him to do, but it seemed evidence of his care for me. Although after what happened with Joseph Kerr, I wondered if I should be allowed near any intoxicating substance.

The doorbell rang; Alan answered it. After the discussion with his family, he'd decided to take over for his father. He knocked on the parlor door, then peered in. "Mr. Charles Hart."

Tony said, "The Patriarch may enter."

I wondered: *why so formal?*

Tony struggled to his feet, leaning on both me and the cane. "The Spadros welcomes the Hart Patriarch."

Mr. Hart smiled, stepping forward to extend his hand, his voice booming so anyone in the hall might hear. "I'm honored to greet the Spadros Patriarch. Welcome to our number."

And I realized that Mr. Hart was the first to officially recognize Tony as head of the Family.

But Alexander Clubb was supposedly our ally. Were he and Julius Diamond waiting to see what happened?

"Please join us," Tony said. "Molly Spadros, the Queen Mother —"

Molly curtsied, as if she hadn't just seen the man a few days prior.

"— and my sister, Miss Katherine."

Katie caught herself in a curtsy, deciding instead to bow.

"A pleasure." Mr. Hart clearly felt amused by Katie's antics.

We all sat.

Tony said, "To what do we owe the honor of your visit?"

Mr. Hart said, "I should ask your Queen —"

All eyes went to me.

"— as she's the one who asked me to come here tonight."

"I did." I took a deep breath. "Because I'm tired of keeping things from people." I looked at Katie. "I think you're old enough to know."

Katie said, "Know what?"

"Mr. Hart is my father."

Clearly Molly already knew, and Tony of course had known all along, but Katie stared at me in shock. "I don't understand." Then she looked at Mr. Hart. "You're the man Daddy hates, aren't you?"

"I suppose I am," he said.

Katie turned to me. "So why'd you bring him here?"

She had to know the truth. "The question you should be asking is why'd your father bring **me** here? You kept asking why people hated your father, why they'd throw rocks at his coffin, why they'd try to burn his house down. This is just a small part of that."

Katie blinked. "I don't understand."

"Your father had me here as a hostage to torment Mr. Hart. That's all he cared about."

Katie sat staring at the table. "You didn't want to marry Tony?"

I shrugged. "Not at first." I took Tony's hand.

But he extricated himself, not looking at me. "Our father was a monster. I didn't wish him dead, but many did."

Molly and I exchanged a glance.

Then Molly hesitated. The rest of us watched, waiting for her to speak. "I should have told both of you this long ago," Molly said to Tony and Katie, "but I was afraid that Roy would find out. I couldn't take the chance that one of you would say the wrong thing."

"What do you mean?" Tony said.

Molly sighed. "Jacqui knows some of this. I originally came to Spadros Manor to marry Roy. But his father Acevedo and I had been lovers for quite some time. Acevedo had a plan. I would marry Roy, who loved nothing but hurting others, and when Roy and his mother were out of the house, we would continue our affair unencumbered."

Katherine's face was a mask of shock.

"At the time, it seemed ideal. But his mother and her servants disappeared shortly after we married. Acevedo blamed me. For a while, he even left me. But I don't know what happened to her. Roy was gone for the first six months of our marriage, and I never asked."

I bound my mother. I kept her in the cottage. But even she screamed in fear of me at the end.

Now it all made sense. The servants in the cottage with no tongues or thumbs, the snipers on the hillside to ensure they never left. "I believe I know where she lies."

Molly sat as if wondering where to begin, then spoke to Tony and Katherine. "I do like things ... rougher than many do." She blushed deeply, and I realized how hard this would be to say to your children. "But that first night ... he forced himself upon me."

"Oh, gods," Mr. Hart said. "I'm so sorry."

Tony and Katie sat there horrified.

"I came with child." She looked at Tony. "This was before Roy Acevedo. Any slight offense would bring a terrible beating." She stared at the floor. "Vedo never knew: he was at the Country House for over a year after Roy and I married." She raised her head then, not looking at anyone. "And even if he had known, what could he have done? I was bound to Roy, not to him! It got so I feared for my life. I was desperate to find some way to calm Roy, get him to see what he was doing. So during that time, I used — measures — to empty my womb. I told Roy his beatings caused it." She gazed at the floor. "He never beat me again, but I vowed never to allow Roy to have an heir, at least, not from me."

Tony peered at her. "What ... I don't understand."

"Roy Acevedo wasn't his son. And Roy murdered him after the boy saw me with Roy's father."

"Oh, gods," Tony said, his face pale and staring. "Oh, gods ..." He buried his face in his hands, breathing heavily.

Katie's face turned alarmed. "Are you okay?"

I put my hand on his shoulder. "Tony, what is it? What's wrong?"

He didn't move. "I was there. I saw it. I saw it!" He sat up, clutching the sides of the chair, face pale, breathing fast, his voice high and terrified. "Oh gods! He ... he ..."

"Tony, it's okay. You're safe," I said. "What did he do?"

Tony didn't look at anyone, his knuckles white. "He broke his neck! With his own hands. He killed my brother!"

"Yes," Molly said, in a voice which spoke of the long nightmare she'd endured. "No one else knew this but Dr. Salmon."

Tony's breathing slowed, and after a moment, he glared at her. "Who let this go on and did nothing."

Molly stirred. "What would you have had him do? Roy had threats for everyone. Who knows what lever he used to move him?"

We sat silent, but I had a feeling that Molly's words had not pacified my husband.

"So after your brother was born, " Molly said, "I continued my liaison with Acevedo, and used the same means to ensure that Roy never had any trueborn children."

"Wait," Tony said, a startled laugh bursting from him. "I — I'm ... my grandfather's son?"

Molly smiled. "Yes, my love," she said. "He was a good man, one of the best."

Which from what she said before was a complete lie.

But Tony seemed overwhelmed by the information.

I felt confused. What was she saying?

"Later, much later, long after Acevedo's murder, I had a brief liaison with Mr. Hart. Just one night. It was at some City Hall party I had to go to on Market Center. Roy wasn't even there. He'd leave for long periods of time, no matter what the obligation, I suppose to play with another captive." She sat thinking for a while, then said, "It was easy to make Roy believe Katherine was his. I just had to make him think he was hurting me."

I realized my mouth was open, and shut it.

"Wait." Mr. Hart focused on Katherine. "She's my daughter?"

Molly smiled at him. "She is."

Katie stood. "This can't be. This is all lies! He was a good dad."

"He was good to you," Molly said. "But didn't you wonder why I always had broken arms, broken legs, bruises on my face?"

"No. You said you fell!"

Tony said quietly, almost to himself, "He has a room where he tortures people. He used to have one here, but I had it closed up after you all left. He might still have some people chained below the Castle, people who might have survived the fire." His face grew pensive. "I should have Ten check on that once he's well." He shook himself. "No, I'll have your Mr. Howell check on it tomorrow."

After all this time without food or water? I doubted they'd find anyone still alive.

Katie turned to her mother. "You whore. You're lying!" Then she turned to us. "You always hated him, Tony, and you too, Jacqui. **He's** my father, not this," she pointed at Mr. Hart, "fat old man."

Mr. Hart looked dismayed.

"You're all against him!" She turned to Molly. "You bitch. You denied him an heir, but I'm not going to let you destroy his memory!" She stormed out.

Molly sat there, stunned.

I stood. "Let me talk to her."

I caught up to Katherine in the middle of the front hall and grabbed her arm. "Wait, Katie. Wait. Please. Don't do this. We're your family! Just think of it. You're Charles Hart's daughter, just like me. That makes us sisters. Real sisters."

She turned to me, her face a mask of hate and rage. "Did you ever think that maybe I didn't **want** to be sisters? I loved you, Jacqui. Loved. You." She looked me up and down in disdain. "But you turned out to be a whore, just like Mama."

"What?"

"I made Tony tell me the other day why you left him those years back. What was his name, this man you left him for?"

I felt bleak. I'd thrown everything away for a man who didn't love me. "Joseph Kerr."

"You betrayed my brother ... for a Kerr? Well, you just wait and see. I'm going to make you sorry!" She ran up the stairs.

Tony, cane in hand, came up beside me. "Katie, wait."

"Let her go. She'll come to reason soon enough."

"Roy wasn't my father!" Tony sounded astonished. "Somehow, I knew. He wasn't my father!" He shook his head, then took a deep breath. "But he was the father I had."

A shock went through me. I squeezed his hand. "Mine as well."

His face turned grim. "I have something I must do. I think it's best you witness it."

The Will

Molly and Mr. Hart stood in the parlor, facing each other. Mr. Hart looked ready to explode. "And how could you tell me this in **front** of her? It's obvious she's had no preparation, no inkling of it. This is horrendous. Her father just died, and you reveal this **now**?" He began to pace, then stopped, facing her. "You know all about our troubles: with Helen's miscarriages, with my son. Why in all these years did you not tell me I had another **child**?"

Molly said, "And risk you doing something foolish? Look at the trouble we have already just from one of your children here. And what if you said or did something to alert Roy? I couldn't risk having my daughter killed!"

Mr. Hart was not deterred. "But —"

Outraged, I stormed up to Mr. Hart, "Of all people, you have no advantage in this round. After all your protestations about how you **loved** my mother, how she was so **precious** to you, how she was your true **wife** ... you betray her with her **friend**?"

Mr. Hart turned red. "I was very drunk. I barely recall it."

"You couldn't have been that drunk. Katherine is the proof!"

I'd thought Mr. Hart couldn't have gone any redder, but he managed. He looked, in a word, mortified.

Tony had stood there silent. "Molly Spadros, as your Patriarch, I rebuke you. How dare you betray your Patriarch, and with his worst enemy? You have dishonored my Family." He handed me his cane, stalked up to Molly, and backhanded her, hard, across the face.

And I was reminded of the time Roy did the same to me.

Molly shrank back in fear.

Then he shook his head, speaking quietly. "And before that, with his own **father.** What kind of creature **are** you?"

"Stop," I said. "Both of you, just stop." I held up a hand. "We're all upset at this ... debacle. But this helps nothing." I wanted the truth out, but this was not at all what I expected.

Raised voices, out in the hall. "Miss Katherine, wait —"

Katie shouted, "No!"

I went to the parlor door; Alan stood there. "I couldn't stop her."

"Did she have a bag with her?"

"No, mum. Looks like she'd gone upstairs for her hat."

I sighed, going back into the parlor.

Molly said, "What's happened?"

I shook my head. "Katie's run off."

Molly sounded alarmed. "She has? Where?"

I shrugged. "She didn't have a bag with her or anything, so she can't have gone far. Maybe ... maybe just out for a walk?"

Molly nodded, the red mark of Tony's hand rising on her cheek.

This had gotten out of control. "Let's just all retire. Once Katie comes home, we can discuss it further."

***

But Katherine Spadros never came home, and a search began.

After she'd left, two of our men trailed her on foot for some time, until she'd gotten into a taxi-carriage, leaving them unable to follow. The taxi-driver said she got off three stops down and ran from there. None of the other drivers claimed to have seen her that night.

Her friends hadn't seen her. The club of girls who dressed like men hadn't seen her. None of the young men who'd sought to come calling — who she'd refused to receive, every one — had seen her.

She hadn't crossed any bridges that we knew of, but that wouldn't deter any real capture. Besides, she was dressed as a man and crafty enough not to give her real name.

Tony had the Manor guards questioned again about her association with Frank Pagliacci, and whether any of them had seen where she'd gone. Or even what the man had looked like.

None of them claimed to remember him. Which was odd, as surely someone had left his post to allow her to have such extensive conversation with the man as to go off with him. But it turned out that the men who did so — the ones manning the side gate who'd claimed earlier they didn't know him either — had been killed in this most recent attack.

Dropped cards, men that the Red Dog Gang staged this attack partially to clean up?

Tony and I were having tea on the veranda. "This is my fault. Ten wanted to put them to the question last year, but I said no. I believed them loyal men." His face fell. "But it seems I was wrong."

I put my hand on his shoulder. "They got their reward." Then something came to me. "We must tell **all** your men about these people, so no one else falls to their wiles."

"Good idea," Tony said. "I'll have a meeting with my men on it."

These insights had been happening more frequently since I'd recovered from drink, and I wondered if the drinking had been hiding the truth about more than that. "Do you think Katie's run away?"

Tony shrugged. "Where? Anyone who recognizes her would know to tell one of my men, if only to let us know they're still loyal and reporting on her safety."

"I don't like to think of the alternative, especially with her association with the Red Dog Gang. She can identify Frank Pagliacci."

Tony got very still. "I've had her with the artist. But yes, that thought worries me as well." He scrubbed his face slowly, with one hand. "I wish we had more men."

"How are the ones from the other quadrants working out?"

"No problems. They're probably spies, especially the Clubb ones, but if they help keep order I don't care what they learn. I have little to hide from them. The real problem is this Mayor, and his District Attorney." He picked up a small sandwich, looked at it, then tossed it back onto the plate. "Burning Spadros Castle shows a definite portion of the people here not only don't want us, they don't fear us, either. At least, they don't fear me." He shook his head. "I never wanted to make people fear me. But ..."

"Perhaps declaring our Knife Man is on the investigation for those who attacked, and that anyone who gives a credible report in the next seven days could earn leniency might — no pun intended — loosen some tongues."

Tony laughed. "My brilliant wife. I'll speak with him about it." He sat quietly for a moment. "I have much to ask him, to be quite honest. About my — about Roy." He let out a breath. "It still doesn't seem real that he's gone. Much less any of the rest."

I hesitated to speak, but I did want to know. "How's your mother?"

Tony's mood darkened at once. "Katie for once had the right of it. How could she betray my father with the man he hated most? What kind of woman **does** that?"

I had no answer. I'd wanted Tony to know Roy wasn't his father. I'd wanted to undermine his mother in his eyes, just a bit. But Molly had done this to herself. It was, in a word, shocking. I couldn't blame him one bit for being angry.

And poor Katie ... to lose your father, then have your home burnt, people throw rocks at the coffin of the man you most loved ...

As I thought the matter through, it became clear what she'd been doing. Why she'd done what she'd done. She loved me as a woman. Perhaps she believed that if I saw her as a man, I'd love her as well?

There was no way to truly know until we found her.

But I'd humiliated her. Then I'd told her the people she'd trusted had betrayed her and murdered her father. Then to learn of your mother's betrayal?

I knew what it felt like to learn — not once, but twice — that the man you thought was your father really wasn't. And I was an adult!

I still didn't think of Mr. Hart as my father. And I thought of Peedro often.

Who could have murdered Peedro? And why?

He was an addict, he was a scoundrel, he was a former cop. But he lived quietly, owned a liquor store, provided a good service. Nothing was taken, not even any liquor. If someone from his past were to murder him, well, everyone knew where he was. Why kill him **now**?

I couldn't help but feel that this was part of something else. "Did Roy ever tell you if he found the man who murdered Peedro Sluff?"

"No," Tony said. He sounded surprised. "He would've told me if he did, if only to gloat that I didn't find him first."

To hear Tony speak of Roy as if he still lived was a bit disturbing. But the funeral had only recently happened. "How's Ten?"

"The surgery went well," Tony said. "Dr. Salmon's supposed to come by later today to check on him."

"Good." It hurt when I used the toilet, and I hadn't been feeling well. I'd speak to him after he saw Sawbuck.

"Mr. Trevisane wants to come by after dinner. He has my father's will to read to us."

I nodded. "I can't see too many surprises in it."

"Well, he's buried," Tony said. "Once the will's read, and whatever provisions in it he wanted are cared for, that'll be that. We can get on with our lives."

He's relieved his father's dead.

"If Katie did run away, she'll be back tonight. I told her about the will reading at the reception, and that I thought our father would have something for her." He sat back, chewing on his lip just a bit. "I hope that wherever she's gone, she's safe."

***

But Katie never arrived, though we waited an hour for her.

Mr. Trevisane seemed put out. "Shall we begin?"

"Very well," Tony said. "Though I'm concerned she's not here."

The dread hung in the room: *could someone have taken her?*

She was an attractive girl. If the Red Dog Gang had found her, our only hope was that they had some use for her. Otherwise, she could be dead, or worse.

Mr. Trevisane said, "Your father's attorney recently died, and Mr. Roy had instructed his office to pass this to me as your attorney." He looked a bit embarrassed. "I haven't actually read it."

Tony said, "We all know what's in there. Just read it so we might be done with this."

Mr. Trevisane opened a sealed envelope, then put on some spectacles to read. "The last will and testament of Mr. Roy Spadros. This supersedes any former testament, and makes any prior agreements or dispensations null and void." He glanced up. "Typical clause, nothing unusual."

"Go on," Tony said.

"I bequeath the entirety of my estate, my lands, properties, riches, duties, and obligations, to —"

He stared at the paper, mouth open.

I said, "To who?"

He shook his head. "I have no idea what this is about." He looked up at us. "Who is 'Master Pip Dewey'?"

The Inheritance

Tony looked entirely confused. "I don't know."

I put my hand on his shoulder. "Tony —"

Molly said, "Why would Roy leave everything to **him**?"

I turned to Mr. Trevisane. "Might we have a moment, please?"

The man glanced at us all. "Very well," he said, and left.

"You know who this is," Tony said to me. "What the hell is going on?"

I sighed, looking at the floor. "Molly, would you like to tell this or should I?"

Molly looked furious. "You wish to have the truth come out so badly, then **you** do it!"

Tony peered at her, then at me. "Jacqui, what's this about?"

So I told him the story, there in the parlor: how Roy had violated Amelia, forced her to bear Pip, continued to harass and terrify her all these years. How she in turn had hated Pip, beaten and terrorized him. How I'd found the boy huddled on the storeroom stair in his blankets and got him a place downstairs with the men so he might be away from his mother. How he'd been abandoned by his parents, even by Peter, the man he thought to be his father. How he'd chosen instead of being a stable-boy to go to the kitchens, where Monsieur Sabacc and Miss Anne had been kind to him.

Tony sat there, mouth open. "All this has gone on in my home, and I never knew of it?"

I felt grieved. "They didn't even tell him where they were **going**! They took his sisters and left him here to whatever fate you might plan for him."

"The poor child," Tony said. "And he's how old now?"

"I don't know," I said. "Thirteen?"

"Fourteen," Molly said.

Tony gaped at her. "And you knew about **all** this?"

Molly's jaw grew tight. "It's what he did." She looked down. "He forced himself on me, that first time. But when he captured someone, had them bound to question ... it was part of his torments."

"Good gods," Tony said. And I could see how his view of the man — no matter how much he'd tried not to feel for him — was turning into utter loathing. "Why did he — how could he **do** these things?"

Molly shrugged, her head still down. "He told me once. Why. But I'm not sure it's something you'd want to know."

Tony drew back. "Then let's not speak of it." He took up the will, which still lay upon the coffee table, and read through it. "My father left the rest of us nothing." He threw the paper down. "Not one thing."

"Well," I said. "This makes one thing certain."

They both looked at me. Tony said, "What?"

I shrugged. "All lands, properties, duties, and obligations? This makes a fourteen-year-old servant — at the very least — lord of Spadros Manor."

***

Perhaps this concept was too much for the others, because rather than going to see the boy that night, they wished to retire. We each went to our own rooms. But I wondered what our new young master would make of all this.

The next morning, we found Pip in the kitchens decorating a large pan of pastries. The courtyard windows high in the ceiling let a beautiful golden-white light spill over his right shoulder as he worked. He wore a workman's cotton shirt and tweed trousers, a full apron over himself.

The pan smelled delicious.

"Pip," I said, "this is Mr. Anthony and Mrs. Molly. Might we speak with you in private?"

He set down the pastry bag he held and glanced over at Monsieur. The man stood at one of the many stoves, stirring a huge pot of what smelled like chicken soup.

Kitchen maids stopped work at all the stations, putting their things down to curtsy to the floor.

Mistress Anne came into the room. "My goodness! What —"

Monsieur gave her a quick shake of the head, then raised his voice. "Everyone, out. Into the staff hall. Now, please."

Once the others had left, Tony said, "Would you like to sit?"

Pip bowed low. "No, sir. That is, unless **you'd** like to sit, sir."

Tony said, "That won't be necessary." He brought out Roy's will, handing it to the boy across the table. "I believe this belongs to you."

Pip wiped his hands on his apron, then unfolded the paper, reading it slowly. Then he looked at me. "I don't understand." Then an edge came to his voice. "I mean, I **do** understand. I can read. But why —?" He frowned. "Can he **do** this?"

"My lawyer tells me he could do whatever he wished," Tony said. Then he hesitated. "I've only just learned what happened to your mother." He stopped then for a moment, and got very still. "She helped raise me. It — it horrifies and disgusts me, what he did to her." At that, he looked at Pip. "And I'm so very sorry for how you've been treated here."

Pip re-folded the paper, lay it carefully on the table, then gave Tony a measured gaze. "I know exactly who you are, sir. In every detail. I see you every morning, up there so cold and proud. I've watched the way you've treated your wife, a woman who's given me nothing but kindness. I bring your food to you at every meal, and you take it without even so much as thanks for the hands which made it. Yet I'd wager that up until this day, you had no idea who I was."

Tony looked abashed.

Pip put his fists upon the table and leaned on it. "How can a man suddenly appear? Hmm? I've gone from being property to having property in an instant —"

Tony gasped, eyes wide.

"— and because of that, I want nothing to do with it." He handed the paper back to Tony. "I'll sell it all to you for a dollar," he said with a sneer, "the minimum for a man of your station."

A short laugh burst from me. That was exactly what Tony gave me all those years to live on each month, and exactly what he'd said to me when he did. I must have told Pip of it once, or perhaps one of the servants did.

Tony's face fell, and he leaned his right hand on the table. "I'm deeply ashamed of what I've done. Please forgive me."

Pip didn't move.

"I never knew I had a living brother," Tony said, "and it's something I've always wished for. I want you to feel welcome here."

Pip scoffed. "Am I? I remember once when Mr. Roy and Miss Katherine were here. I was nine. I could tell he wanted very much for us to meet, to be a family. He suggested she play with me. But she took one look and said, 'Why should I play with some dirty servant?'" He shook his head. "You will never accept me as your master," at this, he pointed towards the meeting hall, "and neither will those people."

He'd grown up with them. But he felt that they'd never accepted him. Whether because he came to life through the violation of someone they held dear, or because they didn't want to take sides in Amelia's treatment of him, this boy had grown up feeling alone.

Tony said, "But you're my brother! Where will you go?

Monsieur had come quietly inside the kitchen, closing the door behind him. "If you approve, Miss Anne and I wish to adopt the lad."

Tony blinked. "But — of course, if that's what he wants to do." He looked at Pip. "Won't your parents be angry over it?"

Pip smiled to himself, shaking his head. "My parents have wanted ever only to be free of me. "

"Good gods," Tony said, defeated. "I'm so terribly sorry."

Pip shrugged.

Monsieur said, "I have a friend in the Cordon Bleu who's willing to sponsor Master Pip's application. He's younger than what they normally take, but I think he'd be well able to pass the entry exam."

I stared at Pip. "You want to go to Paris and become a chef?"

His face softened. "I do."

The room grew quiet.

Tony said, "You don't have to stay down here tonight. Come up for dinner with us. We can find you a guest room."

"Thank you, but no," Pip said. "You mean well. But you've not heard a word I said. This is where I belong." He turned away then, under the stream of light and into the relative darkness of the kitchen. "Mr. Roy disgusts you, I can tell. But I listen to what people say. I've known everything he did." He faced us then. "He was always kind to me. He came down here often, spoke with me, asked if I were well." He stopped then, head down, hands upon the table, and let out a breath. "The Holy Writ speaks of each of us playing their Divine Hand given by the gods. And it says you either play this blessed Hand poorly or well, for evil or for good." He looked at us then, leaning forward in the darkness, the reflection from the table lighting his face from below. "But what if this man's Hand itself was evil?"

All three of us gasped, and my mind reeled. Could such a thing be? It sounded like blasphemy.

Pip seemed unbothered. "Why is such a thing so hard to believe? The Dealer misdeals every day, and other than grief at the child that might have been, no one ever remarks upon it." He leaned once more upon the table, this time out of the light. But he looked at us with those pale eyes. That pale young face, so much like Roy's. "What if his Hand itself was evil, and he played it the best he knew how?"

***

I thought about Pip's words the rest of the day. And I refused to believe it. Many had evil Hands. The quadrant-folk said we in the Pot were discards, or had evil Hands, doomed to the Fire.

Yet Pot-folk never raped, nor murdered, nor tormented others! I felt Pip only excused what was inexcusable, unforgivable.

But what Pip said never left me, not as I did my work, nor as he served us dinner.

This time, Tony thanked him.

Something about that both angered and touched me.

My eyes met Pip's, and he nodded.

That night, Mr. Hart returned. Tony had taken to his bed, claiming he didn't feel well. Molly didn't come down to greet him. But Mr. Hart didn't seem to be disturbed about this as we sat in my parlor around tea; he mainly cared about Katie. "Any news?"

"None," I said. "Our men know she's missing. They've asked, but no one has seen her." Mr. Howell had come by earlier; some of the men had given good suggestions. "I sent a Memory Boy to my contact at the *Bridges Daily* —"

This caught Mr. Hart's interest. Clearly he wanted to know who that might be.

Amused, I continued, "— so we should have something on it in the paper tomorrow. Plus the men plan to go door to door, each to his assigned street." That was one more thing we needed to do: get copies of her portrait made.

No, I thought. There would be one in the paper. I'd have them show that. "I suppose there must be no news in Hart, then."

He looked startled. "I hadn't considered it."

"Well, if one theory is that she's run off to the Red Dog Gang again, and your son is involved ... I mean, surely there must be men of his involved too. Thus, Hart quadrant."

He nodded quickly. "You're right. I'd thought from what you'd told me about this Frank fellow, that she'd go to the Spadros slums where he seems to roam, or even to the Pot. Forgive me; between this horrible attack on my grandson, Etienne gone missing, and now Katherine, I ..."

And suddenly it came to me how very old he was. So many shocks to a man in his middle seventies couldn't be healthy for him.

He leaned forward. "Tell me more of this Red Dog Gang. I recall a few years back when you told Master Jonathan about your troubles with them, and you mentioned them in connection with my son. But why would your husband's sister have anything to do with this?"

So I told him about Katie's transformation. Starting as an innocent young girl, a man from the Red Dog Gang calling himself Frank Pagliacci had begun luring her away from our Family. "I suspect it was some time after I left my husband, from the things she's said."

Mr. Hart nodded.

Frank gave her cigarettes, listened to her woes. Helped her leave the Spadros Manor grounds to steal jewels then pawn them in the Pot. She'd even joined in on the attack upon the Diamond Country House when Lance Clubb and I went to negotiate with Cesare Diamond.

Mr. Hart sat there, mouth open. "And no one knew this? Where were her men?"

"I believe some of them were also taken in by this fellow, allowing him to bring her to these places." Then I had an awful thought. "Your son's men. Surely some of them would have known where he went. Or did they all flee with him?"

Mr. Hart frowned. "Most of his men and all of his Apprentices have left with him. Which wouldn't be unusual. But the ones who remained were killed in the attack on Hart Manor."

"Just like here," I said. "The ones who helped Katherine and Frank. They were killed in the attack." This was too much of a coincidence.

Mr. Hart said, "We need to check to see who was killed in the attacks on Clubb and Diamond."

I felt surprised he came to this conclusion so quickly. Perhaps I'd underestimated him. "I'll ask my husband to contact the Clubbs. Perhaps you might be best to speak with Mr. Julius." Julius Diamond hated Tony, and would surely balk at being asked anything about his men if it came from my husband.

"That I will," said Mr. Hart. He leaned back in his armchair, then his face changed, as if he'd remembered something. "Miss Josephine would like to visit. Apparently her brother came here with a letter but was refused entry? I realize the timing of the matter might have been poorly done. But ..."

What did she know about all this? "Have you questioned her?"

Mr. Hart shrugged. "Etienne never told her he planned to leave. She came to the Racetrack in tears when she heard the rumors of his involvement with this."

This gave me a shock. I could count on one hand the number of times I'd seen her cry, even now, and I'd known her since my birth.

And I realized that every time Mr. Hart came here, it was a many-hours journey over many hundreds of miles, even if he went by public train, which of course a Patriarch wouldn't do. "Very well. But I don't wish to see Master Joseph. And that's final."

"Finally, you've come to your senses."

This surprised me. "Why do you say so?"

His face became guarded. "It's not for me to tell. But I'd advise you to have nothing more to do with the man."

"Is there anything you **can** tell me?"

He leaned forward, eyes distant. "Rumor, mostly. Women who claim he'd fathered their children after proposing marriage, then disappearing —"

I'd heard of those rumors from Jonathan Diamond. Jon went so far as to claim he had a portrait of Joe with a woman Joe had supposedly fathered a child on. But I'd never seen it.

"— men making claim that he owed them large amounts," he looked pained at that, "but failed to pay."

I'd heard those rumors as well. "But doesn't everyone speak ill of the Kerr family? I always passed those off as nothing but envious lies."

Mr. Hart said nothing.

"This is difficult for me. I've known this man since I was born. I grew up with him. So to hear of this is ... it's shocking. I still find it hard to believe."

"So why do you wish not to see him, then? What's happened?"

I sighed, finding it still too near, that day. That look of triumph in his eyes. "I thought he cared for me," I finally said. "But he doesn't."

"Good thing you found out now," said Mr. Hart, "before something worse happened to you."

***

After that, Mr. Hart left. Acevedo cried, and I went upstairs to his rooms to find Daisy tending to him. As she pinned his diaper, she swayed, stumbled, and I caught her. "You must sleep."

"How can I? He's had his medications, yet he won't stop crying."

The girl's face looked haggard, drawn. And I realized Molly had been right: I'd bedded Tony without thinking, then left Daisy to care for the results. "This won't do. You rest; I'll watch him for a while."

Deep gratitude crossed her face. "Thank you, mum."

His cries of pain moved something inside me. I brought the boy to my bed and rocked as we lay crying together, he for his unbearable suffering, his deep and rending grief, and I for all the things I'd lost.

***

The next morning, Tony's leg was hurting more, so we called for the doctor, who had him brought to his office for another x-ray. I went with him this time, and when his leg was exposed to the air, an angry red surrounded his wounds, with redness going forth from them.

Dr. Salmon looked dismayed. "Infection."

Tony and I both gasped.

Then he turned to his nurse. "Prepare for a drainage procedure." He turned to me. "Once I ensure no further fragments lay inside, I must open the wound, wash it, and pack it.

Tony stared at the doctor, horrified. "Will I lose my leg, then?"

"That's possible," said the doctor. "But if I can get the wound cleaned well enough it might still be saved. I'll need to call for my assistants, and for the ether-man."

I said, "So he'll be to sleep, then."

"Oh, yes. You wouldn't want to be awake for this sort of thing."

"Please," Tony said, "if you must take the leg, wake me first? I don't think I could bear waking to find it gone."

Dr. Salmon seemed touched by this. "I promise, dear boy. I won't do anything without your permission."

This is your Patriarch you speak to. "Doctor, where is your Telephonic Telegraph? I must contact our people at once."

While the nurse brought Tony into the ray room, the doctor directed me to the mechanism and instructed me on its use, including how to change who you wished to speak to. "You speak into this tube, and put this other tube to your ear to hear the reply."

"How remarkable," I said. "And it works through wires?"

"Indeed it does. Now, if you'll excuse me?"

First, I called Spadros Manor. Apparently, Pearson hadn't instructed his son in the use of the device, because Alan took some time to reply, not realizing where the ringing noise was coming from. But once that problem was solved, I was presented with another.

"The doctor said that Master Ten should remain in bed for another week, so that the bone in his spine might begin to heal before he moves around. But if I tell him this news," Alan said, "he'll want to go to Mr. Anthony at once."

And who could restrain him? The man literally filled doorways, and had not an ounce of fat upon him. If we tied him to his bed, he'd injure himself for certain. "Don't tell him. Call for Master Bresciane and Mr. Howell to attend me here at once."

"Yes, mum."

I replaced the mechanism in its niche and turned to find the doctor standing expectantly. "His x-ray shows no sign of foreign material inside. As soon as the ether-man arrives, we'll begin."

"Thank you," I said. "But we must wait for my husband's men, so he might give them instructions."

"I almost forgot," Dr. Salmon said. "I heard back from the CCC. The Committee has granted a special dispensation for the surgeons from Azimoff to come here."

Relief swept over me. "Good news at last."

I sat beside Tony in the doctor's private office holding his hand until Mr. Howell and Master Bresciane arrived, each with two men I didn't know with them.

Tony looked frightened, as I suppose anyone would be. But when the nurse came in with the news they'd arrived, he put on his public mask and bade them enter as well as any.

I felt very proud of him that day.

Tony told them both of the doctor's words. "I wish to have you here as witnesses to my wishes in case this goes wrong. Follow my wife as Queen Regent, and the Queen Mother as her advisor —"

I barely restrained myself from scoffing at allowing Molly to advise me on anything. But it was a good plan. Molly had connections I could only dream of.

"— until your Heir is a man." He took my hand and raised it between us. "She has a keen mind and a stout heart. I trust this woman with my life and the life of my son. If you have any love for our people, follow her."

They all looked taken aback at that last part.

"Never fear," Master Bresciane said. "I served your father for over fifty years; may the gods grant me fifty more to serve your son."

Mr. Howell nodded.

This was all very well and good, but nothing stopped Master Bresciane from killing me and Tony, seizing (or killing) Acevedo, and claiming the title of Patriarch for himself. "You have no desire to rule?"

The man's eyes were clear, his voice steady. "I'm no good with fancy words or fine clothes, Mrs. Spadros, and I don't **like** hurting anyone. My only wish since I was a boy has ever been to be left to tend gardens in peace. But the call came, and I have always answered it." His tone made his intent clear: *whether I wanted to or not.*

"And for that we thank you," Tony said.

Dr. Salmon came in. "The ether-man's set up and ready."

"Let's get this over with." Tony rose, walking to whatever doom.

The Surgery

As it turned out, the wound hadn't healed properly, and purulence had set in. But the doctor had been able to clean out Tony's leg and pack it well, and he provided us a wheeled chair to bring home.

Somehow, reporters had learned we were there, all crowding around as I wheeled Tony to the carriage.

"Are you in any danger?"

"None," Tony said. "An issue with the wound is all. I should be perfectly well in no time."

A clamor of questions.

I said, "If you please, sirs, my husband's just been with the etherman. I'd like to get him home to rest."

They backed off, tipping their hats and murmuring apologies. Tony got into the carriage on his own, to the tune of hundreds of cameras. I got in after him, and once the carriage went into motion, he smiled. "You have a way with them."

Heat rushed to my face. "I don't know. I just say what seems right. It was all the truth."

"You're best when you speak true; I've always thought so."

***

Late that afternoon, Josie came to call.

It'd been many years since she'd been there, and I almost refused her to enter. But I knew she'd keep on until I saw her, so I relented. "What can I do for you?"

Josie's eyes widened. "I heard about the surgery. How can I help?"

How could she have heard of it so quickly? "Seems to me you've 'helped' quite enough."

"Jacqui, I don't understand. Joe says you refused my letter. It's clear something's happened between you." She leaned forward, all seriousness, in a way I'd never seen in her before. "Did Joe hurt you? What has he done?"

The triumph in his eyes ... I couldn't look at her. I felt too ashamed. "I don't have time for this now. I've obvious Joe cares nothing for me. And I'm wondering whether or not you even do. I think going to see you was a mistake."

"I was glad to see you." Josie said. "I'm sorry." Her face fell. "I wish you would tell me what happened. I never, ever meant you any harm. I thought the day would make you happy."

"Did you know this was going to happen?"

"I don't understand. Your husband's surgery?"

"The attack on Spadros Manor. Did Mr. Etienne have you ply me with Party Time so I'd not be here when the attack happened?"

Immediately I saw the fallacy of that argument. If Etienne Hart wanted me dead, he'd **want** me with Acevedo and Tony, not safe in Hart quadrant.

"I swear to you, Jacqui, I knew nothing of it!" Tears filled her eyes. "I had nothing to do with it. I didn't even know you were to arrive!"

"So how did you have the Party Time all set up? Why did you put it in my tea?"

She sighed. "My grandfather's friend is a cousin of one of the Apprentices. He brought over the new Party Time when he came to call. Grandpa's doctor said he couldn't have it, so it's just been in the cupboard." She looked into my eyes. "You always liked it before. We thought to surprise you."

I didn't know what to say. I didn't feel well, and I'd had about enough. "It was quite a surprise, thank you. Now I've got a lot of things to do, so —"

Josie rose abruptly. "Of course. I didn't mean to cause trouble. I only wanted to help." Her manner became earnest. "You **will** call on me if you need anything ... won't you?"

I didn't answer. But I did walk her to the door.

It hurt badly when I used the toilet next, a stabbing pain as if a knife went inside me. So I had Alan call for the doctor. "An irritation of the urinary tract," Dr. Salmon said. "Have your kitchens serve you cranberries with honey with each meal."

"And that will cure it?"

"It'll help your body do its job. And lots of water, one cup for every cup of tea. Tea can be dehydrating." He turned away, muttering, "These young women and their tea."

Miss Anne didn't know how to prepare this concoction, so we went to Jane, who stepped right up. "Here, my dear, I know exactly what you need." She turned to Miss Anne. "Cook a cup of them until soft in just a bit of water, just enough to cover. Then when completely cool, mash them into a cup of honey." She turned to me then, face severe. "And you eat it up, every bit."

This amused me. The concoction tasted good, and I thought all would be well.

***

The surgeons from Azimoff arrived the next afternoon. Their clothes were strange, their accents strange, and they carried many boxes of what looked like a soft black metal. "We'll need a large room," their leader said, so we brought them to the dining hall.

"This will do," one said. "Once we remove the table."

So the table was removed, and their own was unfolded from one of the large black boxes. It had many cunning mechanisms to raise and lower the table to the exact height needed.

Air would have loved this. He would have been, nay, should have become an Inventor. But he lived in the Pot, where we weren't even taught to read but by the whims of our brothel's patrons.

And the night I was sold to the Family, Peedro killed him.

I hadn't thought of my childhood friend in some time, and I wondered how his little brother David Bryce fared. Were he and his family safe from those mobs looting the slums?

I sent a letter to them asking them to let me know if they were well.

The chandelier in the dining room was removed along with the table, and the Azimoff men placed their own lamps.

These lamps were like the very bright light the doctor had shone inside me when he diagnosed my pregnancy, with smaller lamps inside the large bulb, and still smaller lamps inside those.

The entire room, even the floor, was encased in thin clear sheets, of a sort I'd never seen before. They felt almost like oiled canvas, if such a thing could be clear enough to see through. One had a large hole near the bottom of it, which the men attached to a machine using a large flexible pipe.

Then equipment was brought in. Small tables which stood to elbow height. A strange device which reminded me of an eye — if it were square and without any white in it — was put upon many stacked empty boxes. Many rolls of blue cloth were encased in the same clear sheets, only these wrappings seemed thinner and more delicate. These rolls were lumpy, as if they contained something inside.

Mechanism after mechanism was assembled and placed inside, ones I don't even know how to describe. They were shiny yet not of newness, but that of well-worn use.

The men sealed the large clear sheets together with strips of bright blue cloth which stuck to the sheets, then whilst some hung yet another row of clear sheets outside of the enclosure, another turned the machine on, sending a smoky gas into the inner chamber.

At this, I stopped one of the men. "What is that gas?"

He smiled at me, obviously amused. "The gas sterilizes the room, so no infection gets into your son's wounds."

I stared at the enclosure, mouth open. "What a good idea!"

But by this time the man was gone, and all his kin.

Tony had gone with them; they were upstairs. Acevedo was crying; I hurried up the stairs after them.

Dr. Salmon was with them, holding the portraits he'd obtained from the ray machine. He held one up in the light streaming through the window, and Acevedo's little bones showed there!

I gasped, and all the men turned to me. Tony came and took my hand. "See there? The bullet is still inside."

I'd never imagined such a thing; seeing a person's actual bones frightened me. "How can you see **bones** in ... in a portrait?"

Dr. Salmon said, "It's an x-ray portrait, mum. That's what it's for."

I nodded, trying to understand. I knew the ray machine showed the bones, but I never imagined they could be seen like **this**! "Can you help him?"

One of the doctors smiled at me wearily. "It's been a while since the attack, and his bones have started to heal wrong, not to mention they're healing around the bullet. So we'll have to deal with that. But we can get the bullet out safely, and give him the best chance. It all depends on what we find, and how well he heals."

I nodded. With doctors you never knew what would happen. Sometimes they died anyway. "Whatever you can do for him, we'll be grateful."

***

The surgery was to take place the next day. We all ate in the parlor, the servants bringing our food up the narrow back stair to the parlor plate by plate.

Tony and me, and Molly. The mood was glum.

The whole city searched for Katie, yet not a sign or clue had been found to where she'd gone. Was she dead? Was she hiding? Had she turned herself over to the Red Dog Gang in earnest and now ran with them? We had no way to know.

From her words, I thought this last theory was most likely to be correct. She'd turned on us, even though all signs were that the Red Dog Gang had murdered her father. If she wished to make us pay, as she'd last said, they were her best hope.

Who might understand the thinking of a girl deranged by grief?

Sawbuck had been fitted with a steel-boned corset under his clothing to brace his back whilst it healed, and he stood guard over Tony once more. But they'd had words about him not being informed about Tony's injuries, nor about his surgeries. Anger radiated from the huge man, and although I didn't blame him, surely it didn't help.

Tony's leg was still red, and the daily changes in the packing hurt him terribly. He seemed paler than usual, with a faint sheen of sweat upon his brow. But he ate, if quietly, so I thought he was doing well. He'd never eat if he felt upset or anxious.

Molly and Tony had stopped speaking to each other. She was angry that he'd struck her, though he claimed it was his duty. She was angry at everyone for letting Katie leave the grounds — as if we could've stopped her. My guess was that she was mostly angry at herself for telling the truth to someone clearly still a child.

Tony was, even still, furious at Molly for what she'd done to Roy. He'd spoken to me about it the night prior, as we sat holding hands in my bed. I wasn't feeling well, and any move made his leg hurt, so we treated each other with great gentleness and care.

Tony had said, "Did you know? About Katie?"

"I never imagined such a thing." I'd hesitated then. "I did know about you, though."

Then it had come to me: the letter. "Remember the letter that Roy wouldn't give you? The day he made us shoot? I still have it." I'd risen, carefully so as not to hurt his leg by bouncing, and rushed to my closets. Finding the panel far back in there, I'd slid the panel up, retrieved the letter, and slid the panel back down. Then, all as before, I'd hurried to Tony and crawled into bed beside him. "See? Even then, he knew about it. It had to be why he ... um —"

"You can say it: killed my brother."

"Your mother told me he caught your brother and his friend acting it out after they saw her and your grandfather in bed together. They were just little children."

"Good gods," Tony had said, appalled. He'd peered at the letter again. "And he got this when I was attacked, after the Party Time shipment was stolen? So at least three years our enemies have known." He'd set it down, a new energy coming over him. "This is why they haven't revealed it!"

"I don't understand."

"They can't. It puts me not as Roy's heir, but as my grandfather's. Illegitimate, yes," he'd let out a laugh, "but that would be more of a technical, legal point. To the people, though, anything my father did would be seen as an aberration. All this gave them was a way to shame my father, cause him grief — but they couldn't use it any further." He'd spun the letter onto the bed. "A few days of scandal in the tabloids, that's all."

Hmm, I'd thought. "Did I tell you about his mother's parents?"

"What about them?"

"Well, they still live, and by all accounts are still furious as to her disappearance." Roy had all but confessed to her murder, but there would be no way for them to know whether she was alive or dead.

"Yes, I remember you saying so," Tony had said. "Do you think they're involved with these actions against us?"

"Dame Anastasia thought so." I'd shifted in the bed to better face him. "She wasn't certain, mind you, but Roy thought that whoever wrote this —" I'd pointed to the letter, "— had access to knowledge only someone quite old and with very good spies might know."

Tony had chuckled then.

"What?"

"Oh, when you said, 'quite old and with very good spies,' my first thought was of Alexander Clubb. But that's silly: he's been our ally for generations."

"Yet he has still to acknowledge you as Patriarch."

"He hasn't come by, no. But I didn't expect him to, not with all that's been going on."

Now, sitting in our parlor a day later, I looked over at Tony, Molly, our half-eaten plates. And the memory of our conversation made me a bit afraid.

We were in desperate trouble.

For the first time in twenty years, we'd let outsiders into our quadrant to help with security. We had an heir, but we didn't know if he'd survive his surgery. A mob had burnt their Patriarch's home, and most of them were still out there.

And Katie was nowhere to be found.

Why had no one come to our aid?

In light of the help the other quadrants had given us and the strenuous efforts of our people to bring about Roy's funeral, perhaps that thought was uncharitable. But Thrace Pike had known to rescue me in the warehouse the night Jack Diamond set it ablaze. And Ma, Benji, Vig ... did none of them fear for my safety?

Yet perhaps they feared to come here, or even to send a card.

But surely Morton would visit, if only to offer condolence! And he'd not so much as sent a messenger boy.

Where **was** everyone?

***

The next day found us in the breakfast room, where we might see glimpses of the dining room and the surgeons there. They'd strung a deep blue curtain of a thin material which felt like paper across the archway, but the lights in there were so bright that the doctors' shadows could be seen coming and going.

Overnight, several women and one man had arrived — their assistants — carrying numerous soft bags much like my carpetbag. They'd asked for large basins and the use of one of our ovens with a stove on top next to a source of water. Then — as Jane told me later — they'd strung much boiled rope, then put their blue material on both sides and the ceiling all the way. This went through the preparation room, down the stairs and along the hall to the kitchens.

Along one side of the material, they'd hung what Alan said looked like rope, but it was clear, with light inside it. "Most remarkable thing I've ever seen."

But this blocked much of the way: the servants had to go through their quarters and up the back stair to get our food to us in the breakfast room.

Monsieur and — now Mrs. Anne — set up a warmer system, where each platter was transferred to a row of pots with small candles beneath them. Our people thus moved back and forth in stages, rather than having one person carry a single platter all the way.

The doctor and his assistants wore loose clothing and what looked like drawstring bags covering their shoes and hair that day, of the same blue as the rest.

Acevedo cooed in the surgeon's arms as the man carried him to his doom. "There, there, my special boy. Aren't you a handsome one."

That made me smile. "You're good with him."

"I like babies," he said fondly, "that's why I treat them."

Then he disappeared behind the blue curtain, and here and there Acevedo would make a small sound, which would each time make my heart pound, but he really seemed happy enough. Then the surgeon said, "Time to sleep now, little one," and all that was left was the sound of the machines.

Each small sound would make us jump, and look round. Mechanisms pulsed and gears whirred, and the doctors murmured inside their clear sheets, and tools clinked. Intensely bright flashes of light appeared through the blue curtains from time to time, and as much as I tried, I couldn't imagine what they were for.

Mr. Hart arrived in the middle of breakfast. I felt glad to see him, and I think Tony was too, but Molly ignored him entirely. After making our greetings, and inviting him to sit, he peered at the blue curtain for several moments, then got his food from the buffet, sat next to me, and ate as if starved.

The plates were taken away, and tea was served. Tony and I sat there, clutching each other's hand, me trying not to imagine the worst.

Tony leaned over to speak in my ear. "All will be well, my love. These are good men; they'll do their best for him."

But what if their best wasn't enough? My poor little baby, who'd done nothing wrong to anyone, lay in there. If I'd only been here, I might have spared him this.

Why had Joe and Josie given me the Party Time, really? Could it merely be as Josie said, a harmless amusement to celebrate her being well? Could Josie be innocent of this drugged seduction, Joe taking her idea to celebrate and allow us time together ... just to use me?

If so, then this was not the man I once knew. He'd tricked me, used me, betrayed my trust. He'd toyed with me in the worst way, and I felt so ashamed of it all. I'd loved him with everything in me, and he'd spat on my love time and time again.

Why did I not see it when he disappeared for all those years after we lay together that first time? Why did I take his excuses, his protestations, his vows of love?

What was **wrong** with me?

Tears fell from my eyes unbidden, and Tony put his arm around me, which made me cry even more. I'd done everything to Tony but kill him myself, and he didn't deserve any of it.

Tony took his arm from around me, reached into his pocket and took out his handkerchief.

For some reason, this made me laugh. "Thank you." I wiped my eyes, blew my nose when I thought no one was looking, then stuffed it into my pocket.

Mr. Hart took my hand. "Come, my dear, let's go for a stroll."

I took his arm and we strolled past servants curtsying or bowing as they might, out to the front porch, now made whole. Today there were few reporters, oddly enough, and no camera-men. I would have thought that either an event such as the Spadros Heir being in surgery at two months of age or the Hart Patriarch on the front porch of Spadros Manor might have been news-worthy. But perhaps Master Bresciane had something to do with this reprieve.

That thought made me smile, if grimly.

"It's good to see you smile," Mr. Hart said. He led me to the left, past the house and over where the stables were. We walked past them, and he put his hand beside one tall black horse's face. "You have beautiful animals here."

"Thank you."

"Sometimes I prefer them. They never betray you. They always try their best, even when provoked." He shook his head. "We don't deserve these gifts the Floorman has given us."

For some reason this brought tears.

He glanced at me and smiled. "Too bad they can't clean up after themselves, though."

Anger sparked in me. "Our stable-man ran off the day we were attacked. We lost twenty men just here. Good men, friends and family. The ones left who weren't hurt too badly try their best, but —"

Mr. Hart appeared abashed. "They're grieving. Forgive me. I was only making light — but I shouldn't have."

We walked for a while, passing along the path that our guests had the day of the event in the meadow, where Roy had sat under that tent, showing our uppers he'd chosen Tony as his Heir.

Then left everything to Pip. Why did he do that?

"Might I ask you something perhaps personal?"

I had no idea what he wanted to ask; it frightened me. "Of course."

Mr. Hart hesitated. "Did Mr. Roy ever say why he hated me so? Even once before he died?"

That brought me back to that horrid day, that terrible story. I felt bleak. "He said that only one man in his whole life had ever been kind to him, and that you killed the man right in front him, simply because he was in the way."

He stopped, there in my gardens, and stared at me, mouth open. "When —?" He put his hand to his forehead, turning away. "I — I ... I've not killed many people in my life. Um, that is, not with my own hands. And I've very seldom even been in the same room with Roy Spadros." He took a few steps along the packed dirt path. "At the Grand Balls." He spoke as if trying to recall. Then he turned to me. "I don't remember even **seeing** him until well after the Bloody Year." His voice sounded distant. "He was barely more than a boy himself — not even as old as you are. But he hated me even then. Fiercely. Enough to murder my entire family."

Then his face took on a look of absolute horror. "Wait. I remember." A bench sat nearby, and he stumbled to it, sitting heavily, his face in his hands. "Oh, gods, I remember. That has to be it." He sounded ready to cry. "Oh, gods ... what have I **done**?"

Concerned, I sat beside him, my hand upon his shoulder. He was almost half past seventy, perhaps too old for such turmoil. "What is it that you've done, sir?"

He sat unmoving, elbows on his knees, face in his hands. Then his fingertips pressed upon his forehead. "I was younger than you. And oh gods, so stupid. I worshipped my grandfather, but he knew very little of warfare. To him, it was all a game. He sent us — my brothers, my cousins — he sent us through Diamond to raid Spadros quadrant. By train, of all ways. He thought it clever, even funny. Looking back, it was dangerous and cowardly." He took a deep breath, let it out, shaky, almost sobbing. "We shot people. We all shot people. They ran from us screaming, but I didn't care. It didn't seem real. I began to feel powerful. Invincible. A group had taken refuge under a wooden table, the sort with benches built in. I passed by, and someone moved, and just like that," he flickered his hand to one side, "I shot him."

I thought of little Ante then. I pictured a small boy, seeing someone he loved, someone who had been kind to him, dying for no good reason, learning the name of the man who killed him, and vowing to make that man pay.

And it grieved me.

His hands dropped. "The instant I did it, I regretted it. I felt ashamed. I knew that man only moved out of fear, or to protect someone beside him. He did me no harm. He probably was never even armed." His head drooped, and he looked dejected. "I killed a man who meant me no harm, and it's haunted me ever since."

"I believe you." But because of that day, I was taken, just to harm Mr. Hart. I was beaten, and cursed, and caged, and subjected to terror, all as a young child. All to make him pay.

I didn't know if I could ever forgive him for it.

Shanna came running up the stable driveway, panting. She was in tears. "Oh, mum."

A bolt of terror hit me; I found myself on my feet. "What's wrong? What's happened? Is my son —?"

She gasped, eyes wide. "No, mum, no! So far as I know, he's well. They — they're not done with him yet." She took a moment to catch her breath. "It's Miss Katherine, mum. They found her." For a moment, her face twisted in grief. "They found her dead."

The Demise

I recall it as if it were yesterday.

We sat in armchairs in the parlor. Mr. Hart, then I, then Tony, then Molly. The sofa to our left, the unlit fire to our right. Two rivermen stood before us, caps in hand. A police constable stood by the door, hat in hand, not looking at us but at the men.

They'd been out dredging the South River, you see, like they'd been doing for the past year. And this morning they found a girl in the river. Face up in the river, dressed in red and green. A red and green dress, quite pretty, her auburn hair streaming out around her. Roses and daisies and holly lay floating round her, and she wore a noose for her necklace, the end broken off some three feet from her body, like it'd snapped.

It was then the constable spoke. "Looks like suicide to me. We need you to ensure it's her," he said, "and to claim the body."

"I'll go," Tony and Molly said, at the same time.

I rose. Katie being dead didn't seem at all real. Her hair was black. She wore black trousers. "Then I best go with you, if only to keep you from coming to blows."

"No," Tony said.

"One of his parents should be here when the surgeons emerge," Mr. Hart said to me. Then he said to Tony, "Might I stay here as well, to wait for them?"

Tony's face softened. "I'd be ever so grateful, sir."

So Molly and Tony got dressed and left. Mr. Hart and I went to the breakfast room, to sit at the table in silence.

At least some of the fault for her death lay with me.

I never took Katie seriously. I never listened to her or found out why she ran after the Red Dog Gang or tried to help her in any way, other than to give her advice she found distasteful.

And now I saw why. She loved me as a woman. And I treated her like a child, made her feel I disdained her. On the top of learning what her mother had done, seeing how her own people hated the man she adored and thought of as her father ... it'd been too much for her.

But why would she dye her hair back to what it'd been? Wear a dress again? It seemed so unlike her.

That's why at first I didn't believe she lay dead in the morgue.

Then Tony and Molly returned.

It was her.

***

Molly had been crying, but Tony looked awful: a grayish tinge to his skin, circles under his eyes, sweating. Alan and Mr. Hart helped him to a seat in the parlor and put another chair under his feet.

Molly would say, "How could this happen?" Then she would cry, sobbing onto the arm of her chair for a long while until she wound down. And the whole thing would repeat again.

Tony just grasped the ends of the arms of his chair, knuckles white, teeth locked.

I didn't dare ask what they'd seen.

My poor little Katie who'd loved horses, and wanted to do anything with me! She'd grown up in that terrible place with those silent servants, those men and women who'd likely had their tongues out by Mr. Roy's Knife Man. Her mother and father had been her life, and both had been shown to be nothing that she'd dreamed.

And I'd betrayed her brother, betrayed her ... gods, what anguish she must have felt!

Mr. Hart sat quietly the whole time, leaning forward, hands in front of him, unmoving.

Gradually, Tony stopped gripping the armchair quite so tightly. Molly was quiet for longer and longer between rounds.

They said she was dead.

How could Katie be dead?

Alan knocked on the parlor door. "The head surgeon," he said, opening the door wide for the man to pass.

The man had his odd tweed suit on now, like ours but not, and smiled when he entered.

Tony leaned forward, knuckles once again white. "How is he?"

"He's well."

We all sighed, relieved.

He turned to Mr. Hart. "And you are?"

Mr. Hart rose, extended his hand. "The boy's grandfather."

The surgeon looked from him to me, and I almost laughed. Was it that obvious?

"Well," the man said, looking at us all, "the procedure went well." He pulled up a chair and sat without shaking Mr. Hart's hand or asking leave, so Mr. Hart sat as well. "However, there's a problem."

Molly looked up, alarmed, as if she'd just noticed the man was in the room. "What problem?"

He smiled soothingly. "We got the bullet out without any problems. It's a miracle there was so little damage to the nerves and vessels. But the bones were shattered, and as I said earlier, had begun to grow back wrongly. We had to break those wrong ties and put the bones back where they belonged, so his hip would work properly." He took a deep breath, let it out. "We did what we could. He's in a new cast now, and we'll see how it goes."

Tony's eyes narrowed. "What does that mean? Will he recover?"

"He will. But it's likely he'll need more surgeries in the future. His case is complex. Babies heal well — in this case, a bit too well — but if we can't get his joint working properly this could affect him through adulthood." He stopped a moment. "Unless, of course, we could get a mechanical joint authorized for him."

That damned Cultural Correctness Committee.

"It'd have to be done in Azimoff," the surgeon said. "It's much too dangerous to try the procedure here."

"I can't risk him leaving the city," Tony said, "and I can't risk him being barred from re-entering once he's gotten the mechanism."

I said, "Didn't Mr. Clubb get his mechanical arm and come back?"

"That was many decades ago," Tony said, "and I'm not sure he got permission beforehand."

The surgeon stood, clearly uncomfortable with the conversation. "Well, we'll send instructions to your doctor and leave medication for him —" For the first time, he seemed to really look at Tony. "What's happened? You look unwell."

Molly blurted, "We just learned my daughter committed suicide."

Tony said angrily, "We don't know anything yet." Then he turned to the man. "My apologies, sir. I was shot in the attack which injured my son, and the leg," he gestured to it, "hasn't healed well."

The man looked concerned. "Let's have those pants off you."

I think everyone else in the room blushed.

Mr. Hart stood. "I'll step outside."

Molly followed, and I wondered what that encounter might be like.

Tony put his feet down gingerly, stood, and eased his trousers off from around his bandages.

The surgeon stopped him from going further, raising the edge of the covering bandage on Tony's leg just a bit. The skin was fiery red, puffy. "Your doctor's been packing this?"

"Yes," Tony said, "after removing a fragment of bullet that had been left behind."

The surgeon nodded, and after a moment's consideration, replaced the bandage. "Go ahead and put your clothes back on, sir." Once Tony did, and sat, the man said, "He's treating this well. But I'll have my nurse give you an injection which should help. I'm technically not supposed to do this." He grinned. "But what the Triple-C doesn't know won't hurt them."

Tony laughed. "You'd do well here."

That seemed to amuse the man. "I suppose I'm too used to my comforts. But it's been a pleasure to visit."

So Tony got his injection, Molly and Mr. Hart didn't kill each other, and Acevedo went back up to Daisy, who cried over him for an hour as he slept. I sat beside her until she stopped crying, and told her how grateful I was for her care of him. Then I went back downstairs.

Mr. Hart had begun his long journey home. The surgeons from Azimoff were packing their mechanisms for their own long journey. Tony was lying down, but not asleep, and I gave him his dose of opium. I went out to the back windows behind his room and gazed out upon my gardens and the meadow beyond.

It was so quiet out there, so peaceful. I could almost forget everything that had happened.

But Katie was dead. Roy was dead.

Anna Goren and Madame Biltcliffe and Marja and Ottilie and Poignee and Treysa and Nina Clubb and Air, all dead.

Herbert Bryce and Stephen Rivers and Maria Athena Spade and Little Ante were dead.

Jonathan Diamond was dead.

My baby had been the target of an assassin.

And Joe didn't love me.

I began weeping, there by the windows. Any peace outside was a lie. My life was a lie. My life was a ruin, and I'd done it all to myself. I'd killed everyone who loved me.

I understood well why Katie would want to die. I'd felt it many times already since that night I fled Spadros Manor the first time, almost three and a half years before.

I felt like even the slightest thing might make me want to die as well. I felt glad Tony had gotten rid of the liquor, both ours and Peedro's, because I wanted some so badly it hurt.

And then Tony was there beside me. "Come lie down with me," he said. "I won't mind it if you cry."

Something in his voice calmed me. I lay in his bed beside him.

I woke to Michaels putting the covers over my shoulder. The tenderness in his eyes almost made me cry once again. "Thank you."

"I'm well grateful to serve such a Lady," he said quietly, "who's always thankful for my service." Then he left.

Tony slept peacefully, and I pulled the covers higher over me to snuggle beside him, feeling strangely moved.

***

Whether it was the surgery or the medications, Acevedo started sleeping better, and seemed happier during the day.

The papers barely mentioned Katie's death, and it seemed to me so sad that one child's passing, even one in such a powerful family, could be almost ignored simply because she took her own life.

It was scandalous, true. Some call it cowardly, forcing a hand you feel unable to play onto an innocent child. Others believe it dooms your hand to burn in the Fire.

I don't know. All I know is that Katherine Spadros was once happy, truly happy. And it all went wrong.

We buried her beside her father, the one place she always wanted to be. Tony forced Molly to take the trip behind us, in a plain carriage, alone. And we stood beside Katie's grave in the rain, not even her friends making the journey.

Molly was looking at Roy's headstone. "The one person he truly loved wasn't related to him at all," she said. "My Katie."

Tony's jaw tightened, his head making a quick, small shake.

I didn't blame him for his anger at his mother. But it did make me wish I'd never spoken of any of it.

***

A few days after we returned home, Pip Dewey, Monsieur Sabacc, and Mrs. Anne left for Paris. The day was overcast, and cool for this time of year. The whole of Spadros Manor came out to wish them well.

Eventually, Monsieur and his new wife went into the carriage, but Pip lingered. "Monsieur said you wish private words with me."

I nodded. Tony said, "We do." He handed Pip the dollar. A formality, really: they'd signed papers long ago. "Please let me pay for your schooling. I feel I owe you that much, for all that you've given our family."

Pip scoffed, shoving the dollar into his pocket. "Whatever you want to give me is on you," he said. "I'll accept it as gift, but I have no obligation. I've given all I care to." He looked at me, then at Tony. "To be frank, I hope never to see any of you again." With that, he got into the carriage, and went away.

Tony stood shocked.

Honor came up beside him. "So our bird has flown."

I was sharply reminded of a time many years back, just after Tony and I were married and Katie was visiting, having recently moved to Spadros Castle.

Molly and I had walked out to the veranda. The day was sunny and hot. Katie was already out there, talking to my little bird. Katie had looked up at me. "What's its name?"

"I don't know."

"Why not?"

I'd smiled to myself. "Because I don't speak bird."

Katie had stared at me, puzzled. Then she'd said, "You should give it a name."

"Well, what if we decided one day that your name was Gertrude, or Penelope, or Aida?"

Katie had frowned. "That wouldn't be fair. I already have a name."

"So does my bird."

Katie laughed. "What?"

Molly had chuckled. "Come on, Katie, let's find something for you to do."

These many years later, my bird now lay under a flat rock outside my apartments. My little Katie lay buried under one as well.

Tony peered down the street after Pip's carriage in the gloom, as a fine mist began to fall. "Why does he hate us so?"

Honor shrugged. "Can you blame him?"

We went back up the stone walkway, and I didn't feel well at all. The ache, low in my belly, had never really left. The cranberries and honey had helped with my pain in the toilet, but a strange greenish-yellow discharge had stained my bloomers that morning.

I had no fever, made no cough, but I often felt cold, sometimes even shakingly so, with little appetite, even — from time to time — a bit of nausea.

I had a sudden horrible thought: could I be carrying Joe's child?

I'd not had my Queen's Rite as yet, and I didn't know if that was normal after bleeding for so long after Acevedo's birth. I wished I'd paid more attention at the Cathedral.

I didn't want Joe's child. I didn't want anything to do with him. But I couldn't tell Molly what I'd done. I just couldn't.

I took Tony's arm and let him lead me to his study. Acevedo cried a bit, far upstairs, and I heard Daisy comfort him.

Tony smiled fondly. "She's good with him, and I'm grateful." He closed the door. "My nurse wasn't nearly so kind to me."

This took me aback. "I'm sorry to hear that."

He shrugged. "It's of no consequence. Come, sit with me."

We sat by the unlit fire, the lamps turned high, and he said, "Now that I consider it, I think it for the best that young Pip and his family have gone."

"I don't understand."

He pursed his lips, let out a breath. "We have no savings left. All those tens of thousands of dollars ... it's all gone."

I stared at him in shock.

"The funerals, the surgeries ... they took it all. It was for the best that they aren't here — I have nothing to pay them with." He leaned upon his good elbow, hand to his chin. "By all rights, I should've paid for Monsieur's honeymoon, but he insisted." He smiled to himself. "He's a good man."

"He is."

He straightened. "But I don't care about the money. I'd do anything to help my son, and those men were the best."

I kissed his cheek. "You're a good man, Tony. And a good father." Tears came to me then. "The best."

He smiled at me, dropping his hand to the armrest. "It helps to hear you say that. Sometimes I wonder if I'm doing the right thing."

"I've never been a father. I've never really had one. But it seems you're doing the right thing. As best you can. For **both** your boys."

He gave me a quick, startled glance.

"Roland's not been here to see you limp and be wheeled about. You didn't let him come here to bullet holes and people throwing rocks. You haven't forced him to visit a quadrant that would surely hate him." I put my hand on his. "Sometimes, as much as it might hurt, **not** being with your child is the best you can do."

***

That evening, Mr. Hart came to see us, and I chided him. "You mustn't make this terrible long trip so often! At least let us meet with you on Market Center."

He chuckled at that. "I've been staying at our Manor until this is all cleared up. I have a son to find, and matters that need explaining."

That made me feel better. "I imagine."

Mr. Hart said to Tony, "Might I speak also with your mother?"

So we waited as Alan was called, and as he went up to speak with Molly, and as she got dressed and came down.

Molly flinched when she saw Mr. Hart, but composed herself and came in, chin high, to sit on the sofa, not looking at any of us.

Mr. Hart said to me, "I spoke with your Mr. Howell. Apparently he's been working on the situation with Spadros Castle?"

"Indeed he is, sir," I said. And I wondered what interest he might possibly have in that.

"I've had a lot of time to think about this." Mr. Hart hesitated for several seconds. "This whole situation is my fault. From the day I shot this man Roy loved, what's happened here was inevitable." For a moment, he seemed overcome. Then he straightened, focusing on Molly. "Let me pay to rebuild your home."

Molly gaped at him for a moment, then said, "How can I possibly live there, after everything that's happened?"

Mr. Hart said, "We've recovered his art, his books. Your men found the room ... downstairs, where he did his work —"

I said, "You mean where he tortured people."

"Yes," Mr. Hart said, "but perhaps that's on me as well. Whatever caused his madness ... that was his home. He built it, he furnished it. And he was the Spadros Patriarch. It belongs to your people." For an

242

instant, he looked uncertain. "Perhaps we can rebuild Spadros Castle to honor his memory, good and bad."

I'd never considered such a thing. Tony and I exchanged a glance.

Tony said, "You mean a museum?"

Mr. Hart shrugged. "I'm sure we might find enough to fill it, if only with the portraits of those he killed."

Molly flinched, hanging her head in shame.

"But let's speak of other things," Mr. Hart said to Molly. "How is our grandson?"

***

The next day, Tony said he might go to his bedroom after tea, and I did too. My headaches, as Dr. Salmon had said would happen, were gone. The cranberries and honey had helped the pain on using the toilet quite a bit. But I'd felt ill off and on all day, and I thought I might just sit by my window for a while.

Dr. Salmon was there almost every day. Why didn't I tell him I still wasn't feeling well?

So much was happening back then. Tony had taken over some of the work, and Sawbuck some, and Mr. Howell some. But a lot of the work still fell to me. Most of all, Katie had just died, and I blamed myself more than anyone else. I passed the tiredness off as too much crying, too much pain.

The Ancient Ones said in their Blasphemous Passages that every death, no matter what the cause, was really a suicide, because the person decided that they were ready to go.

Maybe back then, I did truly want to die.

But I sat there, glumly watching the golden sun play over the back side of the front arm of the house, the shadows move ever so slowly by, the servants and carts move around in the courtyard below.

A knock. "Mum?"

It was Honor. "Come in."

He and Michaels came in and closed the door behind them.

They looked ... normal. But for some reason, I got the feeling that something had quite upset them. "Is all well?"

Michaels stared at the floor. Honor hesitated. "Well, yes and no, mum. Jacob has something to tell you."

He had something to tell ... **me**? "Sit down, both of you."

Michaels paled, glancing at the door to my closets, and beyond that, Tony's room.

"All's well," I said. "Please, sit. I insist."

So they moved my tea-table out just a bit so Michaels might sit in my other chair. Honor leaned upon the window-sill. I'd scooted out from the window some so I might face them, the table just to my right. "Go on."

Michaels hesitated. "I'm not sure where to begin."

I knew that feeling well. "How about at the beginning."

"Yes, mum." He leaned an elbow on the table, and his face on his hand, still staring at the floor. "I suppose you heard of how Miss Daisy came to be here."

"I did."

"She and I spoke, and she told me the story of how it happened ..."

"That she was forced upon, yes." Men were so squeamish about such things, as if they didn't happen to women in this city every day.

"Well," Michaels said, "she never wanted the child, but she didn't have the heart to prevent its birth, even if she'd been able to afford that tea they use. The one that's unavailable now?"

I nodded.

"The baby helped her get her first job as a nursemaid, but, well, after the child weaned, they couldn't afford to keep her. Her and her mother and brother."

"I don't understand. What did she do?"

"She sent the girl to Dickens," Michaels said, "to the Home there. For orphans."

"She sent her baby away?"

"It's a good place," Michaels said quickly, "that's what I told her." He glanced at Honor. "It's where we were, me and Skip. It's how we met, as boys."

"I see."

"That's what I told her. Miss Daisy was sad one day about it. But when I told her how it was with us, she felt so grateful that her girl was being cared for, and maybe could have a good life somewhere. She just wanted the child out of Bridges, away from the creature who'd sired her. She didn't want the man anywhere near the girl."

I felt shocked. "She feared he might attack the **child**?"

"She feared her girl being used in his plans. Being used to make himself look like a good man, when clearly he wasn't. But yes, she feared him as well."

"Then she did the right thing." But I felt as if there were more to the story. And I wasn't sure what it had to do with me or why he told me this. "Was there anything else?"

Michaels flushed red. "Yes, mum, I'm sorry, mum. That was just the start of it. You told me to start at the beginning."

"Go on."

"You see, I talked to Skip here about it, um, Master Honor, mum, and he asked if this were why I'd been acting so strange lately."

I thought back: Michaels had seemed more nervous than usual. And him covering me with the blanket was definitely out of his normal behavior. "And was it?"

"No, mum. I'm sorry." He began panting, as if deeply distressed. "I ... I just, it's hard for me to say it."

Honor put his hand on Michaels' shoulder. "You have to tell her."

This sounded like a discussion they'd been having for some time. "Master Michaels, what is it you must tell me?"

He blurted out, "I murdered your father."

The Disclosure

For a moment, Michaels' pale, tear-streaked face was all I could see. Then I felt someone watching me to my left. There in the doorway to my closets, his face just as pale, stood Tony.

Tony looked appalled, his mouth open. "Why would you kill —" he stopped for a moment, and I could see the gears turn as he thought it through.

Both Michaels and Honor sprang to their feet.

I said, "Peedro Sluff?" And I smiled at Tony, held out my hand. "Come here."

Tony took my hand briefly, then stood behind and slightly on the right side of me, across from Honor. I said, "These men are here at my request. Master Michaels has come to confess."

I could feel rather than see Tony relax beside me, and he said, "You may sit. Please continue."

Tony put his hand on my shoulder. I held it as Michaels continued.

"The fault perhaps is mine," Honor said. "At first it was only a feeling, those days after you were given the Dealer's Gift. But the more I watched you, the more I became certain of the truth. The places you went to, the way you reacted to things that were said —"

"Wait," I said, suddenly afraid he might say something I didn't want Tony to know.

"Let the man speak," Tony said sternly.

Fear coursed through me.

Honor glanced at us both. "Forgive me for speaking out of turn, sir. I thought you knew."

"We can go more into this later." Tony's voice was grim. "Go on."

Michaels had sat there, head bowed, as if he hadn't heard anything Tony said. But then Michaels said, "Daniel was there at the Home too. We were the same age. He —"

"Wait," Tony said, now clearly curious. "Daniel? I've heard that name before."

"He went on to become Master Jack Diamond's manservant."

Tony said, "And Peedro Sluff killed him."

"**Yes!**" The word sounded ripped from Michaels' throat. "Daniel was my best friend. He was my brother. I **loved** him! He saved my life on the way to Bridges, and I owed him **everything**." Fury twisted the man's face. "Daniel meant everything to me. He was murdered in my quadrant, by Mr. Roy's man, and I wasn't there for him."

I let go of Tony's hand, feeling bleak. *Another life that Roy destroyed.* "I'm sorry."

"It wasn't your fault, mum," Michaels said. "You were just a child, dragged here to be enslaved due to that man. But you were kind to us, me and Skip, even though we're just worthless servants." He began to sob. "You were kind to us. And when I'd heard he'd ruined **your** life too, I ... I couldn't take it anymore." He hid his face in his hands. "They gave me a gun at the House Servants Academy. I went to Peedro's store, and I looked in his eyes and I shot him. I didn't see anything of you in him." He raised his head. "But hearing you weep over his death changed everything. He was your father. And I was wrong to take him from you."

I was going to say, "He wasn't really my father" but Tony put his hand on my shoulder. "What is it that you thought I knew, Honor?"

I stood, took a step away, turned to face him. "Tony —"

"No," Tony said firmly. "I command you to tell me the truth, Honor. Now."

Honor hesitated, glancing at us both. Then he said, "I could be wrong, sir. My understanding of this was that though your liaison was welcome, the child which came from it was not."

Tony grasped the back of the chair. "Thank you. You may go."

Once the door closed, he turned to me. "Is this true?"

How could I possibly salvage this? "Tony, I —"

"No! No. **Do** not lie to me again! It's a simple question. Answer me now: yes or no. When you learned you were with child, did you want to be?"

I couldn't say anything else. "No."

"And when you came here the next morning, did you have anything else in mind but ridding yourself of him?"

"Um ... "

"I'll take that as no. And why did you not just **say** so?"

"Because my housekeeper Mrs. Crawford had —" *Oh gods*, I thought. *I can't say this, not now.*

"Had what?" His face turned fierce, desperate. "For gods' sakes, Jacqui! Just **tell** me!"

"I was never barren." I didn't care anymore. If he killed me, well, maybe I deserved it. "My mother had given me the formula to a tea that cleansed the body of the Gift. Caused the construct inside to die." I couldn't look at him. "I've taken it every morning since we married."

If Roy's face was cold during his horrid miserable life, Tony's was glacial. "Go on."

"But Mrs. Crawford switched my morning tea for one which did nothing."

"This explains my father's interest in her. So was this **his** doing?"

"No. I'm sure he was furious about it."

"Where is this woman now?"

Roy must have sent for her. "She was at Spadros Castle when it was overrun. No one survived."

"This woman didn't do this on her own," he said. "Who ordered her to do it?"

I hesitated.

Tony grabbed my shoulders. "Stop. Hiding. The **truth**! If it wasn't my father, then who? Who **did** this to you?"

There was nothing more I could do. "Your mother."

The Doom

Tony stared at me, anguish upon his face. "You never wanted a **child**? You almost **died**! And yet you said nothing! **Why?**"

"I know you love your mother," I said. "How could I break that?" And even my mother had supported her in this.

Tony took me into his arms. "This is not your fault. None of this is." He pulled me away to peer into my eyes. "Do you understand? What is about to happen is not your fault, I promise you."

Not understanding, and more than a bit afraid, I nodded.

Tony went to the door and spoke to someone in the hall. "Find my mother and bring her to my study at once. By force if you must. She is no longer your Queen." Then he turned to me and held out his hand, so I took it.

We went down the back stair, then along the hall to his study. Tony put one chair beside his. Then he took every other chair and put it against the wall, so anyone entering would be forced to stand. "Sit beside me." Then he sat, and we waited.

I could hear exactly where Molly was at any stage of this. She protested, then she cried out as she was — by the sound of it — dragged down the grand stair and to the door. A loud thumping as she tried to escape. Then the door opened and she entered like nothing had happened.

"Come in," Tony said, also like nothing had happened. "Come close to me so I might look at you."

Alan and Honor came inside as well, closing the doors behind them, presumably to stand guard.

Molly was in her house dress, and more than a bit disheveled, but I suppose that was her own doing. "How might I serve my Patriarch?"

Ah. So she wanted to play it **that** way.

Tony didn't rise. "Thank you. You finally acknowledge me. Now you will tell me one thing: did you conspire to murder your husband and destroy his legacy?"

Alan and Honor exchanged a horrified glance.

Molly looked shocked. "Of course not!"

"Then why, after you coerced my wife's housekeeper to trick my wife into conceiving a child against her will, did my father — the one who most opposed it — die outside my door? Then the woman somehow died during a mob attack on the Castle? Hmm? It seems much too much a coincidence."

Molly stared at him, mouth open. "Tony, dearest, you must believe me. I had nothing to do with that ... that destruction! It's unthinkable! And I almost died outside your front door that day!"

"There is that," Tony said. "So you admit to conspiring to prevent my wife from choosing whether to bring us an Heir of her own free will, and that directly against your Patriarch's wishes."

I felt impressed. *Well played, sir.*

Molly stood frozen, eyes wide.

"Well, at least you admit to it. As much as I want to right now, I'd hate to have you put to the question." He spoke as if perfectly serene, but thunderclouds were in his eyes. He stood, a slight tightness in his face still testifying as to the pain in his leg. "You are, as my wife reminds me, my mother. I won't force you into the street. But you are not welcome at my table. You are welcome only in your rooms, and may not set foot outside your door, nor send message to anyone on this green earth, nor show your face to me ever again."

Molly said, "Tony, wait. I can explain —"

"No explanation defies the will of your Patriarch. Since you've defied one, I can only presume you'll defy the next as well. But let me be perfectly clear: the next time I see your face is the day of your death." He sat, making a gesture as if flicking a piece of lint off his desk. "Begone."

Molly wailed, "Tony, please!" She lunged for his desk, but Alan and Honor were quicker, grasping her arms and pulling her away.

Tony put his hand on mine. "I'm so sorry."

"For what?"

"I've failed to protect you time and time again. But I never imagined I'd have to protect you from my own mother." He turned away, stood. "I'm going to my rooms now."

***

The next day, Tony spoke at morning meeting. For direct defiance of her Patriarch, Molly Hogan Spadros was to be stripped of all titles and duties, and confined to her rooms here at Spadros Manor until further notice. A screen was to go over her windows so she might not make message to the street. She was to receive no packages, no mail, nor was she to send any. Any food would be tasted before going to her, and that food would be only that which could be eaten with a spoon. Nothing hot, nor acidic, nothing that could be used to attack anyone was to be given to her. She would be assigned three maids, to rotate so she might have a guard inside the rooms at all times, and three guards would be assigned for the outside hall.

To put it more plainly, she was a prisoner.

Tony was to be notified, day or night, if she tried to escape, or tried to suborn anyone else to aid her. She and anyone who aided her would be transferred to Roy's former torture rooms in the basement to live the remainder of their lives.

Tony didn't say what would then happen to them, but the threat of being confined there seemed to daunt the staff enough.

Her rooms had been searched, and anything that might be used as a weapon had been removed.

After he gave this speech, he went to his rooms and took to his bed.

I didn't blame him one bit.

Apparently, I'd sent an invitation to Gardena Diamond, because they visited the next day, a little after two. Alan had put them in the parlor before telling me they'd arrived. With Gardena was her sister-in-law, Cesare Diamond's wife Furaha.

The Diamond Family, other than some born "under the table," were generally quite dark of skin, with fine features and glossy black curls. Mrs. Furaha Diamond was no exception. She was a tall, stately woman, who bore herself as if she were already Queen.

Gardena, of course, was Gardena: utterly beautiful, with long raven curls and a fine figure. She was two years older than me, but up to then, we'd been as close as sisters.

I hadn't seen nor spoken nor even written to Gardena (other than a card of condolence) since her brother Jonathan's death. I'd felt so lost, so grief-stricken, so overwhelmed with Acevedo's crying, that I let one of my dearest friends grieve her brother alone.

And I felt ashamed.

So part of me didn't want to face Gardena. I feared she'd blame me for Jonathan's death, just as her father had.

Mrs. Furaha Diamond curtsied low. "Thank you for seeing us."

But Gardena rushed to me with a wide embrace. "Oh, my poor Jacqui! To see such murder at your very doorstep!"

My relief was so great that for a moment, I felt dizzy. "You don't hate me."

She pulled back. "Hate you? Whatever for?"

"For Jon."

"Let's sit." Gardena pulled me to a chair, sat beside me, took my hands. "Look at me. I do not blame you. I don't even know all that **happened!**" She leaned back. "Jon's servants said he got a letter, then he called them in, insisted that he take more of his medicine than the doctors said he ought, got himself dressed, and rushed out before they could call my father back."

She sat very still for a moment, gazing away. "We didn't know where he'd gone. But he was scheduled to see a specialist doctor the next evening, and we thought perhaps he'd gone to make some preparation." Then she focused upon me. "The whole matter puzzled us until we got word from your husband that you'd been taken."

"He saved me. They'd sent him a forged letter, supposedly from me, telling him to meet me at that place, then herded us like frightened sheep. Something tore," at that, I touched my still-sagging belly, "inside —"

Furaha Diamond had stood there this entire time, watching us, but at this her eyes widened.

"— and I was bleeding everywhere. There was so much blood, and the pain was unnatural! I've never felt anything like it." I took a deep breath. "I told him not to, but Jon carried me out of there. It wasn't far, ten yards at most, but then he cried out, clutching his chest, and fell." The vision of Jon's face, the sound of his cry ... it has never left me since, even to this day. "I thought he might die, right there before me."

Gardena only nodded.

I didn't want to tell her the rest, about Jon asking me to kiss him. I'm sure that us actually kissing was all over the city by now, but our conversation felt too private to share with anyone.

She seemed to be waiting for more, so I said, "Your people arrived then, and mine, and here we are." I had a ruined body and a son who had no interest in me; she had a dead brother. "I don't think the day went well."

Gardena smiled at that, but her eyes were red. "No, indeed."

It was then I noticed Furaha Diamond wore her jet black hair into a multitude of small, interwoven braids, endlessly forming their Holy Symbol. "Would you care to sit, my Lady? I'd be happy to call for tea, if you wish it."

Gardena said, "We're actually here to see Tony."

I'd guessed they were actually here to see Tony, but it amused me to hear Gardena say so. I rose. "Then I won't keep you. I believe he's in his study."

Then it hit me: Gardena Diamond always called him Anthony. We went into the hall. "I've never heard you call him that before."

She smiled to herself, but it was sad. "He told me that's what he preferred. I never knew."

All these years, they had a child together, yet he never told her? And she never asked? I showed her to his study, and Alan stood there, opening the door for us. He stepped inside. "The Lady of Diamond and her spinster, sir."

Tony looked as if he'd been waiting for them, and rose. He didn't so much as glance at Gardena. "The Spadros Patriarch welcomes the Lady of Diamond," he said to Furaha. "Please, come in."

Furaha had a small, amused smile on. But they came inside, and the doors closed behind us.

I led them to Tony's desk, going to his side.

Furaha and Gardena went to Tony's desk and curtsied low. Once they rose, Furaha said, "Diamond, of course, does not officially recognize the Spadros Patriarch. Spadros quadrant is regarded as occupied lands belonging to them."

She had an accent unlike one I've ever heard, before or since. Tony gave her a nod. "As Spadros regards Diamond."

"**Un**officially," she said, "the Diamond Heir congratulates the Spadros Patriarch on the birth of his son and Heir. And we share your grief at the loss of your young sister." She stopped for a moment, head down, then faced him. "The Diamond Patriarch, unofficially, of course, and in the Diamond Heir's opinion, is, and I quote: 'acting like an unmitigated ass'."

Tony burst out laughing. "That sounds like your husband," he glanced at Furaha. "No offense intended."

She smiled. "My husband indeed has skill with his words." Then she sobered. "The Diamond Heir humbly begs pardon for the unforgivable insult given at his brother's funeral, when our Patriarch refused you attendance at the memorial of your sworn ally, then threatened harm upon you and your Heir."

Tony gave another small nod. "All is forgiven: my quarrel is with your Patriarch, not your people."

Furaha relaxed. "My people are grateful for Spadros mercy." She stopped then, as if considering what she'd just said. "Mercy is not something I expected here."

"I'm not my father," Tony said. "Please, sit."

They didn't move. "We have little time," Furaha said. "Her father knows nothing of our visit."

Ah. Julius Diamond would be enraged if he learned Gardena was here.

Tony said, "How may I help, then?"

"Your wife and I will move our chairs to the hallway," Furaha said, "so you and my sister-by-law might converse. The door will remain open, and you will sit so that both may be seen plainly." She lowered her voice then. "That's the only way I could persuade my Mr. Cesare to allow this."

"Very well," Tony said. I could tell he felt intrigued at this notion. "Let's begin."

So chairs were moved. Gardena sat at one end of the desk, Tony at the other, and Furaha and I out in the hallway. Although the servants seemed to catch a fright at coming round the corner and seeing us, with much gasping and curtsying, I thought the arrangement both novel and pleasant.

Gardena and Tony began speaking at once, in voices too low for us to hear. As usual, they seemed to be arguing, Gardena urging Tony on to some action that he hesitated to make.

Interesting.

Furaha produced a small bit of colorful and elaborate needlework from her handbag and began to sew. "How is your son?" At my stare, she smiled to herself. "A Yuletide vest for my youngest."

"It's beautiful." It wasn't black and white and silver, their colors — but rather greens and yellows and reds, with golden threads interwoven here and there.

"Thank you."

"To answer your question, he's as well as can be expected after surgery." I didn't want to reveal too much; whilst I didn't think she — or even Cesare — would use Acevedo's infirmity against him, others who might overhear them speak of it might. "But he's a strong child. I expect he'll do well."

She nodded. "In my country we have a special healing poultice for children suffering wounds of this type. I'll send the recipe."

I was touched by her kindness. "Thank you."

Tony had his good elbow upon the desk, gazing at Gardena fondly. To see him looking ... happy ... brought tears to my eyes.

"He loves her," Furaha said.

I nodded.

"She has told me so, but I didn't see it until now."

"Amongst my people," I said, "this is not a problem, unless it be hidden with lies. But here ..."

Furaha nodded. "Be at peace. It's good for a man to love his son's mother, whether he may act upon it or no."

I thought of these two, who should have by all rights been married, kept apart only by fear and hatred. "Why are fathers so cruel?"

For an instant, I thought she'd protest, then she said, "Ah. Yes. Cruel is a word I'd use. Roy Spadros and Julius Diamond have had much more in common than you'd think."

And for some reason, I thought of Cesare. "I hope your husband is well?"

She gave a small smile, yet it was sad. "As well as might be expected. That young Master Jack would take his own life —"

This gave me a shock. I'd forgotten that only a few knew that Jack Diamond still lived.

"— well, it struck him a blow. It was most unexpected. And then for his youngest brother to die also ..." She glanced aside, eyes red. "He has many regrets." She shrugged, head down. "It's difficult to see him suffer so."

As far as I might tell, much of the animosity between Cesare and Jonathan had been Cesare's own doing. "Please convey our sympathies. My husband and I miss Jon terribly."

She smiled to herself, not meeting my eye, and I wondered if she'd heard of us kissing as well. "I will."

Then I felt foolish. Of course she had. We never got the Diamond quadrant tabloids, but I'm sure the speculation gave their Family great embarrassment and concern. "He asked me to do it. To kiss him."

She didn't look up from her needlecraft. "Oh?"

"Somehow, even then, he knew he was dying." Grief flooded through me; my eyes and nose stung. "I'm sorry if it caused your people trouble. But I don't regret it."

She'd put down her work and was gazing at me. "You loved him."

I whispered, "I did. I never wanted to admit it. But I did." I bit my lip, not wishing to say more. And I think if I had said anything I'd have begun sobbing, right there in front of everyone.

She nodded. "I wish I would've known him better. It sounds odd, being his sister-by-law, for me to say so. But we spoke so seldom."

"He was a good man. The best." I stared at my hands, wishing I would have thought to bring something to do.

Furaha smiled to herself. "I think this would please him."

"Do you believe the Way of the Cards? That Jon lives on, right now, as part of someone else's hand?"

She shrugged. "I'm no theologian. But I'd like to think they both live, one way or another. Life is too precious for it to vanish forever."

***

Soon after that, Gardena and Furaha left. Tony was quiet and pensive the whole rest of the day, and didn't come to my bed that night. Clearly, something troubled him, but I couldn't figure out what it might be.

Early the next morning, Charles Hart arrived, so we invited him to breakfast. "My men found Etienne last night," Mr. Hart said, "and we've set up a meeting on Market Center at noon. I think you deserve to be there."

I looked to Tony, who nodded. "The doctor doesn't think I should travel again as yet, nor Ten. But you may go, if you take your men."

That seemed ironic, in light of all that had gone on.

Or perhaps Dr. Salmon feared Tony might suffer a setback if he moved around too much. "Of course." Then I said to Mr. Hart, "How many are we allowed?"

"Three each, all armed."

Tony said, "Armed? This sounds like trouble."

Mr. Hart shrugged. "I doubt there will be. Etienne's vision is so poor he'd be hard-pressed to shoot anything not close enough to touch. And I personally sponsored his men; they have no cause to shoot me. Or your wife, for that matter." Then Mr. Hart frowned. "From the sound of it, he felt entirely secure and unalarmed. His attitude was curiosity at why we'd been searching for him."

The man of his who'd been killed in the attack on Hart Manor had likely been his informant on matters here in town. "How much does he know, I wonder?"

Mr. Hart said, "That's what we're going to find out."

***

We rode in Molly's carriage — now mine — and I took Honor and Blitz with me. After some thought, I also chose Mr. Theodore Sutherfield. Mr. Sutherfield had watched over me those years at my apartments, and I trusted him to watch over me in this case as well.

Tony had been surprised by my choices. "I don't understand. Honor and Blitz are servants. Only Teddy's a Family man, and I didn't know you two were acquainted. Who are these men to you?"

So I told him of how Honor had sworn to me, how Blitz and his oldest brother had kept me safe and guided me those years at my apartments. "They're like family, and I know they'd keep me from harm if they might."

"I see." Then he smiled. "You've managed to gather Queensmen before ever having the need. Well done."

That made me think. "What of Molly's men? Won't they object to her capture?"

"They've all been taken and questioned." He put a hand on my shoulder. "Never fear, my love. I won't make the same mistake I made with Katie."

This had sent a chill through me. Tony had taken immediate measures to secure his place, cutting out his mother's rule with a ruthlessness which would've pleased Roy well.

I'd hesitated to mention Michaels and how he'd sworn to me as well, and now I felt glad of it.

I gazed out over the wide gray river. What had the attack on Tony's home, Roy's murder in front of him, his son's injuries, learning of his mother's real character ... what had it done to him?

He'd done things before that made me wonder, but this ... his mother captive, her men now likely in some cell — or perhaps dead — just for swearing to her?

I had to make plans to protect my men and their families, if ever things should go poorly for me. I imagined Master Bresciane and his knife, and shuddered.

My carriage crossed onto Market Center, around the Plaza, to the warehouse district. We were to meet Inventor Etienne Hart at a meatpacking warehouse. An odd place to meet, but my brother was an odd man.

Could he have possibly ordered my baby's assassination?

The Red Dog Gang claimed responsibility in the most outlandish way possible, tossing handfuls of cards in the street for anyone to see. But even if my brother was the Hart wildcard, he was an Inventor, a vastly intelligent man. What plan could the Red Dog Gang have put forth to make him think this to be a good idea?

I couldn't see how this benefited him.

The street was empty. Mr. Hart and his men met us at the door. "I'd like to introduce my cousins," Mr. Hart said.

The oldest, perhaps forty, was Mr. Tong Tau Ershiwu, a stern-looking dark-haired man. Next was Master Chongsan Madiao, a tall, thin man in his middle thirties with a narrow face, even narrower eyes, a shock of bright red hair and a face covered with freckles. The last one was perhaps nineteen and stout: Mr. Hart introduced him as Chipmunk. He had dark hair, ruddy cheeks, and a bright, mischievous grin: I liked him at once.

I introduced Blitz, Honor, and Mr. Theodore, then said, "Shall we?"

"Let me do the talking," Mr. Hart said.

I didn't want to go along with this. "You said I might confront him I have a lot of questions of my own."

Mr. Hart shook his head. "I have no idea what his state of mind is, Mrs. Spadros. If you speak, it might only agitate him."

I had a bad feeling about this.

Mr. Hart looked at the men. "Remember," Mr. Hart whispered, "no shooting unless I command it. We're here to determine if he's mad. But until then, we need him alive."

Like most such places, the building's interior was a cold utilitarian gray. Not knowing what I might face, I'd brought the pistol Jonathan had given me, my favorite boot knife — also a gift from Jon — and the garotte wire Roy gave me long ago.

I carried the dead with me, into a place of death.

We went down a darkened hall, which led to a much larger room. The workbenches had been pushed aside to allow a space some fifteen feet on a side.

Mr. Hart and his men went inside; I hesitated to enter. "I don't like this," I whispered to Blitz. "There's no cover, nowhere to hide should any shooting actually begin."

"If this ends in shooting," Blitz said, "that'll be the least of our worries."

Mr. Hart turned back to gesture to us, so I went in. But what Blitz said worried me. I didn't know these men. They outnumbered mine two to one. If any of them had been turned by the Red Dog Gang ...

And why did Etienne want to meet **here**? Why had he set it up like this? So far as I could tell, there was only one way in or out. I hadn't seen anyone, but he could have men waiting outside. He could kill us all, then say we tried to kill him. It'd cause trouble, true — perhaps even start a war. But no one could prove anything different.

And there was another matter. My stomach twisted; I clasped my hands in front of me to stop them from shaking.

I didn't want to believe it of Mr. Hart, but he'd been agitating for me to leave Spadros quadrant for years now. Nothing stopped him from ordering his men to shoot Honor, Blitz, and Mr. Theodore, then seize me, forcing me to go with him — to his Racetrack or anywhere else — all in the name of "keeping me safe." And with our quadrant in its weakened condition, there was little Tony could do about it.

Etienne Hart already sat there at a smallish rectangular table at one end of the space, his three men behind him. His men already had their guns drawn, their hands by their sides. One of the men stood right behind Etienne Hart. A poor choice: the Inventor would be left partially deaf from the noise were the man to actually raise and shoot his gun from that position.

"Those must be some trusted men," I murmured, hoping my voice didn't shake too badly.

Mr. Sutherfield chuckled to himself.

Blitz nodded.

Mr. Hart and his men took the left corner of this ghoulish triangle, myself and my men the right.

Blitz had his hand on his holster, his knuckles white. But I shook my head, lifting my hands to show they were empty.

At that, the Inventor's men holstered their weapons.

Etienne Hart spoke: "Why all this theater?"

"Enny," Mr. Hart said, "why indeed? You have us meet you in this cold awful place. You give your Patriarch and father no seat, offer this Queen neither tea nor refreshment. Why are you doing this? Where have you **been**?" I could tell he didn't want to have to ask the question. "Did you order the Spadros Family's murder?"

Etienne scoffed. "Of course not! Who told you I did?"

Mr. Hart said, "Then why did you flee?"

Etienne hunched forward. "I never fled. I went on a scheduled visit to the Generators in the countryside to supervise my Apprentices' work. I knew nothing of this attack until days later." He leaned back then, his strange multi-lensed spectacles focusing upon me. "I was appalled by the whole affair, particularly the idea that I would put a hit on a baby."

I said, "But you know something. Who's behind this?"

Mr. Hart said at the exact same time, "Did he tell you he was going to do this?"

Etienne jerked towards him, surprised. "The topic came up, yes."

I felt confused. "Who?"

Mr. Hart waved to quiet me, eyes flickering to the other men.

I blurted out, "Then why didn't you **warn** us?"

Etienne's face turned angry. "I specifically told them **not** to do this! I'm not sure why you blame me — it was never my idea in the first place! It was all —"

Inventor Hart's left eye exploded, glass and blood and brains spraying out. We ducked, men on all sides pointing their weapons to the man holding the pistol behind him.

I shouted, "NO! We need him alive!"

The ordinary-looking man, who'd shot from the hip, looked at Mr. Hart and said, "He warned you what would happen if you told her." Then he moved the gun's muzzle to under his chin, a wild mad ecstasy in his eyes. "I do this for Frank!" He pulled the trigger.

For an instant, we all stood stunned, appalled. The man's body fell.

Then Mr. Hart and I rushed to Etienne.

I screamed, "Call for a doctor!"

The Hart men ran from the room. Honor and Blitz moved the table back. Mr. Sutherfield helped Mr. Hart move Etienne from where he sat to the floor, propping his feet up on the chair.

Why hadn't we brought a doctor **with** us?

Mr. Hart took his son into his arms, blood soaking his jacket. Etienne looked up at his father with his remaining eye, confusion in his face. "Papa?"

Then he lay staring as his father cradled him, sobs filling the cold silence. Blood pooled upon the floor.

So passed the Hart Inventor, my brother, betrayed by his own man.

***

By the time a doctor was found, the police arrived, then the coroner's wagon. The whole time, Mr. Hart wailed over his son's body.

I was supposed to be Queen and all, but I couldn't help crying, too. This was the only brother I'd ever have, and Frank Pagliacci had him murdered to keep him from speaking the truth.

A grim resolve came over me then. These people had killed enough of mine. One way or another, this had to end, and soon, before it destroyed my city.

The coroner's men had to pry the Inventor from Mr. Hart's arms. But once done, Mr. Hart stood, covered with his son's blood, as the men took away Etienne's body. "I had two daughters and a son," Mr. Hart said, "and I've lost you all."

"Not all, sir," I said softly.

Mr. Sutherfield gave me a surprised glance.

Yet if I were to be perfectly honest about it, Roy Spadros was the only father I ever really knew.

The Masked Man had been a child's fantasy: as much as I'd hoped and wished for it, he'd never have come to live with us in the Pot. Peedro Sluff had lied, used me to regain access to the quadrant, then left me to suffer alone.

But Roy fed and clothed me, trained and taught me, punished and rewarded me. He'd given me his heart there at the end, what little was left of it, and shared his most awful secret.

Mr. Hart had just lost his son, though. I had to give him something. "I always hoped the man behind the mask was my father. I think what I need most in this town is a friend."

***

Weary, I returned home, my brother's blood still upon me. I told my panicked Tony what had happened.

Then I thought of Josie.

What would she do? She'd spent everything she had on this wedding. This marriage to a man she didn't love had been her one desperate chance out of poverty, and her chance had been killed along with that madman's bullet.

So I sent a note of condolence. Perhaps it might help to ease her grief in some way, but I doubted it.

Then I gave Tony his dose of medicine — he needed very little these days, but his leg was still quite tender — and lay in his rooms beside him.

In the midst of night, I awoke, shivering. He wasn't there.

Alarmed, I searched our rooms, then drew on a thick robe and house slippers. I went out into the hall behind Tony's rooms, to the window near the back stair, and I saw him.

He walked alone past the gardens, out on the meadow, and something in his stance spoke of great pain.

I hurried down the stairs and outside. Running to him, thinking he needed more medication, or walked in his sleep. But when he turned to me, tears shone on his cheeks, and I stopped still, astonished.

I'd never seen him cry before.

"Tony? What's wrong?"

He took his unbound hand and placed it upon my thick hair, lying loose beside my cheek, and his tear-filled eyes spoke of an unbearable grief. Then he withdrew his hand and turned away. "My father is dead. My sister has taken her life. My son is injured, and may become a cripple." He shook his head, still turned from me. "You ... you long for men who don't love you, and scorn those who do." He sighed, and turned his face to the stars. "Yet who am I to judge you?"

Something's happened, I thought. "Gardena."

His shoulders slumped. "Yes, Gardena ... " Tony placed his hand on his forehead for a long moment. "She came to me ... after you left to chase Joseph Kerr years ago, and confessed her love for me. And I loved her yet a second time. But how can I love her, when I have a wife, who ..." his voice broke. "Who I love more with each day."

Tony's been unfaithful. He's lied to me, all this time.

The thought left me suddenly bereft, as if my only support had been pulled from under me, as if the very ground beneath me began to crumble. This was what Gardena had been urging Tony to tell me. "You should go to her. She's more worthy of you than I am."

"Gardena ... is Gardena." Tony's words sounded far away. "She's light, and air, and a leaf on the wind. I hope she finds a man who can match her brilliance and passion. She deserves an equal." He dropped his hand in a gesture of despair. "I can only be a poor second."

Reaching into his hair, I drew his face down to look into mine. "You are the best, kindest, most gracious man ..." I suddenly thought of Jonathan, and I wanted to be truly honest, "... living today."

I paused, letting go of him. I felt as if I looked down from a terrible height as the earth continued to crumble beneath me. "But I too have something to say."

I closed my eyes and in my heart, jumped. "I bedded Joseph Kerr the day you were shot." Grief, loneliness, and anguish welled inside me as I opened my eyes, and against my determination, I began to cry. "I **betrayed** you —"

Tony raised his hand, but it was only to stop me from speaking further. His voice was calm. "I know."

"Y — you know?"

"Amelia came to me before she left. With her misgivings, her evidence, and your reaction. Your grief these past weeks, greater than any I have ever seen in you, only confirmed her story."

I began sobbing. "It was terrible! The look in his eyes ... " I shuddered to remember it. "He cares **nothing** for me, nothing at all. I was always only an object to be possessed, a token of some victory." I could hardly breathe for crying. "And in your darkest hour, I was in his bed instead of by your side. I shall **never** forgive myself."

"Come to me," Tony said, his voice full of compassion. He held me with his good arm, kissing my hair. "We are utterly lost, you and I."

There, in the moonlight, as the night chirped round me, I felt he spoke true. And I grieved how we'd become lost, together.

"It rent my soul," he finally said, his voice breaking, "when I realized the truth, long ago, that you've never, **ever** returned my love. Yet I've forgiven you. How could I not? You were ripped from your home and family, forced to marry me, forced to endure my attentions, forced to bear my child ..." his voice broke, and he shook his head. "You're a wild and beautiful bird, cruelly tormented on my account."

He let go of me and touched the hair beside my face once more. "Yet I love you! I give thanks every morning when I wake and you're near me. You are my life."

Our eyes met, there in the moonlight, and my heart was stirred.

Then his hand dropped to his side. "But I can't live like this anymore. So I release you from your vows."

What? "I don't understand."

"I will cause no scandal," Tony said. "No one will harm you. My mother and I will care for Acevedo, or you can take him and go, to Azimoff or wherever you wish. I'll pay for your tickets to anywhere in the world. You're free."

Panic rose within me. "But ... so you're sending me away?" Tears filled my eyes. *Just like Ma did.*

He shook his head; pain lay in his eyes. "I will never send you away," he said. "I ... I can't. But I can't bear to cage you any longer." He rested his hand upon the hair curling beside my face once more, yet his own face held anguish. Then he blurted out, "So ... you **don't** wish to leave?"

I shook my head, relief rushing through me. Now that he wanted me to go, there was nowhere else I'd rather be than at his side.

His face didn't change. "No more secrets, no more lies. If you want to stay here, that's what I ask." He fell silent for a moment. "And I must know: Will you ... can you live with me as my wife, and love me in truth?"

Some enormous wall broke inside my soul. In his loving, gentle eyes, the answer had been there all along. "I will."

The Contagion

Tony took my bare hand, the first he'd touched my skin that night, and flinched. "You're burning up! How long have you been ill?"

I shrugged.

He grabbed my arm, pulled me across the meadow.

Sawbuck once told me that someday I'd have to return here, and when I did, I needed a reason to sustain me.

And as Tony pulled me across that wide meadow blazing in the moonlight, it all became clear. Molly, for all her deception and betrayal, had spoken the truth: it was time for me to grow up.

Tony had also spoken truth. I'd chased after Joseph Kerr, a man who didn't love me, leaving behind my dear husband, my precious little child.

No wonder Acevedo wanted nothing to do with me! He was in pain, and I'd neglected and despised him. I'd hated him. I'd wished him to die.

But no more. These people deserved better. I might be an investigator, but I was also a wife and mother. I was the Spadros Queen, and as Ma had said, my best duty was to Tony and our son.

Something my mother had said also came to me as we traversed that cold uneven ground: *and as many more as the gods give you*. And I smiled to myself as Tony hurried me through my gardens, that beautiful light wavering round me. Perhaps more would come one day: boys, yes, but girls also. I was a descendant of the Cathedral: I had much to share with my daughters.

Tony pulled me through the small back side door, and into the hall by his study. "Call for the doctor," he shouted, and everything happened, it seemed, at once.

I was carried upstairs and put to bed.

I'd lain on Josie's bed when I bedded Joe. Could I have caught Josie's fever, that woman's contagion?

My bed was so wonderfully warm and soft. But then I dreamed, and my dreams were anything but pleasant.

***

I almost died once more.

Molly was brought from her exile when the doctor could find no cause for my symptoms. She knew this contagion at once: womb fever.

And when I learned this, I think something broke within me.

Joe had grown up in the brothels. He knew what this contagion was. He knew the signs that a man carried it. I recalled the greenish drip upon the floor the day we bedded. He had to have known.

Yet he bedded me anyway.

Joseph Kerr, the man who swore he loved me, who'd asked me to devote my life to him, who swore he'd never had any other woman but me, had given me womb fever.

Molly saved my life that day. She insisted my mother be brought to Spadros Manor to tend me.

I don't know what happened between Tony and my Ma, but Tony looked awed and more than a bit afraid when he spoke of her. "Facing your mother is like peering out into a howling storm," he said. "This explains much."

I survived. Yet once I woke, and was again well, Dr. Salmon told me and Tony that the damage done to me inside by the contagion Joe carried was so great that he doubted I'd ever have a child again.

And on learning that, I wished, just for a moment, that instead of calling for Ma, that Molly had let me die.

***

It seemed unseemly for Mr. Eight Howell to return to being an Associate after standing second to the Queen, so he became my secretary, with his office at the Backdoor Saloon as before. One day much later, when I'd recovered and was at my apartments, he brought me a large box full of jewelry. "These were from the last group questioned about the attack on Spadros Manor," he said. "What would you like done with them?"

I peered inside. A ring near the top caught my eye. Gold, with elm leaves carved onto the outside and "Forever yours" inscribed inside.

Amelia. "Where did this come from?"

He shrugged, glancing away.

Alan did promise he'd look for her and Peter last. "Can you tell me what became of the Dewey girls?"

Mr. Howell sighed. "Sold to the orphanage in Dickens with the rest. I thought we might learn something more from the older one, but your man Honor insisted."

I thought my heart would entirely break. I struggled to keep my voice steady. "You've done well."

"Well, at least we got something for them," Mr. Howell said. "Once you factor in shipping. Wasn't a complete waste."

I took a deep breath, let it out. The man didn't know those little girls. He hadn't watched them play in my gardens. He hadn't seen how dearly they'd been loved.

And he hadn't been raised by Amelia like I had. He hadn't been taken care of by her, watched over by her. He didn't know what this all meant.

Amelia had been there for me through everything. If this ring was here, she was surely dead.

I dropped the ring back into the box, not wanting to look at it any longer. "Give the best ones to our men who deserve it," I said, "then sell the rest." At this point, we could use every penny.

"Yes, mum. The same with the other boxes?"

I smiled to myself despite how I felt. So he knew I'd want to know, that I needed to see her ring for myself. And he wanted to see how I'd react. I'd chosen well, indeed. "The same."

He turned to go, then stopped, looking back at me. "I'm sorry, by the way. I know she'd been with you for some time."

I nodded, feeling bleak. "Yes, sir. Indeed she was."

***

In the aftermath of the *Bridges Daily* exposé, both the Mayor and District Attorney resigned in disgrace. My long-time enemy Chase Freezout had been defeated at last, a small but long-awaited victory.

The new Mayor would be chosen in the upcoming election, held in the fall. If my guess was right, Frank Pagliacci would reveal himself soon: 'Mayor for life' was too tempting a prize for him to ignore.

Thrace Pike, of all people, became the new District Attorney. And it worried me. What would a Bridger gaining this high office, one with the power to investigate the Four Families, hold for our future?

Diamond and Clubb quadrants never did publicly acknowledge Tony as Spadros Patriarch. We never expected Diamond to do so, all things being as they were. But the Clubbs had been our ally, up to Roy's murder. Neither of us knew what their silence meant, and it troubled us. Tony put extra guards upon the bridges to Clubb, something we'd not done since the Coup.

For some time, Tony fretted about how we would pay for our Midsummer promise to our men. But then Mr. Hart paid for little Acevedo's surgery. To my surprise, he did so publicly, making a statement that he had hopes for Hart and Spadros quadrants to one day ally, and live in true peace.

But there would be no peace so long as the Red Dog Gang existed. And grim as my life felt those days, I couldn't let myself die. Not so long as the people they'd murdered — Roy Spadros, John Pearson, and my brother Etienne now on that ever-lengthening list — remained unavenged.

I didn't know how we'd defeat the Red Dog Gang, but I felt glad I didn't need to hide anything from Tony anymore.

And, as odd as it may seem, I felt hopeful. Maybe, with my husband and the vast resources of both Hart and Spadros quadrants on my side, we finally had a chance.

~~ This ends Chapter 9 of the Red Dog Conspiracy ~~

The Four of Clubs
Part 10 of the Red Dog Conspiracy
Coming October 2023

Acknowledgments

My thanks to Julian White for his beta reading and encouragement. I'd also like to thank Erin Hartshorn for her editing and proofreading.

Thanks also go to my street team, The Commission, without whom this book might not have made it into your hands.

Special thanks go to my Patrons, whose monthly financial support helps make this series possible:

Julian White

Melissa Williams

Laura Prime

Michaelene Alston

Cristina

Eirlys Evans

Jane Kamvar

Aramanth Dawe

Rachel Heslin

Phoebe Darqueling

James Mallison

Danielle Barnes

By Wilson

Kanyon Kiernan

Follow the Red Dog Conspiracy on Patreon

patreon.com/red_dog_conspiracy

About the Author

Patricia Loofbourrow is the NY Times and USA Today best-selling author of the Red Dog Conspiracy steampunk noir crime fiction series. She has been a professional blogger, author, and editor since 2000 and began writing novels in 2005. Her first published novel, *The Jacq of Spades*, released in 2015 and has sold over 20,000 copies worldwide.

A native of southern California, Patricia Loofbourrow has lived in central Oklahoma since 2005. You can see all her books at pattyloof.com

Note from the Author

Thanks so much for reading this far! If you like this series, please leave a review where you bought this.